Merry ... 2018 ..!

Matryoshka

GORAN POWELL

Also by Goran Powell

FICTION:
A Sudden Dawn
Chojun

NON-FICTION:
Waking Dragons

AWARDS:

A Sudden Dawn
   Winner: USA Book News, Historical Fiction 2010
   Gold: eLit Awards 2011
   Gold: IP LivingNow Awards 2011

Chojun
   Winner: Eric Hoffer Award 2013
   Silver: Benjamin Franklin, Historical Fiction 2013
   Bronze: eLit Awards 2013
   Finalist: Book of the Year, ForeWord Magazine 2013
   Finalist: International Book Award 2013

MATRYOSHKA

Copyright © Goran Powell 2013

Cover design: Adrian Nitsch

goranpowell.com

GORAN POWELL

NADIA

Cheapside, City of London, December 1999

The sleek Audi A8 inched forward in the slow moving traffic. In the evening gloom the privacy glass was unnecessary, no one could see George Petersen inside. He was reclining on the rear seat, hands on knees, head tipped back on the headrest, eyes lightly closed, working to get a little freshness back before a final session of paperwork at the office.

He was returning to the City after a press conference in the West End. His driver had chosen to go down Cheapside, it was the shortest route but hardly the quickest and Petersen considered admonishing him. He decided against it. It had been a good day all told and he had no wish to spoil his mood.

He shifted on the unforgiving seat. The Bentley would have been more comfortable, softer and altogether more luxurious, but his publicity expert Geri Harper ('The PR-girl' as he liked to call her) had said it gave out the wrong message: too self-indulgent, a throwback to a bygone age. On the eve of the new millennium, the Audi presented a more understated impression of quality hedged by restraint. It was a better fit, in her words, with the company's 'Ethical positioning in the marketplace'.

He hated Geri and her profession with a passion but he had to admit she knew her job. The press conference had been a big success. The 'jackals' as he called the journalists had lapped it up and bayed for more. And afterwards Geri had said he'd handled them very nicely. He'd been confident, sincere, and open, without allowing them to take control. Coming from her it had been high praise indeed, she was usually full of niggling little criticisms. She'd even smiled, and not for the first time, he'd thought how good it would be to screw her. Or better still, to have her kneeling before him, lips too busy pleasuring him to utter any more niggling little criticisms. For a moment he'd even considered inviting her to ride back in the Audi with him. He would have enjoyed staring at her shapely legs on the seat beside him. But to do so would have been to give her power over him and she had enough power already. She could hail a cab.

A blare of car horns. He opened his eyes. They were still on Cheapside, by St Mary Le Bow Church. The restrained little tower had once been among London's most prominent landmarks but now it fought to be noticed amid the surrounding office blocks. Looking straight ahead down Cheapside, Petersen saw the pale glow of the Royal Exchange, built to resemble a Greek temple. It had once been an important meeting place for city traders but now it was nothing more than an upmarket shopping mall. Beside it stood the equally grand but less welcoming Bank of England, protected on four sides by a high wall. The area was crowded with commuters heading home via the Bank underground station.

Why did they all leave at the same time, he wondered. If they stayed a little longer, worked a little harder, they too might one day be chauffeur-driven in an executive-class automobile instead of clawing for an inch of space on a crowded commuter train. It was nature's way, he reminded himself. The herd was many but the lions few. The wildebeest will never fight like the lion, that's why the lion is king. It was the Law of the Jungle but it governed the City of London as surely as the wilds of Africa.

He took his mobile phone from his briefcase and punched a number. 'Saunders?' He called his wife by her maiden name, a pet-name he still used for her. 'Back late. Press conference went swimmingly. Paperwork awaits. Must dash.'

He punched another number. 'Becky? George. Listen, are you around later? Thought I might pop round. Been a good day. Thought we might celebrate.'

He waited while Becky pretended to check her diary. She was punishing him for not calling sooner. It had been several days since they'd last spoken. He was tiring of his new mistress rapidly. Since when did she think she could start acting like a wife? 'Listen, Becky, I'll call you back. There's a call I have to take.' He hung up.

The driver turned into Old Broad Street and pulled up outside the offices of Havilland Ethical. Petersen glanced up as he always did whenever he stepped out of the car. This was his company, his building, and the size and scale of the tower never ceased to excite him. The 42 floors of glass and steel were a mark of how far he'd risen in the last ten years, taking the company from a two-story factory in Slough to a Times Top 100 company in the heart of the City. The rotating doors were spewing out a steady stream of employees. Anyone else trying to enter would have struggled, but Petersen was the CEO and a path parted quickly for him. He noticed his employees avoided his eye, not wishing to be noticed leaving by the big boss, despite the lateness of the hour. Petersen looked straight ahead. His gaze said he was too concerned with weighty matters to even notice their departure. He rode his private elevator to the 42nd floor where the directors' offices were located. It was late and all the other offices were empty. Only Molly, his personal secretary, was still there, talking on the phone. She looked up and gave him a broad smile as he passed. He hung his jacket on the mahogany hanger in his private closet and poured a small Scotch.

Molly put her head around the door. 'Do you need me to stay, George?'

Molly was one of the few people who still called him by his first name. She'd been with him for ten years and he joked with his senior colleagues that she knew him better that anyone, including his wife. It was probably true. She'd always looked after him with unstinting loyalty and he'd rewarded that loyalty in many ways, though never, he suspected, in the way she really wanted. Petersen was a handsome man and Molly a romantic middle-aged woman. The eye contact held a fraction longer than usual was enough to tell him he could sleep with her anytime, but he was never tempted. Aside from being a little too old and plump for his taste, Molly's adoration was far too valuable to risk losing. In a position like his, where discretion was paramount, there was no better assurance of loyalty than the infatuation of an older woman.

'No, you go,' he told her. 'But thanks for waiting. You're a darling.'

'Your messages are all logged,' she said with a smile.

'As I knew they would be,' he grinned. 'Now go!'

He took his Scotch and stood by the window, looking down over the lights of London. It was a view he never tired of seeing. He was about to attack the paperwork on his desk when there was a soft knock at his door. 'Come,' he called out, wondering if Molly had returned. No one entered. The knock came again. He went and opened the door. Before him stood a woman he didn't recognise dressed in a drab blue cotton shirt, grey slacks and black lace-up shoes – hardly the sort of outfit normally seen on the 42nd floor. Her hair was brassy blond, the kind that comes from low-quality dye. Her almond eyes were dark, almost black. She was well into her thirties but her skin was immaculate save for a small imperfection on her right cheek. Her bronze skin-tone set off the golden hair to stunning effect.

'Security,' she said with a smile.

Her voice was foreign, Eastern European, he thought, but he couldn't be sure.

'I'm sorry to disturb you but I need to look inside,' she added. 'Is that alright?'

'By all means,' he said, holding the door open for her to pass. It took him a moment to realise her outfit was the same one worn by all the other security guards. On her it looked very different.

'No Henry tonight?' he asked.

'Henry is ill,' she said, stepping past him and walking to the centre of the office. Petersen stole a look at her figure as she did. The unflattering grey trousers couldn't hide the long tapered legs and narrow hips. He imagined she'd been an athlete or a dancer before she had become a security guard.

She glanced around quickly and turned to him with an

apologetic shrug. 'I'm sorry, but my instructions were very specific. I have to check every office. I hope you don't mind.'

'Not at all,' he said, throwing up his hands theatrically. 'Security's important.' He frowned with mock gravity. 'So what do you think? Is it safe in here?'

She smiled. 'I think so,' she said, a little of her nervousness vanishing.

She got his humour. He liked that.

'I'm sorry to have disturbed you,' she said, making her way back to the door. 'It's just that this is my first night on the job and I need to be thorough.'

'I completely understand,' he assured her, enchanted by his unusual visitor, who had the grace and poise of a beautiful woman combined with a delicious nervousness of a first-time employee. It was an irresistible combination and Petersen forgot all about the paperwork.

'I love your accent,' he said. 'Where're you from?'

'Romania,' she told him. She was just one step away and he could smell her faintly. It wasn't perfume, that would have been out of place for a security guard, just the subtle waft of soap or shampoo, he couldn't tell which. She smelled fresh and clean. He liked that smell.

'Well, you make a pleasant change from Henry, I must say,' he said, sticking his hands in his pockets and leaning back on his heels.

'That's good, because Henry won't be back for at least a week. Maybe longer.'

'Oh dear, poor Henry. Nothing serious I hope?'

'Food poisoning, apparently.'

'Nasty.'

She was about to step past him but he held out his hand to

prevent her. 'Well listen, I often work late and since we're going to be seeing each other regularly, you'd better tell me your name.'

'My name is Nadia,' she told him.

'Just Nadia?' he asked.

'Nadia Antonescu.'

'Nadia Antonescu.' He repeated the name, making a good attempt at the pronunciation. 'You have such lovely names where you come from.' She smiled at this. He went on. 'Well I've met quite a few security guards in my time Nadia, but I must say, none like you.'

'What do you mean, 'like me'?' she demanded.

'Well a woman for a start. And a beautiful one at that.'

She tried to hide it but Petersen could see she liked the compliment. He continued: 'Mostly it's just old Henry on the night shift – not the most interesting chap in the world, unless you want to know all about London and the Blitz.'

'I don't know anything about a Blitz,' she said blankly.

'I'm sure you don't my dear,' he chuckled. 'So tell me anyway, what brings you to London, Nadia Antonescu?'

'I came here for the same reason that everyone comes, to make a better life for myself.'

'But how did you end up here, in Havilland Ethical, working in security? I'm fascinated …'

'In Romania I was in the army. Working in security was easy for me.'

'You were a soldier?' he said, delighted at the notion.

'A lieutenant,' she said proudly.

He imagined her in a tight-fitting army uniform. It was a good picture – far better than the cheap security guard's uniform she wore now. Then he imagined her out of it – it was even better.

She smiled. He didn't want to let her go. 'Of course,' he nodded. 'It makes perfect sense. Well listen, what time do you finish tonight, Nadia?'

'This was the last stop on my rounds,' she told him.

'Splendid. Now, I know you're a security guard, and a former soldier as well, but it's late, and London's not the safest place at this time of night. I'm just finishing up here too, so why don't I drop you home?'

'I don't think so ...' she began.

'Where do you live?'

'Earls Court.'

'Earl's Court is on my way,' he said triumphantly. 'So it's settled.'

She frowned. 'I don't think Mr. Knowles would be very happy.'

'Who the hell is Mr. Knowles?'

'He is the head of security.'

'Oh, Knowles! Listen, don't worry about Knowles. I'm Knowles' boss.'

'People might talk.'

'Who might talk? Everyone's gone home. And besides, we'll take the Aston.'

She looked at him blankly.

'My own car,' he explained. 'No chauffeur. No gossip.'

He saw she was still unsure. 'Even if someone does find out, what are they going to say? It's hardly a crime to give a colleague a lift home.'

She smiled and her thick red lips curled provocatively. 'A colleague?'

'It's just a lift, nothing more,' he assured her, his hands held up in surrender. 'You have the word of an English gentleman.'

She laughed at this, and he saw he'd won her over. 'I'll meet you in the car park in ten minutes,' he told her.

Twenty minutes later he was still waiting in the car park, and beginning to wonder if she'd changed her mind. He'd been watching the elevator and expecting it to open, forgetting that security staff were not allowed to use that facility. He didn't notice the stairwell door swing open and only glimpsed her approaching figure when she was a few paces from the car. Still, it was enough to see she'd changed into a more appealing outfit, a figure-hugging skirt and jacket and a pair of four-inch heels. The ensemble wasn't expensive – from a high street chain he imagined – but it looked brand new, and with her blonde hair hanging loose and down she looked every bit as good as a catwalk model.

He lowered the passenger window. 'Hop in.'

She leaned inside. 'This is your car?'

'Just a little run-around.'

'You didn't tell me you had a James-Bond car.'

'I thought I mentioned it was an Aston.'

'I don't know this make.'

'Like you said, a *James Bond* car,' he grinned. 'Watch your head when you get in.'

There was no need to warn her. She slipped lithely inside and settled easily into the reclining leather seat. Petersen watched as she turned to reach for her seatbelt. He tried to imagine what she must be thinking now, how unimaginable it must be for a former soldier from Romania to find herself in an Aston Martin V8 Vanquish. He had to admit that despite the cheap clothing and the brassy hair, she didn't look out of place in it, not in the slightest. 'Hold tight,' he said, flooring the accelerator and releasing the handbrake. The tyres screeched their protest, seeking purchase on the smooth concrete before firing the car forward in a cloud of smoke. The force threw her back in her seat, but she didn't cry out or clutch at the door handle in fright, and Petersen sensed she was enjoying the thrill.

Once they'd exited the car park onto the main road, Petersen slowed down. The City of London was the most heavily policed square mile in Britain and filled with cameras that, unlike those inside Havilland Ethical, he couldn't control. Besides, there was no need to speed. The traffic was light at this hour and they progressed swiftly down King William Street and west across the Bank intersection onto Queen Victoria Street. The earlier rain had changed to a dry powdery snow and the Christmas lights twinkled on frosted trees. 'London's beautiful at this time of night, don't you think?' he asked.

'London is a fantastic city,' she replied.

'Is it your first Christmas here?'

'It is, but I'm not staying for the festivities. I'm returning to Romania at the end of this week.'

'So we won't see you again until the next Millennium,' he chuckled.

'I guess not.'

'Will you come back to Havilland Ethical?' he asked.

'I hope so. But if Henry is better, I may go somewhere else.'

'I'll have a word with Knowles if you like,' he said. 'See if we can arrange something more permanent for you. If you'd like that, of course.'

'Why not?' she said. 'Your company is very smart compared to most of the places I've worked.'

'I imagine it is,' he said happily.

'You must be very successful,' she said. He felt her eyes on him, assessing him. It never ceased to amaze him what an aphrodisiac power was to a woman. He had no objection to this. He'd worked hard to get where he was today and beautiful women were just a natural part of the reward.

'We do alright,' he said with exaggerated modesty. 'Most of the time.'

'What do you do in Havilland Ethical?' she asked.

'We make medicines. Herbal remedies, mostly.'

'You make all this money from herbal remedies?' she said in amazement.

'It's a big market, and growing all the time,' he told her.

She shook her head in disbelief. 'In Romania we have herbal remedies too. Every old grandmother knows herbal remedies, but none of them drives around in an *Aston*.'

'It's not just knowing the herbs. It's knowing the market, knowing what people want. And giving it to them.' And what do people want?' she asked.

'We have a new drug just released called Shangri-la. It's already our biggest seller by a country mile.'

'Shangri-la, where people live forever?' she asked, unsure if she'd understood correctly.

He nodded.

You're not serious,' she scoffed.

'About living forever? No. We call it *slowing the signs of aging*. People are going crazy for it.'

'Which herbs do you use?' she demanded.

'That's top secret, I'm afraid,' he said with an apologetic smile.

'So you *are* James Bond,' she smiled.

'Quite right, Miss Moneypenny.'

She was silent. He was aware of her shifting in her seat and crossing her legs, the creak of the leather and the rustle of her stockings against the lining of her skirt. 'It's alright, you don't have to tell me,' she said quietly.

He sensed her disappointment in his lack of trust. He stole another glance at the strange, beautiful woman from Romania, whose idea of herbal medicine was probably a few grasses and weeds collected from the slopes of the Transylvanian Alps, and weighed up the risk of telling her more against the pleasure of finding himself between her thighs later that night.

'Have you heard of ginseng?' he asked.

'Yes of course. Even in Romania we have ginseng.' 'Well this is a unique strain, very powerful, found only in Tibet. It's hellish difficult to get hold of. In fact we have to smuggle the bloody stuff out of the country illegally.'

'That must be difficult,' she said.

'It is. And expensive. Or at least it *was*.'

'Not any more?' she asked lightly.

'No. We found a way of growing the damned stuff a little closer to home.'

'Really? Where?'

'That I can't tell you Nadia, seriously,' he said, nodding to emphasise his point. 'I've told you too much already. If I tell you any more I'll have to kill you.'

Whitmoor Common, Guildford, January 2000

DCI Jeremy Simons squatted beside the car to get a better look at the body. The icy morning had made his knees stiffer than usual, and he cursed the low-slung design of the Aston Martin. The driver's door had been opened and the hosepipe pulled out of the gap at the top of the window and left on the stony ground. The other end was still taped around the mouth of the exhaust.

The body was pale, the eyes closed, the mouth open in one long, final cough. The pallid skin tone seemed out of place beside the expensively tailored suit and the Aston Martin.

Simons heard the crunch of footsteps behind him and turned to see DC Mena Gakhar approaching. She looked frozen, but cheerful nevertheless. Gakhar had been seconded to his team just two weeks earlier, when another young female officer had left on maternity leave. When he'd heard that a young Pakistani woman had been assigned to him, he'd not been pleased. He was aware of the need to improve the force's ethnic ratios – especially the Surrey police – but he'd secretly dreaded having to pussyfoot around a young Muslim girl just to satisfy some politically correct paper-pushers in Whitehall. As it turned out, he needn't have worried. Gakhar's parents might have been from a small village in Pakistan, but Mena had been born and bred in Bradford and apart from the colour of her skin, she seemed no different to any other stout Yorkshire lass.

She'd been first on the scene that morning and had been taking statements from the council workers who'd found the body. She reported what she'd learnt to Simons:

'Workers saw the car and the hosepipe and opened the door to see if he were still alive. Got a right shock when they saw 'im they did.'

Gakhar's thick Yorkshire accent still came as a surprise to Simons. The rolling vowels and clipped consonants seemed out of place coming from such an exotic-looking woman.

'Have we got a name yet?' he asked.

'Just come in. Car's registered to a George Petersen.'

'I know that name.'

Simons searched his memory. Gakhar pulled a mobile phone from her jacket and punched the number keys.

'Who are you texting?' he asked.

'I'm not texting, I'm surfing.'

'On your phone?'

She looked at him blankly, her round eyes boring into his, and suddenly Simons felt like the dinosaur he'd promised himself he'd never become.

'Says here he's the CEO of a company called Havilland Ethical,' Gakhar told him. 'Ring any bells?'

'That's him,' Simons exclaimed. 'I thought I knew the face. His company collapsed just last week, almost brought the whole bloody stock market down with it.'

'Says here company secrets were leaked to the press by an unknown source,' Gakhar said, reading on. 'City police are investigating.'

'Then they might be a good place to start,' Simons said.

Gakhar pocketed the phone and leaned into the car. Simons imagined she might have had enough of the body, but Mena seemed drawn to the dead man. 'Strange that he should top himself though, 'int it?' she said. 'Why would you want do that, with all that money and all?'

'His company had gone down the toilet, Mena.'

Gakhar leaned in further, so close to the body that her nose was almost touching it. Simons knew there would be no smell, it was too soon and too cold, but even so, he found himself put off by her obvious fascination with the corpse.

'Still, he would've had a few quid minted away, wouldn't he?' she said, speaking loudly so Simons could hear her. 'They always have a few quid minted away, don't they, rich people? In one of them places where the Nazis stuck all their gold and paintings – a Swiss bank that don't ask for names. Numbered accounts only. Or one of them off-shore banks in the Bahamas or the Canary Islands.'

'Cayman,' he corrected.

'What?'

She emerged from the car and stepped close, a little too close for comfort, considering how near she'd been to the dead man.

'The Cayman Islands are a tax haven, not the Canary Islands,' he said lightly, feeling a little guilty for correcting her. He hoped she didn't think he was being patronising. She stared at him, her eyes unblinking, the thick shoulders set firm, the ample bosom pointing at him accusingly. 'I still don't know why you'd want to go and top yerself,' she said finally.

'He was ruined. A man like Petersen lives for his reputation.'

'Got mixed up in some dodgy dealings, y'think?'

'Perhaps.'

'Then maybe it's not suicide. Maybe it's murder.'

'We'll let the coroner decide that.'

'And forensics,' she added.

'We're not on telly now, Mena. Wait for the coroner's report. And in the meantime, go and inform the family.'

investigation was little more than a pale-faced boy with lank ginger hair and freckles. Shaking Childs' bony hand, Simons was reminded of meeting one of his son David's friends when David had been a teenager. That had been some time ago, ten years at least. David was married now and living in Australia. Simons smiled at Childs reassuringly, hoping his surprise hadn't been too obvious. Every officer seemed young to him now, it was yet another sign of his age.

'Tea? Coffee?' Childs asked. 'The machine's pretty pants, but it's all we have. They took our kettle away last week.'

'They took your kettle away? How come?' Simons asked in surprise.

'Health and Safety,' Childs answered.

'What on earth did they think you were going to do to yourselves?' Simons asked, happy to start out on a friendly note. Things went a lot smoother if there was a good rapport between the officers involved in a case from different forces. He knew this from past experience, some of it bitter.

'Burn ourselves, I guess,' Childs shrugged. His shoulders moving inside his oversized suit reminded Simons of a bag of bones. Was the young officer simply acting serious, or did he really have no sense of humour?' Simons decided to give it one more try. 'You're based in the Square Mile, number one target of the IRA and every other terrorist with an axe to grind, and they take away your kettle in case someone gets hurt?' He rolled his eyes. 'Brass, eh?'

'It's messed up,' Childs nodded.

Messed up? Simons had only heard that on TV before. American cop shows. He guessed Childs watched them. It was a losing battle. Childs punched the button for tea with extra sugar and the machine set about making it. A thin grey liquid emerged into a ribbed plastic cup. 'Want one?' Childs asked.

'I'll pass, thanks,' Simons smiled.

'Water?' Childs offered in a final bid at hospitality.

'If you're sure it's safe,' Simons said with a straight face.

'No known incidents of disease or death so far,' Childs grinned, handing him a cup.

'Thanks,' Simons said with a grin of his own.

Childs showed him into an interview room so small that there was barely enough room for the table and four chairs inside. The interview rooms in the Surrey Police headquarters were considerably bigger, but space wasn't at such a premium there. Childs put a file on the table and took a ballpoint pen from his jacket that he clicked repeatedly, much to Simons' irritation.

'We found a body this morning, on rough ground just outside Guildford,' Simons began. 'Suicide, by the looks of it. Gassed himself in his car. Car's registered to George Petersen.'

'Ah,' Childs nodded slowly.

Simons leaned forward. 'I know Petersen was ruined, and facing a scandal, but even so it's pretty drastic, killing yourself like that. I'm trying to get a clearer picture of what happened and whether there are any suspicious circumstances we should be looking into.'

'We're still in the early stages of our investigation, but I'm happy to share what I have so far,' Childs said. He stopped clicking his pen and put it on the table, much to Simons' relief. 'Havillands had just launched their new wonder drug called Shangri-la – a new anti-aging drug, herbal based, the next big thing. They'd invested millions in it, done a big publicity push to coincide with the new millennium: press conference, ad campaign, celebrity endorsements, the works. A week later,

The Times ran a story saying the drug was fake. Petersen fought to discredit it, but the paper stuck to its guns, and it turned out to be true. The drug was fake.'

'How did The Times get the story?'

'We're trying to find out, but the paper's holding tight to its sources.'

'Can't you force them to tell you?'

'We could get a High Court summons, but they'll just say it was an anonymous tip-off and we won't be able to prove otherwise.'

'There must be a way to find out,' Simons said.

'I'm pursuing another angle,' Childs said. 'I have an interview with the former PR Director of Havillands this morning.' He pulled out his PDA and brought up his calendar to check the details: 'Geri Harper, eleven thirty.'

'Mind if I tag along?' Simons said.

Childs smiled. 'Sure, inter-force cooperation, and all that.'

Simons grinned at the younger man to hide his irritation. He didn't like having to ask to 'tag along'. Childs was little more than half his age, and only one rank below him. Where were they getting their officers from these days, kindergarten? Worse still, he seemed to be using the same type of mobile phone as Mena Gakhar, and the bloody thing did everything except make the tea. He'd have to get one, and then the fun would start, trying to figure out how the bloody thing worked.

Havilland Ethical, Old Broad Street, London

There were three hundred angry shareholders outside Havilland Ethical when Simons and Childs arrived. They were pushing and shoving, hoping to get inside and recover some assets, however small, or perhaps simply to vent their fury on the management, if they could find anyone. The revolving doors that had once spun automatically throughout the day had been locked, and two security guards were controlling a single side entrance. Simons and Childs pushed through the crowd, badges raised. The security guards allowed them through and they rode the elevator to the 40th floor in silence, unsettled by the scenes outside.

Simons glanced at his appearance in the elevator's mirrored panels. He looked tired. These days he always looked tired. He'd be fifty soon. He still thought of himself as young, but his body had other ideas, and the grey was winning the battle against the brown in his thinning hair. He brushed his short fringe over to the side with his fingers, and straightened his tie. He always wore the most expensive suits and shirts his salary would allow, but in a place like Havilland Ethical, he would always be poorly dressed. But now that an investigation was under way, the cut of his suit didn't matter. Those tailored Savile Row suits and Armani shirts would have to answer to him just as surely as the hoodies and druggies who hung around the town centre in Guildford.

The lift door opened and a petite woman in a grey suit greeted him. 'Detective Childs?' Her smile was rather forced, Simons thought. He pointed her to Childs with a smile and Childs stepped forward and shook her hand. 'I'm Detective

Inspector Childs and this is DCI Simons, from the Surrey Police.'

'Two of you?' she asked.

'There's been a new development in the case this morning, and DCI Simons is partnering us in our investigation,' Childs explained.

She looked from Childs to Simons. Her face was pale and drawn. Simons guessed she'd been crying just moments earlier, and was putting on a brave face for the police. He wondered how the news of her CEO's death might affect her.

She led them through an empty reception area and down a corridor straddled by spacious glass-fronted offices, all vacant now. They entered a boardroom and took seats on the end of the large oval table.

'I'm not sure how much I can help you,' she said. 'Or even if I should be talking to you without a lawyer.'

'You're not under arrest, Ms Harper,' Childs said gently. 'This is an informal interview, at present.'

'Even so, I don't know very much about what went on.'

'Well just try to answer as best you can,' Childs said with a smile.

'Did you know George Petersen was found dead this morning?' Simons said.

She'd had no idea, that much was plain from her reaction. He continued, allowing her time to take in the news. 'It was suicide, by the looks of it. Hosepipe taped to the exhaust of his car.'

There was no sign of personal loss in her face or body language. 'First the share-price collapse, then this. Are you sure it's George?' she said, her lips twitching involuntarily into a frightened grimace.

Simons nodded. 'The car's his. The face matches the photos we have of him. His wife will make the final identification, of course, and the coroner will verify it.'

'What do you need from me?' she asked.

'The company's been in the news a lot recently,' Childs began, turning his pen over and over and clicking the end open and shut. 'First the launch of the new wonder drug, then the rumours of fraud, then the share-price crash. What went wrong, exactly?'

She sat more upright in her chair, marshalling her thoughts. 'Shangri-la – the wonder drug, as you call it – was made from a rare type of ginseng that grows only in Tibet. It was very expensive to farm and import, hence the premium price. George was hoping to grow the plant closer to home and reduce costs. The processing and packaging was done just outside Edinburgh, and I know George was trying to grow the ginseng in Scotland…'

'Where in Scotland?'

'Somewhere in the Highlands, to try and replicate the climate conditions of the Himalayas. The exact location was secret. You'll need to talk to the head of operations up there.'

''He caught a flight to Taiwan this morning,' Childs said. 'The extradition papers are being drawn up as we speak.'

'Really? Oh my God, what have they done?'

'You tell us Ms Harper,' Simons said.

'I had no idea he'd succeeded, that he was growing it already.'

'But someone did, because they told The Times and The Times printed the story,' Simons said.

'Yes,' she said quietly.

'And the story turned out to be true,' Childs said more gently.

Simons sat back in his chair. He had been taking over the younger man's investigation. It was poor form.

'But I had no idea,' she said, her voice tight. She was on the verge of new tears. 'None of us did.'

'Would such a story be enough to cause the collapse of the entire firm?' Simons asked quietly. 'Havilland Ethical sold plenty of other drugs too.'

'Absolutely it would,' she replied. 'You have to understand the pharmaceutical industry. It's all about ethics – hence the company name. A scandal like this undermines the brand to its core, raising questions over every other product in its range.' She fought back the tears that threatened to surface at any moment. 'That story was a death warrant for Havillands, pure and simple. Once the shareholders got wind of it they were falling over themselves to sell. The creditors saw what was happening and started calling in their loans. The company had borrowed heavily to push the new drug. It had little in the way of liquid assets to call on. Within a week the stocks weren't worth the paper they were printed on.'

'Do you have any idea how the information got to The Times?' Childs asked.

'No, but I know George was going crazy searching for the leak. He insisted it must have come from Scotland. He was on the phone to Scotland for hours each day.'

'And how did he seem, personally?' Simons asked.

'Agitated, distant.'

'Not his usual self?'

'Not at all.'

'What was his usual self, Ms Harper?' Simons asked.

'Confident, self-assured.'

'How well did you know him?'

'I knew him well enough professionally, but not personally, if that's what you're driving at.'

'Who did know him personally?' Simons asked.

Geri Harper shrugged. 'Not his wife, that's for sure. The best person to speak to would be Molly Parker. She's his PA – *was* his PA,' she corrected herself.

'Where can we get hold of Molly Parker?' Childs asked, reaching for his mobile. Simons watched as Childs prepared to make a note of the address on his phone. He wondered if his phone could do the same. It didn't look nearly as flash as Childs' phone.

'I'll check the records,' Harper said, opening the laptop on the table. 'I know she lives in Highgate, but if you wait a moment, I'll give you the exact address.'

Highgate Village, London

With its leafy streets, homely pubs and individual little curiosity shops, Highgate reminded Simons more of a quaint Surrey village than a north London suburb.

He parked his police Mondeo in the street next to Molly Parker's and they walked around the corner to her flat. Simons had no wish to give her neighbours cause for gossip. Molly had taken the news of Petersen's suicide badly when he'd telephoned her earlier. There was no need to add to her misery.

When she opened the door, her eyes were small and her mouth was drawn in a tight line. She'd been crying recently, but she was trying hard to stay in control. Simons smiled encouragingly. She let them in without a word. They sat on two floral armchairs and Molly sat opposite on a matching sofa. She reminded Simons of a daytime TV presenter, the neat haircut, smooth make-up, and a body that said she was careful what she ate, most of the time. From the hurt in her eyes he imagined she'd cared deeply for Petersen. He wondered if Petersen had had the same feelings for her.

'Thanks for seeing us at such short notice,' he began gently. 'I know this is difficult, but we need to find out exactly what happened to Mr. Petersen – to George – so we can put the whole matter to rest quickly.'

'I can't believe it,' she said in a tiny voice. 'First that dreadful newspaper report, then the collapse. Now this...'

He nodded sympathetically. 'I understand you knew George as well as anyone. Can you tell us how he was in the last week?'

'He wasn't his usual self, of course he wasn't,' she said, irritated by the question. 'The company that he'd spent years building was collapsing around him. His life's work had been ruined in a matter of days by one stupid newspaper story.'

'How was he different?' Simons asked quietly.

'He was frantic, trying to find the source of the leak. He was on the phone to Scotland for hours. There were arguments, accusations... It was horrible. He was going crazy trying to find that bloody woman.'

'Which woman?' Simons asked.

Molly pursed her lips.

'Please, Ms Parker,' he said softly. 'We'll keep it as confidential as we can, his family's suffered enough. But we need to know.'

'Well it's no secret George was a bit of a lady's man.' She smiled thinly.

'Go on,' he nodded.

'He'd been seeing a new woman recently,' she said, her fingers twisting as she spoke.

'Did you know her? Did you see them together yourself?'

'I heard it from Charlie Knowles.'

'Charlie Knowles?'

'Head of Security, I've known him for years.'

'And how did Charlie Knowles know?' Simons asked.

'Well that's the funny thing. This woman was a security guard, believe it or not, and quite beautiful, apparently. I never saw her myself because she worked the late shift. Charlie said she was Eastern European, Romanian, I think. When the story broke, George got Charlie Knowles to try and trace her, but she'd gone back to Romania by then.'

'Do you have a name for this woman?' Simons asked.

'Nadia *Something-or-Other* completely unpronounceable,' she shrugged. 'Charlie will know. You'd best ask him.

City Police Headquarters, London

The tiny interview room felt more cramped than ever. The large, ruddy-faced man sitting across the table from Simons was Charlie Knowles, one-time Head of Security at Havilland Ethical. Knowles was around fifty, solid and heavyset, with large, blunt fingers that he pressed together while he waited for the interview to begin. With DI Childs sitting beside him, Simons felt hemmed-in in the airless room and wished he had grabbed a cup of water from the machine while he'd had the chance. It was a bit late now, they were all seated and ready to begin. He decided to launch into the interview instead, hoping that once it began he would forget the mild feeling of panic that threatened to overwhelm him.

'Thanks for meeting us here Mr. Knowles,' he said briskly. 'Just so you're aware, DI Childs is investigating allegations of fraud while I'm looking into the death of George Petersen.'

'Anything I can do to help,' Knowles said. He had the calm, clipped tones of someone who had once served in the army or perhaps even the police.

'We understand George Petersen was having a relationship with one of the security guards at Havilland Ethical shortly before the collapse. Can you confirm that?' Simons asked.

Knowles sighed. 'Yes… a Romanian woman called Nadia Antonescu. She was taken on as a temp over the Christmas period to cover for another guard who was ill. When the scandal broke, Mr. Petersen asked me to get hold of her. Said it was urgent. I tried, but she'd gone back to Romania. Petersen got quite insistent. In fact, he was going bloody berserk.' Knowles stopped for a moment and Simons could see that despite the calm exterior, the whole business had hit him hard.

'Did you see them together?' he asked gently.

Knowles shook his head. 'One of my guys saw them leaving late at night in Petersen's Aston Martin. They did it four nights in a row. She never turned up again after that.'

'You think this woman's responsible for the leak?' Childs asked.

Knowles shrugged. 'My guess is Petersen told her things he shouldn't have and the press got hold of it. Maybe she sold the information, or told the wrong people, I don't know. But Petersen was determined to trace her. I got onto the firm that supplied her, Limehouse Security, but they couldn't get hold of her either. No one could. She just bloody well vanished. I even contacted the Romanian police and they checked her out. Turned out Nadia Antonescu was an eighty-year-old woman living in a little village in Transylvania.'

'Is there anything you can tell us about her?' Childs asked.

'I never met her personally,' Knowles said. 'She was on the night shift, I worked in the day, but I do have something that might help. She had a security pass to swipe in and out. All her entries and exits are logged. I collected all the CCTV footage from around the building during the times she was there and went through them.'

'It must've taken hours,' Childs cut in.

'Tell me about it,' Knowles smiled, 'But if it got Petersen off my back, it was worth it. The funny thing was, apart from the fact that she's blonde and has a great figure, it's hard to make out anything about her at all. Either she just happened to be looking the other way whenever she passed a camera, or she knew every damned CCTV in the building.'

'Did you get anything at all?' Simons demanded, struggling

to keep the frustration from his voice.

Knowles reached into his briefcase and took out a plastic bag filled with DVDs and a large envelope. He withdrew a 10 x 8 print from the envelope. 'This was taken in the basement car park on the first night. We'd only installed that camera the week before, so perhaps she didn't know about it. Anyway, it picked up her face, just this one time.'

Simons stared at the grainy image of a woman. Her legs were obscured by an Aston Martin, the same car he'd seen on the waste ground outside Guildford. She was looking into the passenger-side window, a half-smile on her lips. Her hair shading half of her face and the shot was distant and blurred, like a paparazzo shot snapped with a long lens, but Simons could still make out the almond eyes and fine cheekbones of a beautiful woman.

'This is all you got?' he asked.

'I checked every inch of the disks personally, Knowles told him. 'But be my guest and check them again. This is the best shot you'll get of Nadia Antonescu, or whoever the hell she really is.'

'She could be anyone,' Simons said absently.

'One more thing,' Knowles said, waiting until both detectives were looking at him before continuing. 'The security guard she was standing in for – an old chap called Henry who's been with me for years – well it turns out he'd been poisoned. He's still on a life-support machine at University College Hospital. I just thought you should know.'

Retton Road, Guildford

Simons hung up his coat and put his briefcase in the cupboard beneath the stairs. His wife was watching TV in the living room. The door was ajar and he could see what she was watching: a detective show set in Los Angeles. Two handsome young cops were driving a powerful black car and chasing a van. The rear doors to the van were open and two men with machine guns were firing at the cops.

'You're back late,' his wife said.

He put his head around the door. 'Been up in London. A new case. The CEO of Havilland Ethical topped himself last night.'

'Your dinner's in the microwave,' she told him.

He heated up the breaded fish, mashed potatoes and peas, and brought it into the living room. He ate it on his lap.

'I do wish you'd use a tray,' she said without looking up from the TV. He wondered how she even knew.

'I know how to eat without spilling my food everywhere,' he told her, as he always did when she said that.

One of the TV cops was leaning out of the window and firing his pistol at the van.

'We had a phone call from David today,' she said without taking her eyes off the TV. 'He says we should go over to Australia to visit them. He says he sent you an email with some photos of little Matthew. It's his first birthday next week, but he's walking already.'

Simons chewed his food and swallowed before answering. 'I'd love to go and see them, you know that. But we've been through it all before.'

'Tell me again why we can't go?' she said, muting the cop show and turning to face him.

'Do we have to do this now?' he asked. 'It's been a long day.'

'Then when would you like to 'do-this' as you call it? I never see you. You're home late every night.'

'There's a new case,' he said, putting his knife and fork down hard on the plate. 'A bloody Romanian spy is on the loose in London.'

She stared at him as if he was mad. He rose and took his plate to the kitchen, where he shovelled the remains of the fish into the bin and stuck his plate in the dishwasher. He didn't want to watch the American cop show, he'd had enough far-fetched police work for one day. He went upstairs to read, knowing his wife would find him asleep when she came up to bed later.

Surrey Police Headquarters

Simons arrived at the station early the next morning. He liked to get to the kitchen before the rush and prepare his first cup of tea in peace.

Three sullen young men with cuts and bruises were seated in the corridor, brought in the night before for being drunk and disorderly. They'd spent the night in the cells and were waiting to get back their personal possessions before being released. Simons could see the duty sergeant taking his time in filling out the forms, forming each capital letter perfectly before moving onto the next. The sergeant was a bastard. The young men must be desperate for a cup of tea right now. Even more desperate than he was himself. He flicked on the kettle. Unlike the City Police, his station hadn't fallen victim to health and safety just yet and they still had one. The water was already hot. Someone had been in just before him. That person was Mena Gakhar and she appeared in the doorway now.

'Chief, there's someone to see you.'

'What, now?'

Gakhar nodded.

'Where?'

'They're waiting in your office.'

'Well, who is it?' he demanded testily.

She smiled nervously, and for the first time Simons noticed she seemed unsure of herself. 'I spoke to MI5 last night, like you told me to. Asked for any photos they had of female spies from the Eastern Bloc …' She hesitated.

'And…?'

'And they put me through to this woman who asked me to

tell her more. I told her what you told me about this Nadia Antonescu. She asked to see the photo, so I emailed it to her.'

'You emailed a photo?' Simons frowned.

'Yes, I scanned it first, then emailed it.'

'Go on,' he nodded.

'Did I do wrong?'

'Just tell me what happened…'

'Nothing, until I got here this morning. Now there's a George Smith from MI5 here to see you.'

'George Smith from MI5? It's too early in the morning for a wind-up, Mena.'

'Seriously, Guv. She's in your office now.'

'She?'

Gakhar nodded.

Simons had had enough. He took his tea and threw open the door to his office. Inside he found a graceful woman of sixty sitting upright on the chair beside his desk. At least she hadn't taken his chair. The minimal courtesies had been obeyed. She'd been beautiful once, he could see, and even now she was a handsome woman. With her long grey hair brushed to a sheen and tied in a ponytail, she looked more like a high-class lawyer than a spy, but that was a good thing, he imagined, if you really were a spy.

'I'm DCI Simons,' he said. 'What's this about?'

The woman stood with a warm smile and offered her hand. 'Georgina Smith, but everyone calls me George.'

Gakhar hovered outside. Simons ushered her in and sat in his chair. Gakhar closed the door.

'The woman you're looking for in relation to the Havilland Ethical case…' Smith spoke in a breezy tone, as if relaying a little local news, '…I wanted to give you a little "heads-up" about her.'

'A heads-up?'

Smith nodded as she took a file from her briefcase. 'That's what they say these days, isn't it?'' She smiled as she withdrew the photo that Gakhar had sent over and placed it deliberately on the desk. 'This is the woman you're after, yes?'

'Yes,' Simons answered warily. 'You have information on her?'

'You could say that,' Smith nodded. 'This type of case is quite rare but there have been others.'

'What type of case is that?' he demanded.

'Industrial espionage, I suppose you'd call it,' she said absently. She placed another photo of a dark-haired woman beside the first. It was taken in what looked like a large American city. 'Chicago, 1997.' She said, placing more photos of different women on the desk. 'Frankfurt, 1996. Tokyo, 1995. Strasbourg, 1994.'

'Who are all these women?' he asked.

'That is the question,' she smiled. 'All I can really tell you is the woman you're seeking is almost certainly Russian rather than Romanian and what's known as a *swallow* – a Soviet-trained spy specialising in seduction.'

Simons sighed. 'A sex-spy? Forgive me George, but isn't that a bit far-fetched?'

'Not at all. Swallows were one of the Soviet Union's most powerful weapons of the Cold War. *Ravens* too – male spies.'

Simons stared at her. 'Hookers and gigolos?'

'These weren't common prostitutes, Detective Chief Inspector. They were highly-trained agents able to move in the highest circles, mixing with politicians, scientists, NATO brass. The secrets they stole from the West were staggering in their breadth and depth.' She placed photos of more women on the table. 'Cuba 1988, Helsinki 1987, Rome 1986, Washington 1985, France 1984. And these weren't industrial secrets, Inspector. These were missile guidance systems, nuclear launch codes, the names of our own agents in the East. People killed for those secrets. People died for them.'

'That's all very well, but what can you tell us about this particular woman?' Simons asked, stabbing his finger on the photo of Nadia.

Smith put her file on his desk. 'Everything we know about her is in here. It's not much, considering.'

'Okay, we'll take a look. Thank you.'

She regarded him coolly. 'I didn't come here to drop-off a file for you, Detective Chief Inspector. I came to warn you. The woman you're seeking is highly dangerous. Approach her with extreme caution and don't try and bring her in alone.'

Simons couldn't hide his irritation any longer. 'Look I know we're not exactly MI5 here, but we do more than cautioning hoodies in the town centre, you know. We've even managed to arrest a few dangerous criminals in our time, including a known psychopath, without calling in the cavalry.'

Smith's tone softened. 'I'm sorry Detective Chief Inspector, I didn't mean to imply any disrespect. It's just that this woman is not a psychopath, she's a trained killer. There's a big difference.'

'I'll bear that in mind,' Simons said bluntly.

'She's an expert marksman,' Smith went on, ignoring his tone. 'Although I suppose I should say *markswoman* nowadays. She's also lethal with knives, darts, poisons. She can turn ordinary household objects into deadly weapons. And if that's not enough, she'll kill you with her bare hands.'

'She sounds perfectly charming.'

Smith sighed and waited before speaking. 'This is what makes her so dangerous,' she said, regarding Simons with something close to pity. 'The male ego, so fragile, so easy to manipulate.' She shot a glance at Mena Gakhar before looking back at Simons, the annoyance showing in her eyes now. 'You have no bloody idea who you're dealing with, man. Take a proper look at the photos!'

Simons glared at her for a moment, then examined the faces once more. Gakhar joined him and they pored over the images together. Most were blurred, distant, snapped haphazardly or enlarged from a small passport-sized photo. The women were of different ages and types, pale-skinned blondes, healthy-looking brunettes, dark-haired women of Asian origin. Some were businesslike and sophisticated, others young and wild-looking. The only thing they had in common was that they were all beautiful.

'It looks like a model agency's portfolio,' he said bluntly. 'What of it?'

Gakhar turned to Smith with a frown, her voice uncertain. 'They're all the same woman.'

Simons snorted in derision. But one glance at Smith told him Gakhar was right. He looked again at the photos. It was impossible ...

'She can change her appearance almost at will,' Smith told him. 'Change her voice, her age, her whole persona. She's an actress worthy of the West End stage, of Hollywood, even. She can speak any number of foreign languages, create forgeries that no guard will ever spot.' She placed a photo ID card of a young dark-haired woman on the desk. 'This was the closest we ever came to catching her. It was her final mission for the

Soviets in Berlin, 1989. She went up against a CIA station chief called Cleary. When he tried to bring her down she drove a spike through his throat. He still talks in a whisper. We believe she's living in the West now, working for herself, selling her talents to the highest bidder. We think she's been responsible for at least five large-scale cases of industrial espionage over the last seven years.'

Simons stared at the faces swimming before him on his desk. 'Do we even know her real name?'

'Only her aliases, of which there have been many. They're all in the file – the ones we know about, at least. She's no longer considered a threat to national security, so we are no longer actively seeking her. I just wanted to share what I had with you. I hope it helps.' She rose to leave.

'One question,' Gakhar said, pointing to the word, hand-written in Cyrillic script, on the file. 'What does it mean?'

Smith smiled. 'It says *Matryoshka*.'

She saw the blank expressions on their faces and went on. 'It was our codename for this agent during the Cold War,' she explained. 'It started out as a bit of a joke, but then it stuck. *Matryoshka* are those little wooden dolls, you know the sort, Russian dolls – one nested inside the other. We never did find the smallest one. Who knows, maybe you will.'

ANASTASIA

Finland Station, Leningrad, 1980

General Kupchenko mounted the stairs from the underground station, his plodding steps slowing near the top but never quite stopping, until, with a final effort, he emerged into the main hall of the Finland Station. Here the many different peoples of Russia moved across the concourse at different speeds, speeds as different as the people themselves. Smart-suited commuters ran to make their connections and tall, good-looking army personnel walked with determined strides. Station workers in drab uniforms moved more slowly, drawing out their tasks to fill the day with the least amount of work, while thickset country folk in rough peasant garb stood gawping at the whirring departure boards in bewilderment. Kupchenko saw a stout old peasant woman in a brown shawl and a brightly coloured headscarf stop directly in the path of a young businesswoman. The businesswoman stepped around her with a silent curse. The peasant woman was oblivious. Kupchenko was heading for the exit but he changed direction and went over to the woman and touched her arm. 'Where are you trying to get to, Grandmother?'

The woman turned, startled. 'Nowhere,' she answered in a loud country drawl. 'I just arrived. My son said he'd meet me here but I can't see him anywhere.'

'Where did he say he'd meet you?' Kupchenko asked.

'At local arrivals.'

'This is international,' he said politely. 'Over there is local.'

'Lord, how's a person to know?' she demanded loudly.

Kupchenko suppressed a smile. They were standing before a board clearly marked International Arrivals. He spread his hands in agreement. 'How indeed?'

'Bless you,' she said.

He watched her amble across the concourse. Her bright headscarf was the only colour in the monochrome scene. The general had a soft spot for these old mothers of Russia. In the darkest days of the Great War – the 900 day siege of Leningrad, when the army couldn't reach them and the Nazis had been pounding their city to dust – it had been these old mothers of Russia who had fed them and kept them alive. These old mothers of Russia *were* Russia, and always would be, despite all the grand rhetoric about workers spewing from the Central Committee.

Emerging from the station, Kupchenko was greeted by the thin northern light that told him he was back in his home city. It was a light so ethereal that he'd always felt it might flicker and die at any moment, plunging the city into an indefinite twilight. He lumbered across the square to the bronze statue that stood in its centre, and looked up into the familiar lupine features of Vladimir Ilyich Lenin. It was a remarkable likeness, he knew. He'd stood in that very spot sixty-three years earlier when Lenin had returned from exile in Europe and watched him emerge triumphant from the Finland Station and address the crowd, standing atop an armoured car. The bronze captured Lenin perfectly: the right hand pointing to a better future, the left clasped in a fist on his own lapel.

Kupchenko stood for an hour beneath the statue, waiting for old comrades who, he knew, wouldn't come. Last year two had made it to their annual reunion, but since that time he'd received two black-edged letters and attended two funerals. He was the last of them now. He was alone. He had to accept that.

The sun had disappeared by the time he left but it was June in Leningrad and the sun never truly set. This time of year was known as the 'White Nights' and it was celebrated with a festival and a fireworks display that seemed faintly surreal against the bright sky.

He left the statue and crossed the River Neva to the first of the islands in the delta where the river emptied into the sea. The islands were connected by a spider's web of ornate bridges, and in their centre was the tiny Zayachy Island, where Tsar Peter had built the city's first settlement. Kupchenko walked past the stout walls of the Peter and Paul Fortress and the narrow tower of the cathedral within, before crossing the mist-covered Neva again and crossing Palace Square. Here was another statue, strangely at odds with the first: Tsar Peter the Great seated astride a rearing horse. Peter was a symbol of everything Lenin had fought to overthrow – the oppression of the masses by a handful of decadent bourgeois imperialists – and the statue remained now purely for historic and, since it was undoubtedly beautiful, aesthetic reasons.

Turning onto Nevsky Prospekt, the city's main thoroughfare, the general headed for the Hotel Europa where he had a suite for the night. His feet ached from so much walking, but walking was good for his heart, and for keeping the weight off his massive frame, and besides, he could do little else these days. The comfort of his hotel suite beckoned, but across the avenue stood the Kazan Cathedral. Its semi-circular colonnade appeared to be beckoning him, welcoming him with open arms, and he could not resist.

In the cathedral's entrance, a bored security guard examined

Kupchenko's identity card and ushered him in smartly without charging the usual fee. Inside, a curator was lecturing a party of schoolchildren on the shameful excesses of the church before the revolution, pointing out the gold and silver leaf, the priceless statues and paintings, and the complex architectural embellishments that had been lavished on the interior when workers and peasants had been starving outside. Kupchenko had heard this argument countless times in his life and had no wish to hear it again. It was not that he disagreed with it, but that he had gone beyond it. Now those in power lavished millions on other projects far less deserving than a church. He went to the centre of the cathedral to see the icon painting of the Lady of Kazan, after whom the cathedral had been named. He found himself moved by her serenity and grace, as he had been each time he'd stood beneath her portrait and gazed up into her loving eyes.

He had survived eighty years of wars, floods, revolutions and purges and had risen to dizzying heights within the most powerful army in the world. More than that, it had been a good life, a life to be thankful for, particularly after all the evil he'd seen over the years. He had few complaints. He missed his wife Lyudmila who'd been dead for fifteen years but at times like these, he was ashamed to admit, he missed his comrades more. There had been five of them, four boys and he, who had grown up together in this city, that had then been called Saint Petersburg. They had stood shoulder to shoulder when Lenin had made his fiery speech outside the Finland Station. They had all joined the Komsomol youth league on the same day and later, they had all joined the Red Army. They had fought together during the city's darkest days, the 900-day siege of Leningrad, when the Nazi invaders had brought the city to its knees, and they had survived. How all five had done so when over a million had died was nothing short of a miracle. Though none of them had ever spoken of it, Kupchenko knew he was not alone in thanking God for his deliverance. His lips moved in silent prayer. If challenged by an overzealous security guard, it could be dismissed as the mumblings of an old retired general, nothing more – no danger to anyone.

His feet ached. He could no longer stand as he'd once done, proud and straight, on the parade ground. It was time to return to the Hotel Europa across the avenue. He would need a good night's sleep in preparation for the next morning, when he would visit Piskarevsky cemetery and the graves of his comrades. In the afternoon, he would walk among the graves of the citizens of Leningrad who had fallen in the Great War, a task as long as the summer days of the city itself.

Hotel Europa, Leningrad

Kupchenko noticed the KGB agent in the lobby straight away. A tall, good-looking man, Georgian, if he wasn't mistaken. The suit was expensive, but the hard eyes and the unread newspaper in his lap gave him away. He was a low-level agent, little more than a pimp. He was watching out for the prostitutes working in the hotel bar. If he was lucky his girl would entrap a foreign businessman or an embassy official in a sex scandal. Photos would be taken on a hidden camera, or the pimp would burst into the hotel room pretending to be an angry husband. The police would be called, but the officer who arrived would be KGB. This officer would make the scandal go away, but then he would ask for a favour in return. So the dirty business of blackmail would begin. It was standard KGB procedure. Crude, but surprisingly effective.

Kupchenko considered going to his suite but it was still early, and if he closed his eyes now he knew sleep would not come. He went into the bar, taking in the entire scene in a single glance: six foreign businessmen, two Germans (one might have been Austrian), one Briton, one Italian, two Americans, our Russians – all party officials of some form or other including one Politburo member – and two hookers seated at a table near the window. The first Kupchenko remembered from his previous stay at the Europa, but the second was new, young, and quite beautiful.

'Good evening General Kupchenko,' the barman greeted him.

'Good evening Yuri,' Kupchenko grunted, heaving his bulk onto the narrow bar stool.

'A toast to the fallen?' Yuri asked, a bottle of Starka poised over a glass. Starka was Kupchenko's preferred brand and Kupchenko smiled to show his appreciation.

'One,' he grunted. 'And join me.'

'Thank you, General,' Yuri said, pouring two swift shots into the crystal glasses.

Kupchenko raised his glass and looked the young barman in the eye. Yuri was a good bartender, but he was a lousy spy. Kupchenko had noticed him as soon as he'd appeared. He was too talkative with the patrons and too nonchalant when eavesdropping on their conversations. Yuri was likeable, memorable, noticeable. A good spy was none of these things.

'Nazdrovie!' Yuri said with a smile.

Kupchenko drained his glass.

'Another?' Yuri asked.

'One's enough these days. Give me tea instead.'

Yuri busied himself preparing the tea.

In the mirror behind the bar, Kupchenko saw the younger of the two hookers stand. He wondered which patron she'd target. To his surprise, she sat beside him and took a cigarette from her purse which she held in her lips unlit.

'I don't smoke,' he told her reflection in the mirror.

Yuri leaned over the bar and lit the cigarette for her. 'Thank you Yuri,' she said, exhaling a long, slow trail of smoke. 'You're a gentleman.'

Yuri bowed graciously. He placed Kupchenko's lemon tea before him.

'You don't drink, either?' she asked Kupchenko.

'No.'

'Do you at least put sugar in your tea, to sweeten it a little?'

Kupchenko looked straight ahead. He was in no mood for

her games. Not today.

'Would you like me to add it for you?'

'Why would you do that?'

'Out of comradeship?'

Comradeship? He felt the anger rise in him suddenly. A whore dared to call herself his comrade? A whore who knew nothing of such things. He turned to her and was about to tell her to fuck off when he noticed the wry smile on her lips. Close up, she was even more beautiful. He took in the sheen of the black hair hanging straight down her back, the rise and fall of her long lashes over the almond eyes, the blush of warmth in her immaculate skin that spoke of some Tartar ancestry in her past. It was difficult to be rude to such a beautiful woman. He shook his head slowly. 'You're not my comrade.'

'If I'm not your comrade then who is?' She opened a packet of off-white sugar and poured it into his tea. 'And where is he? A fine comrade he is, leaving you to drink alone.'

'My comrades are all dead,' he said before he could think better of it.

'Well that's sad,' she pouted. 'So maybe you could use some company tonight? I'm Anastasia, by the way. Nice to meet you.'

Kupchenko had no objection to whores. He'd used them often enough in the past, and even now occasionally, on his trips to Yalta. A man still had needs even at his age but tonight was not the time. 'I'm not good company this evening. Why don't you go and talk to someone else?'

'Maybe I don't like foreigners,' she said, biting the lemon slice and squeezing its juice into his tea.

'Then there are some Russians for you,' he said. 'The man in the grey suit is a party official. He might not have hard currency, but he'll have plenty of rubles.'

'Maybe I don't like crooks,' she answered. It was the type of comment that could see her continuing her profession in a labour camp instead of the elegant rooms of the Europa.

'You're very choosy for someone in your line of work,' he grunted.

'I like to think so.' She took another long drag on her cigarette. 'You don't think I can afford to be?'

'You're beautiful enough, that's for sure. So tell me, before you fuck off and leave me in peace, why the interest in an old man like me?'

She shrugged. 'You have honest eyes.'

Kupchenko tried to suppress the laughter that rumbled up inside him but failed, and once he'd started, he couldn't stop. Years of unfiltered Armenian cigarettes gave his laughter a deep, rolling rattle that was amplified by his huge frame.

Anastasia looked away in annoyance until he'd finished. 'You like women, I take it?'

'Yes, I like women.'

'And you're not too old?'

He shrugged.

'Men are never too old.'

She stubbed out her cigarette and Yuri removed the ashtray and replaced it with a clean one. 'It's a pity,' she went on, 'Because I think you'd enjoy what I had in mind.' She blew out her last trail of smoke.

Kupchenko was unable to resist. 'And what was that?'

She turned on the bar stool to face him and leaned forward so Yuri wouldn't hear. 'You're an army man, I can tell, despite your smart suit and tie. High up too, if you can afford to stay at the Europa – a general, probably. A man like you is used to giving orders and having them obeyed, so here's what I have in mind: I'd order you to strip naked, completely naked, you understand. Some men like to keep their vest on or even their boots. I hope you're not that kind of man – an army man who likes to keep his boots on?' She waited for him to answer but he didn't respond. She went on, 'Then I'd tell you to kneel and if you did that for me, I'd take off my coat and stroke your head like a good boy. Would you like that, General? I think you would...' she smiled encouragingly. 'Then I'd order you to go down on all fours like a dog while I washed your genitals. No one likes sex with a stranger if they're not clean. If you're lucky, while I'm washing you, I might let my finger slide into your anus. I think you might like that.'

She raised her eyebrows inquisitively. He stared at her. 'Then I'd sit on your back and ride you like a pony, and let you lick my fingers. Then I'd get one of my toys from my purse and use it on you. Would you like to know which one?'

Kupchenko didn't respond.

'Never mind. We can decide later,' she said lightly. 'Next, I'd tell you to lie on the floor, on your back. If you did, I'd unbutton my blouse and take off my bra. If you're lucky, you might see my breasts. Then I would stand over you and step on you.' She leaned forward and breathed in his ear. 'Don't tell anyone but these shoes are not Soviet shoes, they're Italian. Don't even ask how much they cost me, because I can never tell you, but the heel is very pointed...'

Kupchenko sat back on his stool and laughed, breaking the spell she'd been weaving so carefully. She turned away and flicked her soft pack of cigarettes until one popped out. Kupchenko took a book of matches from the bar and lit it for her. 'Don't be angry, Anastasia,' he said, squeezing her arm affectionately, 'I was enjoying your story very much.'

'Now you're laughing at me,' she said angrily.

'No! I'm laughing at myself, if you must know. I'm surprised how well you know me. It's quite uncanny.'

'Now you're fucking with me.'

'I promise you, I'm not.'

'Do you want to fuck me or not?'

'I'm old enough to be your father,' he said, his huge old hand picking up the delicate teacup like a bear's paw.

'More like my grandfather,' she shot back quickly.

He nodded slowly. 'You're right, Anastasia, more like your grandfather... But the truth is I'm here to visit the Piskarevsky Cemetery. I'm going there tomorrow morning. I come every year at this time to pay my respects to fallen comrades. It's a sad time for me, so I hope you can understand when I say I'm simply not in the mood.' He shrugged apologetically.

She had no smart comeback now and he sensed she was about to leave. To his surprise, he found he didn't want her to. It had been a long time since he'd talked so intimately with anyone, not since his wife had died fifteen years ago. He went on before she could go. 'My comrades and I would meet here every year. Five of us, we knew each other since childhood. We fought in two world wars together, in the revolution together. We endured the Siege of Leningrad together. Last year, there were still three of us. This year I'm the only one.'

He sipped his tea. 'Now you know why I was not in the mood for... what you described.'

'Well you might not want sex, but how about some company? It sounds like you need it.'

'Company?'

'You can talk to me instead. A lot of men like to talk. It's more common than you might think.'

'Isn't that what we're doing?' he asked.

'Yes it is,' she said with exaggerated slowness, 'But afterwards they pay.'

'Why would I pay for something I can do for free?'

She looked around the half-empty bar full of strangers. 'Talk is never really free anyway, is it General? Not in our country.'

Kupchenko struggled to suppress another rattling laugh. He took a sip of his tea instead and replaced it with studied care on the saucer. He tapped the counter-top lightly with his fingertips as he fixed her with his eye. 'I've never paid for idle chat before, Anastasia. But I have paid for information often enough. So why don't you tell me about yourself, and I'll pay you.'

'Most men like to talk about themselves,' she said.

'I'm different.'

She looked at him doubtfully. 'Fine, but do we have to talk here? Can't we go somewhere more private?'

'Of course,' he nodded seriously. 'We can go to my room. But I want the truth, Anastasia, nothing less. I only pay for the truth.'

*

Anastasia sat on the edge of the bed, her knees pressed together lightly, her palms flat on the quilted bedcover. She was facing the old man, who'd seated himself by the window on a round-backed armchair. She could have sat in the chair beside him, but she preferred to be in front of him and let him see her. She could move closer later. He might change his mind and want sex, most men did in the end, and then she could charge more. She didn't relish she prospect of trying to get the old warhorse off, that could prove to be hard work, but she needed the money.

She'd avoided several rich punters in favour of this ugly old Russian. Why, she couldn't be sure. He didn't have honest eyes, that was certain, but there was something in them that drew her to him. Perhaps those old eyes had seen a Russia when things had been different, less depressing, more noble, if only for a short time. She was beginning to regret that attraction now, the wily old bastard was proving more difficult to manage than she'd imagined.

'The first thing I should tell you,' she began with a smile, 'which you've probably guessed, is that my real name isn't Anastasia.'

The general nodded impatiently.

'My real name is Oksana, Oksana Mikhailovna Bazan. I was born in Leningrad. My father was from Leningrad. My mother was from the Volga region, near the Caspian Sea, a Tartar by origin. She met and married my father when he was stationed in Stalingrad and they moved back to Leningrad before I was born. My father was in the army. He was often away. We received word that he died on a mission abroad, they never told us where. I was fifteen at the time. Mother wanted to move back to Volgograd to be near her relatives, but I decided to stay here. There's more opportunity in Leningrad. We keep in touch only rarely.'

'That was very young, to be on your own.'

'I can take care of myself,' she smiled. 'This, what I'm doing now, it's only temporary, just a way to get some money, so I can do what I really want.'

'And what's that?'

'Fashion design.'

'What sort of fashion? Soviet fashion?'

'You laugh, but why not? There's no reason why our clothes should be so dull. Lingerie, for example. I know a thing or two about what men like.'

She stood up, reaching to the zip at the back of the skirt. 'Let me show you.' She slipped off her skirt and let it fall to the floor. She turned around. Her panties were still half hidden by her blouse, pale gold satin and cut high at the hips, with delicate frills along the edge. She unbuttoned her blouse slowly, keeping her eyes on his. 'What do you think?'

'They look expensive.'

'They were. I can't tell you how I got them, you might report me to the authorities. You might have me arrested and taken to an underground prison for interrogation.' She opened her blouse, holding it at the bottom edge, revealed first the left side and then the right side of her brassiere.

'What do you think, General?' she asked with a knowing smile.

'You look fit,' he said. 'What do you train in?'

'Dance and fitness,' she said.

'Ballet?'

'No, ballet was never for girls like for me. But I can dance for you if you like.'

'I was only asking,' he said wearily. 'I wanted information about you, remember, not your clothes.'

She frowned. He was a stubborn old fool. 'I train at my local sports centre to keep fit. Some weight training too, to keep in tone. And I used to play handball.'

'Not any more?'

'It's difficult to make regular team practice,' she said, sitting back on the bed and crossing her legs slowly. 'There are too many other things going on instead.'

'How did you get into your current occupation?'

Things weren't going according to plan. The old bastard seemed determined to talk rather than do anything else. 'It was a business decision, pure and simple,' she told him. 'Do you know how much I can make in one night compared to working in a shop, or a factory, or waiting tables, or serving popcorn in the cinema?'

'I see,' was all he said.

She was tiring quickly of the old man. His questions were too searching, too personal. It was not the type of talking she'd had in mind. It was time to wrap things up and move onto another customer, someone younger, more normal, less inquisitive.

'Is there anything else you'd like to know?' she asked with a tone of finality in her voice.

'No,' he said, shaking his head slowly.

'Then pay me and I'll leave you to rest. You have a busy day tomorrow,' she smiled. Kupchenko regarded her silently. Had he changed his mind? 'Or perhaps you *would* like to fuck me, after all.'

'No, I don't want to fuck you,' he said bluntly.

'Alright then,' she snapped. 'Pay me five hundred rubles, it's a lot less than I normally charge.'

'I'm not paying you a single kopek.'

'Stop fucking around,' she said, jumping up and standing over him, glaring.

'I'm not paying you,' he said wearily. 'Look into these honest eyes if you don't believe me.' He stared up at her and the watery red eyes held her gaze coldly.

She realised he was completely serious. 'Fuck your mother,' she shouted. 'I'm going to call the hotel manager.'

'No you're not,' he told her.

'How do you know what I'll do?' she demanded.

'Because you're too clever, Anastasia, Oksana... whatever the hell your name is. And you were right, I am a general in the Soviet army. Do you really think the manager of The Europa will press a general to pay for something that's illegal in his own hotel?'

'He knows it goes on!'

'He knows, of course. But he also knows that officially, your profession does not even exist, not just in his hotel, but nowhere in the Soviet Union.'

It was true, she knew, and even if it weren't, she stood no chance against an army general. She struggled to hold onto her temper, searching for another avenue. 'Why won't you pay me?' she said in a small voice. 'I thought we had an agreement. I thought you were a man of honour.'

'We agreed on the truth. You gave me a pack of lies.'

'What makes you say that?' she frowned.

The general rose from his chair. Even for an old man he towered over her, like a great bear that had lumbered in from the forest, and she had to force herself to avoid taking a step back.

He smiled thinly. 'I've spent a lifetime getting the truth from people, interrogated the best in the world using methods you couldn't begin to imagine, so don't be too upset. You're good. In fact, you're very good – a natural. And you helped a lonely old soldier pass an agreeable evening instead of a depressing one, for which I thank you. If I'd wanted to hear a pleasant fantasy or a fairy story, I'd pay you without hesitation, even though five hundred rubles is an extortionate price. But I wanted the truth, remember? And you lied. Please don't bother to deny it.'

'You son of a whore,' she hissed.

'Don't be angry,' he said with a pained smile. 'I'm going to offer you something worth far more than five hundred rubles.'

'Give me three hundred and I won't call the manager.'

'You won't call the manager,' he said. 'I'm going to offer you an opportunity.'

'I'm not interested,' she spat. 'I'm going to get the manager.' She pulled on her skirt and buttoned her blouse quickly.

'A chance to change your life forever,' he continued.

She stared at him. He was insane. She should have seen it before now. She cursed her own stupidity. 'Pay me two hundred rubles and we'll say no more about it,' she said, holding out her hand for the money.

'You don't want to hear my offer?'

'What can you offer me? A job in the army? Driving a tank? Fuck off back up between your mother's legs you son of a whore.'

She grabbed her purse and made for the door. She could feel her cheeks burning scarlet.

'*Wait.*'

His voice was quiet, but with an edge that stopped her in her tracks. Suddenly she saw how the tired old general had risen to such commanding heights in the most powerful army in the world. She waited, unable to disobey.

'Is this the life you want?' he asked.

'I told you what I want.' She wanted to go now, to be free of him, but he stepped up to her. He was no longer a lumbering bear. His cold grey eyes were those of a wolf, calculating, remorseless, cruel. She stared into the wolf's eyes – how could she ever have called them honest?

'Nobody gets what they want, Anastasia. But a woman like you, she can get men to do what she wants. That is power, *real* power, if you know how to use it.'

It was easy for the general to talk of power. Power came naturally to him. He had no idea what it was to be powerless, to be a woman, an orphan, a whore whose only power was over a man's cock, a power that lasted no longer than it took for that cock to spill its seed and return to its wife or girlfriend. Her fear left her, replaced by an anger she couldn't control. 'Power over every man except you, eh General? Well fuck you, General. Fuck you!'

She turned to go but he reached for her. She tried to beat his hands away but he pinned her arms to her sides with shocking strength while he kissed her lightly on both cheeks. 'I'll send someone for you,' he murmured. 'When they come, go with them.'

'Let go of me,' she cried, tears of frustration rolling down her cheeks.

He released her and she left.

Marshala Zakharova, Leningrad

The squat, three-story block where Anastasia lived was located in a side road off Marshala Zakharova near the southern end of the harbour. The buildings on the main street had been made to look attractive with baroque facades, but in the side streets things were very different. This building was unkempt, though not so derelict as to attract any special attention. The yellowing walls bore the remnants of countless posters put up over the years, and a neon sign, long broken, that said the first half of the word 'cinema.' Few people knew what the building was now, or what went on behind the shuttered windows.

Beyond the basement entrance was a cocktail bar and lounge area with intimate booths and low lighting. Upstairs were the rooms where the girls lived and worked. The place was run by Grigory, with the help of three men from the southern republics who took care of the bar and security. Anastasia's room was on the first floor, at the end of the corridor. It was small and cramped, but it had its own private bathroom, a luxury by any standard in the Soviet Union, and her own TV – an old black and white set that Grigory had given her some time ago. Compared to the other girls, she had the best room in the house.

Anastasia flicked through the channels absently. There was nothing of interest: a war film she'd seen countless times before, a carefully orchestrated talk show, a documentary about athletes preparing for the Olympics that would be held in Moscow that summer, and General Secretary Brezhnev receiving a medal. In the later years of his life, Brezhnev had become fond of receiving medals, and he was regularly

awarded the Hero of the Soviet Union on his birthday, which
came with the order of Lenin and the Gold Star. Today he was
being awarded the Marshal of the Soviet Union, the highest
military honour of all. It was all dreadfully boring. She switched
back to the preparations of the Olympic athletes, where the
swimmer Vladimir Salnikov was being interviewed.

There was a soft knock at her door. She opened it to find a
tall blonde woman with piercing blue eyes standing outside.
The woman smiled, revealing small, brilliant white teeth in a
neat row. 'My name is Svetlana Dimitrieva,' she said. 'Grigory
told me to come straight up. I hope you don't mind?'

'You're alone?' Anastasia asked. She had never had sex with
a woman alone. There had always been a man involved too.

'Is that a problem?' Svetlana asked.

'Not really. What are you looking for?'

'I'm not sure yet. May I come in?'

'Sure,' Anastasia said, standing aside. 'Just give me a
moment to get ready.'

'Take your time,' Svetlana said, taking a seat in the armchair
in the corner.

'You can change the TV channel if you like,' Anastasia told
her.

'I like to watch the athletes,' Svetlana said happily. 'I think
we'll have a good Olympics this time, what do you think?'

'I think so too, especially now the Americans have
boycotted the games.'

'They're afraid of how badly they'll lose,' Svetlana said
sharply.

Anastasia scooped up a pile of clothes from the bed and
folded them away unhurriedly inside a tiny wardrobe. 'I'm
sorry I'm not dressed. You took me a little by surprise.' She

was wearing a long black sweater that came down to her mid-thigh, revealing slim tanned legs.

'It's no problem,' Svetlana assured her. 'I like to see what goes on behind the scenes.'

Anastasia gave her a quick smile and leaned over the dressing table to check her face in the mirror.

'Your make-up looks fine,' Svetlana said. 'You're a very beautiful young woman.'

'Thank you,' Anastasia replied, walking slowly to where Svetlana was seated. She took off her sweater, revealing a pale purple silk negligee beneath, and a glimpse of matching underwear beneath that. Throwing the sweater aside and leaving her tousled hair as it was, she held Svetlana's eye and put her hands on her hips. 'So tell me, what can I do for you, Svetlana Dimitrieva?'

'Surprise me,' Svetlana said breathlessly, leaning back slowly in the chair.

Anastasia sat on the corner of her bed, legs parted, her hands on her knees. 'Okay, but give me an indication, because in all honesty, I don't know a lot about women.'

'You don't object?' Svetlana asked, her eyes wide in mock surprise.

'No, it's just that, well, a woman like you, I imagine she knows what she wants.'

'I do, Anastasia. I want you to guess what I want.'

'It would help if I knew a bit about you,' Anastasia said, playing for time while she tried to figure out what Svetlana was hoping for.

'Why don't you begin by telling me who you think I am?' Svetlana said, blinking expectantly to show she was waiting for Anastasia to begin.

Despite the smile, it was clear Svetlana was a woman used to getting her own way and Anastasia knew she couldn't play for time any longer. She took a final look at the tall slim frame, the tanned skin and the fashionably cut hair – short at the sides and parted on the left with a long fringe swept over to the right. Svetlana could have been a model but that would have been too simple and besides, she sensed Svetlana would be a little disappointed in such an obvious answer. She decided to give her something more provocative.

'You're from Moscow,' she began. 'I can tell from your accent. You're in your late twenties, twenty-eight, perhaps?'

'You flatter me, but go on,' Svetlana smiled, delighted that the game had finally started.

'You're married.' Anastasia went on, speaking more quickly now. 'Your husband is rich, of course, and high up in the party. A minister, perhaps?'

Svetlana nodded encouragingly. 'Go on.'

'You have a big house in the suburbs and a summer dacha, of course, though not in the forest but by the sea. And not by the cold Baltic, I don't imagine. By the Black Sea, in one of those fashionable resorts. Yalta, perhaps?'

Svetlana clapped her hands in delight. Anastasia went on.

'You grew up in a poor family, but it was a family with aspirations, a family from the intelligentsia, who put art and learning above money. They sacrificed a lot so you could study – ballet, at a guess, although I would need to see you walking a little before I could be sure. But you were never really interested in the dancing, just the opportunities it provided…'

Anastasia stopped for a moment so make sure she hadn't overstepped the mark. Svetlana leaned forward and put her chin in her hands, her lips lightly parted, her eyebrows raised, challenging Anastasia to go on.

'…You met your husband when you were still very young. He came to one of your performances, and decided he'd marry you the moment you appeared on the stage. He sent you flowers every evening and returned to every performance. You tried to resist for a while because he was so much older and your parents didn't approve, but he wore you down. And besides, there was something about him you found hard to resist. He was a man of power. For such a man to be besotted with you was intoxicating. You married him.'

'Perfect! Go on,' Svetlana urged.

'Soon, you discovered another side to him, a darker side. It did not come as a complete surprise to you. What surprised you was how you came to enjoy this side of him as much as the other, perhaps more. After the first time, when he brought another woman to your bedroom, you began to discover a new side to yourself, one you barely knew existed. Your husband's money and power enabled you to enjoy these pleasures in a way few could have dreamed of, especially in our country.'

'Remarkable,' Svetlana said, unable to hide a smile of admiration. 'What sort of pleasures, exactly?'

'Let me show you,' Anastasia said, stepping forward and pushing gently against her shoulders until Svetlana was leaning back in her chair. Sitting astride her thighs, she let her long hair fall around her visitor's face as she slowly lowered her lips to hers, stopping just before they touched.

'I sense you've enjoyed many pleasures, but do you know the pleasure of denial?' she whispered.

'Show me,' Svetlana said, her voice husky now.

Anastasia wet her lips with the tip of her tongue and stood up. 'Get up,' she ordered, a new tone in her voice, the tone of command. 'Take your clothes off. All of them.'

'What are you going to do?'

'No more questions,' Anastasia ordered, 'Do as I say, *Little Bitch*.'

Svetlana rose obediently and undressed, revealing a tanned body with just a faint bikini line, ample toned breasts and the neatly trimmed fuzz of blonde hair above the pubis. It was the kind of body men dreamed of, Anastasia knew, but there was something about it that Anastasia couldn't figure out. She'd thought Svetlana had been a dancer, but there was a breadth to her shoulders that suggested something else, an athlete of some sort.

'Lie on your front,' Anastasia ordered, pointing to the bed. Svetlana complied. Anastasia knelt astride the backs of Svetlana's thighs and, taking her wrists, bound them together with a silk scarf from her dresser. The knot was snug but not restrictive. She had plenty of experience in tying knots. 'Roll onto your back, *Little Bitch*,' she ordered.

She raised her hips to allow Svetlana to turn over, then moved forward and sat astride her chest. Her hand came down to cup her cheek affectionately, 'Now I'm going to teach you about having things you don't need, and wanting things you can't have.'

'No,' Svetlana said. Anastasia gave her a warning slap on the cheek. 'Quiet, *Little Bitch!*'

'Really, stop,' Svetlana said.

'I told you to be quiet!' Anastasia said, preparing to slap her harder.

Svetlana's hands snaked out from behind her back and seized Anastasia's wrists. Anastasia hadn't felt her loosen her bonds.

Svetlana pushed her back until she was off-balance and slipped out from under her thighs. 'Enough,' she said breathlessly.

Anastasia stood, awkward now. 'If you didn't like it, you should have said. We could have done something else.' 'Don't worry,' Svetlana smiled, rolling over to the other side of the bed, 'I'm not disappointed. Quite the opposite, in fact.' She sat cross-legged and Anastasia noticed she wasn't in the least embarrassed by her nudity. 'I heard you were good but I wanted to see for myself. The truth is, you're very good. And every bit as beautiful as I was led to believe.'

'If I'm so good, why did you stop?' Anastasia asked.

'I saw all I needed to see,' Svetlana replied.

'What was that?'

'You picked up the signals I gave you. You took my fantasy and developed it. You seduced me, and quite effectively, I might add.'

'Who are you?'

'My name is Svetlana Dimitrieva, as I told you, and I work for the government.'

'What do you want with me Svetlana Dimitrieva?' Anastasia demanded, tiring of the woman's games.

'I want you to come and work with me,' Svetlana answered seriously.

'I work for Grigory,' Anastasia said curtly. 'I think you know that.'

'Don't worry about Grigory.'

'You don't understand. Grigory doesn't fuck around.'

'Don't you want to hear more before you refuse?' Svetlana asked lightly. 'It's not every day you get an offer like this.'

'Why would I want to work for a someone I don't know?'

Anastasia demanded.

'You don't know me, but I know you. I heard about you from a colleague who you met in the Hotel Europa. He sends his greetings, by the way.'

'The old general sent you?'

'His name is General Kupchenko.'

'You're in the army.' Anastasia found she wasn't surprised by the revelation. Something about Svetlana had hinted at some military discipline.

'A branch of the army.'

'Well whichever branch it is, you should be careful. Grigory has connections in high places. I really think you should go.'

'Grigory is a pimp and a KGB informer,' Svetlana sneered. 'I told you, don't concern yourself with him. Think of yourself. Do you really want to stay here? You're young and pretty now, but you'll grow old very quickly.'

'And what type of work are you offering me?' Anastasia demanded.

Svetlana smiled. 'Despite his appearance, General Kupchenko doesn't command an armoured tank division. He works in military intelligence. It has many high sounding titles, but those who serve in it simply call it The Organisation. And you can be part of it, *Evalina Petrovna.*'

Anastasia was stunned. Evalina Petrovna was the name she'd grown up with, a name she'd buried along with her childhood.

Svetlana smiled at her surprise. 'Gathering information is what The Organisation does best.'

Anastasia sat down hard on the chair and breathed out slowly. 'What else do you know about me?'

Svetlana frowned, marshalling her thoughts theatrically.

'Well let me see… you were orphaned from the age of six. Your first orphanage was a house on Dyebenko Street where you were looked after by an elderly matron who took good care of you. Do you remember her name after all this time, I wonder?'

Anastasia thought she did, but she couldn't be sure. She waited for Svetlana to tell her.

'Her name was Zina.'

It was the name Anastasia remembered, though she'd called the old woman *Tyotia* Zina – *Auntie* Zina.

'Zina died less than a year after you came to her, and you moved to a new orphanage,' Svetlana continued. 'You weren't so happy there. You ran away three times towards the end, but each time they brought you back. As soon as you were sixteen you left for good – and ended up here a little over a year later.'

Anastasia sat in silence for a long time. Finally she sighed. 'What kind of work do you want me to perform?'

'Information gathering.'

'How?'

'By any means necessary, Evalina Petrovna. But a woman like you, with your looks and your talents, I'm sure you can imagine how.'

'What you're offering is not so different from my work here then,' Anastasia said, rising and pulling on her sweater.

'There's all the difference in the world, but I don't expect you to understand.'

There was a new edge to Svetlana's voice that made Anastasia stop. She realised she'd insulted the woman. Svetlana rose from the bed with a swift, effortless movement and for a moment Anastasia wondered if she was going to strike her, but Svetlana simply reached for her clothes and began to dress in silence.

'Tell me why it's different,' she said.

Svetlana ignored her, and Anastasia had the feeling she was fighting to keep her feelings under control. 'Tell me,' she said again.

'Didn't you know there's a war on?' Svetlana said sharply.

'The Cold War?'

'From where we fight it, it's not so cold. People risk their lives every day. People die, sometimes in unimaginable circumstances to protect the motherland, to protect you, while you lie here on your back for a handful of rubles.'

Anastasia was shocked by the sudden passion in a woman she'd believed so cold.

Svetlana went on. 'I'm offering you the chance to become a soldier in the war against the enemies of the Soviet people, to fight against those who would destroy our way of life, bring our country to its knees and enslave us. It's a war no one knows about, but it's real, and it's being fought night and day all over the world.'

'And how will I fight these enemies of the Soviet people?' she asked.

'We will train you,' Svetlana said, standing up to her full height, taller, suddenly, than Anastasia had realised, at least two inches taller than she was. 'You'll be trained by the finest minds in the Soviet Union, physically, mentally, psychologically, to levels that you cannot yet imagine.'

'And if I refuse?'

'If you refuse, I will walk out of the door and you'll never hear from me or The Organisation again.'

'Nothing will happen to me?'

'What do you think will happen to you?' Svetlana asked with

a frown.

'You said you're in the secret service. I might be followed, arrested, imprisoned, I don't know...'

'We are military intelligence, not KGB. It probably doesn't mean much to you, but there is a big difference.' Svetlana gave Anastasia a small smile of reassurance. 'Nothing will happen to you. You have my word.'

Anastasia wondered if it counted for anything. She had the feeling it did.

'If I wanted to silence you, I'd do it now,' Svetlana went on, and again, Anastasia had the feeling it was true.

'When must I decide?' she asked.

Svetlana threw on her jacket and reached for the door. 'Now.'

'Wait!'

Svetlana's hand closed around the handle.

'Even if I wanted to go with you, I can't simply walk out of here.'

'Yes you can. Put on some warm clothes and leave everything else behind. The Organisation will take care of everything. It always does.'

'Grigory won't allow it.'

'Leave Grigory to me. Are you coming or not?'

*

Grigory saw the blonde woman called Svetlana descending the stairs and rose from the bar stool with a frown. She'd paid him handsomely to spend the evening with Anastasia but she was leaving early and that made him nervous. He had no wish to return even part of the money.

'Is everything okay?' he asked.

'Everything's fine,' Svetlana assured him. 'Anastasia's exactly who we were looking for.'

'We?' Grigory saw Anastasia appear on the stairs too, dressed in jeans, a sweater and an outdoor jacket. He frowned and turned back to Svetlana, who produced an ID card showing her in a crisp army uniform. 'Lieutenant Colonel Svetlana Dimitrieva, Soviet National Army,' she smiled. 'I need to inform you that Anastasia is coming with us.'

'Wait a moment,' Grigory said. 'There must be some misunderstanding. She doesn't work for anyone else.'

'She does now,' Svetlana answered. 'But don't worry Grigory, we're prepared to compensate you generously for what you might call *loss of earnings*.' She handed him an envelope, far thicker than the one she'd given him on the way in. Grigory squeezed it between his fingers. He estimated 3,000 dollars inside, maybe more.

'Listen, Lieutenant…' he began.

'Lieutenant Colonel,' she corrected him.

'Lieutenant Colonel. Listen, I don't sell my girls…'

'Really? I thought that was exactly what you did do, Grigory. And if you're wise, you'll let this one go now.'

He leaned in closer. His lips tightening into a threatening smile. 'You should know I have connections…'

'In the KGB? Yes, I know,' she smiled. 'It won't make any difference. This comes from higher up.'

'If that's so, then I need time to check it out. Let me make a few phone calls. If everything's in order, she can go with you. Come back tomorrow.'

Svetlana looked away. 'Very well. But when I do, I want no trouble. Is that fair?'

'No trouble,' Grigory smirked, pocketing the envelope and savouring his victory over the army bitch.

The kick impacted his jaw with shocking force and he crumpled where he stood. Svetlana caught him before he hit the ground and placed him on one of the seats by the wall.

'Hey, what just happened?'

One of the punters at the bar had noticed the sudden movement from the corner of his eye. Svetlana put her arm around his shoulder and put her lips to his ear. 'Grigory had a bit too much to drink, that's all. Let him sleep it off.' She turned to Anastasia. 'Let's go.'

She walked unhurriedly towards the exit. Anastasia followed.

'But Grigory doesn't drink,' the punter called after her.

'Who says he does?' the barman asked, noticing Svetlana heading for the door with Anastasia, who was dressed for the outside. It wasn't her usual outfit for that time of the evening.

'The blonde,' the punter told him. 'I think she knocked him over with her foot.'

'Knocked who over?'

'Grigory.'

The punter was a little drunk, but the barman knew something wasn't right. Over the years he'd developed an instinct for trouble – a nose, as he liked to call it – and his nose told him there was trouble now. He strode to the end of the bar and called to his colleague sitting by the exit. 'Hey Marko, stop those two.'

Marko only had time to rise from his seat before a vicious front kick from Svetlana sent him flying through the double doors behind him. She followed him through the doors a moment later to finish him off, and found him seated against the wall fighting for breath. She turned to deliver a kick to his temple, but he drove forward at the last instant and trapped her leg. The power in her kick was shocking but he clung grimly on and pushed forward until his arms circled her waist and he lifted her off the ground.

Anastasia followed through the double doors and screamed when she saw Svetlana in the Georgian's grip, but Svetlana was icy calm. She clapped her hands over his ears and both eardrums burst simultaneously, then dug her thumbs into his eyes and pressed forward. The pain was too much. 'Bitch!' he cried, throwing her aside. Svetlana landed on the balls of her feet like a cat and kicked him hard between the legs. He grunted and folded, but didn't go down. At that moment the barman burst through the double doors, cosh in hand. Anastasia was in his way and he swung the cosh at her. She covered her face with her hands and took the blow on her forearm. He seized her by the throat and slammed her into the wall. 'Stay where you are,' he ordered, before moving on to deal with Svetlana.

The Georgian was bent double before Svetlana, who brought the tip of her elbow down hard onto the back of his neck. He slumped at her feet. The barman swung the cosh at the back of Svetlana's head. Anastasia screamed, imagining Svetlana's skull split open, but Svetlana turned and spun inside the arc of the cosh, seizing the barman's wrist as she did, and suddenly he was flying over her shoulder. He landed hard on the floor and as he did, she drove his head into the concrete with her fist.

'Get in the white Moskvich at the end of the street,' she ordered Anastasia.

Anastasia ran to the main door. 'Aren't you coming?'

Svetlana stepped over the still body of the barman and

stood beside the double doors. 'In a moment.'

'What are you waiting for?' Anastasia whimpered.

The doors burst open and the last of Grigory's security men emerged – Tabidze, a two-metre tall ex-policeman who'd been imprisoned for fraud. In his right hand he carried a KS-23 shotgun that he pointed at Anastasia. 'Stay there,' he ordered.

The KS-23 was used as an anti-riot weapon in Soviet prisons, where its wide shot radius made it a formidable weapon. Tabidze had witnessed its effectiveness first-hand and it had prompted him to secure one for his own line of work. To brandish it in one hand felt good, but tactically it was a mistake. He hadn't seen Svetlana behind the double doors and when they swung shut Svetlana was at his shoulder. Her left arm snaked over his right. She gripped the barrel and twisted away hard, slamming her bodyweight into his prone elbow joint. He squeezed the trigger at the same moment that his elbow snapped. His roar of pain was drowned out by the shocking blast.

Anastasia fell against the door in shock, but the shot was sent high and wide by Svetlana's brutal manoeuvre. Svetlana continued to twist, wresting the gun from Tabidze's useless arm and without arresting the motion, she smashed the stock down in a scything motion into his knee. His leg buckled and he collapsed. Tabidze bellowed in rage. She swung the stock again and struck him square across the face. After that, he lay on the floor in shock, his shaking hands holding his shattered face, blood running between his fingers. Svetlana reloaded the shotgun and pressed it to his throat.

'Consider this a friendly warning. Don't follow me or things will get serious.'

She turned and strode down the corridor towards Anastasia.

Her eyes bored into Anastasia's angrily. 'I thought I told you to get into the Moskvich.'

Anastasia flung open the door and ran outside. She wanted to be sick, but Svetlana was right behind and she dared not stop. She swallowed down the bile and ran to the white Moskvich at the end of the road.

The passenger door was unlocked and she jumped inside. She found it difficult to breathe in the closed space. She wondered whether she could open a window. She didn't know if Svetlana would allow it. She began to cry. Svetlana opened the driver's door and slung the shotgun onto the back seat. 'Cover it with the blanket,' she ordered. Anastasia saw a thick old blanket on the back seat and did as Svetlana had said. Svetlana gunned the engine and drove away smoothly to the end of the street, where she stopped, signaled and waited for a space in the busy traffic. Anastasia glanced over her shoulder, expecting to see Grigory and his men at any moment, but they didn't appear, and then Svetlana turned into the fast-moving traffic on Marshala Zakharova. Now she glanced at the woman who had single-handedly broken her out of the prison she had built for herself. Svetlana turned to her with a frown. 'Are you alright?'

'I'm okay,' she said in a small voice.

'Good' Svetlana smiled. It was a cold smile. A deadly smile. And all of a sudden, Anastasia knew she was more afraid of Lieutenant Colonel Svetlana Dimitrieva than she had ever been of Grigory, or his men.

*

She was a child, walking hand in hand with Auntie Zina once again. The old woman's hands were misshapen, the skin thin and brittle like autumn leaves, but she loved those hands – hands that cooked for her, dressed her, and brushed her long black hair – hands that led her from the orphanage to the Summer Gardens in the centre of Leningrad. Auntie Zina often took her to stroll through the delightful grounds and visit the statue of Krylov, the fable-writer whose stories Zina read to her at bedtime. It was one of her earliest memories, a happy memory. After that, her memories were not so happy. Now she was standing barefoot in the corridor of Zina's house. Two burly ambulance men were taking Zina away on a trolley. They hadn't bothered to cover the body and she could see the dreadful expression on Zina's face, the mouth open wide, screaming a silent warning. A taciturn woman had arrived soon after and taken her to a big house on a hill in a different part of the city. No one ever mentioned Zina again.

Now she was entering a cold room filled with silent children and broken toys. The walls were stained grey, the paint peeling, the cot mattresses hard plastic, the smell of urine so pervasive that the air itself tasted bitter. Some of the staff were kind-hearted, like Irina, who would smuggle in a piece of fruit for her 'Pretty One,' as she called her. Some were uncaring, like Magda, who would lock the children in their dormitory for hours while she went out for cigarette or a chat with the nurse. And some were cruel, like Veronika, who would beat them and threaten them with Ward Six if they misbehaved further. Ward Six was the children's ward in a hospital for the criminally insane. And then there was the Director, a distant figure whom she glimpsed on dim corridors. He would smile and pat her on the head as he passed but he never spoke to her. Without

Auntie Zina she'd felt a solitude so deep that she thought she might never emerge from it – until the arrival of a mischievous boy called Alexei.

Alexei was a year older than her, with a mop of dirty blond hair and a toothy grin. He was given a cot beside hers and they quickly became friends. Soon she grew to love him like the brother she'd never had. She would cry when he got punished, which was often. Alexei peed in the linen closet. Alexei put Lego in Veronika's shoe. Alexei drew a crude picture in the mist on the windowpane.

Life was bearable with Alexei as company, until the day Magda forgot to lock the door when she went for a cigarette. Alexei noticed immediately and urged her to come exploring. Emboldened by his carefree smile, she followed him down the stairs and out of the front door. The garden was different from how she remembered it. The last time she'd seen it had been when she'd arrived in the winter. She had not left the house since. Now it was summer and the garden was filled with flowering bushes and unruly weeds. Alexei was running in circles. She was following him, oblivious of the trouble they'd be in when they were discovered. The director's new Lada was parked on the sloping driveway. Alexei tried the door and found it unlocked. He climbed in and sat in the driver's seat. After much urging, she joined him on the passenger seat. Alexei was turning the heavy steering wheel left and right. Now he was sitting on the edge of his seat and pressing the pedals with his toes, making the noises of a car engine. She'd never seen him so happy. Now he was tugging at a lever between their seats. Then they were rolling down the steep driveway, and she was screaming, convinced they would end up in the street and crash into the busy traffic. But the wheel had been turned to the left and the car had simply veered on the driveway and thudded into the concrete gatepost with a sickening crunch.

*

Anastasia woke with a start to find herself in the stationary Moskvich. Svetlana was dozing beside her. She had no idea how far they had driven, or any recollection of Svetlana pulling into the gravelled parking area cut into the birch forest. She peered into the surrounding trees. The pallid bark reflected the dawn rays weakly and immediately beyond the first row of trees was impenetrable blackness. With the engine turned off, the Moskvich's heating had gone off and she could see her icy breath inside the car. Svetlana had thrown the blanket over them both but even so Anastasia was frozen to her core. She looked over onto the back seat for the shotgun and saw it was concealed in the footwell beneath an opened out newspaper. Svetlana was nothing if not thorough.

She remembered leaving the sprawl of Leningrad and following signs for Novgorod, the first major city on the way south to Moscow. They still hadn't reached it, as far as she knew. The road had been littered with potholes and the Moskvich's dim headlights had barely lit the way before them. In places, whole sections of the road had been washed away by the winter rains and the tyres had spun on wet mud and gravel, but Svetlana had kept the car moving steadily, ever southwards.

Anastasia didn't remember falling asleep. Her arm throbbed and she touched it gingerly with her fingertips wondering if it was broken. Her mind went back to her dream and to Alexei. A specialist from the Commission for Mental Evaluation had come to the orphanage to assess him a few days after the incident. The specialist had declared Alexei to be suffering from pronounced cretinism and incurable. Alexei had been removed from the orphanage and taken to Ward Six. She had been punished too but she could not recall her punishment now. It had been negligible compared to the loss of Alexei. She had never seen him again but kindhearted Irina had gone to visit him three times in Ward Six. Each time she'd told her less about Alexei and after her third visit she'd reported that Alexei hadn't recognised her. She never went again.

'How's your arm?' Svetlana asked without opening her eyes.

'It hurts,' Anastasia told her.

'Let me see,' Svetlana said, sitting up and holding out her hand. Anastasia rolled up her sleeve gingerly and Svetlana took her arm by the wrist. 'Can you move your fingers?' she asked quietly.

'A little.'

'Does it hurt more than before or less?'

'Not as much.'

'Good.'

Svetlana worked her fingertips gently along the forearm, feeling the bone. 'It's not broken. I think you caught a glancing blow, but we'll get it X-rayed in Moscow to be sure.'

'Do you think Grigory will come after us?' she asked.

'No.'

'How can you be sure?'

'Grigory will check up on Lieutenant Colonel Svetlana Dimitrieva, and when he does, he'll realise it's best to keep his money in his pocket and his mouth shut.'

Svetlana turned the ignition key and coaxed the reluctant engine into life.

'What will he discover?' Anastasia asked.

'That I am an officer of the *Glavnoye Razvedyvatelnoye Upravleniye* – the GRU for short.

'But no one calls it that, just *The Organisation*,' Anastasia said.

'That's right,' Svetlana nodded. 'And you are part of it too now. You are safe.'

Anastasia smiled. It felt good to be safe. The Moskvich gained speed slowly on the straight empty road.

'There is one thing you should know,' Svetlana said quietly. 'Once you have joined The Organisation there is no going back. Don't try to leave. Not now. Not ever.'

'What will happen if I do?' she asked, unable to resist the question, knowing the answer even before it was said.

'If you leave, or run away, or even go missing for an hour, I will find you and I will kill you. I hope you believe me, Evalina Petrovna. Do you believe me?'

Anastasia looked into the cold blue eyes and turned away, unable to hold their gaze. 'I believe you,' she whispered. And it was true. She did believe her.

Tsaritsyno Suburb, Moscow

The windows of her new apartment were sealed shut, though whether it was deliberate or due to the ice outside, Anastasia didn't know. The window panes were small squares, double-glazed, with wool stuffed around the edges as further insulation. She'd noticed the cold was different in Moscow. In Leningrad it was a damp, shivering cold that rolled in off the Gulf of Finland and soaked through the outer clothing to the skin. In Moscow it was a deep, numbing cold that lacked the moderating influence of the sea. Instead it crept up from the frozen ground and penetrated through to the bone.

The view through the windows was one of uniform communal blocks known as *Kommunalka* – the great Soviet housing solution. On the architect's plans each six-storey block had been gaily painted and surrounded by gardens and play areas for children. The reality of the hastily-erected concrete warrens fell far short of the drawings. Anastasia's block, and all the surrounding ones, housed army personnel and as such were in good repair. The elevators worked, albeit reluctantly, and there was at least one light bulb on the corridor of every floor. The apartment had been designed around a single kitchen and bathroom, as all apartments were, with four bedrooms of varying size set aside for one family, one couple, and two singles. However there was no one else in their apartment. She and Svetlana had the place to themselves.

They'd arrived in darkness the night before, exhausted after three days of driving. She'd woken when they'd entered Moscow, but she'd seen none of the sights she'd been expecting: no Kremlin, no Red Square, no onion domes of St

Basil's Cathedral, just endless grey streets, poorly lit. She'd been surprised at how provincial Moscow appeared, almost village-like in places, compared to the monumental scale and grandeur of Leningrad.

She'd woken to find the apartment empty and had set about exploring her new home. The kitchen was small and tight, with an old fashioned stove and bronze marks on the wall where the flames had licked the off-white paint. The cupboard was well stocked with black bread, eggs, onions, spiced sausage and good cheese – food that could only be obtained from a special store. The bath was old, showing the signs of years of scrubbing with harsh scouring pads, and the hot water, when it finally came, was scalding. Svetlana had warned her that it came on intermittently, but it always came on and if she was vigilant, she would get a hot shower at least once a day.

Svetlana had given her the room reserved for a couple, though her bed was a single bed, and she wondered how a couple would ever be able to sleep on it. She opened the wardrobe and the drawers at the foot of her bed. The hollow echo of the wood reminded her how little she had in the world, nothing but the clothes on her back and a few toiletries in her bag. She opened the bag now and laid out her make-up on top of the drawers, thankful that she'd brought two combs, so they could occupy more of the empty space.

Svetlana had taken the family bedroom. Anastasia went in to look while Svetlana was out, but didn't stay long. A swift glance inside the wardrobe revealed army-issue uniforms, plain blouses and skirts, twill trousers, walking boots and a pair of flat shoes, nothing to suggest the glamour of which, she was sure, Svetlana was capable. She left quickly, feeling that Svetlana would know if she stayed any longer. She tried the doors to the other two rooms and found them locked. A set of keys hung in the kitchen, but none opened either door. She cooked an egg, which she ate with two slices of black bread, and Svetlana arrived just as she was finishing.

Svetlana was carrying an armful of bags with labels she didn't recognise. 'I got you some clothes. I think you'll like them. Come and try them on.' Svetlana took a key from her pocket and opened one of the locked doors. Anastasia saw the room was arranged like a theatre dressing room, with a wardrobe full of coats, hats and elegant gowns, a cupboard of wigs, drawers filled with make-up from Paris and New York, and a chair set before a mirror with scissors and hair products arranged before it in the style of a hair salon.

'Go and wash your hair,' Svetlana ordered. ' I'm going to give you a new look. It'll be good to work with such a lovely model.'

Anastasia obeyed, and soon she watched in silent misery as Svetlana turned her lovely long hair into a short, unfashionable cut. Svetlana seemed to cut well enough, but she had no eye for style, that was clear. Anastasia guessed it was her military background. She dared not complain.

When the haircut was complete, Svetlana turned her away from the mirror to begin her make-up. She treated several areas of her skin with a cotton-tipped stick, then worked with a foundation brush over contours of her face, leaving the eyes and lips aside and concentrating on the brow, the cheekbones, the nose and the chin.

'Do you know what is *Maskirovka?*' Svetlana asked as she worked.

'Disguise?'

Svetlana exhaled sharply through her nose to show her

displeasure. 'Maskirovka is far more than wigs and make-up. It's an art form, and a weapon, as deadly as any in the arsenal. An enemy is never more vulnerable than when he doesn't know he's under attack.' She bent down before Anastasia so their faces were at the same height, and Anastasia felt her studying her as a sculptor might study a statue as it emerged from the marble. She seemed satisfied with her work, and set the foundation brush aside. 'The Soviet army specialises in misleading the enemy,' Svetlana went on. 'We can hide anything, from microchips to missile silos, not simply by camouflage, but by deception, by making the enemy look elsewhere.'

'Like a magician?' Anastasia said.

'Yes, just like that.'

Svetlana began working around Anastasia's eyes. 'Tell me, what is the most powerful weapon of all, Anastasia?'

'A nuclear missile,' she answered.

Svetlana laughed and she could feel her warm breath on her cheek. It smelled sweet and medicinal. She wasn't sure if she liked it or not. 'The answer is older,' Svetlana went on. 'Much older. So old, it's in the bible.'

'I've no idea,' Anastasia replied.

'Who presses the button that launches the missile?' Svetlana asked lightly, applying a dark pencil beneath her eye now.

'The president.'

'Very good, *Little One*.' Svetlana said, brushing a stray lock of hair off her forehead and cupping her face gently beneath the chin. The irony of Svetlana's term of endearment wasn't lost on her. She'd called Svetlana *Little Bitch* just days earlier. 'And what is the president?'

'A man.'

'And who presses the buttons of a man?' Svetlana whispered.

'A woman.'

'Yes, a woman, but not just any woman. For every man there is one woman. For Samson there was Delilah. For David, Bathsheba. For Anthony, Cleopatra.' Svetlana laughed softly. 'A will of iron can be turned to water by a woman. Not through sex, through something far more powerful – the most powerful weapon of all.'

Anastasia didn't want to say it. She waited for Svetlana to say it, but Svetlana just smiled and moved Anastasia's head from left to right, and up and down, admiring her artistry. She gripped the chair and turned her around so Anastasia could see herself in the mirror. The face in the mirror was one she barely recognised. The eyes were small and sunk deep inside dark hollows, the eyelashes short and sparse. Even the shape of the eyes had changed, the tapered almond lines gone, replaced by round eyes, plain eyes. The nose seemed wider and flatter, the lips pale, the cheeks fleshy. The skin was sallow with red blotches where, she guessed, Svetlana had irritated the skin with a chemical.

'What the hell have you done to me?'

'*Maskirovka*,' Svetlana said, putting a hand on her shoulder in sympathy. 'A woman like you is far too noticeable, Little One. Now you'll blend in.' She handed Anastasia a pair of thick, black-rimmed glasses. 'Put these on. Then you'll look every inch the dedicated student, ready to begin your lessons at the Institute.' She opened the door to leave. 'I'll give you a moment to get acquainted with yourself.'

Anastasia stared at her new self. She took off the glasses and peered closer in the mirror. The sallow skin and sunken eyes reminded her of the time around her fifteenth birthday when she'd fallen seriously ill. The nurse in the orphanage, a thickset peasant woman from Belarus, had made light of her stomach pains for weeks, telling her all women suffered from such things. Only when she'd collapsed in the dining hall had she been taken to hospital. For several days the doctors had been doubtful of her recovery, but she had recovered. She never found out from what; no diagnosis had ever been given to her.

On returning to the orphanage she'd been summoned to the Director's office. Professor Fyodor had told her of all the phone calls he'd had to make and all the favours he'd had to call in, just to get her seen at the hospital. Then he'd requested a favour in return. It turned out to be the first of many. She'd run away three times, but there were few places to hide in a city where homelessness was forbidden by law, and each time the police had returned her to the orphanage.

When she reached sixteen she'd left and not returned, moving instead from one workhouse to another, living with the meanest members of society, though a young woman with her looks never went cold or hungry. There was always a man willing to share his food and his bed.

One night in the summer, she had gone to the port with one of the women from the factory where she worked, and returned with thirty rubles in her pocket. It was more money than she'd ever seen before. Soon she was earning five times that amount in the smarter quarters of the city. Then she'd met Grigory, smooth, handsome, Grigory. Grigory had taken her away from that life, if only for a short while. She had loved him for that. Loved him so deeply that she missed that love even now, a love as short as the Leningrad summer.

Svetlana reappeared with a camera, a foreign make Anastasia

didn't recognise. She put her glasses back on and Svetlana snapped a photo. A moment later a square of paper emerged from the camera.

'Polaroid,' Svetlana explained. 'American. Convenient if you're short of time, but the quality is poor.' She waved the paper in the air for a few seconds and handed it to Anastasia, who saw her new image developing before her eyes. Svetlana opened a drawer and took out a square of white plastic, a roll of clear plastic, and some scissors and glue. Taking the photo back from Anastasia, she cut a square around the face and glued it to the thick plastic, then covered the whole piece with the clear plastic. She took a small machine from the cupboard and pushed the plastic card through it, sealing it closed.

She handed the new ID card to Anastasia. 'Meet Tatiana Zykova, student at the Marx Engels Institute of Foreign Languages and Political Science. And my new flat-mate.'

Anastasia examined the card. 'It looks so real.'

'It is real. It's one of the things you'll learn, but not at the institute. I'll teach you that myself, among other things.'

Suddenly she smiled with what seemed like genuine warmth and extended her hand to Anastasia. Anastasia took it cautiously and Svetlana shook it firmly. 'Hello, my name is Svetlana Dimitrieva. And you must be Tatiana Zykova. I'm very pleased to meet you.'

TATIANA

Marx Engels Institute, Moscow 1981

Svetlana had parked the Moskvich at the entrance to the Marx Engels Institute. The building had been created in the grandiose neo-classical style favoured by Stalin after the war. The long facade was punctuated by columns and balconies to soften the austere lines. Beyond the main building were smaller blocks, less conspicuous in design, and beyond them a grass field and the sweep of a cinder running track.

'How's your arm today, Tatiana Zykova?' Svetlana asked. She'd been repeating the name over and over to ingrain it into her mind.

Tatiana flexed her fingers and made a fist. It didn't hurt like before. Svetlana had taken her to a hospital the day before, a hospital very different from the one she'd visited in Leningrad. She'd been shown to a comfortable private room. A pretty young nurse had arrived promptly to X-ray her arm. A doctor had come five minutes later to reassure her that her arm wasn't broken. He'd spent twenty minutes mixing a paste for the bruising and applied it himself, touching her arm as if holding precious china. He'd even created a sling for her, which she'd removed as soon as she'd left. 'It's better now, thank you,' she told Svetlana.

'Good. Now don't be nervous on your first day,' Svetlana told her happily.

Tatiana looked out of the window at the institute. The students gathered on the broad steps outside were laughing gaily, so full of confidence. Her own education had been little more than basic lessons at the local school and she had found them tedious in the extreme. 'Tell me again what I'll be studying?' she asked, suddenly unwilling to get out of the car.

'English, mainly, but also French, Italian, German, enough to get by in those countries, so I hope you have an ear for languages.'

'I don't know,' Tatiana answered honestly. 'I never took any exams.'

Svetlana put her hand on her knee and squeezed it gently. 'This is different, Tatiana Zykova. The teachers here are the best in the world. You have a sharp mind. I don't need exam papers and qualifications to tell me that. I know it, trust me.'

'What else?'

Svetlana smiled. 'Marxist Leninist theory, of course, but also world politics, economics, science, literature, art and drama. By the time you graduate, you'll be able to discuss anything with anyone, anywhere in the world, Tatiana Zykova. Oh, and you'll learn SOMBO too. I think you'll like it.'

'SOMBO?'

'Unarmed combat.'

'What you used against Grigory and his men?'

'That, and some other things,' Svetlana answered evasively. Are you ready to go in?'

'I think so,' Tatiana sighed.

'There are some things you should know before you begin,' Svetlana said, suddenly serious. 'As far as the people of the institute are concerned you are on an army scholarship. They won't ask any questions, but the other students... tell them nothing about yourself, or me, or The Organisation.'

'I won't,' she said.

'Don't get too friendly with any of them,' Svetlana said. 'Be polite, but nothing more. I hope you understand, it's for the best.'

'I do.'

Svetlana paused and looked her in the eye when she spoke again. 'There will be young men studying with you. Don't get involved with any of them.'

Tatiana said nothing.

'If you want sex it's not a problem,' Svetlana went on quickly. 'I'll arrange it. There are plenty of handsome young men in the army. Tell me and you can meet them. Just don't get involved with anyone intimately, do you understand?'

Tatiana shrugged.

'I'm serious,' Svetlana said, her voice turning hard. 'Don't get involved. Is that clear.'

'It's clear,' Tatiana said.

Svetlana sat back in her seat and looked out through the windscreen to the moody autumn sky. Her fingers traced unseen patterns on the steering wheel as she spoke. 'Do you know what happens to the most beautiful and gifted of the graduates from this institute?' she said, her voice little more than a whisper. She didn't wait for Tatiana to answer. 'They go on to a new school in Verkhovnoye, in the desert near Kazakhstan. It's a long way from Moscow, a long way from anywhere. In their first lesson they're ordered to strip naked and examine one another's bodies. In the second, two of them are ordered to have sex in front of the others. In the third, all of them have sex, whether they want to or not.' Svetlana's voice was even, but Tatiana noticed she was breathing heavily as she spoke. 'At first it's shameful and humiliating. Women are forced to sleep with women, men with men. No taboo is left unexplored. By the end of their time at Verkhovnoye, those young men and women no longer consider their bodies their own. They are the property of the Soviet Union.'

'You were one of these students,' Tatiana said with certainty.

Svetlana gave her a fixed smile. 'You're fortunate Tatiana Zykova, you won't need to undergo such training when you graduate. You're not ashamed of your body. You know how to use it already. You can go onto more interesting lessons straight away.'

'Where will I go?' Tatiana asked.

'You will go to Little England,' Svetlana replied.

'I've always wanted to visit England,' Tatiana smiled.

'Then study hard. Study like your life depended on it. It might do, one day.'

Tatiana tried to hide the fear that rose in her at the sound of those words, but Svetlana must have seen it in her eyes, because she took her hand and the warm dry heat soothed her anxiety. 'Don't look so worried, Little One,' Svetlana's smiled. 'You won't be doing this alone, none of it. I'll be with you. Always. I hope you'll come to think of me as a friend, a sister, even. I never had a sister. I'd like that very much.'

Tatiana stared into the cold, beautiful eyes. 'I'd like that too,' she said, and part of her meant it.

Tsaritsyno Suburb, Moscow

'You said nothing about killing,' Tatiana said angrily.

'Didn't I?' Svetlana frowned. 'Well forgive me, Tatiana Zykova. Do you object?'

Tatiana stared into the open wardrobe. Svetlana had unlocked the fourth bedroom. It contained nothing more than a single bed, a wardrobe and a chest of drawers. The surfaces were bare save for a plastic lamp and an ashtray on the drawers. There had been nothing remarkable about the room until Svetlana had opened the wardrobe to reveal every shelf filled with handguns and, on the floor beneath the bottom shelf, neatly stacked cartons of bullets.

'Of course I object.'

'Maybe that's because you don't know how to do it yet,' Svetlana said taking a pistol, cocking it and aiming it at the window, one hand supporting the other, her grip rock-steady. She pulled the trigger and there was a loud click. 'It's a fine art.'

'I won't do it,' Tatiana said.

'Don't be so melodramatic,' Svetlana laughed. 'Your missions will not be assassinations, we have specialists to take care of such things. So before you get too moralistic about it, consider this: your missions will involve taking secrets from powerful men. Important secrets, secrets that could win or lose a war. How do you think those men will react when they discover what you've done?

Tatiana was silent. Svetlana held out the pistol to her, 'Do you want it now?'

Tatiana refused to take it.

'It's a Makarov, standard Soviet issue for the army and

police, single or double action. It's good because it's simple. When you're in a firefight and someone's trying to kill you, the last thing you need is complications.'

Svetlana returned the Makarov to the shelf and took out another pistol, similar in shape, with a dark grey barrel and a dark brown hand grip. 'Browning High-Powered, made in Belgium,' she went on. 'Many of today's guns are based on this design, so it pays to know it well.' She released the safety, unloaded the magazine clip and reloaded it, her fingers moved in a blur over the hard metal. 'The truth is you'll rarely carry a firearm in our line of work but if you do, it will probably be a foreign make like this one.'

She replaced the Browning. 'We use guns from Finland, Spain, Yugoslavia. ' She withdrew another pistol. 'This is the Ceska CZ75, Czech-made, cheap, accurate, reliable, popular all over the world.'

Svetlana gripped Tatiana's hand and placed the gun in it. Tatiana turned the compact killing machine over. It was heavier than she'd expected, so much heavier than the plastic guns she played with in the orphanage with Alexei.

Svetlana took the gun back and handed her another. 'Beretta 92SB, state-of-the-art Italian design. Single or double action. Short recoil. 9mm. Fires 15 rounds before reloading. It's being trialed by the US military now and our sources say they're about to place a big order.'

Tatiana ran her fingers over the dull steel, feeling the awful precision of the engineering that had gone into it.

'It's so heavy.' It was all she could think to say.

'No, it's a normal weight,' Svetlana said, taking the Beretta back and handing her a long barrelled stainless-steel revolver with a wooden handle. 'This is heavy. It's a Colt Python, .357

Magnum, a classic revolver design. It takes only six bullets, but it's smooth, accurate and reliable. Plenty of people use them even now, especially in law enforcement.'

Tatiana held the revolver, not knowing what to do.

Svetlana took it from her and flipped open the cylinder. Taking a single bullet from a carton in the wardrobe, she put it in one of the chambers. 'Have you ever heard of Russian Roulette?' she asked, closing the chamber and placing the barrel at her own temple. Tatiana didn't answer. Svetlana pulled the trigger. There was a quiet click. She pulled it again. Another click. Again. Again. Tatiana closed her eyes.

Click.

Svetlana flipped the gun open to reveal the bullet waiting to enter the barrel.

'Relax Tatiana, I'm fucking with you. I didn't spin the chamber, so I knew where the bullet was.' She removed the bullet. 'Stop gaping, Tatiana Zykova. 'Even though I'm fucking with you, this isn't a game. You need to pay attention. I'm going to teach you to count how many bullets you fire, and how many your enemy fires, even in the middle of a fire fight.'

'Like Dirty Harry?' Tatiana said, knowing it would annoy Svetlana.

'Who?'

'You must know, the movie, with Clint Eastwood.'

'I don't know.'

Tatiana knew she was lying. She smiled innocently. 'It's a Hollywood movie. He fires a big gun like this one, a forty-four Magnum — *the most powerful handgun in the world* — that's what he says.'

'Well this Harry is wrong,' Svetlana sneered. 'The Udar 12.3mm is the most powerful handgun in the world. It has armour-piercing capabilities of up to five millimetres.' She pried the revolver from Tatiana's hand. 'Where did you watch such a movie anyway?'

'Grigory liked American movies,' Tatiana answered.

'A pimp – no wonder he was so susceptible to that horse-shit.'

Svetlana closed the wardrobe and locked it, pocketing the key. 'I'll teach you about handguns, but the truth is, you're more likely to use a different weapon. Go ahead and choose one now.'

'Where from?' Tatiana asked, looking around the stark bedroom.

'Anywhere,' Svetlana replied. 'Imagine I'm about to kill you. Arm yourself, quickly!'

Tatiana hesitated, then seeing the dark look in Svetlana's eyes, she lunged for the chest of drawers and threw open the top drawer. There were no weapons inside, just kitchen utensils. She seized a chef's knife and wheeled around just as the lamp in Svetlana's hand caught her on the temple.

She woke to find herself on the floor inside the tiny bedroom. Svetlana was kneeling over her, the chef's knife behind her and out of reach.

'I'm sorry Tatiana Zykova,' Svetlana said. 'I promise not to hurt you like that again, but I needed to show you something you must never forget. Everything is a weapon. Your hand is a weapon. Every part of your body is a weapon.' She stroked Tatiana's hair. 'You chose a deadly weapon, but I chose a closer weapon. I could have used the ashtray instead. I could have used the pen in my pocket. I could have used my bare hands.'

'You're a bitch, Svetlana Dimitrieva,' Tatiana said angrily.

'I hurt you with love in my heart,' Svetlana said, her hand cupping Tatiana's cheek. Tatiana brushed it away.

'You don't believe me but it's true,' Svetlana said, offering Tatiana her hand to help her up.

'Fuck off,' Tatiana said, standing on her own.

Her head spun and Svetlana caught her by the shoulders and held her steady. Tatiana noticed a small smile on the face of her tormentor.

'Why are you smiling?'

'Because I like to see this fire in you, *Little One*. When you're angry, you're no longer afraid. The little mouse is willing to stand up for herself. That's good.' She squeezed Tatiana affectionately before letting go. 'If you're too afraid, you can never be a good soldier. And I want you to be a good soldier, Tatiana. It's what I want more than anything.'

Petrovsky Park, Moscow

Miriam Gavrilova took a seat in the café opposite Petrovsky Park and ordered lemon tea. She'd arrived ten minutes early for her meeting with Svetlana Dimitrieva. It paid to arrive early rather than late in these circumstances, and the overcrowded Moscow buses couldn't be relied upon.

She caught her reflection in the cracked mirror on the wall beside the counter. How old she looked. She didn't think of herself as old. She still thought of herself as that ambitious young actress who'd studied under the great Stanislavsky himself. Stanislavsky's system had been copied in the West, where it was called 'method acting', but Miriam knew his method could never be mastered by a Westerner. Didn't those people know that drama was life, and life was suffering. No nation knew suffering like Russians. How could a Westerner, no matter how talented, ever plumb the depth of human emotion as a Russian could?

Miriam Gavrilova knew suffering. She'd married young, to Sergei Dvorkin, fifteen years her senior, a successful dramatist in the Moscow theatre. They had been happy together, until one of his plays had been denounced as 'anti-Soviet' by a jealous rival. Sergei had been arrested and the two of them had been resettled in a labour camp near the arctic circle. Sergei had been forced to work on the White Sea canal, a project so dangerous it was known as the canal of death. Sergei had never been strong or healthy. He had survived less than a year before succumbing to typhus.

After four more years alone in the north, Miriam had been allowed to return to Moscow and begin her rehabilitation.

She'd taken part in plays again, successful plays, sanctioned by the Party's strict Cultural Committee. Stalin himself had sat in the audience on more than one occasion. Her talent had been noticed, and she'd been invited to teach drama in the Marx Engels Institute. It had been an invitation she could not refuse.

Some of her students had proved more talented than others. Recently a new student had arrived who excited her like none before. Tatiana Zykova was not only beautiful – although she didn't seem to know it, hiding behind her plain hairstyle and thick glasses – she was also a natural actress of astonishing ability. Miriam was still thinking about her new protégé when Svetlana Dimitrieva slipped silently into the seat opposite her.

'Your new student is simply wonderful,' Miriam told her with an extravagant wave of her hand. 'She's like some sort of Asiatic Marlene Dietrich, with a face that can appear different every day. A blank canvas on which to paint your own picture. A mirror to reflect your own soul.'

'You really think she's that good?' Svetlana asked, surprised by the drama-teacher's excitement. Miriam Gavrilova was usually so thrifty with her praise.

'The best I've ever come across. Better even than you, Svetlana Dimitrieva,' Miriam said with a twisted smile. 'Where on earth did you find her?'

'In a brothel.'

Miriam eyed her suspiciously. Svetlana returned her gaze until Miriam sighed.

'Well it makes sense, the girl has suffered, she has lived. Not like those spoilt young sons and daughters of party officials.'

'How long until she's ready?' Svetlana asked.

Miriam stirred her tea slowly and tapped the spoon against the lip of the cup, watching the droplets fall away, waiting until the last one had fallen. 'Why are you always in such a hurry?' she asked quietly. 'I've only had her for a year. At the moment she's just raw talent. Give me two more years and I'll give you a master.'

'We don't have that long,' Svetlana answered.

'These things can't be rushed,' Miriam said with a shrug.

'How's her conduct in other respects?' Svetlana demanded.

'She's good in everything. Works hard. Learns fast. And I've heard no complaints from other staff.'

'Any unwarranted liaisons?' Svetlana asked casually.

'You mean has she made any friends?' Miriam said, unable to stop the flash of annoyance even after so many years of keeping her thoughts to herself.

'Tell me now or it'll be worse in the long run,' Svetlana replied evenly.

Miriam picked up her tea and took a sip, then replaced the cup on the saucer and pushed it away. 'She's been working closely with Andrei Karlovsky. They work well together. He's talented.'

'You think they're more than comrades?' Svetlana probed.

'I think they are friends.'

'Lovers?'

'Just friends.'

'But you believe there may be some mutual attraction.'

'Oh go to hell Svetlana Dimitreiva,' Miriam said, rising from her seat, too angry to consider the repercussions. She seized her heavy overcoat off the back of her chair and left without pausing to put it on.

Svetlana finished her tea before returning to the Moskvich parked around the corner. She drove onto the main street and stopped in front of the bus stop where Miriam Gavrilova was waiting. Miriam ignored her for a few moments, then opened the door and climbed in.

'Quite an exit,' Svetlana said quietly.

Miriam looked straight ahead and remained tight-lipped as Svetlana pulled out into the busy Moscow traffic.

Tsaritsyno Suburb, Moscow

Svetlana entered the elevator and Tatiana followed, pulling the heavy inner grate across until it clicked shut. The outer door closed slowly, creaking loudly as it moved. Inside there was barely enough room for the two of them and they were forced to carry their large kit bags vertically to fit them in. When the outer door finally closed, Svetlana hit the button for the basement. The elevator dropped six inches in freefall before beginning its painfully slow descent. The air inside was close and sickly despite the icy weather outside. The elevator came to a juddering halt and the door opened half way before sticking. Tatiana heaved the inner grate open and shoved the outer door until it opened fully.

The gym in the basement was open to all residents of the building, though in practice only a handful ever used it, and most of those were special forces. The gym itself was small, dank and airless. The plastered walls remained unpainted and there were no mirrors. The concrete floor was only partially covered with old pieces of carpet, and one corner was covered by old wrestling mats. There were no changing facilities and the single toilet had stopped working long ago. Despite its meagre appearance, it was well equipped with free-weights and machines, gymnastics equipment, pads, boxing gloves and two hanging punch bags. Five young men were training inside, officers of the Red Army from neighbouring flats. The men greeted the new arrivals courteously. They had seen the fighting ability of the blonde lieutenant colonel. Some had even sparred with her and bore the marks to prove it.

Svetlana ignored their greetings. She opened her kit bag and put on the traditional heavy red top of the SOMBO player. Tatiana did the same, though her top was blue. Svetlana handed her a head-guard and boxing gloves. 'You're quiet this evening,' she said.

Tatiana tied her head-guard tightly so it wouldn't slip when the sweat began to pour. She eyed Svetlana as she spoke. 'There was a student in my class, Andrei Karlovsky. He was there yesterday – today he's gone.' She picked up her gum-shield but didn't put it in her mouth. 'No one knows why he left or where he went. When I asked in the office there was no record of him ever being there.'

'He was a friend of yours?' Svetlana asked lightly.

'He was a fellow student,' she answered, staring hard at Svetlana, who was unwilling to meet her gaze.

'Who knows what happened,' Svetlana shrugged. 'I'd forget it. I told you before, the institute is not a place to make friends.'

'You had him removed,' Tatiana said deliberately.

Svetlana put in her gum-shield. 'Are you ready?'

'You did! Admit it.'

Svetlana held out a glove. It was customary to tap gloves before they sparred. Tatiana ignored it.

A sharp left struck her on the forehead and a lightning fast right caught the side of her chin. She stumbled back. Svetlana came forward. A vicious right uppercut to the body caught her in the solar plexus. She bent double. A hard hook caught her on the temple.

Svetlana stepped back, giving her time to recover. The eyes gave nothing away, no indication of the extra aggression in Svetlana's sparring that night. She felt the fury surging through her limbs and exploded forward, feinting with the left before swinging a hard overhand right. The punch caught Svetlana flush on the jaw, spinning her head and sending her gum-shield flying. Svetlana tried to step back and recover her senses, but she followed her, pressing her advantage. Svetlana's right foot lashed out in a front kick that stopped her in her tracks and now it was Svetlana's turn to attack. Three fast punches forced her back against the wall and Svetlana drove a powerful low-kick into her thigh. She unleashed a right hook in retaliation, but Svetlana ducked it, throwing a shocking left hook to her floating rib as she did. The shot took the air from her and she gasped. She saw Svetlana's hand reload for another hook and dropped her elbow to protect her side. It was a mistake. Svetlana redirected the hook to her head and caught her flush on the jaw. She fell forward, seizing Svetlana's shoulders to help her stay on her feet. Svetlana attempted a foot sweep, but she countered and turned in with a reaping throw of her own. To her surprise, she caught Svetlana perfectly, sweeping both Svetlana's feet high into the air and landing on top of her. But Svetlana had held on tightly and used the momentum of the throw to roll her. Now Svetlana was on top.

She tried to maintain her grip on Svetlana's neck, but with the bulky boxing gloves it was impossible and Svetlana pulled free. She turned into her, working to get her knees between them and create space to move in. Svetlana swept her knees aside and spun smoothly around to her side, holding her in a cross-body pin. Unable to escape, she offered her arm as bait, waiting for Svetlana to seize it. As Svetlana did, she rolled up into her and freed her arm. Svetlana rolled away and they both rose to their feet. But Svetlana seized her behind the head and kept her head down. She felt a blinding pain across her forehead. Svetlana had kneed her in the centre of her head-guard. It was a mark of Svetlana's ability that she hadn't smashed her in the face. She knew that breaking her nose was the last thing Svetlana wanted, and this knowledge enraged her further. She drove two fast punches into Svetlana's face, feeling the sharp impact through the padding in her gloves, then feinted a low kick. Svetlana raised a shin to block but she sent her kicked high instead. Svetlana reacted at the last second, jerking her head away, but even so her shin clipped Svetlana's temple and Svetlana fell to her knees. Now she rained punches on her tormentor. Svetlana covered her head with her bulky gloves and rose slowly taking the onslaught on her gloves and arms. She punched until she was too tired to punch any more.

Sensing a lull in the onslaught, Svetlana swung a sharp blow at her chin that stopped her in her tracks. Dazed and suddenly exhausted, she felt her anger leave her. Her arms were so heavy she could no longer hold them up. Her lungs were unable to draw air. She ripped her gum-shield from her mouth and gasped, and when Svetlana rose up before her, she knew she was finished.

Svetlana drove a front kick into her solar plexus and she felt herself suffocating. She began to panic. Svetlana drove a shin-kick into her liver. Her body locked up in a spasm, immobile. She stood helpless as Svetlana hammered four heavy low kicks into her thighs. She buckled but Svetlana caught her and held her so she could unleash more punches. She felt the pain of each blow like a knife and waited for the blow that would end it, stealing her senses and sending her to a welcome oblivion. That blow never came. Svetlana held back so each blow would be felt. Finally she heard the voice of a man somewhere nearby.

'Don't you think she's had enough?'

It was one of the young men training in the gymnasium. He was smiling nervously at Svetlana, and Svetlana's eyes were boring into his. Then her beautiful face broke into a broad smile.

'We get a little carried away sometimes, don't we, *Little One?*' she said, patting Tatiana on the shoulder affectionately.

Tatiana limped away. She ripped off her gloves and head-guard and sat down heavily beside her kit bag. Svetlana sat beside her and offered her a bottle of water.

Tatiana ignored it and drank her own.

'You fought well,' Svetlana said happily, ignoring the snub. 'You got angry. That's good. People say not to fight in anger, that it's too draining, that it blinds you and makes you vulnerable. Such people know nothing about fighting. I say get angry and let hatred fill your soul.'

Tatiana took another pull on her water. Swallowing hurt her ribs and she grimaced in pain.

'What do you think?' Svetlana went on. 'How did you feel when you fought me with anger in your heart?'

Tatiana hated Svetlana then, her beautiful tormentor, who offered friendship yet took away her friends, who encouraged her to fill her heart with hatred and offer love but never give it. Svetlana was changing her into someone she didn't know, someone powerful, someone cruel, a stranger she didn't know whether to admire or loathe.

'I think I was angry and you still beat me,' she answered defiantly.

'Only because I've had more training than you. And a better teacher.'

Tatiana tried to hide her curiosity, and failed. 'Who?'

'You'll meet him one day.'

Tatiana stood and untied her belt, opening her SOMBO tunic slowly. Her ribs were painful. Svetlana helped her to remove it. 'You weren't angry,' Tatiana said quietly.

'What was I then?' Svetlana asked.

'You were simply different, more intense.'

'It's called channelling. It's true that you must be angry, but you must also control that anger and channel it into aggression. If you don't it can blind you, make you miss things. Do you understand?'

Tatiana shrugged.

Svetlana smoothed a strand of sweat-soaked hair from Tatiana's forehead. 'I could never be angry with you, *Little One*. How could I be? I love you. Haven't I told you that before? Haven't I always told you love is the most powerful weapon of all?'

'Stop fucking around,' Tatiana said.

'Why do you think I'm fucking around?' Svetlana demanded with a frown.

Tatiana was tired of her games, deeply tired. 'What do you want of me exactly, Svetlana Dimitrieva? What do you want? Tell me, because I don't know.'

Svetlana leaned closer so the men in the gymnasium wouldn't hear. 'I want you to be a good soldier, Tatiana Zykova. The best. Better even than me, and I'm the best there has ever been. I won't be able to go on forever. One day you'll take my place. I want you to serve our country as I have done,

Tatiana Zykova. I want you to bring our enemies to their knees, as I have done. And one more thing – which you might not believe but I promise you it's true – I want you to live, Tatiana Zykova. I want you to live.'

Red Square, Moscow

The familiar domes of St Basil's Cathedral came into focus through the viewfinder. The sensuous curves and gaudy colours seemed all the more surreal beside the austere square lines of the Kremlin and Lenin's Mausoleum. Tatiana pressed the shutter and it snapped the cathedral with a satisfying click. It would make a nice picture when it was developed, the kind she'd imagined two years earlier when Svetlana had told her they were going to Moscow. It was the Moscow of Magazine covers, news reels and picture postcards, the Moscow she'd been denied, until now.

The day before she'd graduated with distinction from the Marx Engels Institute. Svetlana had been in the audience, clapping as loudly as any proud parent or guardian when she'd gone up to receive her diploma. Afterwards they had attended a lunchtime party in a nearby restaurant and on returning to the apartment in the afternoon, Svetlana had presented her with a box wrapped in fine gold paper. Inside she'd discovered a camera, a high quality Russian-made Zenit, brand new, the latest model. The smooth precision engineering of the lens and the solid workmanship of body felt good in her hands. That evening they had strolled to nearby Tsaritsyno Park and snapped pictures of the unfinished palace built by Catherine the Great that stood in the grounds. She'd learned to use a camera at evening classes, and how to develop her own film. Nevertheless Svetlana had given her more advice on how to get the best from the Zenit, and promised her some more exciting subjects to photograph the next day.

True to her word, Svetlana had woken her early with the

announcement that they would be making an excursion into the centre of Moscow. They'd left shortly afterwards, parking just south of the Moskva river and crossing Bolshoy Moskvoretsky Bridge northwards towards Red Square. They'd stopped on the bridge itself so Tatiana could photograph the outer walls and soaring towers of the mighty Kremlin on the north bank of the river. Strictly speaking no photography of the Kremlin was allowed, but she carried an amateur photography permit obtained from her evening classes, and besides, Lieutenant Colonel Svetlana Dimitrieva was with her to smooth over any misunderstandings if she were stopped by security or police. As it was, no one seemed to notice and they continued over the bridge into Red Square. Five large water trucks were spraying the vast expanse of grey cobblestones before the square became too crowded with tourists and the cobbles glistened in the morning sunshine, adding to the already magical vision that greeted them. Tatiana zoomed in on the cathedral and snapped another image of St Basil's colourful domes. She invited Svetlana to stand in the picture, but Svetlana refused with a smile and Tatiana didn't press her. She snapped the giant clock on the Spasskaya Tower on the Kremlin wall, the ornate GUM department store on the eastern side of the square, and the squat step-pyramid that was Lenin's Mausoleum, before joining Svetlana in the rapidly growing queue to enter Lenin's tomb.

They descended into the dimly lit basement in a slow procession of visitors, speaking in hushed tones beneath the watchful eyes of the security guards. Lenin's body lay in a crystal casket. He appeared surprisingly small and quite unreal, a shop dummy made to look like a man rather than a real dead body. His hands had been laid awkwardly on his hips, and his beard was little more than a few wisps of hair on his chin. It was hard to believe this pale flesh had once moved a nation to rebellion. Emerging into the light a minute later, they circled the northern wall of the Kremlin, passing through the pretty Alexander Gardens, to the looming Troitskaya Tower and the entrance to the Kremlin itself.

The fortified citadel had been the seat of power in Russia since the expulsion of the Mongols, eventually coming to rule lands from the Baltic in the west to the Pacific in the east. Inside the Kremlin's massive walls, Tatiana discovered an array of buildings of such beauty and splendor – and such seemingly impossible contradictions – that her mind struggled to take it all in.

Tsar Ivan the Terrible had been crowned in the Cathedral of the Assumption and he had prayed in the Cathedral of the Annunciation. He lay buried in the Cathedral of St Michael the Archangel. A stone's throw from these places the Communist Party now ruled from the Kremlin Palace and the modern Palace of Congresses. Long black Chaika limousines passed silently beneath Ivan the Terrible's Bell Tower and the Tsar's Bell, the largest of its kind in the world. Red Army guards stood by the historic Tsar's Cannon, the largest ever made. The Kremlin contained all the beauty and turmoil of Russian history in one small square of land, a square so filled with power, both ancient and modern, that the very air itself seemed to crackle with charge. The contradiction of old and new had not prevented progress. If anything, it had enhanced it, and the new lords of the Kremlin ruled an empire far beyond anything even the most ambitious Tsars of antiquity had ever dreamed of ruling.

They ate a simple lunch of cheese-filled *pirozhki* in the quiet of the Alexander Gardens before walking northwest on October 25th Avenue. Tatiana wondered where Svetlana's city tour would take her next. Wherever it was, it would be hard to compete with the excitement and drama of the Kremlin.

The avenue finished at a broad square with a statue in its centre and three-story building of yellow stone on one side.

'This is Dzerzhinsky Square,' Svetlana told her. She pointed to the statue in the centre, 'And that is Felix Dzerzhinsky. Do you know who he is?'

Tatiana shook her head.

Svetlana smiled. 'The building is Lubyanka.'

Tatiana had heard of Lubyanka. Everyone had heard of Lubyanka. 'KGB headquarters,' she said with growing unease.

'Yes,' Svetlana said happily. 'And Felix Dzerzhinsky was the founder of the secret police, the Cheka, which became the KGB.'

Tatiana nodded, eager to be on their way, but Svetlana's expression had hardened and suddenly she knew her enjoyment was over.

'I want you to take a photo of the building,' Svetlana said. 'Use your camera. Once you've done it, get it developed and bring it to the Hotel Metropole this evening.'

Tatiana stared at her. 'How can I? There are guards outside.'

Svetlana nodded, 'There's also a prison in the basement. They'll take you there if they catch you. If they do, there'll be no point telling them your name or mentioning The Organisation. They'll find no record of you. They'll hold you as a foreign spy and no country will claim you.'

Svetlana turned to go.

'Wait,' Tatiana begged.

'Do you understand your orders, Comrade Zykova?'

Svetlana said icily.

Tatiana hated her like never before. She couldn't bring herself to speak. Svetlana took a step closer and touched her arm. She snatched it away instantly.

'You have everything you need to carry out your mission,' Svetlana said more softly. 'Just remember your training.'

Svetlana turned and walked a few steps before stopping and turning back. 'And make it a good picture, showing the building clearly, not snapped from a moving bus or a faraway building. That won't do.' She smiled. 'I'll meet you in the Metropole at eight. Don't be late.'

Hotel Metropole, Moscow

Tatiana sat beside Svetlana on the old leather seat facing the bar and handed her a manila envelope. Svetlana did little more than glance at the photo inside before putting it in her purse. It didn't pay to be seen looking at pictures of Lubyanka, especially not in a notorious KGB haunt like the Hotel Metropole. Svetlana turned to her with a happy smile. 'How did you get it?'

'With the help of one of the guards,' she answered drily.

'Really? What was his name?'

'His name was Boris.'

'And his surname?'

'I don't know. I didn't ask. Why?'

'Because he must be reported,' Svetlana said stiffly.

'Really? What will happen to him?' she asked, fearing for the simple guard she'd tricked into posing for her while she took his picture. The guard, Boris, had been too preoccupied with the pretty young photography student to notice that one of the portraits she took of him – the one where she had him gazing heroically over his left shoulder – had missed him altogether and shot the building over his left shoulder.

'He'll be court-martialled and shot.'

Tatiana was about to protest when she saw the hint of a smile on Svetlana's lips. She pursed her lips. 'What'll happen to him, really?'

'Nothing will happen to him. We can hardly tell the KGB that we duped one of their own guards, can we?'

Tatiana smiled, relieved. Svetlana raised her hand to attract the waiter and ordered two glasses of champagne. 'Where did you get the film developed?' Svetlana asked once the waiter had gone.

'I found an underground lab that does erotic photography,' she answered. 'I told the technician I was a model and needed some prints for an urgent casting. I insisted on using the lab myself, but I promised him copies when I was finished.'

The waiter arrived with the champagne and Tatiana waited until he'd gone before continuing. 'When I finished, I told him the prints hadn't come out. He was furious, but what could he do?'

Svetlana raised her glass. 'Fuck him,' she grinned.

'Fuck him,' Tatiana laughed, raising her glass too.

Svetlana replaced her glass on the table and Tatiana noticed her gaze shift to the bar. She was staring at the Asiatic businessman and seemed unable to take her eyes off him.

'You like him?' Tatiana asked in surprise. She'd never seen Svetlana take interest in a man before.

'He's handsome, don't you think?'

Tatiana took a closer look at the man. He was a little over medium height, and thickset. His shoulders and thighs bulged beneath his grey suit. She guessed his weight to be 90kg, as she'd been taught to do by Svetlana. When he placed his briefcase on the floor, his jacket fell open and she saw his flat stomach. It was then she realised the bulk inside his suit was entirely muscle. He was dark-haired and swarthy, with a hint of grey at the temples, and a shadow across his heavy jaw despite being close-shaven. His skin was honey brown, his nose broad and flat like a boxer's, and his eyes, black and hinting at a family origin somewhere east of the Urals.

'He's attractive,' she said with a shrug.

'He's not your type?' Svetlana asked lightly.

'What is my type?' Tatiana asked, intrigued by the new playfulness in the woman who was usually so serious.

'Tall and blond, a little feminine, I imagine, like one of those pretty boys from Duran Duran.'

'Nonsense.'

'It's true.'

'How can it be? No patriot could possibly admire a Western imperialist. The Communist Manifesto forbids it.'

'Well said Tatiana!' Svetlana chuckled.

Tatiana found the sound of Svetlana's laughter faintly disturbing. She'd never seen her in this mood before and wondered how much she'd drunk before she'd arrived. Svetlana took her hand and squeezed it affectionately. 'I have one more task for you today, *Little One*. A small one, don't worry.' There was a mischievous grin on her face. 'Go and talk to that man at the bar and find out his name.'

'That's all?'

'That's all.'

'Why him?'

'I have reason to believe he's a person of interest to the state,' Svetlana answered evasively.

Tatiana shrugged. She rose and examined the man again as she approached him, seeking clues that would tell her more about her new target. He was dressed like a businessman, but he didn't look comfortable in his suit and she sensed he wasn't a man who pushed paper. The hardness of his features made her wonder if he was a gangster, or a soldier out of uniform, but he had none of the stiffness or military bearing she'd expect from an officer, and he was too well dressed to be a regular soldier. He sipped his beer and she had the feeling he wouldn't have another. It wasn't much to go on, but it didn't matter. All she needed was a name. She put her champagne glass down on the glass-topped counter beside him and leaned both elbows on the bar to steady herself. 'If you ask me, champagne's over-rated.' she said, the hint of a slur in her voice, 'Don't you agree?'

He smiled but didn't reply.

She nodded at his beer. 'I guess you do. You've got a beer, after all, not champagne. Although, maybe you've got nothing to celebrate. Me, I'm twenty-one today and I'm having a party at my place, later. Want to come along? Everyone's invited.'

He shook his head.

'Not your thing? I understand. I'm Ursula, by the way. Nice to meet you.'

She hoped he would say his name, but he said nothing.

'Are you staying in this hotel?'

'Yes,' he answered. His voice was rich and deep, surprisingly soft for such a roughly chiseled face.

'I'm not staying here in the hotel. I just like this bar. It's not the smartest place, but I like the old fashioned style, and you get to meet some interesting people. How about you, you're not from Moscow are you?'

He shook his head. There was the hint of a smile on his lips. Her act was amusing him.

'You don't say much, do you?' she went on. 'Well, it's okay. I talk enough for two people, everyone says so. So, anyway, why are you here? Not in here in the hotel, but here in Moscow? I know why you're in the hotel – you need a place to sleep, obviously – but why are you here in Moscow.'

'Business,' he said.

'Business. Okay. Confidential business, I imagine.' This was proving more difficult than she'd expected. It was time to try a more direct approach. 'You don't want to say more, I understand. Some things are best kept confidential. But listen, you're a good-looking man, you're here alone, in the hotel, why don't you come to my party, eh? Would you like to come along?'

She saw his eyes wander over to Svetlana. 'My friend over there, she's coming too. She's beautiful, isn't she? Tell me your name and I'll introduce you.'

The man didn't reply but simply smiled at Svetlana, who rose from her seat and sauntered over to join them. Tatiana extended her hand to welcome her: 'Svetlana Dimitrieva, meet...' she turned to the man with a smile. 'You never did tell me your name.'

'Didn't I?' the man said, taking Svetlana's proffered hand and shaking it happily.

Svetlana turned to Tatiana. 'Who is this handsome man you've found, Tatiana?'

'He's here on business,' Tatiana said lamely.

Svetlana gave her a look of disapproval. 'You've been talking to him all this time and you don't even know his name? Why are you making such a meal of it? Let me show you how it's done.' She stepped closer to the man so her leg was touching his thigh. 'Tell me your name and you can sleep with me,' she said, just loud enough for Tatiana to hear.

'Vasili,' the man grinned.

'Full name, if you please.'

'Dimitriev, Vasili Ivanovich. Colonel, Soviet National Army,' he said playfully in the clipped tones of a simple soldier reporting to a superior.

Tatiana finally got it. The man had the same surname as Svetlana, but in the masculine form.

Svetlana squeezed her arm playfully. 'Tatiana, meet my husband. He's from Voiska Spetsialnogo Naznacheniya, but it's such a mouthful that we just call it: *Spetznaz*.

Marx Engels Institute, Moscow

Tatiana had been paired with Xenia Galina for SOMBO training. Xenia was a tough girl from Estonia who was very aggressive, if lacking in technique. Normally Tatiana could beat her but today Xenia had thrown her twice already. Tatiana's mind was elsewhere. She was still thinking about the night before in the Hotel Metropole. Svetlana had given her the keys to the Moskvich and spent the night with her husband in the hotel. Tatiana had driven home but been unable to sleep. She had found herself strangely unsettled to learn that Svetlana was married.

Suddenly she was spinning in the air for a third time and hit the unforgiving mats hard. Xenia landed on top of her and she struggled to breathe. Xenia moved to secure a hold. She twisted her hips away and drove her knees into Xenia's torso. Xenia tried to pass around the side but she wrapped her legs around Xenia's waist. Her hands slipped inside Xenia's collar. Xenia rose, knowing a strangle was coming, and secured Tatiana's left hand with her right to prevent it. In a feat of considerable strength, she lifted Tatiana to slam her into the mat. However with her hands down she'd left her neck exposed. Tatiana's right leg circled it to form a classic triangle choke. Squeezing her thighs together, the blood to Xenia's brain was cut off swiftly. Xenia slammed her onto the mat, hoping the impact would shake her off, or better still knock her out, but she hung on grimly. Xenia tried to lift her again, but she was too weak now. Tatiana gripped the back of Xenia's head and pulled it to herself to increase the pressure. Xenia would be unconscious very soon. 'Tap,' she ordered.

Xenia refused.

'Tap!'

She felt Xenia go limp. She wondered if Xenia was faking. If she released the choke, would she fight on?

A man's voice came from nearby. 'She's out.'

She hadn't noticed him squat beside her. She couldn't see his face, but she saw his hand lift Xenia's hand and release it. Xenia's hand fell like a piece of meat to the mat. She was out cold. Tatiana released the choke and the man rose and walked away. She hadn't seen his face but she knew he wasn't one of her usual instructors. The rest of the class had stopped fighting some time before. They were all watching the stranger. Tatiana turned to Xenia slumped before her and tapped her face lightly. Xenia's eyes opened and she looked around in surprise. She wasn't so aggressive now, just dazed and a little embarrassed. 'You should have submitted,' she whispered to her.

Xenia ignored this and instead stared at the stranger. 'Who's that?'

The man turned and Tatiana saw it was Svetlana's husband, Dimitriev. He was dressed very differently now, in a simple green T-shirt and combat pants rather than the smart suit of the night before. The T-shirt was stretched tight across his barrel chest and veins on the insides of his forearms stood out, indicating exceptional fitness.

'You're trying too hard to win,' he told the students with a pained expression, as if he had witnessed something deeply distasteful. Tatiana felt a stab of resentment. The standard of their SOMBO was considered very high and their class contained several national champions.

'Try not to win and see what happens,' Dimitriev said with a wave of his hand. Nobody moved.

Finally Oleg Murzin spoke up. Murzin had recently won a silver medal at the Pan-Soviet Games. 'You have to try and win.'

'No,' Dimitriev said dismissively.

'I disagree,' Murzin said.

'If you don't agree with me, then try to beat me,' Dimitriev said with a sigh. His voice was so quiet and relaxed that Tatiana wasn't sure if she'd heard him correctly.

'You want me to beat you?' Murzin asked.

'Yes. You, anyone, all of you. Try and beat me.'

No one moved. Dimitriev walked among them. Tatiana estimated there were twenty students on the mat. His head was bowed, his eyes on the floor.

'Come and try,' he said more loudly. 'Once you've beaten me, you can take the rest of the day off.'

Still no one moved.

'Submit me. Or try and knock me out if you prefer. It's all the same to me.'

'First may we know who you are?' Murzin said, standing to face Dimitriev. Dimitriev smiled. 'My name is Dimitriev, Vasili Ivanovich,' he answered.

'And your rank?'

'Colonel.'

Murzin looked away in annoyance.

'I understand your reluctance,' Dimitriev said evenly. 'You don't want to attack a colonel. Usually it's not such a good idea, I agree. But in this instance, I gave you an order, and I expect you to obey it.'

Still no one moved.

'A direct order... to all of you. I won't issue it again.'

Murzin shot forward low and fast, his body a blur across the mats. Murzin was a big man and immensely powerful but it was his aggression that had won him so many titles on the SOMBO circuit. Tatiana had seen the ferocity of his fighting and watched in dismay as he hurled himself at Dimitriev. She hoped they wouldn't all be punished for what Murzin did to Dimitriev. So she was surprised to see Murzin sprawled face-first at Dimitriev's feet a moment later. Two more students had also come forward but they had stopped when Murzin attacked, expecting him to take care of the colonel. Dimitriev reached for the first of them now, his arm extended in what seemed like a greeting, too slow to cause alarm. His hand snaked around the student's neck and with a twist of the hips, he sent him flying into his comrade and across the room.

'So far only three of you have obeyed my order,' he said with a pained smile.

Murzin rose and threw himself at Dimitriev's back. Dimitriev kicked behind like a mule and Murzin was sent flying. Dimitriev shook his head in disappointment. 'Still only three.'

A gang of four rushed him at once and he disappeared from Tatiana's view. The fool would pay for his arrogance now, Tatiana thought. The four students punched and kicked at Dimitriev, who disappeared beneath a hail of blows. She closed her eyes, wondering at the shit-storm that they would get over this, wondering what she would say to Svetlana when she saw her next. When she opened her eyes Dimitriev was before her, throwing the last of his four assailants aside. The other three lay on the floor already, taken out by strikes unseen. Dimitriev advanced towards her, kicking another bystander out of the way and sending him flying. Tatiana seized the moment to fire a straight punch at his face. She felt her fist guided away by the slightest touch before being seized in a crushing grip. Snaking his arm over hers, he took his own wrist and spun, sending her crashing into Xenia, who was standing beside her.

The students who had not yet attacked knew their best chance was to attack together. They descended on Dimitriev like a pack of wolves. He moved through them, striking as he passed, his movements of evasion and striking as one, moving always to the weakest point of the mob, finding its weakness as water finds its way through rock, striking as water strikes when it falls from a great height. At one point Tatiana saw him on the ground, his body writhing like an eel, his arms covering his head and neck, his legs working to propel him away from the apex of the storm, to trip and unbalance. One student fell into another and Dimitriev rose to occupy his space. Then he moved through his attackers, striking with his hands, his arms, his elbow and even his shoulders, until it seemed there was no part of his body that was not a weapon. The students fell away around him until they were all gone, and only he remained. He beckoned to her, a carefree smile on his face, as if calling an old friend to join him for a drink. She hesitated, knowing the fate that awaited her if she agreed, then lunged forward, feinting with the left and throwing a fast overhand right. The trick had worked once before against Svetlana, perhaps it would work once again against her husband.

She woke a moment later, seated on the floor. Dimitriev was supporting her and massaging the side on her neck gently. 'Good morning Tatiana Zykova,' he said, his voice warm and soft as honey. 'Svetlana has taught you well, better than most. Can you stand yet?'

'I think so,' she said. Her voice sounded thin and faraway.

'Good, then come with me,' he said, helping her to her feet.

They walked together through the bodies of the students sprawled on the ground, nursing their injuries, or groaning quietly to themselves. Some were still unconscious, but those that were awake watched the colonel pass as if seeing a ghost.

'Where are we going?' she asked.

'To complete the final part of your training,' he answered.

'But where?'

'Svetlana didn't tell you?' he asked in surprise.

'Svetlana said I'd be going to Little England,' she said.

'That's right,' he grinned. 'Little England.'

*

The giant Antonov took off from Sheremetyevo airport and climbed slowly into the sky above Moscow. Tatiana and Dimitriev were the only two passengers, but the cavernous cargo bay was filled with 150 tonnes of army supplies that strained the four mighty Lotarev engines to their limit. Dimitriev had taken a row of seats to himself and, sensing he wanted to be alone, Tatiana had taken another row at the opposite end of the small passenger compartment. She'd closed her eyes but despite her tiredness, sleep had taken its time in coming.

Now, finally, she was walking in Leningrad, with Grigory, beside the River Neva. It was their first date. They'd met the night before, in a bar on Nevsky Prospekt. Grigory had been urbane and charming. He'd talked about her favourite things, films, music, books, fashion. At the end of the evening he'd invited her to go to the cinema to watch Stalker. He'd seen the film several times before, but it was so good that he didn't mind seeing it again. Was it good? She couldn't tell. Her mind had not been on the film but on the handsome young man beside her. They were discussing it now. She'd thought herself an able film critic, but beside Grigory she felt like an amateur. Grigory knew all about the movie industry, the actors, the director. He talked about plot and subtext. She let him talk, she liked the sound of his voice.

Her face felt flushed by the cold Baltic wind coming in off the wide open river. Fine snowflakes swirled in the pristine night sky. Grigory took her by the hand and led her into the warmth of a bohemian little café where the owner greeted him warmly. They drank tea and talked about other films that she liked. Grigory was like no man she'd ever met before. He was polite, courteous and charming, not like the boys from the orphanage, or the men from the workhouses, or the punters she met in the hotel bars. Grigory listened when she spoke, he laughed at the things she said. He made her laugh. He paid for everything, the drinks, the cinema, even the tea. She'd been enchanted by this warm, handsome stranger. It was the most magical night of her life.

As the hour approached eleven and the café began to close, Grigory invited her to his apartment, and she went with him. He turned out to be a generous lover. The next day he went to work. He managed a nightclub, he told her. She was welcome to stay in his flat, if she liked. She agreed, wondering what Grigory would say if he found out her profession, but Grigory never asked and she had the feeling he already knew.

It was only when she visited Grigory's nightclub a week later that she finally understood. The club was filled up with rich businessmen, military types, and party officials, some young but most middle-aged or older, and beautiful young women.

The atmosphere was so relaxed and charming that it took her a moment to realise what this place was. She had never encountered a brothel like this one before.

She confronted Grigory angrily. He acted surprised and a little hurt that she should be upset and told her not to be so naïve. It was the way of the world, there was no point in denying it. Better to accept it and profit from it like everyone else. She'd left, but Grigory had found her and soon they were together again. He took her to the best restaurants and bought her new clothes. They went to the theatre and the ballet together. Grigory always had money. She didn't need to work. She moved in with him. They lived happily together for two months before their first serious argument. She'd slapped Grigory, and he'd knocked her to the floor. Afterwards he'd been remorseful, and she'd forgiven him, but the arguments happened more frequently after that. Then Grigory told her there was someone he wanted her to meet – a party official he owed a favour to. She'd known it was coming, but even so it cut her like a knife.

*

She was woken by turbulence. Outside the window, a grey dawn revealed snow-capped mountains stretching into the distance and beyond them, vast tracts of virgin forest, the firs tipped with frost despite the Spring season. She rose and sat opposite the slumbering Dimitriev.

'Where the hell are we going?' she demanded.

His eyes opened lazily.

'You told me we were going to England.'

'I told you Little England.'

'Those mountains are the Urals, not the Alps.'

Dimitriev nodded.

'That means Siberia,' she said.

'Also correct.'

She held onto her temper with difficulty. 'Tell me where we're going, please, Colonel.'

Dimitriev sat up in his chair and squeezed his eyes with his thumb and forefinger. 'The place we're going has no name.'

'No name, so we're going nowhere?'

Dimitriev sighed. 'We are going somewhere, but it has no name, no number, no classification.' She regarded him blankly. 'Officially, it doesn't exist. So no record of it exists anywhere, and no mention is ever made of it. Otherwise, it would exist. Do you see?'

'What will we be doing in this place that doesn't exist?' she demanded.

'Training.'

'What sort of training?'

Dimitriev's expression darkened and for a moment Tatiana saw the same blankness in his eyes she'd seen in the gymnasium at the Marx Engels Institute. She smiled. 'Tell me Colonel, *please*.'

Dimitriev leaned back in his seat, his eyes assessing her coldly. 'There's no point. You'll see for yourself soon enough.'

'Then tell me how long will we stay in Siberia?' she demanded, unable to stop herself.

'As long as it takes.

'To do what?'

'To learn what Siberia has to offer.'

Tatiana could hold her temper no longer. 'Oil, gas and snow – that's all Siberia has to offer, unless you count the Gulags.'

Dimitriev stared at her until she looked away. She had no wish to anger him, not at the beginning of their time together, not when he was her only link to Moscow, to Svetlana, and to The Organisation that she still knew so little about. Not when she was so very far away from home.

Krasnoyarsk, Siberia

The Antonov landed in Krasnoyarsk in central Siberia. The day was bright and cold and snow was piled high by the side of the runway. A young lieutenant was waiting for them inside the empty terminal building. He took them to a car parked nearby and drove them through a white landscape of densely forested tracks until, shortly before nightfall, they reached a base surrounded by snow covered firs.

They got out of the car and entered the guardhouse. A sergeant saluted Dimitriev and searched his case swiftly before inviting him to pass through. He had Tatiana put her suitcase and papers on the table. He sealed her identity card in a manila envelope and labeled it with an eight-digit number. Next he made a careful inventory of the contents of her suitcase and tagged it with the same eight-digit number before setting it on a shelf behind him.

'Go through,' he told her.

'I need my bag and papers,' she said.

The sergeant stared at her, his grey eyes void of understanding.

'I need them,' she repeated.

'Everything you need will be supplied,' he said. 'Please go through.'

She looked to Dimitriev, waiting impassively at the far end of the guardhouse. She sighed and went to join him. The lieutenant was waiting in the car outside and drove them through what looked like urban streets. The road signs were written in French, then Italian, then German. Then they were on a street with an English name: Park Road. There was a pub on the corner called the Red Lion.

The car pulled up a few doors past the pub outside a residential house. The lieutenant turned and handed her an envelope. She examined it. There was nothing written on it.

'Open it,' Dimitriev told her.

Inside was a key-ring with two keys and a tag reading 8B.

'Home,' Dimitriev smiled.

She stared at him blankly.

'Go on,' he nodded. 'I'll meet you here tomorrow evening at 17.30.'

The lieutenant shifted in his seat. She realised he was waiting for her to get out. She looked at Dimitriev again. His face gave nothing away. She got out and stood on the neat square slabs of paving stone beside the smooth tarmac road and watched the car drive away.

*

Her new home was a flat on the upper floor of a two-storey Victorian-style house, a style common throughout England. She left the front door ajar, expecting someone to appear and tell her which rooms she could use and which she couldn't. No one came. She shut the door and bolted it.

The kitchen was the first room off the hallway. A plain white cupboard was stocked with tea bags, tins of beans in tomato sauce, and plain biscuits. The fridge was filled with luxuries: cheese, butter, fresh milk, eggs, sausages, bacon. In the top was a small freezer compartment with colourful boxes of breaded fish, battered chicken pieces, potato chips covered in oil, and frozen peas. On the counter was an electric kettle with an unusual three-point plug.

In the bedroom, she found a small double bed with freshly laundered bed-clothes in black and white stripes. The wardrobe and chest of drawers were filled with new clothes with labels she had never heard of. She sifted through them slowly, knowing each item had been selected by Svetlana, knowing that each one told her something about the woman she was expected to become. These clothes said she was a woman of modest means – none of the labels were designer names – and that she was conservative in nature. Most of the wardrobe was made up of casual clothes, long skirts, woolen jumpers, denim jeans and comfortable shoes, the typical garments of an English student. Only a small section held a few colourful dresses. In a box on her dressing table she found costume jewellery and make-up. In the drawers were more clues to her new identity: a collection of leotards, leggings, sweatshirts and sweatpants. She guessed she was a woman who took her health and fitness seriously.

In the lounge there was a small colour TV that played English channels, a video recorder, and shelves filled with English books. Among them she discovered Animal Farm and Nineteen Eighty-Four by George Orwell, and The Gulag Archipelago by Aleksander Solzhenitsyn, all banned in the Soviet Union. She wondered whether she should read them or whether she was being watched and tested for anti-Soviet behaviour. Another shelf was stacked with newspapers and magazines of all kinds including pornography, and there was more pornography among the videos on the bottom shelf.

Returning to the kitchen, she noticed a square of paper pinned to a cork board behind the door. It was weekly a timetable beginning on Monday morning with *Newsagent, 06:30*. Other listings included *Café, 07:00, School, 08:30,* and *Bank,*

12:30. Each lunchtime a different place was listed: *Doctor's, Chemist's, Bank, Grocer's,* and *Pub* on a Friday. Every morning and afternoon said *School* and every evening it simply said *Training.*

*

After a fitful night's sleep, she emerged from her new flat fifteen minutes before her first appointment. The newsagent was only a few doors from her own, but she wanted to explore her new home in the daylight. Above her the sky was a vast uniform blue, so solid that it seemed to sit over the base like a heavy blanket, keeping everything in place beneath it. She didn't have time to admire its grandeur, her attention was taken by the short street in which she found herself. In the clear morning light, its ordinariness made it all the more surreal. The newsagent was at the beginning of the street and beside it was a chemist's shop. Opposite was a café imaginatively called The Number One Café and beside it the Red Lion pub she'd noticed the night before. At the end of her street a barrier had been lowered with a 'Stop' sign on it. There were no guards and it would have been easy to walk around the barrier but she knew it would not be a good idea. She walked instead to the other end of the street. Most of it was filled with houses similar to her own, 22 in total, with odd numbers on the left and even numbers on the right. Each house was painted a little differently and planted with a small garden at the front. A single yellow line ran the length of the road beside the curb. At the end of the street was a gate marked 'School' with a small building beyond. Beside it was a bank with a sign of a black horse. Opposite was a restaurant called The Red Fort that looked Indian in design, and beside it a small cinema. A tiny, empty children's park stood at the end of the road. Around the far edge of the park rose a five-metre fence topped with razor wire, and beyond that the darkness of the Siberian forest.

The street was still empty when she approached the newsagent, but as she passed the door to number six, it opened and a middle-aged woman emerged wearing a smart grey suit and carrying a black handbag on her shoulder.

'Morning!' she said in English with a cheery smile.

'Good morning,' Tatiana replied in English.

'You must be our new neighbour. We heard someone was moving in. I'm Vivian, by the way. Nice to meet you.' The woman did not proffer her hand and Tatiana fought the urge to offer her own, recalling the British reluctance when it came to bodily contact.

'Yes, I just arrived last night. My name is… Tania.'

'Such a lovely name. Is it Russian?'

Tatiana saw the woman's calculating eyes behind the innocent smile.

'No, it's from Poland,' she said lightly.

'How lovely,' Vivien replied. There was a singsong lilt to her voice, a contrived cheeriness. 'Well I'd better get on. Things to do … people to see … places to go, you know how it is.'

Tatiana smiled and stepped past her, feeling a weight lifted off her shoulders the moment she was free of the strange woman. The sign above the newsagent said *Silk Cut*. She had no idea why. The window was filled with colourful posters announcing Bingo, magazine giveaways, and TV programmes. On the door, small hand-written cards hung in the pockets of a single plastic sheet, offering the services of a window cleaner, a child-minder, a painter and decorator and a gardener. Inside she was greeted by a kaleidoscope of colour. An entire wall was filled with glossy magazines, another with chocolate bars and fizzy drinks, and in the middle of the shop, taking up most of the space, were two rows of shelves stacked with tins, jars, packets and boxes. Behind the counter were cigarette brands from all over the world including, she noticed, *Silk Cut*. Beyond these, beneath a hand-written sign saying *Off Sales*, were two shelves of beers, wines and spirits. The shopkeeper was a small man of sixty, bald except for a wisp of curly grey hair above his ears and a neatly trimmed moustache and beard. He looked over the thin gold-framed spectacles on his nose and raised his eyebrows and spoke to her in a language she had never heard before.

'I beg your pardon,' she said, flustered.

He repeated his sentence, and this time she could just make out the English, twisted almost beyond recognition by his tortuous pronunciation. *Can I help ye, missy? Ye look a little lost, if ye dinna mind me sayin'. Was it somethin' in particular ye were wantin'?'* He was waiting for a reply. Unlike the woman outside, there was no falseness or coldness in his eyes, but he too was assessing her.

'Good morning,' she said brightly, 'I just wanted a newspaper.'

'Then ye've come to the right place. We've lots of newspapers. Which is yer daily?'

She scanned the titles quickly, searching for one she might recognise. 'The Times,' she said, reaching for a copy and placing it on the counter between them.

'That'll be 25 pence, luvvie,' he said.

She regarded him blankly. She had no money. 'I'm such a fool! I've left my wallet at home,' she said, rolling her eyes.

'Yer wallet?' he said quickly. 'Do ye really carry a wallet? Only most ladies I know carry a purse.'

'Oh yes, my purse,' she grimaced. 'Silly me.'

'Ye're not from round here are ye?' he asked suddenly.

'No, I'm from Poland,' she said. 'I just moved in yesterday. I live at number eight.'

'Well no matter about the money dearie. Take the paper and ye can pay me tomorrow,' he smiled.

'Thank you,' she said. 'You're very kind.'

She noticed the paper was two days out of date. It took time to ship the latest English papers to Siberia.

'I'll pay you tomorrow, don't worry,' she assured him.

'Aye, I'm sure ye will,' he nodded. 'And if ye don't, I know where ye live.'

She stared at him, unsure whether he was serious or joking.

'Ahm only kidding luv,' he said at last.

'I'm sorry, I don't understand English humour yet,' she said.

'Well Missy, the first thing you need to understand about my humour is that it's not English, it's Scottish. But I'll let ye off just this once, what with ye being foreign and all.'

'Thank you,' she laughed, feeling her cheeks reddening despite herself. 'I didn't mean to be rude. I was wondering where your accent was from.'

'Well now ye know,' he nodded sternly, 'So ye won't make the same mistake again. And since yer new to the area, I'll let ye in on a little secret. There's a bank, at the other end of the street where ye can open an account. And if it's shut, ye can get money out of the cash machine, wi' yer bank card. It's easy. Go along and they'll show ye how it works.'

'Thank you,' she said, grateful for the tip.

'Ach, it's nothin'. Will ye be needing anything else? Fags…

Booze… Marmite?'

She looked at him in bewilderment.

'Sorry,' he grinned mischievously. 'I forgot you weren't from round here.' He pointed as he spoke: 'Cigarettes? Alcohol? Marmite, to spread on yer toast?' He lifted a flap at the end of the counter and came out into the store and reached for a squat black jar from a shelf behind her. 'Try it. It's a very British thing. People either love it or hate it. See what ye think.'

She accepted and, making her excuses, hurried from the shop before the shopkeeper could invent any new games or tricks for her. The shopkeeper waited until she was out of the door and then reached for the pen and paper under his counter and began his report.

*

She went to The Number One Café for her next appointment at 7:00. Inside were two small tables, both occupied, the first by a young man in a black workman's jacket reading a newspaper, the second by a well-dressed middle-aged man reading a book. The workman was eating a large plate piled with bacon, sausage, toast and beans, while the middle-aged man was eating scrambled eggs on toast. Both had large white mugs of tea before them, which, Tatiana knew, was the staple drink for such a place.

The dour-faced woman behind the counter waited for her order without a word. It took her a moment to realise it was the same woman who had played Vivian, her neighbour. The smart suit and beaming smile had been replaced by a grubby chequered overall and a bored expression. The woman's pen hovered over a small brown notepad expectantly. She scanned the menu, scratched on a blackboard in coloured chalk, and saw words she'd never encountered in the lecture halls of the Marx Engels Institute, *Hash Browns, Black Pudding, Cumberland sausage*. Beside it on the wall, coloured card had been cut into the shapes of stars and labelled with even more baffling names: *Toad in the Hole, Bubble & Squeak, Welsh Rarebit*.

'Breakfast Option One,' she said hopefully.

'Beans or tomatoes?' the woman fired back.

'Tomatoes,' she answered.

'Black pudding's twenty pence extra today,' the woman told her.

'Okay,' Tatiana smiled, unsure what to expect, but guessing the woman wanted her try it.

'How many sugars?' the woman asked, pouring tea from a large metal teapot into a chipped white mug and reaching for a glass sugar jar with a spout.

'One, thank you,' Tatiana said.

The woman poured an endless stream of sugar into the red-brown liquid and stirred it once. It was not nearly enough to dissolve the sugar, but she handed it to Tatiana, who took it without complaint. Tatiana looked at the tables hesitantly, wondering which diner to sit opposite. 'Sit anywhere,' the woman told her. 'I'll bring it over when it's ready. Go on, they won't bite.'

Tatiana approached the young workman. His clothes were different from a Soviet worker's clothes, but even so there was no mistaking his profession, it was the same uniform the world over, the course, roughly-hewn garments of a physical labourer.

'Do you mind if I sit there?' she asked sheepishly, nodding at the chair opposite him.

'Be my guest, love,' he answered without looking up from his newspaper.

She sat and examined the upside-down paper that was little bigger than a magazine. It showed a topless girl in black panties and a witch's hat with the headline *Happy Hollyween*. In the bottom corner she read *Holly from Norwich, aged 20*. The man made no effort to cover up the pornographic picture or make any room on the table for her. She placed her folded copy of The Times on the corner and examined the remainder of the two pages he was reading. There were two smaller pictures of scantily clad women and the word 'sex' appeared five times in various headlines and smaller headings. It seemed almost comical, and for a moment she wondered if some Soviet wit had created the paper as a joke to mock the depravity of the West. She looked at the name of the paper: *The Sun*. She recalled seeing the bright red label among the titles in the newsagent, and several others similar to it. She decided it must be real.

The man ate his breakfast greedily without looking away from his paper. She wondered what was expected of her. She was here to learn, and this man, this agent, this actor, this spy, whoever he really was, had been put before her deliberately. She needed to engage with him.

'Do you always read this newspaper?' she demanded suddenly.

He looked up absently. 'Yeah, what of it, darling?'

'I'm just asking, because it doesn't seem to contain much news,' she said.

'It's got the football results,' he said with a shrug. 'That's all I'm really after.'

I don't see much football in it either,' she said with a smile.

'It's got other stuff too,' he grinned. His eyes left hers and roamed her body lazily. 'I haven't seen you round here before. If I had, I would've remembered. Pretty girl like you.'

'I've just moved in,' she smiled.

He didn't ask her name. 'Pretty enough to be a Page Three Girl,' was all he said.

'What's that?' she asked.

He tapped the bottom corner of the page. 'Page three. There's always a girl on page three. Every day, in The Sun.'

'Is there? I wouldn't know. I don't read that sort of paper,' she said coolly, wondering if there really were such men in England – he was certainly not the English gentleman of popular myth in the Soviet Union.

'Oh, other rags have girls too, don't get me wrong,' he said seriously, 'The Mirror, The News of The World, you know, but the Page Three Girl is unique to The Sun.' He spoke affecting a posh accent to emphasise the scientific nature of his analysis.

She stared at him, wondering what sort of answer he was expecting from such a statement.

'I dunno how you read that bloody thing,' he went on, nodding at The Times. 'Too big to open out, even in here, let alone on the bleeding bus or train.'

Tatiana sipped the sweet, tepid tea. The milk gave it a sour, curdled aftertaste that turned her stomach. She set it aside carefully. The woman from behind the counter appeared by the table with a large oval plate. She waited impatiently while the man moved his paper then put the plate before Tatiana. She returned a moment later with a side plate containing two perfectly square slices of toasted white bread painted with glistening yellow butter.

'Excuse me but I didn't order this,' Tatiana said, pointing to two pieces of thick black sausage on her breakfast plate.

'Yes you did, pet,' the woman said tersely. 'Black pudding… remember? I did ask you, but I can take it off if you like.'

Tatiana blushed – she'd expected a pudding as a second course, which she'd considered strange, but which she'd been willing to try. She'd not expected slices of what looked like blood sausage – 'Of course I did. Silly me! It's fine,' she smiled.

The woman shook her head and left. The man opened his mouth to speak but it was full with egg and beans in a rich tomato sauce and he was forced to chew several times and swallow first.

'You're not from round here, I take it,' he mumbled at last.

'I'm from Poland,' she told him.

'You're a Pole,' he smiled.

'I guess so,' she answered.

'You're not a dancer too, by any chance?'

'No, why do you ask?'

'Only that would make you a pole-dancer, wouldn't it?' he grinned.

'Is that some kind of joke?' she demanded.

'Listen, no offence, eh love? Only we English, well we love to joke around you see, with words and suchlike. It's a national pastime. You'll get used to it.'

She ignored him and ate her food. Despite the generous portions of sausage, bacon, egg and grilled fresh tomato – all rare, high-quality foods reserved for party officials in the Soviet Union – the taste was remarkably bland. Only the blood sausage seemed to have any flavour at all. She sprinkled salt and pepper over her plate but it made no difference and she chewed her food miserably.

'Try some ketchup,' the man suggested, handing her a red

plastic bottle in the shape of a tomato.

'No thank you, I don't like ketchup,' she said, having tried it before in Moscow on several occasions.

'Brown sauce, then,' he offered, handing her a thin brown plastic bottle. She squeezed a little onto her plate and tasted it. It tasted of spiced soya beans and vinegar, but it was better than ketchup, and added a little extra flavour to the otherwise bland offering.

'Well I better be off,' he said, rising. 'I'll be late for work, again.'

'What do you do?' she asked.

'I'm a High Court Judge,' he told her seriously.

She stared at him.

He laughed loudly. 'I'm a plumber darling. What did you think I was?'

'Very funny,' she said icily.

'Yeah, well it's gotta be done, ain't it? Let me know if you want me to take a look at your pipes sometime, eh darling? Right, I'm off. I'll probably see you tomorrow.'

*

The school was no more than a single classroom in a neat prefabricated grey block. Tatiana stepped inside. There was no one around. A row of children's paintings stretched around all four walls, each with a letter of the alphabet beside it. There were four tiny desks and chairs plus a larger desk and chair, presumably for the teacher. Tatiana sat on one of the tiny chairs, her knees each side of the desk, and waited. A woman breezed in. It was Vivian and the café owner from earlier. She looked very different again – this time wearing a blonde wig with tortoiseshell glasses, a casual skirt and a thin woollen cardigan.

'My name is Mrs. Moffat and I'm your new teacher,' she said in a cheery voice, addressing the room rather than Tatiana directly and rubbing her hands together enthusiastically. 'Perhaps we should begin with all of you telling me your names?' Her eyes scanned the empty room as if seeing a classroom full of children, then came to rest on Tatiana. 'Let's start with you.' She pointed at Tatiana with a beaming smile.

'Tania,' Tatiana replied.

'What a lovely name. And do you have a second name Tania?'

'Zilinski,' Tatiana answered, thinking of the first Polish surname that came into her head.

Mrs. Moffat wrote the name in her register and placed a deliberate tick beside it. 'Good. Everyone's present, so we can begin.' She taught Tania to recite the letters of the alphabet and how to write them, both as capitals and small letters. Next she showed her how to join the letters together in the English style of handwriting, rather than that used on The Continent. The way Mrs. Moffat said the word *Continent* showed it was clearly far inferior to all things English. Next, Mrs. Moffat had her new student draw pictures in crayon of her home and family: her mother, her father, her brother and her dog. After this, she fetched a guitar and they sang songs about an old farmer called McDonald, a black sheep with three bags of wool, and an old woman who swallowed a fly. When they had finished, Mrs. Moffat beamed with delight and Tatiana smiled back. She'd pleased her teacher, that was good. She glanced at her watch, wondering how much longer the lessons would continue.

'Are you wearing a watch, Tania?' Mrs. Moffat asked

suddenly.

'Yes,' she answered cautiously, instantly aware that she'd done something very wrong.

'Why are you wearing a watch? You can't tell the time, so what's the point?'

'I don't know, Mrs. Moffat.'

'Come here,' Mrs. Moffat said, her voice cold and shrill now, her finger pointing rigidly to a spot on the floor before her.

Tatiana went and stood on the spot Mrs. Moffat was pointing at. She was a head taller than the stout middle-aged woman before her, but she felt she was six years old again and standing before one of the staff at the orphanage. She fought down the fear of what the woman might do to her.

Mrs. Moffat held out her hand. 'Give me the watch.'

Tatiana didn't want to give up her watch. It was the only one she had, and she needed it. She didn't know where she could get a new one on the base. 'I can't,' she told her.

'Give it to me right now,' Mrs. Moffat demanded shrilly. 'I won't tell you again.'

'My mother gave it to me,' she blurted out. 'She'll be angry if I lose it.'

'You won't lose it. It's being confiscated, that's all.'

Tatiana glared at her.

'You can collect it at the end of the day,' Mrs. Moffat said icily. 'Now give it to me!'

Tatiana unfastened the watch and handed it over. It was a cheap watch that Svetlana had bought for her when she'd first arrived in Moscow, but she'd grown used to it. It suited her. She hoped the agent would remember to return it later, as she'd promised.

Mrs Moffat took the watch and put it in the pocket of her

cardigan. 'Now hold out your hand, palm up.'

Tatiana did as she was told, and Mrs Moffat slapped her palm with a plastic ruler. 'That's for answering back.'

It stung for a moment. Tatiana had no idea what to do next. Mrs. Moffat smiled, her stern mood instantly forgotten. 'I don't like disciplining children, but once in a while I have to do it. There was a boy here last week who did something much naughtier than you. He got six of the best.'

'What is six of the best?' Tania asked warily.

'Six good whacks on the backside,' Mrs. Moffat said, indicating the low, horizontal blow with her ruler.

'What did he do?' Tatiana asked.

'He asked too many questions. Now off you go for lunch, and take these books to read at home. I want you to know all these stories by tomorrow.' Mrs. Moffat handed her a tall pile of children's books. On top of the pile was her watch.

*

When she returned to the school in the afternoon the classroom had changed to a university-style lecture room with a white board. A man in his late forties was waiting, balding, with steel rimmed spectacles and a creased lab coat. Without acknowledging her in any way, he began drawing two diagrams in marker pen on the board. When he'd finished, he removed his spectacles and addressed his lecture to the ceiling.

'There are two principle types of device to consider, the first of which uses fission and the second of which uses fusion. Fission devices of the kind deployed by the Americans at the end of the Second World War are commonly known as *Atomic* bombs and have a blast yield equivalent to 15,000 tons of

TNT. Fusion devices of the kind released by the Soviet Union over Novaya Zemlya in 1961 are commonly known as *Thermonuclear* devices. The device that we detonated over Novaya Zemlya released a blast equivalent of 50 million tons of TNT.'

Tatiana noticed a misty look in his eyes. He was recalling a fond memory. 'That device was over a thousand times more powerful than the combined bombs dropped on Hiroshima and Nagasaki. In fact, it was ten times more powerful than all the explosive devices detonated during the entire Second World War.' He shook his head wistfully, and caught Tatiana's eye for a moment before looking away. She had the feeling he didn't want her to see him becoming emotional. 'We intended the yield to be twice as large, 100 million tons, but we had to reduce it because the pilot who dropped the bomb would not have escaped the blast. Even so, it was the most powerful device ever detonated in the history of mankind.'

His eyes settled on her for the first time. 'Tell me young lady, have you ever visited the Kremlin?'

'I have, Professor,' she nodded.

'You saw the Tsar's Bell and the Tsar's Cannon – so called because they are the largest ever made in the world?'

'I did,' she smiled.

'Well our device had many names and codenames, but do you know what we called it? The *Tsar Bomb*. A good name, don't you think? Do you see the joke? It was just our own little attempt at humour, but rather good, I thought.'

*

When she returned to her house, Dimitriev was waiting outside. He was dressed in a grey double-breasted suit, with a white shirt, red tie and red braces, in the English fashion of the day.

'Comrade Colonel,' she said in Russian – the first time she had spoken Russian that day – 'I'm just returning from my lecture. Sorry if I'm late.'

'You're not late, I'm early,' he replied in fluent English. 'And please, call me Vasili.'

'Do I have time to get changed, Vasili?' she asked, switching to English.

'Of course,' he smiled. 'Plenty of time.'

'Would you like to come in? I have tea.'

'That would be nice, but I prefer coffee.'

She showed him to the kitchen and he sat at the little square table in the centre. She took the jar of Nescafe from the cupboard. Freeze-dried coffee of this kind was highly prized in the Soviet Union and was only available in shops reserved for Party members. She opened the lid and popped the foil cover. She'd never drunk instant coffee before and was unsure how to make it. She thought about asking Dimitriev, but Dimitriev might be testing her. If he was, she didn't want to make a mistake. 'How strong do you like it?' she asked casually.

'One teaspoon is fine for me,' he said happily. She added a teaspoonful to his cup and the same to her own.

'Do you have any biscuits?' he asked.

She'd seen a packet the night before and reached for them now. 'Rich Tea,' she said hopefully.

'Super,' he said with a smile.

She laid out the biscuits on a plate and put it before him on the table. 'I'll get changed while we wait for the kettle to boil,' she said. Then she hesitated, 'Are you going to change too?'

'No. Why do you ask?'

'I thought we were going to train.'

'We are.'

'You're dressed very smartly for training. What should I wear?' she asked.

He grinned. 'During your time with Svetlana, I imagine she taught you how to dress like a lady.'

'Among other things,' she answered warily. It had been a long day and she was growing tired of the games.

He bit into a biscuit and munched on it quietly before answering. 'Then wear a nice dress and a pair of heels.'

She went into the bedroom and put on a dark blue dress with some costume jewellery and chose the shoes with the lowest heel she could find. When she returned to the kitchen, two more biscuits had gone and Dimitriev's coffee was finished. She took a sip of her own coffee. It tasted wonderfully smooth, if a little sweet for her liking. She would need no sugar in the future, the rich creamy milk would be quite enough. She took another sip.

'Don't rush,' he told her. 'We've got plenty of time.'

She wanted to ask what their training would entail, but she knew that despite his friendliness Dimitriev was assessing her, and she didn't want to appear nervous. She guessed he wanted her to learn to fight in restrictive clothing, the kind she might wear on a mission. In his ample suit, Dimitriev would have a huge advantage in terms of mobility. He would have a huge advantage anyway. His fighting ability was little short of miraculous. Nevertheless, as she sipped her coffee she made a mental list of the weaknesses in his attire. His collar and his tie could be used to strangle him, as could his suit lapels, which could also be gripped like a SOMBO jacket for a throw. He had no belt which she could slip off and use against him. The stretchy braces would make a poor substitute, however they might be enough to distract him so she could feel in his pockets for something she might use against him: a pen, a lighter, a penknife, if he was carrying one. Dimitriev noticed her eyes on him and smiled. She finished her coffee and returned his smile.

The gymnasium was behind the cinema and invisible from the street. There were no windows. No one outside would be able to see what was happening inside. There would be no one to help her, no matter what Dimitriev had in mind. He flicked on the long neon strip lights and she glanced around the hall quickly, searching for clues as to the training he had in mind for her. There were no mats, no punch bags, no pads or gloves, no skipping ropes or striking dummies. There was no training equipment of any sort, just a large cassette player plugged in at the wall.

Dimitriev closed the door. She kept her arms by her sides, but her weight was evenly distributed on each foot and her senses hyper alert, waiting for his attack. He saw the readiness in her stance and blinked in surprise, then bent and pressed a button on the cassette player. A loud hiss came across the speakers for ten seconds and then a playful Viennese Waltz blasted out, filling the hall. Dimitriev extended his hand to her, raising his voice to be heard above the music. 'Would you care to dance, Miss Zykova?'

*

The Red Fort restaurant was dimly lit inside and smelled of aromatic spices. The walls were decorated with brightly coloured prints of Hindu temples, bejewelled Gods and elephants decorated in colourful brocade. The waiter who greeted them at the door wore a pristine white turban. He turned to show them to a table before Tatiana could get a good look at his face but later, when he handed her a menu, she saw the eyes of the Scottish newsagent behind the dark make-up and full black beard. The Indian waiter was one of his finest roles. He answered her questions about the menu patiently and with good humour, explaining the complex ingredients and spicing combinations in each dish with practiced ease. Tatiana listened in delight to his performance, thinking how her drama teacher Miriam Gavrilova would have admired him too. The man's accent was the least of it, he really did appear to be a different person. Once he'd taken their order and left, Tatiana sat back in her chair and pressed her eyes with the heel of her hands.

'Is everything okay?' Dimitriev asked.

She stared at him, wondering how to answer. Could she confide in him, or would that be taken as a sign of weakness? Was she expected to endure this entire test alone? The waiter returned and laid a tray with two large crisp pancakes before them, along with some small jars of chutney and brought them each a small glass of cold Danish beer. She sipped it gratefully. She needed to relax.

'Listen, Colonel…'

'Vasili…'

'Sorry, Vasili. I have no idea what I'm doing here. If you can tell me anything I need to know, please tell me now.'

He held her gaze for some time before answering. 'This is

training, Tatiana, plain and simple. Think of it as that, nothing more.'

She smoothed down the napkin on her lap. 'But what happens if I fail?'

'Why do you think you'll fail?' he asked, matter of fact.

Tears welled in her eyes and she fought to hold them back. 'I don't even know where I am.'

'Everyone feels the same,' he said lightly. 'Just have faith.'

'Faith in what?'

He shrugged. 'In yourself. In The Organisation. In Svetlana and me. We don't let our people down.'

The waiter arrived with a trolley of stainless steel dishes and laid them out before them, announcing the name of each as he did.

'I know nothing about The Organisation,' she said. 'Svetlana didn't tell me anything.'

'That's good,' Dimitriev said.

'Do we still work for General Kupchenko?' she asked.

'Kupchenko?' Dimitriev said in surprise. 'Kupchenko moved on some time ago. We report to General Levkov now. He's the Chief of the Foreign Directorate.'

'I met General Kupchenko in Leningrad,' she said. She felt the need to tell Dimitriev. She needed to feel some connection, however tenuous, to home.

'I know,' he said.

'The general decided I would be good at this type of work,' she said, biting into the subtly spiced food, too preoccupied to taste it.

'I heard,' Dimitriev smiled.

'Do you think he was right?' she asked.

'That remains to be seen,' he said evenly.

She smiled. 'Of course. We've only just met, and not in the way I would have liked, I might add.'

'Sometimes Svetlana has a cruel sense of humour,' Dimitriev said, leaning back in his chair. 'But she thinks very highly of you, if that helps.'

'It does. And what about you, Vasili? What can you tell me about yourself – only information you can divulge without having to kill me, if you please.'

He laughed. He was handsome when he laughed, more handsome than she'd first thought. The brutality of his features was gone for a moment, and he seemed warm and inviting. 'I joined the army straight after college. It was all I ever wanted to do. After two years I was given the opportunity to test for Spetznaz and passed the selection process. I was already into martial arts and competed in many of them, karate, judo, SOMBO. I had good instructors, the best in Russia, or so I thought. But the trainers in Spetznaz were something else. They showed me things I'd never seen before, techniques that could never be used in competition, and levels of conditioning that I couldn't have imagined.'

'The way you fought at the Marx Engels Institute – it wasn't like anything I've ever seen.'

He shrugged.

'Which art did you use?' she persisted.

'All of them,' he replied.

'But aren't they all different?'

'No. They're all the same.'

'You combined them all into one?'

'Something like that,' he said, and she felt he was tiring of the topic. It was no use, she couldn't resist pressing him for more details. 'Do you have a name for your martial art?'

'No,' he sighed. 'It's simply a system that works for me.'

'Will you teach me your system?' she asked. 'While we're here, on the base? I'd like to learn it. What you did at the Institute, it was astonishing. Maybe we could schedule some time after the dance class?'

He shook his head.

'Why not?' she asked. 'Isn't that what you're supposed to be doing – teaching me to fight?'

'The system is not something I can teach you.'

'Then who can?'

'You must teach yourself.'

'How can I teach myself? At least tell me that,' she urged.

'I'll do better than tell you. I'll show you,' he smiled.

'Thank you,' she beamed. It would be incredible to fight like the colonel. 'When can we begin?'

He smiled at her eagerness but when he spoke he was serious. 'We have already begun.'

*

They danced for hours, every evening, for one month. Every so often Dimitriev produced a new tape with different rhythms and tempos. Tatiana quickly saw that Dimitriev himself wasn't much of a dancer. Apart from the basic waltz and the salsa, he knew no other set routines, and simply used the music to improvise his own steps. Usually he led and Tatiana followed, but occasionally she led and he followed. Soon she'd learned to respond to the slightest pressure of his hand, the turn of his head or movement of his eyes. On some occasions, it felt it as if she was even responding to his thoughts. They moved as one, with no leader and no follower, male and female in perfect harmony, moving with one mind.

The music finished and the tape hissed a static fizzing in the air. Dimitriev took his hands off her slowly, his eyes still connected with hers. 'Touch me with your fingers,' he told her.

She placed her palm on his chest.

'Touch me everywhere, quickly, use both hands.'

She complied, touching his face, his neck, his arms and shoulders, his stomach and legs.

'Faster,' he urged. She complied.

'Wait.'

He turned the tape over and the music began again. 'Continue,' he ordered.

Now her hands beat out the relentless rhythm on his body. 'Use your feet too,' he ordered. She beat out a flowing series of attacks on his head and neck, flicking kicks near his groin and his knee joints, moving around him gracefully as she did.

'Stop!'

She waited.

'Now I'll touch you, and you must prevent me,' he told her.

He reached for her, his fingers extended for her throat. She brushed his hand away easily. His other hand reached out. She parried that too. 'Touch me too, as you did before,' he ordered, reaching for her again. She blocked his hand and touched his cheek.

His left hand flashed out quickly. She parried and touched his arm. His hands reached for her, one after the other. She parried, tapping him as she did. He moved forwards. She slipped to the side. His foot came towards her stomach. She brushed it aside and turned him, tapping his kidney. His hands became fists. He threw punches from all angles. She dealt with each easily, knowing they were coming long before they landed. Kicks came now. She felt the approach of each one. Dimitriev attacked with flowing combinations, slowly at first, then with growing speed. Nothing could touch her. He sped up and she matched him. They moved around the gymnasium, fighting as they had once danced, in perfect unison. Then Dimitriev changed up a gear and attacked at speed – not the speed she had witnessed in the Marx Engels Institute, she was not ready for that yet – but at a speed that a normal assailant might employ. She matched him again, her limbs moving as swiftly as her mind in dealing with the blinding array of punches, kicks and strikes, in finding openings and striking home to Dimitriev's body, moving so fast that she was unaware of individual actions, merely aware of her hands and feet acting on her behalf while her mind remained free to process the next attack, and find her next target.

An unbearable excitement rose inside her. 'Unbelievable!' she cried out wildly.

Dimitriev's punch caught her hard on the chin and she sat down heavily on the gymnasium floor. She tasted the bittersweet blood in her mouth.

'Are you alright?' he asked, squatting beside her.

She looked straight ahead, ignoring him.

'Tatiana?'

'I'm fine,' she said in a faraway voice, turning to him slowly. 'I see it,' she nodded. 'I saw everything. We weren't fighting, we were dancing.'

He smiled.

That's your system,' she said, breathlessly.

'Not my system,' he said, helping her to her feet.

'Whose then?'

'One day I will show you.'

'When?'

He ignored the question, reaching instead for her lip and pulling it down gently to inspect the cut. She felt his rough fingers inside her mouth and his hot breath on her cheek. She opened her mouth so he could see inside.

'It's not too serious,' he said, matter of fact.

'When will you show me?' she persisted.

'When you're ready. There are other things we must cover first.'

'What things?' she asked warily. He sighed, and she sensed he was about to evade her question. 'Tell me please, Vasili.'

'The final part of your training is designed to prepare you in the event of capture and interrogation,' he answered. 'Sadly, it is not as pleasant as dancing.'

Yenisei River, Siberia

The noise of the motor horn sounded again and Tatiana woke, realised it wasn't in her dream. Outside her window she saw Dimitriev sitting astride an enormous motorcycle. It was early on Sunday morning, the day she normally had to herself to recover from the ordeals he put her through during the week. Her heart went into her mouth, as it did every time she saw him now.

It had begun with Dimitriev binding her and covering her head with a hood. Her task had not been to escape, as it had been with Svetlana, but simply to endure. Dimitriev had given her a signal, three slow taps, to use if she could not bear it. In the first morning she had tapped twice, once in panic, feeling unable to breathe, and once to urinate. In the afternoon Dimitriev had told her tapping was no longer an option and she had lain hooded and bound on an icy concrete floor throughout the afternoon, wondering if Dimitriev was watching, wondering whether, if she tapped, she would be released. She had wondered for hours, the question her only companion, holding onto it like the conversation of a cherished friend. Was he with her? Did he care? Did he feel remorse for what he was putting her through? Should she tap? It would answer the question. End the maddening conversation in her head. But to tap would be to fail. She did not want to fail. So she endured, holding onto the question as a Zen monk holds a *koan* in her mind, using the riddle to occupy her thoughts to the exclusion of all else. In her case, to the exclusion of her real enemy, panic.

In the evening Dimitriev had removed her hood and given

her a cup of water. He had transferred her to the boot of a car before securing her hood once more and shutting her inside. It had been a few degrees warmer than the hut, but the confined space preyed on her mind far more than the cold had done. She had thrashed inside and screamed at Dimitriev through her gag. She had tapped, and tapped, and tapped, until she felt herself lifted from the boot and dragged inside the shed once more. Her hood was removed roughly and Dimitriev tore the gag from her mouth. She gasped in the precious cold air.

'Is it air you want?' Dimitriev had demanded. She'd not dared to reply. He had dragged her to a basin of icy water and held her head under for two minutes until her struggling had ceased.

When she'd come around he'd been kneeling over her, his lips close to hers, water dripping from them. 'You live longer if you don't struggle,' he'd said, lifting her and manhandling her towards the basin once again. She had struggled with all her might but she was weak from her ordeal. She had pleaded with him, begged him not to… He had thrust her hard against the basin, locking her body in place with his own, holding her until she was still. His hand cupped her throat and he drew her ear to his mouth. 'Show me you are alive. Tap out the seconds with your hand and keep a count.' Then he plunged her head into the water once more.

And so her training had begun. The first day had been easy compared to what came after but she had done as Dimitriev had wanted, she had learned to face death readily rather than run from it. So much so that lately, she had felt herself peering over an abyss, curious to see how far out she could lean out without falling. Each time she ventured a little further, only to be brought back by Dimitriev. In those days of endless cold, he had held her life in his hands so often that she had come to think of herself as living at his pleasure and dying at his whim. He had never once expressed regret for what he had put her through. Nevertheless she had seen happiness in his eyes when she emerged from unconsciousness. And perhaps something more, she could not be sure. Lately other men had come in the night, dragging her from her bed, binding her, tormenting her, questioning her for hours, each time longer and harder than the last. The last time they had locked her in a brightly lit windowless room for days, until she had lost all track of time. Then the questions had begun. Finally they had drugged her and she had no recollection of what happened after. That was the last thing she remembered.

She wondered how long she had slept since then. She had the feeling it was days rather than hours. And while she had slept, something had changed. The sun was out. The short, hot Siberian summer had arrived. Something else had changed too: Dimitriev had smiled as he'd held up the spare helmet. She splashed water on her face to waken herself and dressed quickly, then flew down the stairs, eager to be away from the base, if only for a few hours.

The roads were clear and dry and the surfaces remarkably good. Many had been newly built to connect the giant science-cities of Central Siberia. Dimitriev pushed the powerful IMZ Ural hard through the forested hills and she clung on behind him, exhilarated not only by the speed but by the beauty of the country and the sudden rush of freedom. After two hours, Dimitriev turned off the main road and sped along a rough mountain track heading into higher hills. The Ural's rugged suspension had been designed for such conditions and coped with ease. When he reached a cutting near the top of the hill, he parked the giant motorcycle and led Tatiana into the forest. The path meandered through larch and fir. Sunshine streamed in rays through the foliage into the dark forest beneath. Insects swarmed around them and Tatiana brushed them away good-naturedly. They troubled her, but nothing could spoil the pleasure of walking with Dimitriev in the forest, away from the grim base, and she smiled to show she didn't mind.

'Once you asked about the system,' he said as they walked.

'I did,' she said.

He smiled. 'Tell me, do you love your country, Tatiana?'

'Yes,' she answered honestly.

'Good, because who could not love this country?' He looked around at the surrounding birch forest, the pale bark shimmering in the mottled sunshine. 'Russia is all about land, land so vast it's unimaginable to people from other countries. We have so much land that we don't know what to do with it all. We're lost in it, in awe of it. It is a powerful land, land that can kill us easily, but beautiful land, land that can feed us, clothe us, protect us.'

'I've rarely been out the city,' Tatiana said quietly.

'But now you can truly see Russia,' he said, his voice filled with excitement. He put his hand out. 'You can feel it. Can you feel the wind?'

'Yes,' she said.

'But can you really feel it?' he asked, his voice suddenly urgent. The answer was important to him.

'I can,' she assured him.

'Close your eyes.' He held her hand and led her through the forest. 'Can you hear the rustle of the leaves … smell the damp earth … taste the pine in the air … feel the leaves beneath your feet?'

She walked, trusting him, allowed her senses to be filled by the forest. She could hear wind in the trees and the song of two different birds. The wind tasted of resin and beyond that she detected the subtle scent of summer blossoms. The leaves creaked softly beneath her feet. She sensed they were walking up a gentle rise. Dimitriev's hold on her arm became lighter, until she felt only his fingertips upon her.

'We use our eyes too much,' he whispered, not wanting to overpower the sound of the forest. 'We need to feel with other senses, with our skin, with our bodies, with our hearts, with our souls.' Tatiana felt the ground even out beneath her feet. They had come to the top of a rise. Dimitriev stopped and she stopped with him. 'Open your eyes,' he told her.

She saw a giant river sweeping through a wooded canyon, so broad that its water was blue like the ocean. 'Which river is this?' she asked, awed by its peaceful grandeur.

'The Yenisei,' he told her.

'It's beautiful.'

'Sometimes, a sight is worth opening your eyes for,' he smiled.

'Come,' he said, leading her down the slope towards the river. They followed the water's edge for a mile before picking up a new path. The narrow forest track took them through a patch of sparse silver birch and onto a muddy country road rutted by cart tracks and marked by horse's hooves.

'I promised to tell you about the system,' he said. 'It is difficult, not because I don't want to, but because it is hard to explain. The power of the system is not to know things, it is to feel things, to become part of things – part of everything. If you use the system to overpower an enemy, first you must become one with him, if only for a moment, before you destroy him.'

'That's how you beat the students at the Institute,' she said quietly.

He laughed. 'Those students were easy to read. I trained the people who trained them. They were all pages from the same book. But to read an enemy who knows how to disguise his intent, that is more difficult.'

They came to a pasture where a small herd of sheep grazed. The ground beneath their feet grew wet and they were forced to pick their way around long puddles. A small barn marked the end of the pasture and beyond it stood a row of low houses.

'How can you know such an enemy?' she asked. 'A stranger who you've never met, someone who you don't even know exists?'

'Sometimes you can't,' he answered. 'But once you know the system, you're rarely surprised by an enemy. To know the system is to know what's going on around you, not just on the surface – what you see with your eyes, but beneath the surface – what you feel with your heart.'

'Intuition?' she offered.

He nodded. 'You can call it that.'

'Female intuition?' she offered playfully.

'Any intuition. Develop it, trust it, use it. It is far more powerful than any facts you might think you know. It will save your life one day.'

'Your system is based on intuition,' she said, hoping to grasp what he was telling her.

He shook his head. 'It is not my system, and I don't call it intuition.'

'Then whose system is it?' she asked sharply. It wasn't like

Dimitriev to be coy. She wanted answers.

'It was revealed to me by someone. Someone who I will introduce you to now.'

'Here?' she asked in surprise.

'Yes.'

'He lives in this little village in the middle of nowhere?'

'He has a house here,' Dimitriev answered.

She was going to say more, to make light of the man's dwelling place, but she sensed Dimitriev thought highly of the man and held her tongue. She would show a little respect, if only out of respect for Dimitriev.

The track opened out to a wider gravel road until it reached the start of the village. Here it had been concreted over for the entire length of the village, little more than a hundred yards. There were no people on the street, just a small pack of dogs that foraged in the piles of trash between the houses.

They were almost through the village before Dimitriev turned off onto a tiny path that led into a copse of trees. In among the trees was a small wooden structure that could have been mistaken for a shed had it not been for the dome-shaped top and the cross above its entrance. Dimitriev stepped inside the little wooden church and she followed him. She found herself in a single room no bigger than a living room, made of planks and rough-hewn beams. There was no one else inside. The walls were hung with icon paintings of assorted saints and madonna and child. They had been placed so close together that they created a chequerboard of warm hues that almost covered one wall. The paintings were illuminated by the light of a single large window high on the opposite wall. The sun's rays caught the gilding beneath the warm bronze and ochre paintwork, giving the icons a glow that warmed the atmosphere inside the otherwise bare church.

'Tell me what you know about this type of painting,' Dimitriev said quietly.

'We studied icon painting at the Institute,' she said. 'It began in the Holy Roman Empire in Byzantium and was later perfected by Orthodox monks in Russia.'

'But what makes an icon different from a more realistic portrait?' Dimitriev probed.

'It isn't intended to be realistic, but symbolic – an icon.'

'An icon of what?' he persisted.

'An icon designed to elicit a religious feeling, a connection to God,' she said, repeating what she'd been taught at the academy. She waited for him to say more but he simply nodded. She wondered why he'd been so insistent with his questioning.

'Which is your favourite?' he asked.

Tatiana examined the paintings carefully. The lines were crude, the colours monotonous, the compositions naïve and lacking in any correct depth perception or perspective. The sizes of the figures were disproportionate and the features pinched. The face of the Baby Jesus standing on Mary's lap was that of a middle-aged man. From her lectures at the Institute, she knew that it was the childlike quality of the icons that made them so endearing. Just as a child paints those it loves most in the world, its mother and father, so the icon painters had painted Jesus, Mary, Saint Nicholas, St Basil and St John the Baptist. She herself had never painted her family, or if she had, she had no recollection of it. No images of her own came to mind. In fact, she had no idea who or what she might have painted, other than an old woman called Auntie Zina who had been kind to her once, a long time ago. Her eyes settled on a small wooden board, eighteen inches square, near the end of the wall. It looked ancient, even older and more worn than the others. The paint had peeled off in many places revealing tarnished gold leaf beneath, and the gold itself was worn away across one side so there was an oval patch of dark, weathered wood in the corner. Nevertheless the simple beauty and symmetry of the depiction of mother and child stood out from the other icons. 'This one's the best,' she said, pointing to it.

Dimitriev lifted it off the wall and turned it around. It was painted on two thick planks that were joined together by a third that had been crudely nailed across the back. Barely visible on the dark wood, she saw the remnants of a signature carved into the wood: *Rublev*.

She stared closer. It was impossible. Rublev was a Russian master who had lived in the fourteenth century. 'This is a genuine Rublev?'

Dimitriev smiled. 'You have a good eye.'

'But what's a Rublev doing here? What are any of these pictures doing here? It doesn't look like a museum to me.'

'It isn't,' Dimitriev said.

'Then what is it?'

'A church,' Dimitriev said.

The truth hit her then. 'The villagers come here to worship?' Her voice was hushed.

Dimitriev nodded. 'The censors rarely venture far from the big cities, Tatiana. Do you think they're going to check every village in Siberia to make sure no one worships God?'

'But religion is banned!' she said.

'You can't ban God, Tatiana.'

She looked at him incredulously, realising finally where all his talk was leading. 'You're a believer.'

Even as she said it, her mind was reeling at the risk of his revelation to both himself and her. Dimitriev seemed untroubled and simply held the Rublev at arm's length, admiring it as he spoke. 'In the old days, icons like these were beloved of the warriors of old Russia. These men who freed us from the yoke of the Mongols and forged our nation were *Bogatyrs* – Christian knights, Men of God: Ilya Muromets, Alexander Nevsky, Dimitri Donskoi. They fought with God on their side. Did you know they would literally carry their icons into battle? Perhaps that's why so many are damaged,' he said wistfully. 'Why the colours are the way they are: mud-stained, tear-stained, blood-stained. The colours of the battlefield.'

'You're *insane*,' she said, shrinking from him. She strode to the door, then stopped. She couldn't leave him now, she would be alone in Siberia, unable to return to the base without him. She had to reason with him. She turned and watched him replace the Rublev with care among the other paintings and wondered what to say to him, where to even begin.

'Russia is a powerful country,' he said, almost to himself. 'And powerful countries have powerful enemies, never more so than today. Throughout history we have been under attack from all sides: Tartars and Mongols to the east, Napoleon and Hitler to the west, Turks and Cossacks to the south. For a man to stand in battle against such enemies requires more than courage. It requires a deep-rooted belief, one that a warrior can share with those standing by his side. God provides that belief, that strength and protection that the warrior craves. Who could go into battle believing in nothing, Tatiana?'

'The Red Army did just that against Hitler,' she said. 'And

won.'

'The Red Army believed in Communism. What can it believe in now?'

For a moment she wondered if he was testing her. She hoped he was, but one look in his eyes told her he wasn't.

She shook her head sadly. 'Oh Vasili, I wish you hadn't told me. I wish…'

'You asked to know my system,' he interrupted. 'Now I am telling you. Here is my system, my sword and my shield: I put my body, my heart and my soul in the hands of God, and he guides and protects me. If you wish to follow my system you can do the same.'

'You could be shot and so could I,' she said angrily.

'Yes,' he nodded deliberately. 'One word to the base commander and I'd be finished.'

'And would God protect you?' she demanded harshly.

'God guides me,' he said with a smile. 'He guided me to trust you.'

'To trust me?' she scoffed. 'You shouldn't have told me any of this Vasili! Does Svetlana know?'

'Yes, she knows.'

'She worships too?' Tatiana asked, unable to believe it.

'No, Svetlana is not a believer.'

'Yet you want me to worship God, here, now, with you?'

'I offer you that choice,' he said quietly. He knelt before the wall of icons. 'Come, pray with me,' he said, extending his hand to her. She stared in dismay at the man who had once seemed so powerful, who now abased himself before a wall of ragged old paintings. His hand retreated, joining the palm of his other hand. She heard the words of a brief unfamiliar prayer tumble from his lips. His hand extended to her once more. 'Yesterday you died, Tatiana. *Three times.*'

She didn't reply.

'When you died, where did you go?'

'I left my body,' she said quietly. I saw nothing else.'

'You returned to God,' he said softly. Still she made no move towards him.

'I prayed each time, and each time he returned you to me,' Vasili said.

She hesitated, then stepped forward despite herself, trying to identify the reason as she did. It was close, but she could not see it, not yet. It was not through any desire to find God, that much she knew. It was more that she could not abandon Dimitriev, not now, after he had placed such faith in her. She took his outstretched hand and knelt beside him. His prayer filled the enclosed space of the little church. She gazed up at the icons. No religious ecstasy overcame her. No bands of angels came down. No heavenly choir could be heard. She looked at the man beside her, a man who believed in something when there was nothing left to believe in, a man who risked his life to share something with her. She was reminded of Alexei, the boy at the orphanage who'd been her playmate for a short time, before being taken away from her. It was dangerous to play with her, dangerous to trust her. She feared for Vasili then and held his hand firmly as he prayed.

*

An urgent telex was waiting for them in the guardhouse. Dimitriev scanned it quickly before handing it to her. She read the faded dot-matrix type twice, wondering what to make of it:

Comrade Zykova is required to return to Moscow immediately for urgent duties in the field by order of Major General Levkov FCD.

She looked at Dimitriev in dismay.

'You have your first assignment,' he told her with a smile.

'It's too soon,' she said, speaking quietly so the guard wouldn't overhear, 'I'm not ready.'

'You are ready, Tatiana Zykova.' He took her hand and covered it with his own. The steady warmth soothed her and she felt her rapid heart-rate come back under control.

'Are you coming with me?' she asked.

'No, the message is for you alone.'

'So when will I see you again?' she placed her free hand over his, not wanting to let go.

'Our paths will cross again,' he smiled. 'Go and pack your things. There's a flight out of Krasnoyarsk at 23.00 hours. I'll have them hold a place for you.'

She blinked and straightened up, knowing the guard was watching. 'Yes, Comrade Colonel.'

He gripped her lightly by the shoulders and kissed her on both cheeks. 'Take care, Tatiana Zykova,' he whispered. 'I will pray for you.'

Twelve hours later, when the giant Antonov touched down in Moscow, Svetlana was waiting on the tarmac.

HELENA

St. Christol Airbase, France, 1983

Michel Benoit turned the ignition key and the little Peugeot roared to life. The 1.9L fuel-injected 205 was a new model and a joy to drive. The journey to work and home on the twisting roads of the Vaucluse was the highlight of his day. Sometimes he felt it was one of the few pleasures he had left that came without a price. Once he'd enjoyed his job, working on projects that other engineers could only dream of, but eventually he'd learned that such a job came with a high price. The carefree days with his young wife were gone thanks to the suffocating security inside the airbase and the constant pressure of the anti-nuclear protestors outside. Ever since the arrival of their first child, she'd been begging him to find work elsewhere. More recently, she'd been urging him to replace the two-door coupe with a more convenient four-door version. He'd have to do it soon, he knew, but not yet. He wanted to hold onto it for just a little longer.

He approached the gate slowly, giving the guards time to come from the guardhouse beside the gate and get into position. The tall gates glided open and stopped, leaving just enough gap for him to pass through, while the guards stood on either side to prevent the protestors from entering. Benoit inched forward. The protestors formed a line to block his exit as they always did. They were mostly women with long unkempt hair and hippy clothes, and they were there every morning and evening without fail.

Michel Benoit worked at St. Christol Airbase in Provence – the site of France's only land-based nuclear deterrent, housing 18 nuclear missile silos. The protestors wouldn't move of their own accord, he knew. He nosed his car forward steadily, as he always did, forcing them to step aside or be crushed slowly beneath his grille. They drummed on the bodywork as he passed. He was almost through when one woman stood directly in his path and he was forced to stop or run her down. She was a newcomer, he'd noticed her first appear a few days earlier – she was hard to miss. Her long brown hair hung in loose curls past her shoulders, highlighted with gold from long hours in the sun. She wore a sleeveless kaftan and her slender arms were tanned a golden brown. Even with no make-up and an angry snarl on her face, she was quite lovely. He held his hands up to her. What the hell did she want him to do? She hammered on the front of his car, shouting words he couldn't hear. He wondered why she hated him so much. Finally she stepped aside and he drove past, ignoring the final insults hurled his way as he passed.

He turned right and floored the accelerator. The little Peugeot surged up the tree-lined road northwards towards the distant heights of Mount Ventoux. The beacon on the summit was visible on top of the pale limestone slopes that made the mountain appear snow-capped even in summer. It was a place of silence and solitude that beckoned him, far from the chaos below. He changed down a gear and the Peugeot raced up the slope. He passed the array of giant satellite dishes at the northern end of the base and then he was flying through fields of wheat that swayed in the wind of the high plateau. It was fifty kilometres to his home in Carpentras but despite the twisting roads he would do the journey in under an hour.

He'd cleared the rise and was driving hard when he noticed the steering pull to the left. Next he felt a juddering coming up through the wheel. He slowed. The car began to wallow. He opened the window and heard the flapping of a deflating tyre. He swore and pulled over. The Alpine wind that gusted across the exposed plateau had an icy edge to it despite the evening sunshine. He got out and swore again. He tried to reach his breakdown service on his brand new mobile phone but there was no signal. He tossed the handset back inside the car.

Benoit was good with the principles of engineering, but not so good with the practical. He didn't relish the prospect of changing the tyre in the cold wind. He scanned the road for traffic, but there were no vehicles anywhere. Resigned, he opened the boot and reached for the jack when he heard the whine of an engine in the distance. He straightened up, hoping it was someone from the base who could give him a lift. When he saw an old yellow Mini approaching, his heart sank. It didn't belong to anyone on the base, more likely it belonged to one of the protestors. He hoped there weren't many of them in the car. They might recognise him and things might turn ugly. As the car came closer, he shot a furtive glance at it and saw the driver was the only occupant. He looked away hoping the driver wouldn't recognise him but the Mini slowed as it passed by his car. The driver must have recognised his Peugeot. He looked up and saw the new woman from outside the airbase looking directly at him. He expected her to stop and hurl more abuse at him but she drove on. He watched the back of the Mini move on up the road. He leaned back into the boot to get the spare wheel when something made him look at the road again. The Mini had stopped thirty yards away. He waited to see what the woman would do. She got out and leaned against the driver's door, her arms folded. She was waiting for him to come to her. He hesitated. She shifted her weight from one foot to the other to show her impatience and raise her chin, as if daring him to accept her help.

He locked his car and strode towards her. She got in before he reached her. He waited a moment, wondering if he should forget it and go and fix his own car, but he was already there, his hand hovering by the door handle. He opened the door and got in. They sat in silence for thirty seconds before he spoke. 'I suppose I should thank you,' he said with a thin smile.

'I suppose you should,' she answered in passable French.

'You're English,' he said in English. His English was fluent. It would be easier for both of them if they spoke English.

'Right again,' she said flatly.

'You don't look it,' he said.

'My parents were Italian,' she told him, starting the engine and pulling away.

'My name is Michel, and my parents are French,' he said with a smile.

She didn't react.

'And your name is…' he prompted.

'Helena Rossi.'

'Well thank you, Helena, for stopping to help me.'

'Where do you need to get to?' she asked.

'If you could take me to Sault I can get a bus from there.'

'I'm going further than Sault. Where do you live?'

'Sault will be fine, thank you.'

She turned to him with a frown. 'What's the matter? Are you worried that if I know where you live I might come in the night and set fire to your house?'

There it was, that anger again, never far from the surface.

He found it faintly disturbing that such a lovely young woman could be so angry with him. 'I don't know,' he said. 'Will you?'

'Oh yes, of course I will. We're capable of anything, aren't we?' She shook her head in frustration and her lips pinched tight. 'Even giving a stranded motorist a lift – imagine that.'

He looked out of the window. The high plateau had given way to wooded mountain slopes, descending into soft ochre slopes, but they were still a long way from the nearest town. He didn't want to fall out with this woman now – then he really would be stranded. 'If you must know, I live a long way from here. I didn't want to put you to any trouble. That's why I asked you to drop me in Sault.'

'Okay. But just so you know, what we do isn't personal,' she said. 'It's about principles.'

'That's nice to know,' he said.

'It's true. But if you want me to drop you in Sault, I'll drop you in Sault.'

Benoit was surprised to feel a tinge of disappointment that she'd given in so easily. Sault wasn't far and part of him would have enjoyed spending longer in that old cramped car with the lovely angry English girl. There was a wildness about her that he found compelling. How could she be so free, so unburdened by society, by duty, by financial concerns that she could stand outside an airbase all day, every day, for a cause that she believed in – however misguidedly.

She drove fast on the zigzag road, but she handled the car with a confidence that put him at ease. They arrived all too quickly at the bus shelter in Sault and he got out to check the timetable. She joined him by the notice board. 'Your bus doesn't leave for another forty minutes,' she said, confirming what he'd just realised.

'I'll wait in the bar,' he told her.

'Okay, well I guess I'll see you tomorrow then,' she said. She gave him a small smile at the irony of it, and beneath the harsh exterior, Benoit caught a glimpse of a shy young girl, embarrassed and uncertain. He wondered if she would beat his car with her fists again tomorrow.

'Let me at least buy you a drink to say thank you,' he said. The words tumbled out before he had a chance to think twice, and now she was looking at him, trying to decide what to make of him. 'Keep me company while I wait for the bus,' he added. 'A last good deed for the evening.'

She shrugged. 'I guess I always was a sucker for lost causes.' And suddenly they were laughing together.

'One drink,' she warned.

'One drink,' he promised.

They found a table by the back wall, far from the window. The irony of their action – that of forbidden lovers – were not lost on either of them. Helena flipped a coaster over and over in her long fingers, then bit the edge of it lightly with her front teeth. 'If anyone sees me with you, I'm screwed.'

'Not as screwed as me,' he laughed. 'Fortunately this is a local bar. There are no peace protestors or arms manufacturers in here, just farmers and shepherds.'

The waitress took their orders without comment and returned swiftly with two small draught beers.

'Here's to farmers and shepherds,' Helena said, raising her glass.

'Farmers and shepherds,' he grinned, taking a long drink. The chilled Kronenbourg hit the spot nicely.

Helena put her glass down carefully on the coaster. Benoit noticed she'd taken a long drink too. He guessed she needed it as much as he did.

'That tastes good,' she smiled, running her thumb through the droplets of condensation on the outside of the glass. 'And to tell you the truth, there's only so much nettle tea and spliff you can do before you go seriously nuts.'

'You sound pissed off,' he said.

'I am. I came here from Greenham Common to get away from the politics, but it's as strong here as it ever was.'

'Politics among anarchists?' he asked with a wry smile.

'Like you wouldn't believe,' she sighed.

'You should try the air force if you want politics,' he said, taking another long pull on his beer.

She looked so sad that she seemed about to cry. 'Among women, too?' he probed gently. 'What sort of politics?'

'Oh there's always some old bull-dyke in charge, who guards her territory like, well, a bloody bull.'

Benoit's English was good, but not good enough to follow her meaning. She noticed the puzzlement on his face and smiled. 'Don't ask.'

'No tell me, what is a bull-dyke?'

She looked away and he noticed a delicious blush of pink on her cheek. Then she seemed to regain her confidence and she leaned forward, waiting until he had leaned closer too before speaking in a low voice. 'A lesbian. A butch one, you know, a masculine type.'

'A bull-dyke,' he nodded, repeating it to embed it in his memory. 'I must remember this. It may come in handy one day.'

Then they were laughing and their eyes meeting for a fleeting moment before she looked away again.

'You don't like bull-dykes?' he asked, suddenly fascinated by the internal politics of the women who protested outside his workplace.

'They don't like me,' she said.

'Why not?' he asked, 'I would have thought they would like you a lot. You're a beautiful woman, after all.'

She looked down, avoiding his eye, but Benoit saw she liked the compliment. Beneath the hard shell she was just a shy young Englishwoman and still unused to Gallic forthrightness.

When she looked up, she was smiling. 'They don't like me because I'm straight,' she said. 'You know what that means, I think?'

'Yes, I know what it means,' he assured her, draining his beer happily. 'It means you like to make love with a man, n'est ce pas?'

She couldn't help laughing at this. 'I suppose it does,' she said, the last remnants of her embarrassment still lingering on her cheeks, the English reluctance to talk about sex, so unlike the French women. What a pity she was on opposite sides of the fence in every way, he reminded himself reluctantly. And what a pity he was married.

Rue de Teinturiers, Avignon

'He's a prime target,' Helena told Svetlana without preamble.

They were seated at a small pavement café in the Rue de Teinturiers, within site of the old city wall of Avignon. To any casual passerby they were simply two women meeting over coffee, work colleagues perhaps, or friends from the university catching up on the latest gossip.

'Go on,' Svetlana ordered.

'He feels guilt for the deaths he caused,' Helena continued. 'Especially the deaths of French allies in the Falklands. He wants forgiveness. He hates his bosses, hates the military hierarchy. He thinks they've been using his work for financial gain, selling his ideas to the highest bidder, irrespective of who they are or how his work might end up in the hands of rogue states and enemies of the free world.'

'He said all this in your first meeting?' Svetlana asked, doubtfully.

'Not in so many words, but it's the feeling I got from him.'

'You need to verify that your feeling is correct,' Svetlana said seriously.

'Of course,' Helena answered, struggling to keep the irritation from her voice.

'I take it he's attracted to you?' Svetlana said.

'I believe so,' Helena nodded.

'I knew he would be,' Svetlana smiled. 'How about his home life, did he say anything?'

'He spoke a bit about it. His wife hates his work and hates where they live. They're from Paris, and they're made to feel like outsiders by the locals. I think it bothers her a lot more than him. She's also terrified that the peace protesters will find out where they live and target them. The arrival of the baby has made things even worse.'

'They sound like a family at breaking point,' Svetlana said happily. 'That's good. You've made good progress. Just be careful of trusting your instincts too much. We need hard facts too, remember.'

'I will.'

'I know you will.' Svetlana smiled and took her hand and stroked it gently. 'Who wouldn't fall in love with you, Little One?'

'You're very kind,' Helena said.

'It's simply the truth.' Svetlana squeezed her hand once more. 'We'll increase the pressure, make some vague threats, nothing too serious, just enough to frighten the wife and drive them further apart. Let me know when he contacts you again.'

St Christol Airbase, Provence

She watched Benoit's car enter and leave the base each day. She was careful not to draw any undue attention to herself now, but remained close enough when he passed that she would see if he tried to give her a message. Ten days passed before he caught her eye one morning, and stopped for a moment so she could read the note scrawled on his dashboard: 'Farmers and shepherds, same time'.

That evening she drove to the bistro in Sault where they had drunk to farmers and shepherds on their first meeting. He was in his car when she arrived, with the window down. His expression was serious. She hurried over to him. 'Is everything alright, Michel? You look worried.'

'Something happened,' he said. 'Will you get in so we can talk?' She hesitated.

'I just want to talk, I promise. I don't want people to jump to the wrong conclusions.'

She got in and he started the engine. 'Where are we going?' she asked.

'Have you ever been to the ochre quarry in Roussillon?' he asked.

She shook her head.

'The hills are all different shades of ochre. It's very picturesque.'

'It sounds good,' she smiled.

He took a minor road that cut south through the Javon forest, avoiding returning via the base and the protestors who would still be thronged outside.

'There is something I need to ask you,' he said. 'Something

delicate.' He hesitated, then the words tumbled out. 'A week ago, someone scratched a CND symbol on our front door. Our house is far from the base, but someone knew exactly where we lived.'

'Listen, Michel,' she cut in. 'If you think I had anything to do with that …'

'That's not what I think,' he said quickly. 'I just wanted someone to talk to about it. I was hoping you might know something …'

'I told you before, our protest is about principles. It's not personal.'

'For you, no. But for others, maybe?'

'I don't know, Michel. I don't know everything that goes on.'

'Okay. Please don't be angry.'

They continued through the village of Saint Saturnin les Apt and drove in silence until they passed a sign for Roussillon. Restaurants and souvenir shops began to appear on the roadside. The town itself was coloured in ochre, a tribute to the land it was made in, and the squat square houses created a patchwork canvass of warm yellows, reds, purples and golds. Benoit parked in the town square and led Helena up the hill to the quarry. He paid the small toll at the entrance and they followed the wooden steps that descended into the deep cliffs of the quarry. The shades of ochre sat in layers so even they might have been man-made, like the layered sands in the bottles found in the souvenir shop.

Benoit sighed. 'You might be surprised to hear this, but I don't know many people around here. Only work colleagues, and believe me, they're not the kind of people you can talk to about personal matters.'

'What do you mean by 'personal' Michel?'

'When my wife Valerie saw the symbol, she went crazy. She thinks all our lives are in danger. She thinks they are going to put a firebomb through our door. She's terrified for the baby. I told her she was over-reacting, but she wouldn't listen. She took the baby and went to stay with her mother in Paris.'

'She left you?'

'Yes, and she won't come back while I work at the base,' Benoit said, tight-lipped.

'Have you gone to the police?'

'There's nothing they can do. They can't watch our house twenty four hours a day.'

'I can't promise anything,' she said, 'But I'll try and find out who did it, and see if I can put a stop to it.'

'You would do that?'

'I'll try, but like I said, I can't promise.'

He took her by the arms and kissed her on the cheek. 'Thank you, Helena.'

'There's no need to thank me,' she said quickly, flustered by his touch. 'I'd do it for anyone.'

'Okay, but I'm just so grateful. Sorry if I've embarrassed you.'

'It's alright,' she said, the trace of a blush on her cheeks.

'Let's walk to the top of the hill,' he said. The view from the top is amazing, you can see right across the Vaucluse.'

'You know, Helena, it's strange but when I really wanted to talk to someone about all these things that have happened, I realised I didn't have any real friends in this whole place. Out of all the people I knew, the only person I found myself wanting to see was you. Isn't that strange?'

'It's pretty sad,' she said, 'But I know what you mean.

Sometimes it's hard to connect with people. Especially when the situation around you is so tense.'

'Exactly,' he said.

They stood on the top of the hill and looked across the valley to the white slopes of Mount Ventoux in the distance. She put her hand on his shoulder and squeezed it reassuringly. 'It's beautiful here,' she said. 'Thanks for bringing me, really.'

'It's my pleasure.' He said. He seemed happy that she liked the view.

'Listen, Michel,' she went on. 'There's something I think you should know. Despite what you do – which by the way is inexcusable – you seem like a nice guy. I just don't want you to get the wrong idea. I mean, you're married…'

'Yes, I'm married,' he smiled. 'And I'm also the enemy, n'est ce pas?'

'You're not the enemy, Michel…'

'I'm joking, Helena. But seriously, all I'm hoping for is that we might be friends.'

She looked at him dubiously. 'There's something else you should know,' she said. 'When I said my protest was nothing personal, that wasn't strictly true. My reasons are very personal.'

'I understand,' he soothed.

'I don't think you do,' she said sharply. She waited, gathering herself before continuing. 'Four years ago my little brother David joined the navy. He was eighteen. Mum was so proud, seeing him looking so smart in his uniform. And dad, well he was an old navy man himself, so he was practically walking on air when his son decided to follow in his footsteps. A year later David's ship joined the task force that set sail for the Falklands War. He was aboard the HMS Sheffield.'

Benoit flinched at the name. 'His ship was sunk by an Exocet missile, fired from an Argentine plane, but built here in France.' She swallowed hard. 'David never came home. So now you know why I do what I do.'

He nodded seriously. 'I know about the Exocet, of course.' She noticed he didn't say how well. That was good. Svetlana would be pleased. Svetlana told her that once the deceit had begun it grew like a cancer, taking over the man, destroying him. Benoit had been the brains behind the radar guidance system that made the Exocet so effective. Now he was also working on far larger and deadlier weapons pointed at her people.

Benoit regarded her seriously. 'I can tell you most sincerely, as a friend, that a lot of people including myself were deeply unhappy that Argentina ended up with our weapons.'

'The tragedy is that I believe you,' she said softly.

'The missiles are bought up by third party dealers, who then sell them on to someone else, who sells them to someone else, until they can end up anywhere.'

'They ended up in the hands of the enemy, Michel! Britain's enemy, not France's, agreed – but our countries have been allies through two world wars. Our armies are joined in NATO but it doesn't stop French weapons killing British soldiers, does it?'

'There need to be tighter controls,' he said breathlessly.

'Controls aren't the point,' she said, raising her voice to be heard above the wind. 'The point is that we can't trust controls. We can't trust the money men and politicians who run things not to cheat, to compromise, to follow the money instead of doing what's right.'

'It's not that simple,' he said.

'But it should be!' she said, tears of frustration appearing in her eyes. He couldn't bear to see those eyes filled with tears.

'Yes, it should be,' he said softly. She looked at him, blinking back the tears, assessing him.

'It should be,' he repeated.

'I'm sorry to bring all that up, but I wanted you to know,' she said.

'I understand, really I do.'

'I'll see what I can find out for you regarding the harassment,' she said. 'You'd better give me your phone number. We can't keep driving to Sault every time we need to talk.'

'Of course,' he said, taking a pen and paper from his pocket and writing it down for her. 'How about you?' he asked, handing the paper to her.

'The phone in the commune's dead. No one ever pays the bill. But don't worry, I'll call you as soon as I know anything.'

'I'd be grateful,' he said. 'It's very good of you, considering.'

'You seem like a good man, Michel,' she said ruefully. 'Apart, of course, from building weapons of mass destruction that could wipe out the planet.'

He grinned. 'Seriously, I'm grateful.'

'Consider it a favour from a friend.'

Carpentras, Provence

Michel Benoit hunted for the phone beneath the piles of washing stacked on his sofa, swearing loudly inside the empty house. By the time he'd found it, the ringing had stopped. It rang again a moment later and he snatched up the receiver. He heard the pips of a public phone box, then her voice: 'Michel, it's Helena Rossi. Is it a good time to talk?'

'Yes, of course. I was waiting for your call.'

'Sorry I couldn't ring sooner. It wasn't something I could rush.'

'I understand,' he said impatiently.

'How are things with you? Did your wife come back?' She asked. Her voice sounded small and far away.

'No, she won't come back. She says she can't live like this any longer.'

'I'm sorry to hear that,' she said. 'Maybe this'll help: I made some enquiries. I found out who scratched the CND symbol on your door. I had to wait till he was drunk and stoned before asking about it. So I hope he won't remember our conversation. Anyway, he said they were just trying to scare you, nothing more. They don't want to get a reputation of being too militant. I don't know if that helps?'

Benoit shrugged.

'It sounds like it won't make any difference to your wife,' she said.

'I don't think it will.'

'I'm sorry,' she said.

'There's nothing for you to feel sorry about Helena,' he said. 'Thank you for your help.'

Silence. She waited. 'How are you, anyway?' he asked finally.

'Not good, if I'm honest. Things at the commune are getting pretty …'

The money in the pay phone ran out. He heard pips. 'Helena, are you there?'

'I don't have any more coins. I'm sorry Michel, I should have brought more.'

'Don't worry. You were saying things weren't so good at the commune. What's up?'

'It's the people, I guess,' she sighed. 'Even though there's so many of them, I feel like I don't know anyone.' There was a short pause. 'I'd better go.'

'No, wait! It's Saturday. Why don't we meet up? We can talk properly. We can go for a drive, visit some more sights. It's a fine day.'

'I don't know …'

'We can meet in Roussillon and see the arena in Arles where they have bullfights.' As soon as he'd said it, he knew it was a mistake.

'I hate bullfighting, Michel.'

'How about the Pont du Gard?' he asked hurriedly. 'It's a roman aqueduct, very old.'

The pips returned and this time her voice didn't come back. Benoit hung up the receiver angrily and kicked over the pile of clothes sitting on the sofa. He surveyed the living room. It was a mess. In the past it had been a mess of plastic toys, nappies and cushioned mats that squeaked whenever he stepped on them. Now it was a different kind of mess, a grim, lifeless mess that wouldn't go away. He felt a sudden anger at his wife, for letting the place get into such a state. He worked long hours to afford all the things she'd bought for the baby. Did she think it would be easy to find another job in a field like his?

He went outside, slamming the door behind him and fired up the Peugeot. The engine screamed into life and the tyres roared on the gravel drive. In less than thirty minutes he was in Roussillon and entering the car park slowly, searching for the yellow Mini. It wasn't there. He sat on a nearby railing and smoked a cigarette, a habit he'd given up until recently. He knew Helena wasn't coming. She lived far closer to Roussillon than he did. He finished the cigarette and stubbed it out deliberately. When he looked up he saw a flash of yellow at the entrance. He hurried over and threw open the driver's door. 'I'm glad you came.'

'I'm not sure I should have,' she said.

'No, it's good. Where shall we go?'

'I don't really want to go anywhere,' she said. 'What I really want is a drink.'

'A drink?' He liked the idea even better than a trip to the roman aqueduct. 'There's a bar just across the road,' he grinned.

*

When they emerged from the bar four hours later, he was drunk. Helena was far less drunk than she appeared, but tripped in the dark car park nonetheless. He caught her and she held onto his arm gratefully. When they got to her car they stopped and he put his lips to hers. Her mouth was still for a moment before responding, slowly at first, but then she returned his kiss with a passion he hadn't expected. He stepped forward, pressing her against the Mini, eager to feel her lithe, slender body against his own. She felt great, every bit as good as he'd imagined.

'Come back to my house,' he said between kisses.

'It wouldn't be right,' she said.

'Fuck what's right,' he said, taking her by the hand and leading her to his car. He opened the passenger door and she got in. He hurried around to the driver's side before she could change her mind and gunned the engine. The car surged out of the car park and down the twisting road towards Carpentras.

'Fuck what's right,' he repeated. 'I don't even know what's right or wrong any more, you know?'

'Me neither,' she slurred.

'All I know is you're lonely, I'm lonely, you're beautiful and, well…'

'And you're handsome,' she giggled.

'Thank you,' he said with a grin.

Her hand moved across to rest lightly on his knee. He glanced at her in surprise. The car swerved dangerously.

'Am I distracting you, Monsieur?' she asked innocently.

'As a matter of fact, yes,' he laughed.

'Shall I stop?'

'No, please don't.'

Her hand brushed lightly on the inside of his thigh. Her fingers worked their way slowly to his groin. 'Oh, what's this?' she asked, running her fingers over the hardness in his jeans.

The headlights of an approaching car appeared in the blackness, and then the blare of a horn as it passed. He pulled over in a lay-by, a small area of rough stones by the roadside, nothing more. He switched off the engine and the headlights and pushed his seat back to create some room. She climbed onto his lap. His hands worked at raising her long skirt so he could feel the smooth warm marble of her thighs. His fingers traced her tight curve. The sensation made him feel even more drunk than he was. Her soft lips descended on his once more, and as they kissed, his fingers reached between her legs and she sighed in his ear. He reached further, seeking the spot that would give her the most pleasure. She gasped at his touch and writhed on his lap. He wondered how long it had been since she'd been with a man. It might have been a long time, living with a bunch of lesbians as she did. Her hands came up to her shirt. She unbuttoned it. She wore no bra beneath, just a tight vest which she slipped up to reveal her taut breasts. The dark nipples were erect and awaiting his mouth. His fingers massaged until she moaned uncontrollably. He pulled her panties aside and slipped a finger inside her easily. He added another and fucked her slowly with his hand.

'Oh Jesus,' she moaned, tugging at the hair on the back of his head so hard that it hurt. Suddenly she reached behind and took his hands away, then sat back on his lap and opened his jeans. She tried to pull them down, but the car was cramped. He raised his hips obligingly and she tried again, this time it was enough. She withdrew his penis and worked it firmly with her fingertips. 'This is what I wanted,' she said, her voice deep, and he felt her hot breath on his cheek. It smelled of beer, warm and sour, and beyond it he could smell the scent of her body. There was no trace of deodorant or perfume, it was simply the smell of her skin, her sweat – the scent of her just as she was. It was better than any perfume he'd ever smelled. 'Take it,' he sighed.

She moved forward again, hovering over him lightly, and he felt the tip of his penis touch tantalisingly at the mouth of her vagina. She held it there for a second, prolonging the anticipation, and fleetingly he realised his first impression of her had been true: beneath the outer shell she was a passionate girl. That passion had been bound up, until now. Now it could be released. Then all thoughts of previous impressions vanished as he felt himself enter her and heard her groan deliriously. All he knew then was the simple sensation of her on him, of being inside her, of the two of them together at last. It felt better than anything he'd felt in a very long time.

*

Helena was woken by the chimes of a nearby church bell announcing ten o'clock. She slipped from Benoit's bed and glanced down at his sleeping form. His face was pale and puffy from the night's drinking, but still handsome enough. The thin quilt was draped over his hips up to his waist. He was in decent shape, for someone who worked in a lab, long limbed, a flat stomach, skin smooth and nicely tanned. His body had felt good against hers – very different from the heavy, out-of-shape bodies that had visited her in Grigory's brothel, and different too from the pale, iron-hard bodies of the Spetznaz soldiers who had visited her on occasion in Moscow, by arrangement through Svetlana. Benoit was different in another way too. He was funny and charming. He listened to her. He made her laugh. He was a young man who, for all his faults, including infidelity, wanted her for who she was – or at least who he thought she was. He was a young man who felt himself falling in love with her. She felt a stab of regret that she would have to hurt him so badly.

She pulled on her shirt and went into the bathroom to shower. When she had finished, she opened the window to let out the steam and examined her face in the mirror. She looked tired. She'd not drunk as much as Benoit the night before, but she'd drunk enough. She pushed her hair back and splashed cold water on her face to tighten the skin. The eyes that looked back at her were small and hard. They were eyes that didn't like what they saw.

When she returned to the bedroom, Benoit was awake. He lay with one hand propped behind his head and a happy grin on his face.

'If you can wait until I've showered I'll fix us some breakfast,' he said.

'Sure,' she said, sitting on the lower corner of the bed, not wishing to get in again. It was the bed where Benoit lay with his wife. It was the marriage bed.

He sensed her train of thought and rose quickly. 'Make yourself at home in the living room, I won't be long.'

She watched his naked form stride to the bathroom: the smooth back, the tanned legs and the white band around his middle where the sun had not penetrated.

She pulled on her clothes and went through to the living room, examining his bookshelves and thumbing through his magazines. There was nothing in the house to suggest a man who carried the secrets of France's nuclear weapons in his head, weapons that could, if launched, kill 60 million of her people. She had to remember this fact, along with the fact that if she failed in her duty, one more Russian might die too.

Palais des Papes, Avignon

The two women walked side by side in the gardens of the palace that had once been the seat of power of the Pope himself. The imposing walls and pointed watchtowers gave the appearance of a forbidding Gothic fortress rather than a house of God. The grandeur of the interior only added to the impression that God's appointed representative on earth had had more than the needs of the poor and the sick in mind in the building of his home.

Beside the daunting palace, and dwarfed by its massive neighbour, was the Cathedral Notre-Dame des Doms, where the work of God was still carried out as it had been for centuries. Helena found it strange to see churches that were not museums dedicated to exposing the decadence of religion. Quite the opposite, they were working models dedicated to the glory of God. They were places where people came to worship, and to confess their sins and receive forgiveness, and blessings. They were places where men and women came to marry, where parents came to baptise their children, where families came to bury their dead. She wondered what Dimitriev would make of the cathedral. She imagined he'd be thrilled to see such splendor dedicated to God, but she could not be sure. Perhaps he might prefer his humble wooden church hidden from the eyes of the world in the Siberian forest, so secret that only he and God knew of its existence. He, God, and one other now.

'You're thinking of Vasili,' Svetlana said.

Helena was startled. Was she really so easy to read? Or had it been an obvious deduction, since they both knew of

Dimitriev's faith. Either way, there was no point in denying it. 'I was wondering if he'd like it here,' she said casually, unwilling to reveal her surprise at Svetlana's insight.

'I think he would,' Svetlana nodded. 'He has a weakness for such things.'

'A weakness you don't share?'

'Religion is the opium of the masses,' Svetlana said, repeating Marx's famous maxim that had been drummed into them. 'You know that.'

'I do,' Helena assured her.

They passed a group of Japanese tourists taking photos of one another in the beautiful palace gardens. They were both silent until they were out of earshot again.

'I love my husband,' Svetlana began, 'But he's a fool. I can't change him, so I protect him.'

'I understand,' Helena assured her.

'I'm sure you do,' Svetlana said. 'If anything of his views on this subject were to come to light, he would be finished. So would those around him. That includes me, and that includes you.'

'There's no need to concern yourself,' Helena said quickly. 'I would never betray the Colonel.'

'Everyone would betray anyone when they're lying naked in a basement cell in Khodinka and the specialists go to work,' Svetlana answered dryly.

Khodinka was the headquarters of The Organisation in Moscow, a place Helena had heard of but never seen. 'Well, we're far from Khodinka,' she said lightly.

Svetlana walked in silence for several paces and then nodded, her mood lightening visibly. 'Yes, we are.'

'Where is he now?' Helena asked. 'Are you able to say?'

'He's in Tehran. That's all I know. It's a dangerous place. I worry for him.'

Helena felt Svetlana's pain. She also felt resentment. Svetlana had Dimitriev to love. It was a good love. A pure love. A love sanctioned by the faceless men at Khodinka. Who did she have?

'Perhaps we should pray for him,' she said lightly.

Svetlana shot her a withering look and she reached for Svetlana's hand. She felt Svetlana resist for a moment, then relax.

'Colonel Dimitriev is capable of taking care of himself,' Helena told her.

'I know,' Svetlana said with a faint smile. 'But thank you anyway. Pray for him if you wish.'

'I would,' she answered. 'But I don't know how.'

'Perhaps it's for the best,' Svetlana said, stopping to put her other hand on Helena's and look her in the eye. 'Don't fall in love with Benoit.'

'Don't worry,' Helena answered. 'I've got it under control.'

'Benoit is an attractive man and the two of you are very physical together,'

Helena wondered how Svetlana knew. The Organisation had the most sophisticated devices in the world. She knew spy cameras and microphones must have been placed in Benoit's flat for quite some time, but she had put it from her mind until now. She wondered where they had been placed. She was tempted to search for them. She imagined Svetlana watching, listening, as she and Benoit made love. She wondered who else might be with her, a surveillance expert from The Organisation, she imagined. She wanted to ask how much Svetlana had seen and heard, but she knew Svetlana wouldn't say.

'Keep your distance, emotionally,' Svetlana continued. 'This is a mission, remember.'

'How could I forget?' she said sharply.

'It's easier than you think,' Svetlana said with a faint smile.

Helena didn't reply. It was hard to imagine Svetlana feeling for anyone else. Her love for Dimitriev was total and complete. They stood at the far end of the palace gardens and looked out over the River Rhone, where the remains of the half-built Pont Saint Bénezet ended abruptly in the middle of the water.

'We've been monitoring Benoit's calls to his wife,' Svetlana told her, interrupting her reverie. She felt a pang of annoyance that Benoit was still calling his wife, and fought to hide it from Svetlana. 'What have they been talking about?' she asked casually.

'Don't worry,' Svetlana said with a smirk. 'He's stopped asking her to come back. I think we both know why.'

'Why?'

'Because he's enjoying fucking you a lot more than he ever enjoyed fucking her. Why did you think?'

'So what are they talking about?' she asked.

'About the baby, mostly. They argue about everything else. She's insisting he give up his job and go to Paris, live with her parents until he finds another job. He's refusing. She's calling him stubborn. He's saying she's being unreasonable.'

'What if she decides to come back?' Helena asked.

'We'll stop her,' Svetlana answered.

'How?'

'We'll find a way. Don't concern yourself.'

She turned to look at Svetlana. Would Svetlana really kill a mother and baby, she wondered, and if so, how would she do it? An assassination would draw too much attention. A road accident would be simpler. A large 4-wheel drive vehicle would drive the woman and child off the road, most likely once she'd entered the steep, narrow roads of the Vaucluse. She saw the figures of Benoit's wife and baby thrown clear of the wreckage at the bottom of a ravine, too far to see any blood or injuries on their bodies, lying as if asleep on the warm rocks, beside a bright blue stream that twisted along the floor of the ravine.

They left the cathedral gardens and walked down the narrow cobbled streets outside towards the spot where Helena had parked. The street was busy with tourists visiting the souvenir shops and art galleries, or picking up the local delicacy of black truffles from the market stalls.

'How much longer before Benoit's ready?' Svetlana asked.

'One more week,' Helena answered.

They reached the yellow Mini and Svetlana took Helena's hands in hers. They kissed one another on both cheeks and Svetlana squeezed her hands affectionately.

'One more week,' she smiled.

*

The lavender fields had come alive seemingly overnight, creating an expanse of startling blue across the region. Backed by soft ochre hills and bathed in warm spring sunshine, they might have come straight from a landscape by Paul Cezanne, but neither Benoit nor Helena noticed the painterly scenes. They could only look straight ahead as the car hurtled along the road. 'Tell me again what happened,' he said, barely able to believe what she'd told him on the phone.

'I don't know how they found out. Someone must have seen

us together when we met in Roussillon.'

'And what did they say exactly?' he demanded.

'They gave me a day to get my stuff together and get out.'

'They can't do that,' he said, slamming his palm into the steering wheel.

'They can Michel, and they did.' She stole a glance at his profile. His lips were drawn tight, his eyes staring intently at a point in the distance.

'Come and live with me,' he said evenly.

'I can't Michel, I won't. It's your family home. I'm not moving in with you.'

'Then where are you going to live?'

'Nowhere. I'm going back to England. I have no choice.'

'You have a choice,' he said, the annoyance beginning to show in his voice.

'No I don't. I have no money, no job, no home. I won't be a kept woman Michel. I won't. And besides, I still have my protest to think about. I still want to make a difference.'

'Then stay here,' he said.

'How can I?'

'I'll think of a way.'

'What sort of way?'

'I don't know, yet. Maybe they'll change their minds.'

'I tried to get them to change their minds. I practically begged them, Michel. I don't want to leave, believe me. You don't know what they're like, those in charge, so fucking self-righteous. And they're as low as the bosses on your side when it comes down to it.'

'What do you mean?'

'Nothing.'

'Tell me.'

She turned to face him. 'I can't even bring myself to say it.'

'Say it!'

'They hinted that there would be a way for me to stay, but what they were suggesting is impossible.'

'What is impossible?' His eyes bored into hers, searching for the slightest glimmer of hope.

It was time.

'They wanted me to spy on you,' she said quietly.

'To spy on me? How? Why?'

'Not on you personally, Michel. On what you do, at the base, to get secrets off you. Can you believe it?'

'What do peace protestors want with secrets?' he asked incredulously.

'One of the leaders came to my room late at night. She told me you specialise in missile guidance systems like the ones used in the Exocet. She said you're working on new projects now, even bigger and more dangerous. She hinted that she has contacts in the British secret service. I think she's some sort of fucking spy, Michel!'

'And she wants our technology?'

'She went into some big long story about how NATO allies should share their technology so it can't be used against other member states, like the Exocets were. About how they're supposed to do it anyway, but rarely do because of arms sales. I didn't even understand half of what she was telling me, Michel. She said if we couldn't achieve total disarmament, then we were at least safer this way.'

'And what did you say?' Benoit demanded.

'I told her she was fucking insane. I couldn't ask you to do that – not ever.' She looked across at him, and saw his jaw tighten. 'It's not true is it Michel, about the Exocets?'

'Of course not. I had nothing to do with them.'

There it was. He had lied.

'But you work on missile guidance systems?'

'Yes, Helena. I do. You know I work at the base. I don't want to lie to you.'

It was the beginning of the end, now that he had lied.

'I knew she was full of shit,' Helena smiled. Benoit smiled back at her.

'This is so totally fucked up,' she said loudly, her hands balling into fists around her long skirt. 'I've got to leave, Michel. Let's go somewhere nice, just one more time. Take me to one of your places. I love the places you take me. Look at the lavender fields Michel! Look how pretty they are. Where shall we go? Think of somewhere. I want to go somewhere nice with you one more time before I go.'

*

Three days later a courier arrived at the commune with a package for Helena. He asked to see some ID and she produced her student card. The courier made a note of the number and checked her signature before handing over the package.

An hour later, in a lay-by on the road to Avignon, far from the commune and the airbase, she stopped the yellow Mini and opened the package. Inside were detailed plans of the missile guidance systems used in the new S3 intermediate range nuclear missiles recently introduced at the St. Christol Airbase. There was also a brief handwritten letter from Benoit. He hoped she would take the information as a mark of the sincerity of his feelings for her. He stressed that his name must remain confidential. And he trusted she would ensure the information ended up in the right hands.

Autoroute de Soleil, Provence

The golden hills of the Vaucluse had disappeared far behind them, giving way to the low-lying coastal plain that would remain all the way to Marseille. Helena had left her car in Avignon and they had taken Svetlana's Renault south to the airport.

On the A7 autoroute, known as the 'Road to the Sun', Svetlana had pulled into a remote service station and parked away from other vehicles. She had leafed through the contents of the envelope quickly before resealing the papers inside.

'I agree with your assessment,' she smiled. 'This should make our scientists very happy. And you will receive a medal for this.'

'What will happen to Benoit?' she asked.

'Don't concern yourself with him now,' Svetlana answered.

'I want to know.'

Svetlana's blue eyes bored into hers, daring her to ask again.

'Tell me.'

'He will commit suicide,' she said, her mouth set in a hard smile.

'Why can't you leave him alone? No one needs to know what he's done.'

'I told you not to concern yourself with Benoit now. Cut yourself off from him. That is an order, Lieutenant Zykova.'

Helena was stopped in her tracks by the sudden use of her old name. It was a sudden reminder that they would soon be flying north to Moscow, where the warm soft lavender fields of Provence would soon seem like a distant dream.

'He'll search for you,' Svetlana explained. 'When he can't

find you, he'll go crazy. He'll talk to the protestors and eventually he'll realise what's happened. Then he might report it to the army, or the army might see him acting strangely and investigate. Either way, he'll be able to identify you. The West will find out that we have an agent capable of such a sophisticated deception and be on its guard in the future. This way is safer. No comebacks.'

'You'll stage his suicide?'

'There is no need to concern yourself with details,' Svetlana said coldly. 'Just remember what he is – a traitor, a man who betrayed his country to satisfy the hunger in his prick, an enemy of the Russian people. He deserves what he gets.'

In Marseilles airport, Helena made her excuses and headed for the rest-rooms where there was a line of public telephones. She lifted the receiver and dialled Benoit's number. She had no idea what she was going to say to him. A warning, that was all she would give him. A single warning with no explanation, just a chance to get away, a small chance to save himself.

There was no answer. She wondered if she was already too late. When she replaced the receiver Svetlana Dimitrieva was behind her. 'Disobey my order again and you will die too.'

She hated Svetlana then like never before. Her hands shook by her side, a twitching that she could only stop by balling her fist. She would happily have struck Svetlana, beaten her until her fists were bloody and raw, or until Svetlana overpowered her and put her into sweet oblivion, but it would not save Benoit. None of it would save him from the fate that was now his for having loved her. She turned and ran into the rest room where she vomited until there was nothing left to expel.

On the long flight to Moscow she sat apart from Svetlana and mourned for Benoit. She had not loved him – it was hard

to love a traitor even if he was little more than a gullible fool –
but she had shared intimacies with him. She had kissed his lips
lingeringly and they had tasted of sweet wine. She had thrilled
to the touch of his hand on her skin and the sensation of his
smooth body between her thighs. She had caressed his back
and dug her fingers into his shoulders. She had felt him lose
himself as he climaxed inside her and in that moment, that
briefest of moments, she had loved him.

She went into the aircraft washroom and examined her face
in the mirror. The face of Helena Rossi had disappeared,
replaced by a new face, a pretty face, of course, but she did not
like it. It was the face of a deceiver, a snake that had shed its
skin, a viper that would bite any man who came near it. Could
a snake bite itself, poison itself? She wondered. She didn't
know the answer. But she knew some insects died after one
sting, while others were able to sting again. If she were to carry
out more missions she must learn to keep her heart out of it or
have it torn each time. If she did not she would be useless to
The Organisation, nothing more than a dangerous liability, and
one The Organisation would not allow to remain.

When the captain announced that they had entered Soviet
airspace she returned to the empty seat beside Svetlana.
Svetlana offered her a magazine and she took it with a smile,
grateful for something to occupy her mind as they began their
slow descent into Moscow.

NADIA

Surrey Police Headquarters, Guildford, 2000

It had been six weeks since the woman known as Nadia Antonescu had brought about the collapse of Havilland Ethical, one of Britain's biggest drugs companies, and the suicide of its Chief Executive, George Petersen. In that time, all attempts to trace her had come to nothing. Detective Chief Inspector Simons scanned the coroner's report that had come in the post that morning. It confirmed what he already knew – that Petersen had taken his own life. There were no suspicious circumstances worthy of investigation. He called DC Mena Gakhar into his office and handed the report to her.

She read it carefully before replying. 'Looks like you were right, Chief. Suicide, not murder.'

'It depends how you look at it though, doesn't it?' he replied.

'Sir?'

'Petersen took his own life,' he said. 'But this woman, this Nadia Antonescu, she practically signed his death warrant. She went in there with the specific intention of seducing him, learning his secrets, and exposing them to the world. For a man like Petersen the scandal was more than he could take. Her actions led directly to his suicide.'

'She's a super-bitch if that's what you mean,' Gakhar nodded, 'But what's that got to do with anything?'

'Strictly speaking we could close the case on Petersen now,' Simons said. 'But I don't like the idea of her being out there circling around looking for her next victim.'

'Neither do I,' Gakhar said. 'But she's disappeared without a trace.'

'She's disappeared,' Simons nodded, 'But not without a trace. Someone out there knows who she is, or at least knows someone who knows someone who knows who she is. We've just got to stop looking for Nadia Antonescu and start at the other end of the trail.'

'The other end of the trail is The Times, but they won't give up their sources. You told me that yourself.'

'I told you a lot of things, Mena. Doesn't mean it's always true. I'm not always right, you know.'

'I thought you were,' she said with a deadpan stare.

Simons grinned. He was beginning to like his new assistant despite his earlier misgivings. 'How do you fancy a pub lunch?' he asked. 'I know a lovely place in London, by the river, with views of the old docks.'

'Sure, but why go all that way?' she asked. 'There's plenty of nice pubs around here.'

'This one's near The Times headquarters,' he answered. 'And no one enjoys a lunchtime pint more than a journalist.'

Prospect of Whitby, London

The pub was one of the oldest in London, built on the waterside with views across the Thames to the Old Salt Quay at Rotherhithe. Simons paid for two fruit juices and went with Gakhar onto the terrace. They took a seat at a table for four at the far end of the terrace, away from the other customers and waited for Declan Capaldi to arrive. A thin pale man with a mop of unruly black hair streaked with grey approached them two minutes later. Neither Simons nor Gakhar were in uniform, but Capaldi obviously had little trouble in spotting police officers. Simons had called him an hour earlier and offered him the choice of an informal chat in the pub or a formal interview at the police station. Capaldi had agreed to the pub.

He looks a lot older than his picture in real life,' Gakhar muttered, recalling the photo of Capaldi she'd found on her BlackBerry on the way over.

'They always do,' Simons grinned.

Capaldi set his pint down on the table. 'I wouldn't give up my sources even if I knew them, which in this case, I don't.'

'Like I said on the phone, this is just an informal chat,' Simons said. 'Please take a seat, Mr. Capaldi.'

Capaldi sat.

'Your story caused a lot of damage, perhaps more than you were expecting. We're trying to find out exactly what happened, so anything you can tell us, in good faith, would be helpful at this stage.

'Fine,' Capaldi said with a pained smile. 'I'll tell you what I can – in good faith. I got a phone call, it lasted no longer than a minute. Anonymous. Said they had proof that Havillands were being less than ethical about where its new wonder drug was coming from. Told me to check my email in the next five minutes and hung up.'

'So you got an email too,' Gakhar said.

'Yes, and you're welcome to see it. It was from an address that was just a random bunch of numbers and letters. I had to go into my junk to fish it out.'

'Into your *junk*?' Simons frowned.

'Yeah, junk, spam, you know, unsolicited mail.' Capaldi stared at him like he was insane.

'Go on,' Simons nodded.

'I guess it was sent from an internet café,' Capaldi said. 'I tried replying several times but never got anything else back.'

'And what did the email say?' Mena prompted.

'It gave the address of a farm in Scotland. I drove up and checked it out. Turned out it was owned by Havilland Ethical, and that they were growing their so-called Tibetan ginseng there. I got threatened by a guard with a fucking big gun for my troubles, but I managed to get a sample from one of the fields. Got it tested in a lab when I got back to London. Turned out the tip-off was true.'

'Anything else you can tell us?' Gakhar asked.

'That's it, honestly. Get a high court summons if you like, I won't be able to tell you anything more than I've told you already.'

'You have no idea where this leak came from?' she persisted.

'None whatsoever.' Capaldi took a sip of his beer.

'How about a wild guess, strictly off the record?' she asked with a smile.

Capaldi shook his head. 'I'm not one for guessing, but I can tell you this: Havilland Ethical was a big drugs company operating in a cut-throat market. It could've been any disgruntled ex-employee with an axe to grind, or it could have been any one of their competitors who got hold of the information somehow or other.'

'By fair means or foul?' Gakhar said.

'Quite.'

'Which do you think?' she asked.

'I think I've told you everything I can,' Capaldi said, rising from his seat. 'And now I'm going to finish my pint in peace.'

'People are dead because of your story Mr. Capaldi.' Her voice was suddenly hard. 'Doesn't that mean anything to you?'

Capaldi's mouth set hard. 'Listen, I'm sorry about Petersen, alright. But the truth is the truth. I just put it out there in the public domain. If he didn't want to be exposed as a fraud, he shouldn't have tried to cheat people, should he?' Capaldi turned to go, but the question had riled him and now he wanted to say his piece. He turned back. 'And quite honestly, his death sells more papers. So *no*, I'm not sorry. Quite the opposite in fact, it's been one of my biggest coups.'

He began to walk away.

'One last question,' she called after him. He stopped and waited with forced patience. 'The anonymous caller, was it a man or a woman?'

'A man,' he said. 'It was a man.'

Soho Square, London

Simons entered the small gated park in the heart of Soho. The grass was crossed by two paths and there was a wooden hut in the centre. He sat on a bench and watched the office workers cross the square to fetch their lunch. In the summer the park was filled with people enjoying their sandwiches in the sunshine, but today winter retained its grip and it was too cold to sit out. That was good, because Simons knew the person he was meeting had no wish to be seen with him.

Geri Harper appeared at the gate on the far side of the square. He couldn't help noticing the shapely legs of the former PR Director from Havilland Ethical as she approached and did his best not to stare. For a moment he regretted she hadn't asked to meet somewhere more intimate, a cozy pub or café, perhaps. He rose to shake her hand. She seemed different now, more confident, less shell-shocked by Petersen's death and the whole collapse. She smiled as she sat beside him.

'We're still looking for the source of the leak,' he told her.

'You didn't get anything from The Times?' she asked.

'Nothing much.'

'I didn't think you would.'

'The press, they're a bunch of...' he stopped himself before he said something that might offend her. The press was her livelihood, after all.

'Oh you don't have to tell me, Chief Inspector,' she smiled. '*Jackals* – that's what George Petersen used to call them.'

He grinned. 'I don't know how you can work with them.'

'It's an occupational hazard,' she smiled. 'If it's any consolation, I don't know how you do your job – finding

George's body, all the ugliness that goes with it.'

Simons nodded his thanks. It was good to be appreciated.

'I'm going to tell you something 'off the record' if I may,' he began. 'We believe someone paid a woman to seduce George Petersen and find out about his new drug. This woman wasn't a simple prostitute, she was a highly-trained industrial spy. She didn't kill George Petersen, not exactly, but she wounded him and fed him to the jackals. Not only that, but she caused the meltdown of a major British corporation. Worse yet, she's still at large and so far, the only lead we have is a bogus name and this...' He produced the photo of Nadia from his briefcase and handed it to Harper. Harper examined the picture of a woman leaning into George Petersen's Aston Martin. 'She doesn't look very dangerous,' she said absently.

'That's exactly why she is.'

She handed the picture back to Simons. 'When George was alive, we used to joke about the jackals. *Keep them fed on scraps and they won't feed on you.* That was what I told him. George liked that one. He remembered it. He even added it to his *Laws of the Jungle.*' She smiled at the memory.

Simons waited for her to explain.

'He had these laws,' she laughed. 'Stupid laws – you know the sort of thing: most people are the herd, only the few are lions – that sort of thing. Schoolboy nonsense, mostly.'

'You miss him?' Simons asked gently.

She shook her head. 'George was an arrogant fool, a liar and a cheat, but charming in his own way. No, I don't miss him, but he didn't deserve to be exposed quite so brutally.'

'No he didn't,' Simons said.

She sighed. 'He would have been easy prey for a woman like her.'

Simons nodded.

'Have you thought about releasing her picture to the press?' Harper suggested.

'Start a witch hunt for an unknown foreign seductress? It'd be a circus.'

'Not necessarily. Not if you handle it correctly. *The police are seeking the whereabouts of Nadia Antonescu in connection with the recent collapse of Havilland Ethical.* Keep it low key. Don't mention George, or his death, and you might avoid a feeding frenzy.'

He considered the idea. He didn't like it at all.

'I can see you hate the press as much as George did,' she smiled, rising from the bench. 'But if you want to catch an insect, you need to start lifting up some rocks.'

'Another of George's sayings?' he asked.

'No, I just made it up,' she smiled.

'More like stirring up a hornet's nest,' he said grimly.

'Oh it won't be pretty,' she nodded. 'But when the dust settles, you may find something new has turned up.'

He watched her cross the square and waited until she had passed through the gate and out of sight. The idea troubled him, but the unknown seductress troubled him more. He reached for his phone and dialed Declan Capaldi at The Times.

Heathrow Airport, London

A stack of assorted daily British newspapers left the loading bay beside Runway Three on a trolley train and was delivered to the open tailgate of a waiting Airbus A320. Here it was loaded, along with twenty five sacks of airmail bound for Russia, and a little over five hours later, the same stack was unloaded at Domodedovo International airport in Moscow. The airmail was swiftly sorted for onward distribution while the newspapers were transported in a van directly to the Khodinka airbase in the northwest of Moscow.

The papers were taken directly to the Analysts' room on the second floor, where a small team of experts pored over the contents of each newspaper, as they did every day. One hour later, a sharp-eyed young analyst picked up the phone and dialed the number of Colonel Vasili Dimitriev. He'd found a follow-up piece on the collapse of Havilland Ethical, a subject the colonel had asked him to watch for, and he thought the colonel might be interested. As he waited for Dimitriev to answer, he looked again at the photo of the blonde woman taken in what looked like an underground car park. She was standing by a sports car, an Aston Martin if he wasn't mistaken, and peering into the window. Though the photo was blurred, she looked quite beautiful and he wondered if the colonel knew her.

Khodinka Airfield, Moscow

The old airstrip in the north-western suburb of Moscow had once been busy, but planes landed only rarely now and when they did, it was usually to deliver some specialised new cargo for testing. The airfield was surrounded by restricted buildings specialising in aviation and rocket technology and patrolled day and night by guards and attack dogs. Inside this outer perimeter, shielded from outside view and accessible only by a narrow passage through a 10-metre high wall, was the headquarters of The Organisation.

Dimitriev passed quickly through the sophisticated scanning equipment. He knew the drill and carried no metal objects of any sort, no bag or briefcase, he even wore elastic braces instead of a belt buckle, and held nothing but a copy of The Times newspaper, London edition, under his arm. The guard saluted him with a smile. Dimitriev was highly respected within the walls of Khodinka.

He went directly to the office of General Levkov, the Head of the First Directorate running agent intelligence. He knocked once and entered without awaiting a response. Levkov rose from his desk and turned to unlock the steel cabinet behind him. He took out a bottle of Russian Standard and filled two glasses, handing one to Dimitriev without a word. Dimitriev rarely drank, but he accepted the vodka and downed it in one with Levkov. Levkov was not only the Head of the First Directorate, he was also his mentor and the man who had first recruited him to The Organisation – a man he admired and trusted. Levkov refilled their glasses and sat down. Dimitriev sat opposite. Levkov placed his glass heavily on his desk. 'You look like shit, Vasili Ivanovich,' he grunted. 'You were fit and handsome when I brought you in. Now look at you.'

'You don't look so good yourself, Gennady Fyodorovich,' Dimitriev smiled, using Levkov's first name and patronym – something few people did nowadays.

'This business in Chechnya is a fucking shit-storm,' Levkov muttered. 'But I don't think you're here to talk about Chechnya.'

'No.' Dimitriev leaned back in his chair, marshalling his thoughts before beginning. He would only get one chance to convince Levkov of his idea. Levkov was not a man to go over things twice. 'Have you heard of a British drugs company Havilland Ethical?' he began.

'Recently collapsed after a scandal in the press,' Levkov said.

Dimitriev nodded. Levkov was as well-informed as ever. 'The Times just ran a new story saying the police are seeking a woman in connection with the collapse.'

'What about it?' Levkov eyed him coldly. So far he'd heard nothing to concern The Organisation.

Dimitriev opened his copy of The Times and placed it on Levkov's desk. Levkov examined the blurred photo of a woman leaning into the sports car. 'It could be anyone,' he said bluntly.

'It's her.'

Levkov stared at him. Dimitriev held his gaze. 'Tatiana Zykova? How can you be sure?' Levkov demanded finally.

'I spent a year with her in Siberia, remember.'

'That was a long time ago, Vasili Ivanovich. A lot has happened since then.'

'It's her.' Dimitriev placed his palm on Levkov's desk. 'I know it.'

'This is personal,' Levkov said coldly. It was a statement, not a question, and there was no room for personal business in The Organisation.

'You're right. It's personal,' Dimitriev nodded, knowing there was no point in lying to Levkov. 'But if I can trace her, I can interrogate her, find out what happened in Berlin.' Levkov closed the newspaper and handed it back to Dimitriev. 'Berlin was a long time ago, Vasili Ivanovich. We have other priorities now within our own borders.'

'Ten years isn't so long. And whoever betrayed her might still be at large in The Organisation,' Dimitriev added.

'You really believe she was betrayed from the inside?'

'I do.' Dimitriev exhaled slowly. 'I want to know what happened in Berlin. I want answers. I know my personal feelings aren't important but if there's a traitor in our midst, that is important.'

'You believe you can find her?' Levkov demanded. 'She was trained by the best to disappear without trace. She was trained by Svetlana. By you.'

'Who better to find the student than the teacher,' Dimitriev said. Levkov waved his hand dismissively. He wasn't buying it.

'This picture is the first solid lead we've had on her in years,' Dimitriev went on. 'It's worth pursuing.'

Levkov blinked slowly, evaluating all the options and possible outcomes before replying. 'You're ignoring the obvious: that she betrayed us herself.'

'I don't believe it,' Dimitriev said.

'Because you spent a year with her once, fifteen years ago?'

'Yes.'

'She's changed since then. After France she was never the same. It was documented in Svetlana's reports.'

'She grew a hard shell. Who wouldn't in such a role? But betrayal wasn't in her nature.'

Levkov shrugged. 'How can you be sure? She was trained to betray. It was second nature to her.'

Dimitriev leaned forward and spoke in a low voice. 'Over the years there have been several high profile missions gone to shit, many smaller ones compromised. For years we've suspected there might be a traitor in these walls. Tatiana Zykova may lead us to him. She may not. But are you prepared to gamble more lives on not finding out?'

Levkov eyed him dispassionately. Dimitriev held his gaze, knowing the slightest hesitation would give Levkov all the reason he needed to refuse. Finally Levkov reached for his vodka and waited for Dimitriev to do the same. He drained it and placed the glass down hard on his desk. 'If there's a traitor in our midst and you believe this woman can lead you to him, then what the fuck are you doing sitting here in my office drinking vodka, Vasili Ivanovich?'

Dimitriev leapt from his seat and stood to attention smartly.

'Go to London,' Levkov ordered. 'Find her. And find out what the hell happened in Berlin.'

*

One floor below the Head of the Sixth Directorate in charge of Signals and Surveillance, General Prokop, replaced the receiver on his telephone. He had just been informed of the meeting taking place between Levkov and Dimitriev. Like them, he had also seen the article in The Times and suspected it might be the work of Tatiana Zykova. However unlike them, he had a very different reason for wishing to find her.

MARIANA

Kurfurstendamm, West Berlin, 1989

The transvestite took his final curtain call. The crowd had demanded four encores, and he was exhausted now. The make-up glistened on his smooth face, making his enlarged features all the more grotesque. Colonel James Cleary applauded with the rest of the audience in the review theatre. He knew the fastidiousness of the Germans when it came to manners, and like any good spy, he had no wish to stand out from the crowd, though privately he found the man-woman deeply repulsive. Rather than applauding him, he imagined beating the grossly-painted features to a pulp with his fists. He swiftly put the thought from his mind. There was no point in fantasising about things he couldn't do, better to think of things he could do.

Now that the cabaret was over, the actors and showgirls would come out from backstage to mingle with the politicians, the businessmen, the high-ranking police officers and the prostitutes in the intimate bar. Sexuality was always open in West Berlin, far more so than in other parts of Germany. The citizens of West Berlin seemed to enjoy flaunting their permissiveness in the faces of their austere Eastern neighbours, a final act of defiance, knowing that if the massed ranks of the Warsaw Pact ever moved west, this solitary half-city deep inside enemy territory would be the first to succumb.

Cleary surveyed the throng. He noticed the new prostitute straight away. She was young, mid-twenties, medium height, dark haired, beautiful, perfect. She wore a skin-tight black dress, high heels and costume jewellery that caught the spotlights when she moved. She was drinking champagne and listening to an overweight politician who was talking at her. It wasn't her beauty that caught Cleary's eye, but the darkness around her left eye, carefully concealed with make-up, but visible nonetheless to an expert eye like his own. He moved closer, circling, watching. She noticed him. She was aware of another of her kind, drawing near. He raised his glass and she smiled. There was a hint of vulnerability in her that he liked. She excused herself from the overweight politician and stepped away. Cleary closed the gap in two strides. 'How about we get out of this place?'

'What are you looking for?' she asked.

She didn't appear to be taken aback by his forthrightness. That was good. It was important to be cool. 'Something different,' he answered.

'How different?'

He grinned. 'I like to play a little rough.' He looked at her blackened eye. 'Looks like you do too.'

'That doesn't come cheap,' she answered, her expression turning a shade harder.

'How much?'

'A thousand West-marks.'

It was an outrageous amount, but there was little else to spend his money on in Berlin, and he had the feeling she'd be something special. 'Do you have a pass for the East?' he asked.

'Yes.'

'Then let's go.'

'There's a hotel nearby we can use,' she said. 'It's very discreet.'

'I prefer my own place,' he told her. He liked to keep control. He knew the tricks of the East German secret police – the dreaded *Stasi* – they had tried to blackmail him often enough, without success. His own home was the only place he knew was clean. It was swept for bugs once a fortnight using the latest CIA scanning devices.

We can go to my apartment if you don't want to pay for a room,' she said.

'My place is better, trust me,' he smiled coldly.

She hesitated.

'I insist,' he said quietly, knowing that for a thousand West-marks, it would be well worth the hooker's short trip into East Berlin.

She waited a heartbeat. 'If you insist.'

They crossed Kurfurstendamm, the main shopping thoroughfare, where the giant Kaufhaus des Westens towered over the surrounding shops and boutiques. The stores were closed but their windows were still brightly lit, showcasing the latest fashions and electronics from around the world. While the shopkeepers slept, the club owners, bar girls and prostitutes worked their trade – Kurfurstendamm was also the centre of West Berlin's thriving red light district.

They walked down the tree-lined avenue. The August sky was holding onto its faint glow despite the lateness of the hour. Cleary led the way down another side street to where a blue VW Passat was parked. She knew the vehicle, but made sure to wait until Cleary unlocked it before going to it.

'Why do you live in East Berlin?' she asked as she took her seat beside him.

'It's where my work is,' he answered.

'What do you do?'

'I work in the American Embassy.'

'I think you got posted to the wrong side of the wall,' she said lightly.

He drove off smoothly over the dark newly laid tarmac. 'Oh I don't know, the East isn't so bad. I mean sure, the place is a fucking joke, but where I live it's pretty nice, peaceful, quiet at night. And you know what they say about East Berlin, right?'

She waited for him to tell her the answer.

'You can sleep easy knowing there's a secret policeman on every corner.'

'I don't think the Stasi are a joke,' she said seriously.

'Hell, the Stasi aren't so bad once you get to know them,' he grinned. 'They're polite for one thing, not like the cops in DC.'

'You have an unusual view of the Stasi, especially for an American,' she said.

'Ah, don't worry, I know all about the Stasi. All I'm saying is it doesn't bother me too much, living in the East. You get used to it.'

'Where do you live?' she asked.

'Pankow.'

'No wonder you like it. That's where all the Politburo members live.'

'Exactly. If you want the best of something in the Eastern Bloc, just follow the leader, right?'

They turned off the brightly lit street running east from the Kurfurstendamm and the Passat's headlights illuminated the brutal barrier that appeared at the end of the road and blocked out all advance. Mariana had seen the Berlin Wall plenty of times since arriving in Berlin, but the sight of it still disturbed her. She was no stranger to restrictions – restricted areas, restricted buildings, restricted streets – but the cities of

Leningrad and Moscow were large and open, and beyond them was a country so vast that you could travel for days without seeing a single wire fence. But here was a whole city, restricted. Go far enough down any of the leafy boulevards and you would find yourself up against an impassable barrier. The wall didn't divide the city, it encircled it, cutting it off completely from the world outside and containing the good life of the West Berliners in a goldfish bowl that was looked upon with a dangerous mix of envy and loathing by those outside.

Cleary turned right into a street that followed the line of the wall southwards towards Checkpoint Charlie, the crossing point set aside for foreigners wishing to enter the Eastern zone. The lighting here was already different. Gone were the street lamps, the colourful neon signs and the bright shop-windows, giving way to the sickly yellow glare of the towering arc lights that lined the wall. The only colour in this grey scene was the graffiti scrawled on the wall. The arc lights illuminated the area of no-man's land between the outer wall and the inner wall in the East containing a series of obstacles that made up what was known as The Death Strip. Those wishing to escape from East to West faced a scramble-proof fence of barbed wire and beyond this, beds of nails, attack dogs leashed on long wires, and watchtowers where guards had orders to shoot on sight. Just before the final hurdle of the wall itself was a concrete ditch, designed as a crash barrier to prevent heavy vehicles from smashing through the wall. Finally the wall itself was over three metres high, with a smooth half-barrel at the top to make climbing more difficult. Since its construction, over 150 East Germans had died trying to cross it.

Cleary inched the Passat forward in the queue at the border. It was the perfect car for a spy, common and non-descript. She had watched him for weeks, entering and leaving the American Embassy on Neustädtische Kirchstrasse from a block away through a telescopic lens. Following him would have been a mistake. The chances of him spotting her were too high. Instead, a team of four agents had been assigned to tail him constantly. They had been able to report on all his movements. Cleary was a pro and didn't try to shake them. He'd grown used to the constant surveillance and was unlikely to commit any clandestine contact or meeting under such circumstances.

She had focused the powerful Zeiss Jena lens on his face, seeking to read his character, his soul, from the brief moments when he emerged from his work or his home. Like all good spies, he was distinctly unremarkable: medium height, medium build, short cropped greying hair, cut in a simple military style. His skin was leathery, a rough shade of red, weather-beaten by the long northern winters of Berlin. He had no moustache or beard, no noticeable birthmarks, scars or features. His grey-blue eyes were wide spaced and neutral, revealing nothing of his intentions. His wide face tapered to a heavy jaw, the chin pronounced, with a cleft in its centre, yet there was nothing to reveal his inner nature. She imagined that living under the constant observation of the East German Stasi, he had learned long ago to affect a neutral appearance in public, knowing that he could be under observation at any time.

Now she had a chance to study him close-up. In the theatre he had revealed more of himself already. He had approached her with no preamble or small talk and insisted she come to his home despite her unease. His lack of social skills, his desire for control, and his lack of empathy marked him out as a dangerous adversary. She turned to snatch another look at him. His profile was silhouetted against the eerie yellow glow of the arc lights. She couldn't see his eyes, but she'd seen them earlier in the theatre, seen the emptiness of a predator preparing to close with its prey. She exhaled slowly, silently, forcing herself to stay calm, to stay cold and clear, to remember who was the real hunter, and who was the real prey.

The border guard waved them through. Fifty metres further on, the East German Grenzpolizei – *Grepo* as they were known – took longer examining their papers, their faces frozen in an unwelcome stare, and took their time in raising the barrier before allowing Cleary to pass.

The change was instantaneous. Smooth tarmac roads lined with Mercedes Benz, BMW and Volkswagens had given way to rough cobblestones filled with the ubiquitous East German Trabant. The garish paintwork of the Trabants' fiberglass bodies flared in the beam of the Passat. The brightly-painted shops and buildings of the West had given way to concrete blocks that still carried the scars of the allied invasion more than forty years earlier. The neon shop signs were replaced by hand-painted boards proclaiming the function of the shop: 'Butcher', 'Grocer', 'Hardware'.

'You really enjoy living in East Berlin?' she asked.

'Not all Americans are capitalist pigs,' he said with a grin. 'Besides, it beats having to wait at the border twice a day. How about you, where do you live?'

'I live in the West. It's where my work is.'

'Understandable,' he said. 'But where are you from originally? You don't look German.'

'My parents were Hungarian.'

Her cover story was already ingrained into her psyche so deeply that she could recite her family history and her childhood memories as convincingly as any real Hungarian.

She knew that her cover was backed up with the appropriate documents, listed in the archives of the West Berlin records office, should he decide to check.

'That explains it,' he said.

'You like my looks?' she asked, matter-of-fact.

'Yes, I do. There's not many like you.'

She crossed her legs and settled back into the seat, knowing that Cleary would catch the movement, that the subtle parting of her thighs would add to the anticipation he was feeling, an anticipation that had been heightened considerably now that they had passed through the Berlin Wall.

The car turned into a wide, tree-lined avenue in Pankow, the up-market district of East Berlin, and came to a halt outside a detached house surrounded by a high wall and security gate. It was the type of place that the CIA insisted on, more difficult to observe and to bug. Their technicians carried out a weekly sweep of the premises for bugs, Mariana knew. The last sweep had taken place two days ago.

Cleary opened his car door. She waited, forcing him to go around the car and open her door too, knowing he would enjoy his games of dominance all the more if they involved taking down her arrogance as they played.

'You never told me your name,' he said as she rose from the car and pulled her coat around her shoulders.

'Mariana.'

'Welcome, Mariana,' he said with mock gallantry, extending his hand to his home as he took his key and unlocked the gate.

*

An hour later she lay on the bed, forcing her breathing to return to normal, massaging her throat and fighting down the waves of panic and nausea that rose in her as she struggled to take a breath. Cleary had gone to the bathroom to shower. She waited for a few more breaths, until her heart rate returned to normal and she felt able to move. She rose and reached for a tissue to clean the semen from her chest. She fought down her revulsion at what she had undergone. She had not had sex with one of her targets since Benoit in France, and Svetlana's advice had proved correct. The most powerful seductions were based on the promise of love, rather than love itself. But Cleary was different. She'd known from the start that he would be closed to love. Sex would be the only seduction open to her, and already she knew her initial impression was correct. Cleary would never fall in love with her, never betray his country for money or blackmail. She would have to use sex as a means to get close to him, close enough to discover any potential weakness that she might exploit to get the information she needed.

She rolled over and stood, her body aching as it hadn't ached since she had fought with Svetlana and Dimitriev during her combat training, but this ache was different, the dull ache of internal violation, a dirty ache that would take days to leave her. Cleary had taken his time in commencing the sex, embarking on a long drawn out role play that involved her committing a crime and being caught. He had begun by slapping her, stinging the flesh on her thighs and buttocks until they were raw. As his arousal grew, he had turned her around and forced her onto her knees before him. Gripping her tightly by the hair, he had forced her mouth open with his hard fingers, and when she had closed it again, he had slapped her hard across the face and forced it open again, until she was waiting obediently for him to extract his penis from his pants. His erection had been full and hard as he pushed it between her lips. When her hand came up to hold his shaft he had slapped it away, unwilling to give her any control over the act. He'd begun slowly, but as his excitement had mounted he'd begun to thrust deeper into her throat until she'd gagged. He had allowed her a moment to recover, then begun again. Fortunately he had climaxed quickly once this had begun. She had sensed his annoyance that he had not lasted longer. However, it was good. There were more things he had intended to do to her, acts that he would want to perform in the future – unfinished business, left until the hunger returned.

Now her throat felt raw and swollen from the damage he'd inflicted on her and she massaged it slowly, fighting down the tears that were close to the surface. She had only two minutes, three at the most, before he would reappear. She searched the living room quickly, seeking a place near the phone where a listening device might remain unnoticed. She'd already planned where to place the device, on the underside of the shelf beneath the TV that housed his DVD player. It would be well below Cleary's eye-line and in deep shadow. She returned to the bed and sat on the edge of it lightly. Cleary reappeared from the bathroom a minute later. The easy manner of earlier had gone, and he wouldn't catch her eye. He wanted her to leave.

'I'd like to take a shower,' she said quickly. 'I won't be long.' She needed the harsh caress of scalding water over her skin, to scrub herself clean of all traces of him. She couldn't bear the thought of travelling home with traces of him still on her.

'Go ahead,' he shrugged.

She locked the door and turned the powerful shower to maximum, relishing the fierce needles that would erode all trace of him from her tainted flesh. When she emerged from the bathroom, fully dressed again, only her hair wet, he had a whisky in his hand.

'You can pay me now,' she said.

He took a roll of notes from his breast pocket and handed it to her. She didn't bother to count it, knowing it would be correct. She pocketed the roll and strode to the door.

'Wait,' Cleary ordered. 'How can I reach you again?'

'Get my number from the review theatre,' she said, pulling the door shut behind her.

Friedrichstrasse, West Berlin, 1989

Mariana pushed through the shoppers on the busy Friedrichstrasse and took a seat in the café opposite Svetlana. They were in the Western zone but from the outside the café was indistinguishable from those further along Friedrichstrasse in the Eastern zone. The difference was the smell. The waft of damp raincoats was the same in any café at that time of year, but here it mingled with fresh waffles, good Italian coffee and smooth Western cigarettes instead of the acrid Eastern brands. The place was busy and the hum of conversation constant, making it safer to talk openly without fear of eavesdropping.

The small colour TV at the end of the counter was tuned to West German News. It was replaying footage from Gorbachev's recent visit to East Germany – unimaginable scenes of the Soviet president being greeted like a saviour by ordinary East Germans. Mariana watched in disbelief as they waved and shouted to him: 'Gorby, save us!'

'Listen to those fools,' Svetlana said icily. 'The West adores him, treating him like some sort of movie star, and now the East Germans think he's going to help them.' Her lip curled down in disdain at the sight of Gorbachev shaking hands with an endless line of stiff German dignitaries, his jovial manner out of place among the stern Teutonic faces.

'Maybe he will,' Mariana said lightly.

'Nonsense. *Glasnost, Perestroika* – what does he think they will achieve? The man is the worst kind of fool,' Svetlana hissed.

'What kind is that?'

'The kind that thinks he can change the world.'

'Maybe he can.'

Svetlana snorted in disdain at the notion.

'You don't think we could do with some changes?' Mariana said.

Svetlana stared hard at her and she returned her gaze evenly. The days when Svetlana intimidated her were gone. Five years had passed since her first mission in France. Svetlana had returned to her former duties, too valuable an agent in her own right to remain a handler for a young protégé. Mariana had worked with a new handler, an older male agent named Chopiak. They had completed four successful missions together in Washington, Rome, Helsinki and Santiago de Cuba before Chopiak had been forced to retire due to ill health. Svetlana had been brought in to act as her handler in Berlin and Mariana had found she didn't mind. In the most dangerous mission of her life she needed someone she trusted and she needed the best. Svetlana was both.

'The Soviet Union needs order, not chaos,' Svetlana said with a shrug.

'Our system is run by a political mafia,' she replied.

'That mafia maintains order,' Svetlana answered. 'What does it matter if a few of them get rich along the way?'

'It's not the theft that bothers me so much as the hypocrisy. All the talk of moral superiority while they line their own pockets, and those at the top have the deepest pockets of all.'

'You're a romantic at heart,' Svetlana said with a wry smile. 'You always were.'

'Then what do you believe in?' she asked Svetlana.

'I believe Gorbachev's reforms will lead our country into anarchy. The system will collapse. And who'll remain in charge when the dust settles? The mafia, that's who. Those people will always run our country one way or another.'

Mariana examined the face of the woman she had once admired and feared in equal measure. Now, after so many successful missions of her own, she was no longer in awe of her one-time teacher. Svetlana was just an agent like any other. When Chopiak had informed her that Svetlana would be her handler in Berlin she'd protested, but Chopiak had set her straight. She should be pleased, Svetlana was the best. And when she'd been briefed on her target in Berlin, she'd understood why the best had been assigned to her. To target a scientist or an industrialist was one thing. To target a CIA chief was quite another. Colonel James Cleary was an old hand, a pro – a 'spook' as the Americans called it – and a good one. In the past Cleary had run agents in Sophia, Budapest, Warsaw and Moscow. In Berlin he had agents in the police, the army, even in the KGB. The East German Secret Police, the *Stasi*, had tried for years to turn him with bribery and blackmail, but Cleary had proved immune. In recent years Cleary had uncovered four East German agents who had penetrated high into NATO command, positions so secret that his information could only have come from within the *Stasi* or The Organisation itself.

She and Svetlana had spent weeks studying Cleary from a distance, reading the files amassed on him over the years and devising an entry route to the man and what he knew. That background research had been vital, but now she had the final piece of the puzzle, the most important piece. She had spoken with him, touched him, and been privy to his innermost fantasies. Only she could confirm if their initial assessment had been correct.

'So tell me about Cleary,' Svetlana said with forced brightness.

Mariana smiled thinly. 'Our initial assessment was correct. He can't be bribed, blackmailed or seduced by normal means. The best I can hope for is to maintain his interest sexually. If I can return to his house, I can plant a listening device near his phone. It might give us some clues to his agent in the Stasi.'

'It's risky,' Svetlana exhaled. 'His house is swept regularly for bugs. It might be discovered. Is there no other way? You don't think he'll fall in love with you and give up the information voluntarily?'

'No.'

'What makes you so sure?'

'He's dead inside.'

Svetlana sipped her tea and held the cup close to her lips as she spoke, 'You're sure?'

'I am. He won't fall in love with me. And he will never betray his country. But he will want me back.'

'Why?'

'Because there are few women who could withstand the way he likes to have sex. This was the first time for us and it was over quickly. Even so, it was brutal.'

'I can see,' Svetlana said, eying the fresh bruising around her cheeks and on her forearms. She lowered the cup carefully onto the saucer and frowned. 'I'm sorry you had to go through that.'

'It's no problem, you trained me well.'

'Even so…' Svetlana frowned.

'I can take care of myself, but thank you for your concern.'

'He bought your cover story?'

'Yes.'

'He'll investigate you, but don't worry, your background is watertight. The paperwork's in place. Every document is genuine,' Svetlana smiled reassuringly.

Mariana looked away. Svetlana was enjoying the hunt. It was something she'd never learned to do herself. Her only fulfillment was in playing the most elegant strokes to achieve victory. But Svetlana, she knew, relished the deadly games they played.

'Do you have the device we spoke about?' she asked. She expected Svetlana to reach into her handbag and produce it but instead Svetlana opened her hand to reveal a transmitter no bigger than her fingertip.

'The latest from our specialists,' Svetlana said. 'They say it operates at a frequency the CIA scanners won't pick up.'

She took the bug and examined it in her cupped hand. It weighed almost nothing. One side was covered with removable tape so it could be stuck on the underside of a table or shelf. She put it in her pocket and rose to leave.

'I almost forgot, Vasili sends his greetings,' Svetlana smiled.

'He's well?' she asked casually.

'Very well, he tells me.'

'Please send him my love,' Mariana smiled.

*

She sat alone in the basement flat in Kurfurstendamm, nursing a cup of instant coffee in a chipped yellow mug. The tiny kitchenette had only two rings and one small cupboard. There was no room for anything else. In the cupboard was a small loaf of rye bread, some Danish salami and a jar of pickles. She would have enjoyed milk in her coffee, but there was no fridge in her apartment. The irony of her situation wasn't lost on her. She was living in the West now, in one of the most exclusive districts of West Berlin, yet she was no better off than when she'd lived with Grigory in Leningrad.

Each night she waited for the phone call that she knew was coming. Her only company was the TV set that showed endless old American movies and German soaps, quiz shows and news of growing unrest in East Germany. Since Gorbachev's visit, the East Germans had been demanding change. Hungary had opened its border with Austria. Thousands of East Germans had flooded through the gap to the West. And thousands more had taken to the streets in Leipzig, Dresden and East Berlin.

Mariana watched the latest demonstration, the biggest yet. An uneasy stand-off existed between the Volkspolizei and the half-million demonstrators outside the town hall on Alexanderplatz. It was strange to think it was all taking place less than a kilometre away on the other side of the wall. The picture zoomed in on the East German riot police waiting with batons drawn before the ragged crowd. In one scene, replayed over and over, a demonstrator and a riot-policeman spoke amicably. The demonstrator even lit a cigarette for the riot-policeman, who smoked it happily with his visor raised as they surveyed the scene like comrades in arms. Then somewhere unseen the order to disperse the crowd must have been given. The policeman tossed the cigarette aside and lowered his visor slowly to give the demonstrator time to get away. The scene cut to an overhead shot of a police charge, followed by close-up footage of batons falling on citizens and bodies being bundled into waiting vans.

The phone rang, startling her. It could only be Cleary. The

number had only been given out to the theatre where they had met. She breathed slowly to steady her nerves.

'Guten Abend.'

'Mariana?'

'Who is this?' she demanded, switching to English.

'I think you know.'

His voice was soft, purring, playful again, as it had been the first time.

'Maybe you could remind me?' she said, not wishing to make it too easy. A hunter needed to enjoy the chase.

'Jim Cleary. We met a few weeks ago in the review bar,' he said, playing along.

'Yes, I remember you,' she said. 'How can I help you, Jim?'

'I thought we could meet again.'

'Can you come to the Western sector?' she asked, knowing the answer.

'That would be difficult. Perhaps you could come here?'

She was silent before answering. 'This time it will be two thousand Marks.'

'That's a lot of money,' he said, the first signs of annoyance in his voice.

'Last time things got quite physical. What did you have in mind tonight?'

'I thought we could pick up where we left off,' he said casually.

'That's what I imagined. And that will be two thousand.'

He exhaled. 'Do you need me to collect you?'

'No, but remind me of your address.'

Cleary gave his address and she replaced the receiver without a word.

She took a long shower. Sitting in front of the mirror with

her hair brushed back and no make-up, she saw a face many called beautiful. To her it was the face of a woman she barely knew, a stranger, and there was fear behind the eyes that stared back at her. She took up a make-up brush and began to apply the smooth, easy strokes that would recreate the face of Mariana – the rise of the cheekbone, the curve of the jawline, the shadow around the eye. She worked steadily for half an hour. It was work she usually enjoyed, in the way a craftsman enjoys turning clay pots or carving ornaments, in the way a warrior enjoys cleaning, oiling and sharpening his weapons. The blood red lips were done now, the picture almost complete. The eyeliner pencil hovered close to her eye. A tremor in her hand made her stop. This had never happened before. She breathed out slowly and allowed her hand to rest on the dressing table before bringing the pencil to her eye once more. The tremor was gone. She worked quickly before it could return.

Stadtmitte, East Berlin, 1989

The border crossing into the East had taken longer than usual. A large crowd of West Germans had gathered at Checkpoint Charlie in support of their East German cousins who were demonstrating on the other side of the wall. Mariana walked north on Friedrichstrasse towards the underground station at Stadtmitte. Helicopters circled overhead, filming the growing crowds in the streets around her. She saw the faces of the *Volkspolizei* – the People's Police – taut and pale in the harsh lamplight. She descended swiftly into the U-Bahn and caught the train north to Pankow.

Emerging from the underground thirty minutes later, she was struck by the stillness of the northern suburb compared with the milling streets of the centre. Only the pretty linden trees on Berlinerstrasse moved in the faint evening breeze as she made her way to Cleary's home.

He opened the door with a smile. She stepped inside and waited for him to remove her coat. He hesitated, knowing that to do so would be to abdicate a small but vital amount of power to her. She waited, knowing she needed to establish some control at the outset, before they began the next round of Cleary's brutal fantasy. He took her coat and hung it on a hook.

'Do you want a drink?' he asked. 'Scotch... Bourbon... Cognac... Vodka?'

'Scotch, a small one,' she said, needing the hit to steel herself for what she knew lay ahead. He poured two neat measures and raised his glass in a silent toast before downing it in one go. 'What do you have in mind tonight, Jim?' she asked.

'I thought we could play it by ear,' he replied.

'I find it useful to establish certain parameters before we begin, to avoid misunderstandings.'

'We already agreed your fee, which is extortionate, by the way,' he said coldly. 'What else is there to discuss?'

'There's plenty to discuss,' she said, placing her glass firmly on the glass coffee table beside her and pressing it down with her fingers.

'For two thousand West-marks, I think I get to call the shots,' Cleary said sharply.

'You do, up to a point,' she answered quickly. 'I know you like it rough,' she began.

'I think you like it too,' he cut in.

'What I like is irrelevant. There are certain realities to consider. My body and my face are my livelihood,' she paused, looking him in the eye. 'No fists on my face or body, no broken bones, no tools or implements of any sort on my body, or inside it. And if you want to come inside me, you need to use a condom.'

Cleary blew out a long breath. 'Jesus Mariana, I think you're over-reacting. I'm not into that kinda extreme stuff, really I'm not.'

'I just wanted to be clear before we begin,' she smiled.

'Fine, but there is one thing I'd like to do,' he said slowly, the hint of a smile on his lips. 'I'd like to bind you – your hands and feet.'

She stared at him for a long moment. She could escape most bonds in seconds – she'd been taught by Svetlana – but she needed him to think she was considering it.

'You have bondage equipment?' she asked finally.

'No, I don't own that sort of stuff,' he said with a shrug.

'But I have some rope kicking around.'

'Okay,' she nodded slowly.

'Great,' he said, rising.

'You should have mentioned it on the phone,' she smiled. 'I would have brought some.'

'Maybe next time,' he grinned.

*

An hour later, Cleary was showering in the bathroom. Mariana had been left gagged and bound on the floor in his hurry to cleanse himself and as punishment for her earlier attempts at taking control.

She waited until she heard the bathroom door click shut. Her back and ribs ached from where he had struck her, but this pain was nothing compared to the ache inside her. Cleary had finished his painful games by sodomising her, and she wanted nothing more than to lie still and hold onto the feeling of shame and humiliation that threatened to gush from her in a river of tears. Instead she knelt up and loosened the rope around her feet. She blinked, trying to clear her vision. Cleary had been as good as his word and he'd not punched her, but he'd slapped her hard enough to leave her with tunnel vision. Her hands trembled as she worked the rope loose, just loose enough to slip her feet from their bond. She stood, not bothering to remove the gag or the rope around her wrists, there was no need and it would only waste precious seconds. She felt an overwhelming urge to gather up her clothes and run into the street. She could see rain falling outside – how good it would feel to have the rain cleanse her of all traces of him – but instead she reached for her jacket and took the tiny transmitter concealed in the lining. She had five minutes at most, ample time to do what she needed.

Cleary emerged from the bathroom to find her lying on the bed in the position he'd left her in, her hands and feet tightly bound. He knelt beside her and removed the gag. She proffered her hands in supplication and he untied the rope around her wrists. She said nothing as Cleary worked with steady efficiency, focusing on the knots and never once looking at her.

She wanted to go, to run, but she fought the urge. Cleary must suspect nothing. She needed to act as before. 'I need to take a shower,' she said as he untied her feet. 'I won't be long, I promise.'

Cleary nodded. 'You know where it is.'

She turned the temperature as hot as it would go, scalding her skin, until the redness of her welts and the gathering bruises blended with the rest of her, if only for a short time. When she stepped out of the shower, the bathroom mirror was misted over. She wiped her hand across the glass and brought her face close. Her reflection was visible in the stripes left by her fingertips. Her left eye looked a little puffed and there was a cut on her lip. She needed to repair her face before she left. A black eye might get noticed. A cut lip might be investigated. It might compromise her mission. She filled the sink with cold water and held her face beneath the surface. She was reminded of Dimitriev and the time during the long Siberian winter when he'd taken her training to new levels: sleep deprivation, choking, drowning. She recalled his hard hands on the back of her neck as he'd held her head in a sink of icy water. She recalled him seated behind her on the hard gymnasium floor, his arms encircled her neck, his legs locked around her waist.

He had applied the 'sleeper' strangle and she had resisted, tensing the muscles in her neck to prevent them from collapsing under the pressure. She recalled the sensation of his hard body against her back, the awful life-crushing power of his arms, the sweet, acrid smell of his sweat in her nostrils, the prickle of his dark stubble on her cheek, the heat of his breath on her neck. Alone together in that dimly lit gymnasium, their bodies entwined in this subtle exercise of pain, she had never felt closer to anyone. She had never wanted any man so badly, and never known such despair, that she should love the one man she could never possess.

She heard the telephone ring in the lounge and rose from the basin of cold water. She put her ear to the door but could hear no more than a murmur from Cleary's conversation. She reapplied her make-up swiftly. Something was wrong. It was the tone in his voice when he'd spoken on the phone. She felt it strongly and she'd learned to trust her instincts a long time ago. She pulled on her slacks and buttoned her blouse, listening for Cleary's movements in the next room. She heard a drawer opening and shutting.

She stepped through the door swiftly, her hands tying up her hair behind her head. Cleary smiled but it was not the smile of a happy man, rather it was the smile of a hunter who had cornered his prey. She smiled too, taking the opportunity to get three steps closer before he raised his revolver.

'I found this,' he said, holding up the transmitter in his left hand. 'It wasn't here before you came.'

'What is it?' she said, coming closer to look.

'Stop where you are!' he ordered, aiming the revolver at her face.

Her eyes filled with tears. 'I can explain,' she began. 'The

Stasi, they made me …'

'Don't,' he interrupted. 'You're a Soviet agent in my home. That's all I need. I'm within my rights to shoot you, so tell me everything now if you want to live.'

A sob of terror burst from her lips. Cleary hadn't expected her to break down like this. She collapsed. As she did her hand descended from behind her head. A weighted hairpin flashed silver and embedded itself deep in his throat. He was so shocked by the dull thud and the surprising lack of pain – pain would come later – that his finger froze momentarily on the trigger. He clutched at the pin with his left hand. The movement threw his aim off by two inches. He fired. Mariana surged forward to finish him. She felt the bullet graze her upper arm. Her right hand slammed into the flat back of the hairpin, driving it further into his flesh. Her left seized his pistol. He pulled the trigger again. The bullet went into the ceiling above them, the noise so close to her ear was deafening. She jerked the hairpin out and made to stab him in the eye but Cleary was combat-trained. He seized her wrist. They were locked face-to-face. She could hear the rasping in his throat as he struggled to breath. She drove her knee between his legs. Cleary grunted but knew not to let the pain deter him. If he did it would be his end. He compartmentalised it, setting it aside for later, and head-butted her. His hand drew her hand, still holding the pin, across his body to stab her other hand. Seeing his intent, she redirected the pin into his wrist. He stepped forwards and, taking her balance, drove his elbow into her face, stunning her. She stumbled back and lost her grip on his pistol. He pulled the trigger again, and the force of the shot made her lose all her senses. Her face was on fire. Falling, she wondered if it was the pain of a bullet in her skull. Was this her final moment? She was still wondering a moment later. She was not dead. She must fight on. Seizing Cleary's leg, she smashed her weight above his knee joint and the force sent him over onto his back. Another round went into the ceiling. Four had been fired in total. She spun away and was across the room in less than a second, but Cleary rolled swiftly onto one knee and had her in his sights.

'Stop.' The word came out little more than a hiss, the sound of blood bubbling in his throat. She was one step too far to make it to the door. He would put a neat hole through the centre of her back if she tried. She didn't want to be interrogated, to betray her country to this man, knowing he would kill her afterwards. She had no wish to go through that. She was about to take that final step when she felt a subtle draught of cold air from the hallway. Someone had entered the house. The door flew open and Svetlana stepped in, her pistol clasped in rock-steady hands, her face set hard and cold. Mariana was in her firing line. She pushed her aside as Cleary fired his remaining shots.

The bullets drove two ruinous paths through Svetlana's chest. Svetlana fired but her bullet missed Cleary by an inch, driven high by the impact of his shots. She hit the floor and stared at the ceiling in surprise.

Mariana heard Cleary reloading. She snatched up Svetlana's pistol and turned to kill him but Cleary's form was disappearing into the kitchen. She fired but her bullets thudded harmlessly into the doorframe. She held her aim on the door waiting for him to reappear. She wanted to see him, to shoot him, to end him.

He did not come.

She stole a glance at Svetlana. The life force was leaving her.

Mariana felt her heart go in her mouth. Svetlana's eyes were locked onto hers. She wanted to kneel and comfort her, to hold her, but Cleary could appear at any moment. She moved forward, her pistol trained on the kitchen door. She would have to deal with Cleary before she could save Svetlana.

'Wait!' Svetlana's voice was weak. 'Wait.'

She stopped and looked back at her one-time teacher, trainer, tormentor. Svetlana had given her life for her without a moment's hesitation. She wondered if she would have done the same for her. Her lip began to tremble.

'Don't cry Little One,' Svetlana whispered, a weak smile on her lips.

'I'll get you out of here,' she promised.

'No.' Svetlana's voice was suddenly stronger. 'Get yourself out of here. I'm already dead. Leave me. That is an order.'

'I won't.'

'Do it.'

The wail of sirens in the distance broke the stalemate.

'Go!' Svetlana said, her voice weak again. 'Go, please. I'm asking you. I'm begging you.'

'I won't leave you.'

'Drink a glass of Starka for me with Vasili,' Svetlana smiled.

'Be quiet! Save your breath,' she said harshly, waiting for Cleary so she could kill him. But Cleary had heard the sirens too. He knew his best chance was to wait for reinforcements.

'Go now, Tatiana Zykova. Do not disobey my final order.'

Svetlana's eyes pleaded, then fixed on a spot on the ceiling. Mariana watched as a shallow breath left her bloody chest for the last time. She saw the spirit ebb from her body and the emptiness of the flesh that remained. Then she was outside in the thin rain that stabbed at her like cold needles, running.

*

The safe house was a tiny apartment they'd rented four weeks earlier. It was located just five blocks from Cleary's home but the neighbourhood was a world apart from the pristine streets of Pankow. Mariana climbed the stairs in the dank, unlit building, not trusting the elevator at a time like this, and fumbled with her key at the door. Inside, she threw the bolt and attached the chain. The act was symbolic, no bolt or chain would prevent the Stasi from entering if they discovered her location.

She switched on the light. The flat was stark and cheaply furnished, but she and Svetlana had prepared it well. She wished Svetlana were with her now. Her iron will would have given her strength and security. But she was not and never would be again. She was alone now with no way back to The Organisation. She stumbled into the bathroom, her mind spinning. Cleary had seemed certain she was a Soviet spy rather than East German. Someone within The Organisation had telephoned Cleary, had betrayed her. She had no idea who. All she knew was there was no way back now.

She examined her face in the mirror. Her right cheek was blackened and her right eye almost closed from the powder burns of the pistol shot that had exploded inches from her face, but apart from the burn, there was no bullet wound on her face. Her arm was a different matter. She removed her coat and blouse carefully and examined her wound, gasped in pain as she washed away the blood. No bullet was lodged in her, it had cut through her flesh and ricocheted off the bone. She took the medical kit from the cupboard above the sink and swallowed a handful of the strong painkillers contained inside.

Next she sat in the empty bathtub – it would be easier to remove the blood later – and pressed the wound tightly, waiting for the painkillers to take effect.

After twenty minutes, she began to clean the wound, gasping in silent agony, desperate to scream but fearful of drawing attention from the neighbours. She applied a line of surgical glue to hold the skin together, then removed the needle from its sterile packaging and stitched as best she could with one hand. Finally she wrapped her arm in a fresh bandage and went into the kitchen. Ignoring the food supplies, she reached for the bottle of vodka and drank.

In the single bedroom was a small dressing table beside the wardrobe, the only furniture in the bare room apart from the bed itself. She opened the drawers and saw the tools of her trade that had been put in there some weeks earlier, the make-up and brushes, the wigs and jewellery. Beneath the linoleum of the middle drawer she found the blank identity cards and papers that would create her new identity now that her current skin had to be shed. Who would replace Mariana? She didn't know yet. It was too much to think about now. She sat heavily on the bed and lay back. The vodka mixed with the painkillers. Her head began to spin. She heard new sirens growing louder. She half expected the sound of heavy boots in the stairwell, voices in the hall, the crash of the front door, brutal hands dragging her away. Part of her would have welcomed the end to the loneliness of her existence. The sirens receded. She would have to continue.

Outside the combined forces of the CIA, the Stasi and The Organisation were scouring the streets of East Berlin for her, watching every station, every airport, every border crossing. It was a time to lay low, to rest and recover, to remain out of sight until the maelstrom abated and she could escape. But escape to where? She'd been betrayed by her own side. She couldn't stay in East Berlin, she couldn't return to Moscow. She was wanted by East and West now. She closed her eyes and felt herself cast adrift, floating in a warm sea, blown by the wind and taken by the ocean currents to... where?

She had no idea.

Checkpoint Charlie, Berlin Wall

Sergeant Albrecht Zimmermann entered the command hut and stood before Captain Holz's desk expectantly. Holz was on the phone, but Zimmermann could see he was on hold, as he had been twenty minutes earlier. He looked out of the window at the growing crowd and shifted his weight uncomfortably. Something would have to be decided soon.

As a *Grepo* – 'Grenzpolizei' border guard – Zimmermann had seen his fair share of incidents on the Berlin Wall. He'd discovered refugees hiding in the boots of cars or clinging on the undersides of lorries. He'd shot at graffiti artists daubing paint on the wall (though his aim was never very accurate on such occasions). He'd even pulled frogmen from the canal running between East and West, but he'd never expected to see what he saw now. The wall that had been a permanent feature of his city ever since he could remember was coming down before his eyes. He looked again at Captain Holz. The once-fearsome Holz seemed to be watching the event unfolding around them with equal surprise and helplessness. Holz had telephoned headquarters repeatedly seeking orders, but no one would take responsibility for the situation.

The crowd outside the command hut had begun to arrive after a press conference earlier in the day when Günter Schabowski, a government spokesman, had promised a relaxation of border controls to ease the pressure in the city. Asked when this would take effect, the ill-prepared Schabowski had replied 'Immediately.' The citizens of East Berlin had taken Schabowski at his word and arrived in their thousands to visit their cousins in the West. Fortunately the mood of the crowd was upbeat and festive. They had waited over forty years for this moment and they didn't mind waiting a little longer. They knew the potential danger of pressuring the border guards all too well.

'Captain, the crowd is growing every minute. Should we let them through?' Zimmermann asked loudly.

Holz rested the receiver down slowly on his desk. He looked up at Zimmermann with a frown. 'Ten minutes ago I spoke to HQ. They said no action will be taken against those wishing to cross the border. I'm trying to get that confirmed now.'

'If no action will be taken, then we should let them through,' Zimmermann said with studied care. Holz nodded, knowing Zimmermann was right. His instincts were telling him the same thing. It was time to let the crowd through before things turned ugly. He didn't want the blood of his own countrymen on his hands. He replaced the receiver and gave Zimmermann a single nod of agreement.

It was all Zimmermann needed. He left the hut and raised the barrier to a roar of approval by the crowd. They surged through the border, flashing their identity cards so quickly that there was no time to check them. The citizens who had once feared and reviled Zimmermann patted him good-naturedly on the back as they went through to be greeted on the other side like long lost brothers and sisters. Zimmermann could hear music playing and the sounds of a giant street party nearby. West Berliners came up to the border and sang happy songs. One handed him a beer and in this night unlike any other, Zimmermann accepted it and drank.

He saw Captain Holz receive a beer too and smiled at him. Holz shrugged and took a slug from the bottle. Neither recalled the paper pinned on the wall of the command hut marked 'Alert, Highest Priority' bearing the description of a wanted fugitive: female, late twenties, medium height, slim build, dark hair, attractive, bullet wounds to upper left arm and face. If they had, it would have made no difference. The woman described bore no resemblance to the woman passing by Zimmermann now. Only if they had stripped her and removed her make-up would they have seen the livid scar on her arm and the powder burn on her cheek. But they did nothing more than sip their beers as she passed by, just another jubilant Easterner passing through to the West.

LILIANA

Holland Park, London, 2000

Liliana Marshall emerged from the underground station at Holland Park and waited for the traffic to ease before crossing the busy Holland Park Avenue. She turned into a side street and the change was instant. This was the London of books and movies, of quiet mews and grand three-storey houses, of black iron gates, tall bay windows and climbing ivy, of gleaming cars and children with nannies. It was the London she'd imagined when she'd been a student – not at the Institute of Fine Art in Sarajevo as her papers suggested – but at an institute far to the north, where fine art was only one of the subjects she'd studied. Her papers said she was a refugee from the Bosnian Crisis, and that she'd arrived in Britain in 1992 with no ID of any sort, having left everything behind fleeing the war. She'd entered through the port of Dover with a large group of Bosnian refugees who had come via France and Germany. At the immigration centre she'd changed her name from Ljiljana Matijevich to Liliana Marshall to make things easier for the overworked clerk, and pronounced her first name 'Lily-Ana' to spare inflexible British tongues from running two syllables together.

On arriving in London she'd found work quickly, first as a cleaner, then as a waitress, then as a shop assistant in a series of ever more prestigious stores. Finally she'd seduced the owner of a small gallery in Pimlico specialising in Oriental art. He'd employed her as his assistant and she'd learned the trade with astonishing speed. Three years later she left him and set herself up as an independent art consultant specialising in Russian iconic art and Avant Garde. She quickly gained a long list of clients demanding her expertise in evaluating the art treasures that were fast emerging from the former Soviet Union. Her list included corporations in the USA and Germany, private collectors in France, Switzerland and Japan, and several so-called 'New Russians' who had made billions selling oil, gas, diamonds, arms and uranium on the newly-free markets of their motherland.

Liliana kept a small office in one of the quiet streets off the main avenue. It was in an old building but well maintained. Her office was kept clean and tidy while she was away, often for extended periods. Her telephone messages were carefully logged and her mail was always waiting for her in neat bundles, wrapped with a thick elastic band. The cost of this simple service was surprisingly high, she could have enjoyed a larger office and a similar service for half the price, but Liliana had chosen her location for reasons other than efficiency.

The receptionist looked up and smiled as she entered. 'Hello, Liliana,' she beamed. 'Lovely to see you again. Your mail's waiting for you and I've got your telephone messages whenever you're ready.'

And there was the reason: no questions about where she'd been, or what she'd been doing. No reasons for Liliana to invent a reply that might later be recalled, investigated, discredited. This level of discretion came at a premium, yet it was a price she could easily afford. She had just concluded another very large commission in the City of London and her fee had been paid into a numbered account in Switzerland.

The commission had been even easier than anticipated and her fee had been the largest yet. She returned the receptionist's smile.

'Hello, it's nice to be back.'

Mile End, London

Declan Capaldi was almost home. He'd had several pints after work with another of the journalists from The Times and he'd stopped to get fish and chips from the shop at the end of his road. When he emerged, he noticed a familiar looking man standing across the street, middle-aged and swarthy, fit-looking, tall and broad-shouldered. Capaldi wondered where he'd seen him before. He guessed the man lived nearby and he'd seen him on the street. His fish and chips smelled good. He was looking forward to eating them in front of the telly. He wondered whether to bother putting them on a plate, or simply to eat them from the paper that they were wrapped in. Eating from the paper meant there was no dish to wash afterwards. He decided to eat them from the paper. He fumbled his key in the door, turning it the wrong way several times before finally succeeding in opening it. As he stepped inside he was suddenly aware of someone behind him. He imagined it was one of the other tenants from the flats above, but when he turned it was the swarthy-looking man he'd seen across the street. Only then did it click where he'd seen him before. The man had been waiting outside The Times building when Capaldi had emerged earlier that evening. The same man had also been in the pub when he'd been drinking with his colleague. It was only now, when the man shoved him inside with shocking force that Capaldi finally realised the dreadful danger he was in.

'Be quiet and you'll live,' the man said in English, though he spoke with an accent, a Russian accent, Capaldi thought.

Christie's Auction House, London

Liliana Marshal emerged from Green Park underground and walked eastwards on Piccadilly beneath the grandiose arches of the Ritz. On the other side of the road were the offices of Aeroflot. She didn't glance in their direction. There was no reason a Bosnian art critic should pay the Russian airline any special attention. She turned into St James Street and continued down towards Pall Mall. This area of London was where the rich came from all over the world to play at being English gentry, taking tea in the Ritz and buying tweeds in Savile Row. She found the whole area faintly repulsive, a grotesque fairytale land filled with pantomime objects: gentlemen's shooting outfits, silver snuff boxes, shotguns, walking canes with swords inside. There were no prices in the windows and no friendly welcome upon entry. These were shops reserved for the right kind of people, people who knew someone who knew someone, who went to the right schools, the right universities, and the right clubs. It reminded her of home – not of Sarajevo, which she'd only visited as a tourist – but her real home, far to the north, where the elite had enjoyed similar shops reserved for their own private pleasure.

Liliana was going to Christie's Auction House to view a new painting that had come on the market recently, causing quite a stir. It was a Kandinsky, from his abstract period, one of the first purely abstract pieces ever painted in the world. She had been hired by a private collector from Russia who was eager to acquire it. He'd written to her, asking her to view the painting when it went on display at Christie's and, if she believed it to be authentic, to bid on his behalf up to a value of ten million pounds sterling. If the painting was being sold by Christie's it was unlikely to be a fraud, and with such a budget it was also unlikely she would be outbid.

She turned onto King Street and entered Christie's, climbing the wide sweeping staircase to the gallery. The idea of seeing the Kandinsky thrilled her, and the gallery on the upper floor was buzzing with similar anticipation. Scanning those present automatically, she took in everyone she'd expected to be there: the curators, the specialists, the collectors, the press, and the ordinary art enthusiasts who had come to simply stand before the Kandinsky. From the undercurrent in the room she knew the bidding would be ferocious, but ten million pounds was enough to see off all but the most determined bidder. She caught her reflection in a gilded mirror at the top of the stairs. She had no need to check how she looked, she knew the face, the body and the persona of Liliana Marshall so well by now – the long dark hair that was never quite tidy, the thick black glasses that made her eyes look small, the hastily-applied make-up that meant her face seemed to lack definition. Her skin was pale and smooth, her teeth less than brilliant white, the result of years of smoking, although she had quit now, and a capped metal tooth was visible on the upper right side when she smiled, a reminder of the cheap dental work she'd never got round to fixing. The ill-fitting trouser suit gave her a shapeless, almost masculine outline. Liliana's straight-talking manner was not everyone's cup of tea, especially in England where people rarely said what they thought, and even more so in the art world that was built on flattery, hot air, and puffery. Yet there were others who admired her for exactly those reasons, and none more so than her clients, who valued her forthright approach in an arena where it was often difficult to get a straight answer.

The curator in charge of the auction was Amy Richardson. Amy had positioned herself at the entrance to ensure she could greet the attendees personally. When Liliana appeared on the staircase she hurried to greet her. Liliana had been a valuable client over the years and as a specialist in Russian art, she was also a potential bidder.

'Liliana, darling! We called your number several times. I'm so glad you could make it.'

'I've been away,' Liliana said. 'But I'm back now.'

Amy beamed. 'And might I ask if you're an interested party?'

It was poor form to ask a consultant such a direct question, but Amy knew Liliana well enough to know she would not object.

'I'm always interested in a Kandinsky,' Liliana answered. It was all Amy needed.

'Let me show it to you...' Amy said, taking her arm. 'It's simply staggering...'

'No,' Liliana said, extricating her arm with surprising ease. 'I prefer to view it alone. And you have your guests to greet,' she said, treating Amy to a winning smile to make up for the rebuff.

'Of course,' Amy smiled, returning to her post at the top of the staircase.

Liliana headed for the bar, scanning the crowd as she went. There were already forty-seven people in the gallery. Twenty-one of them she knew. Twenty-six were strangers. She logged each new face into her memory and placed each in a likely category: 'dealer', 'collector', 'artist', 'art-lover', marking each in terms of threat level, noting size and weight, physical presence, persona. She was unlikely to encounter a real threat in a place like Christie's, but old habits die hard.

She took a glass of champagne and went to stand before the Kandinsky. She'd seen it in plenty of books and periodicals, but that was no substitute for the real thing. To stand before the canvas that had been touched by the artist himself, and the paint, mixed and applied by his own hand moved her as few things could. The canvas contained the soul of the artist, and the soul of an artist like Kandinsky was that of a seer, one who saw the world in a unique way, a way that others would follow years later, though never better. The painting was undoubtedly an original. There was no need for sophisticated testing and authenticating, she had seen countless examples of Kandinsky's work before, and this was his, unquestionably. Painted at the height of his genius, after making the final leap from abstracted forms to purely abstract images, the first of its kind anywhere in the world. She felt herself profoundly moved by the painting.

A sharp scratch on her arm brought her back to reality. She turned. It was not a face she had logged earlier, however it was one she knew, albeit different now. The needle had punctured her skin at the one moment when her mind had been elsewhere. Few people in the world would have known to strike then. Only one she could think of and he was here now. He must have followed her inside, waited downstairs while she surveyed the crowd, and come up only when he knew she would be distracted by the painting. His timing was as perfect as it had always been. In another second she would feel faint. Her motor skills would become severely impaired. She would lose the power of speech. Her legs would buckle beneath her. Within fifteen seconds she would be incoherent.

'You.'

Her lips were already slack. She felt spittle on her chin.

His face was more tanned than she remembered, the hair a little greyer, but still thick and short, cropped closer to his scalp now. The thin gold-rimmed glasses made him look distinguished. His clothes were expensive, Italian silk suit, tailored English shirt and polished brown brogues, a thin Mackintosh with pockets deep enough to conceal a needle with ease. 'The avant-garde artists had more in common with the old icon painters than one might think,' he said amiably in the perfect, stylised old-world English that was so commonly heard in the galleries of West London.

She did her best to strike him, to shout to the idiots standing around her like rocks, unaware. She was furious with them for not seeing what was happening. She dropped her glass. Her legs deserted her. He caught her arm, turning with an apologetic smile to those around them. 'Oh dear, I think Lily's had a little too much champagne.'

Amy Richardson appeared at her side, anxious to help. She and the Russian sat Liliana in a leather armchair in the corner of the room. The well-spoken Russian thanked Amy politely, talking quietly, discreetly. 'It's my fault,' he confessed. 'I insisted on meeting Lily for drinks before we arrived, even though she wasn't feeling well. She told me she's taking antibiotics but I insisted. I was so excited about the Kandinsky.'

Amy smiled at the stranger. Anyone who could bid on the Kandinsky was a man of considerable means – one she'd wish to do business with again.

'Look,' he continued, his expression pained, 'Why don't I get her home? My driver's outside. It's the simplest way.'

'Perhaps we should call an ambulance?' Amy said half-heartedly – the idea of paramedics in her gallery held little appeal.

'I really don't think it's necessary,' he assured her. 'But if she's not feeling better by the time she gets home, I'll take her to the hospital. It's the least I can do under the circumstances.'

Liliana stirred in her seat and threw her head forward, trying to rise, but her legs refused to carry her and she slumped forward. She slurred a sentence, the words starting quietly and getting louder. They were incomprehensible, but loud enough to draw more attention from across the room. A line of spittle dripped from her chin into her lap.

'Lily will be deeply embarrassed by this,' the Russian said urgently. 'Please, I think it's best for all concerned if I get her out of here discreetly, don't you agree?'

Amy was unsure. The Russian handed her a card. She didn't recognise the name, but it was Russian, and the quality of the card told her everything she needed to know.

'Give me your card and I'll call you later this evening to reassure you,' the Russian said. The statement was no longer a request, but a command. Amy handed over her card. The Russian smiled, then gripped Liliana by the shoulders and raised her from the chair. She could barely walk, but Amy was surprised to see the Russian was able to guide her quite easily from the gallery and down the stairs with one arm around her waist. She'd never known Liliana to drink too much before, but people were strange. They had their secrets, and perhaps Liliana's was drink. If it was, she wouldn't be the only person in the art world with such a secret.

Harlesden, North London

She tried to move and failed. A wave of nausea came over her and she was sick. The thin liquid splashed down onto her chest. Her hand moved to wipe herself and failed. She was bound to a chair. She spat to clear her mouth, but vomit remained in her nasal passage, and the smell made her gag again. Years of training kicked in, and she took hold of her breathing, working around the panic and concentrating on longer, slower breaths, feeling her heart-rate slowing as she did. The thudding in her chest receded, allowing her mind to assess her situation rationally.

She'd been taken by Dimitriev. Even knowing his abilities as she did, she was surprised at how easily he'd done it. She surveyed her surroundings. She was on the ground-floor of a house, empty of everything save the chair she was on and the thick, rough curtains that had been drawn across the window. It was daylight outside, but she had no idea of the time. She looked down to examine herself. She was seated on a heavy chair, and bound so firmly that she knew there was little point in straining against her bonds. The Organisation was expert in securing its victims for interrogation. It was the secret nightmare of every agent, to find the tables turned, to be the interrogated instead of the interrogator, the accused instead of the accuser. She felt the panic threaten once more, and forced herself to change her thinking, to consider every option for escape, no matter how small. She needed to believe it was possible to reason with Dimitriev, to play on a closeness they had once shared long ago.

Dimitriev hadn't covered her head or gagged her. It was a

good sign – a sign that he wanted to talk, at least to begin with. He appeared with a kit bag and a bucket of water. He cleaned her face with a damp cloth, then wiped the vomit from her blouse. 'I'm sorry I had to bring you here in such a way,' he said quietly.

'You didn't have to,' she said. 'I would have come with you. We needed to talk.'

'I didn't want to take that chance.' His tone was distant, clinical. It was a bad sign.

'How did you find me?' she asked, hoping to begin a conversation, a connection, any connection to her would-be interrogator, her potential executioner.

'I saw your picture in the newspaper,' he answered, matter-of-fact. 'Letting yourself be photographed – it was a serious mistake. After that, I spoke to the journalist who wrote the original article about Havilland Ethical. He wasn't hard to find.'

'Capaldi? He knew nothing about me.'

'Capaldi knew who hired you.'

'He had no idea.'

'He guessed – correctly, as it turned out – once I persuaded him to try.' Dimitriev unzipped the kit bag revealing pliers, a chisel, a scalpel, and the handgrip of what looked like a Glock pistol. 'I showed him how freedom of speech has a different meaning where we come from. After that, I simply followed the trail, until I found you.'

'What do you want to know?' she asked quietly.

'I want to know what happened in Berlin, before you betrayed your country.'

'I didn't betray my country. My country betrayed me.'

'You should know better than to try and evade my

questions, Tatiana Zykova. Tell me quickly and make this easier for both of us.'

'You'll kill me afterwards.'

'Yes. But tell me quickly and your death will be swift and painless, that much I promise you.'

'For old time's sake?'

'Something like that.'

'Do you remember how we used to dance together, Vasili?' she smiled, reliving the memory – a happy memory. 'I loved dancing with you.'

'And I loved dancing with my wife.'

She swallowed hard. Dimitriev was right. Svetlana had died because of her. 'If I knew who betrayed us, don't you think I would have said something, got a message to you? The truth is I don't know. It could have been anyone in The Organisation. It could have been you.'

'Perhaps you don't know anything. Or perhaps you just wanted out. You'd had enough of doing your duty for the motherland. You forgot there's no 'out' in our line of work.'

'Things have changed Vasili. The world has changed.'

'Some things never change.'

'I don't have an answer for you,' she said quietly.

'Don't make this difficult,' he said, his voice lower, menacing. He took the scissors from his bag. She closed her eyes, preparing for the first cut, but he only cut away her blouse, discarding it on the floor, then snipped through her bra and removed it too.

'A victim who feels naked is more likely to confess,' she said, citing an interrogation fact well known to The Organisation. 'Do you really think that being naked will worry me, Vasili? After all the training I was given?'

'Your body's still beautiful. A shame to disfigure it,' he said, taking a packet of Benson & Hedges cigarettes and a box of matches from his kit bag. He lit a cigarette and, she noticed, inhaled deeply. He was steadying his nerves for what he was about to do. He didn't want to hurt her. That was important, it could save her life. She had to change his mind now. Once the torture began, she was more likely to end up dead. A tortured victim becomes less than human, easier to kill.

'This is your last chance to die cleanly,' he said, seizing her hair suddenly, the speed of his hand and the power of his grip as shocking as it had always been. He was close to her now, close enough that if she were to attempt an escape, now was the time, but Dimitriev's face and neck were out of her reach and any attempt to bite him would have been fruitless, merely angering him. He brought the cigarette close to her breast. She could feel the first prickling of the heat on her skin, a sensation that would soon be amplified a thousand times.

'Torture me and I'll give you names, all sorts of names, as many names as you want Vasili, but they won't be the right names. I don't have a name. But let me go and I'll tell you what I know, I swear. We can work together to make things right.'

'You're right,' he smiled, stepping away and throwing the cigarette aside. Reaching into his bag he pulled out the pistol – a Glock as she'd thought – and held it to her temple.

'Tell me or don't tell me, it's up to you. Either way, you're going to die. Tell me and I'll avenge Svetlana's death and your betrayal. It's up to you.'

'I have no wish for revenge. I left that life behind a long time ago.'

'You can never leave it behind.'

'I did.'

'And you make a living now doing what?'

'I make money. No one dies.'

'George Petersen died.'

She blinked 'I didn't imagine he'd kill himself.'

'Last chance,' Dimitriev said quietly. 'If not for yourself, then for Svetlana. She loved you.'

'I know,' she said. 'But I won't tell you for Svetlana. I'll tell you for you. If it will bring you some peace, I will tell you, Vasili.'

He waited, the gun still at her temple.

'Cleary got a phone call just minutes after I planted the listening device. That call alerted him to the device, and to me.'

'Are you sure? Did you hear the conversation?'

'No, but I felt it, Vasili – like you taught me to feel, to listen to my feelings. It was the call that alerted him to the transmitter, I know it.'

Vasili nodded grimly. 'Go on.'

'When he confronted me, he knew I was working for the Soviet Union, not the East Germans. The call must have come from someone within The Organisation.'

'There were only three people who knew about your operation,' Dimitriev said. 'You, Svetlana and Gavrilovich, the East Berlin station chief.'

'If Gavrilovich knew about it from the start, why did he wait until that moment to inform Cleary? Someone else must have found out. Someone who only realised when the transmitter signal went live. Someone in Signals, perhaps.'

'There was only one man monitoring the listening device for security reasons and that was Prokop,' Dimitriev said. 'But Prokop knew no details of your operation.'

'It doesn't matter,' she replied. 'When the transmitter went live he recognised Cleary's voice. If Prokop was Cleary's source inside The Organisation, he would have spoken with him. He realised it was Cleary who was being monitored and contacted him immediately to alert him.'

Dimitriev's mind was racing, but Liliana's was faster and put his thoughts in order for him. 'Prokop called immediately so Cleary could say he'd caught me planting the transmitter. It was a quick way to stop the operation in its tracks. Prokop was Cleary's mole.'

Dimitriev's face turned pale.

'What is it?' she asked. She'd never seen Dimitriev like this before.

'Prokop is a General now,' Dimitriev said slowly, the thoughts tumbling one after another as he spoke, 'He is the Head of the Sixth Directorate. He knows about my mission. He knows everything.'

A tinkle of breaking glass in the next room. A thud. A canister rolling. Dimitriev launched himself across the room and rolled to the door, slamming it shut just as it exploded to slow the penetration of the gas. The window erupted in a hail of bullets, shredding the heavy curtains and sending glass flying across the threadbare carpet. Liliana threw herself on her side, the heavy chair hit by two bullets and splintering beneath her. She looked up at Dimitriev. He'd led the traitor to her, and if he didn't kill her himself, the traitor's assassins would. Dimitriev aimed the gun at her head once more.

'Do it, Vasili,' she pleaded. 'Don't leave me to them.'

More bullets erupted, thudding into the worn carpet inches from where she lay. From the patterns of the gunshots, there were two submachine guns being fired into their window. Only the rapidly disintegrating curtain meant the shooters weren't targeting them directly. Prokop had sent an Alpha team to take her and Dimitriev down together, and sever all links to his betrayal. Two more were entering the house now from the back, one would be watching the side for escape, and one guarding the vehicle in which they would later get away.

Dimitriev frowned, his finger tightened on the trigger. She closed her eyes. Then she felt her bonds being severed quickly by his utility knife and his powerful grip dragging her to her feet.

Metropolitan Police Headquarters, London

'Multiple gunshots at Drapers Road, Harlesden.'

Aisha Obaru's emergency switchboard was alight with waiting calls, but she'd already heard enough to alert the Armed Response Unit. Her call was taken by specialist firearms officer Max Gerard and moments later three flame red BMWs were on their way to Drapers Road. Each vehicle carried three officers armed with the standard-issue Glock 17 pistols and contained two Heckler and Koch MP5 semi-automatic carbines in the boot.

'Details,' Max demanded.

'Neighbour across the street called it in,' Aisha told him. 'Two others callers have confirmed it. Reports vary from two to six men outside a detached house at the end of the road. The first caller said he saw six men getting out of a blue van. He didn't get the number plate. I asked him to call back if he can get it without putting himself in danger. The second caller saw four men burst into the house. She heard two explosions and gunfire, both single shots and machine gun fire. The third caller said he heard explosions and gunfire, and saw two armed men at the back of the house.'

'Sounds like a gangland thing, drugs war, probably, fighting over territory.'

'The first caller also said he heard the men talking in a foreign language. I asked if he knew which one. He said he didn't recognise it. It wasn't French or German, but it might have been Russian.'

'Good to know, thank you. Keep me updated, I'm on my way,' Max said.

'Good luck with this one,' Aisha said. 'It sounds like the Wild West out there.'

'More like the Wild East,' Max said, reaching for his keys and his firearm.

*

'Cover the stairs,' Vasili said, tossing the Glock to Liliana. 'I'm going to check the back.'

The Alpha team had waited ten seconds for the gas to clear before entering and in those precious moments, Liliana and Vasili had made it to the first floor. They could hear four agents checking the ground floor. When no targets were found, they would begin searching upstairs.

Liliana knelt in the entrance to a bedroom that provided a line of fire down the stairs. 'Do you have another gun?' she asked. 'No, but more ammo,' he said, tossing her three bullet clips from his bag. 'And this.' He tossed her a sweatshirt from inside the bag and she put it on quickly. It smelled of him. Vasili carried only his knife as he went into the back bedroom.

She breathed slowly, smoothly, waiting for the first agent to appear on the stairs. It had been over ten years since she'd fired anything more than an air-pistol – British anti gun laws made it difficult to keep in practice – and she knew the target would be armed, moving fast, and shooting back. She could hear them below her, stepping quietly in the hallway, though not quietly enough. Vasili appeared from the back bedroom and motioned to her to join him. He led her to an open window and she looked out over the back garden. Vasili held up four fingers and pointed downstairs, then two and pointed outside. He was guessing, she knew, but she felt the same numbers based on the gunfire, and the size of the team likely to be sent to take down two agents. They would all be Spetznaz, which meant they would be six of the most lethal soldiers in the world. She looked at Dimitriev and saw a faint smile on his lips. Part of him was enjoying the situation, the thrill of facing the best of the best, the challenge to see if the trainer-of-trainers could outsmart a team of young protégés. He put his mouth to her ear. 'There was one patrolling the back a moment ago. He's moved around the side now to check we're not escaping from there. Hold them on the stairs for one minute while I take care of him, then come out of the window.'

He slipped through the open window. She leaned out after him, pistol at the ready, covering him, but there was no agent in sight. Dimitriev glided down the old iron drainpipe in seconds and disappeared into tall nettles growing beside the house.

She returned to the landing just as the first of the Alpha team appeared on the stairs. She surged forward and fired, aiming for his head, knowing he'd be wearing body armour. He vanished. She felt she'd missed. The Glock had lacked the hard kick she'd been expecting. A storm of bullets erupted up the stair. She dashed into the back bedroom and took cover behind a sturdy old wardrobe. The door erupted before her eyes and bullets passed through the thin wall and embedded in the wardrobe. One half-inch of oak was all that separated her from death.

Outside, Sergeant Anton Saburov heard the shooting coming from the rear of the house and ran into the back garden to cover the window. Dimitriev ended his life with the ridge of his hand, smashed across his throat so hard that no breath could penetrate the deformed tissue of his larynx. In his final moment Saburov felt Dimitriev's razor-sharp knife sever his carotid artery. His final thought was one of admiration for his killer. He had underestimated Dimitriev. For a hunter to underestimate his prey was always a mistake, in this case a fatal one. His last sensation was one of strong hands dragging him into tall nettles that stung his skin. To his surprise, the sting of the nettles was the most painful part of his end.

Inside the shooting stopped. Liliana knew what was coming next: a grenade. Tossed into the bedroom, it might not kill her but it would stun her enough to allow the Alpha team to enter safely and finish her. She lunged for the ragged door and slammed it shut as the grenade was thrown. The grenade bounced off the door and rolled back down the stairs. She heard the Alpha team shout and leap away as it exploded. She looked back at the open window. Had it been a minute yet? Not quite. She needed to hold them off a little longer. She threw open the door and took up a firing position at the top of the stairs. The blast markings of the grenade showed it had gone off at the top of the staircase, too high to have caused the Alpha team any serious damage. The muzzle of a machine gun appeared at the bottom of the stairs. She opened fire and it disappeared. She emptied her clip down the stairs before returning to the bedroom and disappearing through the open window. If Dimitriev had failed to take the agent outside she would be dead in a matter of moments, but Dimitriev was waiting below, machine gun in hand, and the prone body of an agent in the nettles nearby. The bedroom window exploded under machine gun fire but she was already out and down the drainpipe in less than a second.

She followed Dimitriev over the fence and away. They vaulted fence after fence. A dog attacking her. No time to fight it, just run. Shouting behind them now, the Alpha team was in pursuit. Another fence. The Alpha team following, just a few gardens behind. Dimitriev flying over the fences beside her. A sense that despite their speed, the Alpha team was gaining. Another dog. A child, watching in silent surprise. A man with a lawnmower, shouting angrily. Over the final fence and into a short cul-de-sac, just five houses on either side. Mournful sirens drawing near.

They ran across the road and took cover behind a sturdy pickup truck. She reloaded the Glock and watched as the Alpha team cleared the last fence and took cover behind the cars parked in driveways, spreading out along the short street to get a broad range of fire. Their guess had been correct – there had been six agents. Now there were only five. A red police BMW roared past the cul-de-sac, then reversed fast and parked on the road to block the exit. The Alpha team opened fire, eager to get their kill before the police could stop them, and the pickup rang with bullets. Dimitriev was about to return fire but Liliana stopped him. 'No, hide the weapons. The police will shoot.'

'Will they?' Dimitriev demanded.

'They will,' she told him, hiding the Glock in her waistband. 'Do it.'

Dimitriev hid the machine gun in the wheel arch of the pickup.

A voice came over a loudspeaker. 'Armed Police. Put down your weapons and surrender immediately or we will use deadly force.'

'We're unarmed,' she shouted to them. 'They're trying to kill us. Help us, please.'

A shot came from across the road and a bullet ripped into

Dimitriev's shoulder. He fell back, rolling to get out of the agent's sights. Liliana saw the agent, who'd rounded a white van to get a line of fire, and saw the van sprayed red with his blood as a police marksman's bullet entered his brain.

A hail of bullets followed, raining down on the Alpha team. She used the moment to drag Dimitriev to his feet and through the front door of the nearest house. An old woman cowered terrified in the hallway. They burst out of the back door and scaled one more fence. She ran into the road and stopped a slow-moving motorist with the palm of her hand. She dragged him from his car, silencing his protest with a palm strike to the neck that sunk him to the curb, unconscious.

On the other side of the houses, in the cul-de-sac, the Alpha team didn't return fire. Their mission would have to be completed another day, and killing British police would make it more difficult than it already was. Instead, they melted away in the opposite direction, making for the backup van parked nearby for just such an occasion.

Liliana drove slowly, fighting the urge to speed, knowing that unless they drew attention to themselves, they would be just another couple in a silver Toyota driving in Harlesden. 'The bullet exited?' she asked the silent Dimitriev.

'Yes,' he said calmly, though she knew he was using all his strength to remain so.

'I thought so. Anything broken?'

'It feels clean.'

'Then you can survive without a hospital.'

He nodded, his palm pressed on the wound.

'I have a locker ten miles from here. You can hold on until then.'

It was a statement, a fact, a truth for Dimitriev to hold onto.

She had been wounded herself. She knew how the mind needed something to hold onto. 'There's money in it, and new ID,' She went on. 'I'll buy medical supplies and fix you up. I'll dump this car and hire a new one. No need to steal one, is there?'

Dimitriev nodded. A stolen car would only alert the police to their trail. Renting a car was less conspicuous, and Liliana's new ID would be watertight, he knew. There was no need for words, no need to interrupt his ongoing battle to master the pain of his wound, the fear of bleeding out, of dying, before they could reach safety.

Liliana parked on the second floor of a car park in Paddington, choosing a bay deep in shadow that would be unseen by other customers and CCTV. She left Dimitriev to his private battle with the pain and returned fifteen minutes later with bandages, alcohol, strong painkillers and a new sweater and coat to replace his bloodstained garments. She worked quickly, expertly, applying a field dressing and helping him into his new clothes. Leaving him once more, she returned thirty minutes later in a newly rented car and helped him into the passenger seat. Dimitriev took more painkillers and leaned back in the passenger's seat, sleeping fitfully as the endless streets of West London gave way to motorway, and finally, to countryside.

It was midnight when the car stopped and Liliana half-carried and half dragged him from the car. He noticed the air was cold and fresh, fresher than he'd breathed for a long time. He wondered where he was, but couldn't summon the strength to ask. In a final effort he climbed the single step at the front door. He had the impression he was entering a little white cottage like something from a fairytale, but he couldn't be sure.

He felt her arms around his waist, reassuringly strong, and felt himself laid on a bed. She fed him more painkillers. The stillness of the bed was a blessing compared to the rolling of the car. The pain eased sufficiently for him to give into his exhaustion. His last sensation before drifting into sleep was the warmth of her body beside his, the touch of her skin, the soft caress of her breath on his cheek, blowing away his fears, ushering in happier dreams.

Surrey Police Headquarters, Guildford

DCI Simons saw a new message waiting in his inbox and clicked to open it. It was from his son David. He read a short paragraph about a recent trip to the Gold Coast and downloaded several photos of David, his wife, and their little boy Jack, playing in the sand. There was little in the pictures to suggest they were in Australia, no tropical rainforest or grand ocean vistas. Even the sky was overcast. It could have been a bucket-and-spade holiday in Devon but instead they were ten thousand miles away. They looked happy. David was sitting behind Jack, encircling him with his legs. They both had sand on their faces, stuck to the heavy sun block they'd used on their fair skins. Both wore a goofy smile.

He felt the same stab of resentment he always did when he thought of his son, the quiet little boy he'd loved so much, who'd slowly grown into a silent teenager and now corresponded only rarely, who talked happily with his mother but had little to say to him. Simons knew David had only sent the email to him because they had no computer at home. His wife didn't even know how to use a computer. Simons printed out the email. He would show it to her that evening. He downloaded the photos onto a disk that he'd take to the graphics shop on the high street. His wife would enjoy seeing the prints in a few days' time. He was about to compose a reply when Mena Gakhar flung open the door without knocking. 'There's just been a gun battle in west London, Chief,' she announced breathlessly. 'Eight shooters in total. Armed response unit reckons it was a gangland shootout. Foreign, probably Russian. And there was a woman among them.'

Simons blinked, trying to marshal the flood of information coming his way.

She went on, 'Six men, firing at a man and a woman. Two of the six died at the scene. The man and woman escaped. Armed response units lost them, say they're still at large. I spoke to the officer in charge, Max Gerard. He said they were highly trained. Said he hadn't seen that kind of shooting since he was in Hereford, whatever that means...'

'Hereford's where the SAS train,' Simons explained.

'Well that explains that,' she smiled.

'Show his team our pictures of Nadia, see if they recognise her,' Simons said.

'No point. Their description was of a dark-haired woman with thick black glasses, attractive rather than beautiful. They'd never make the match.'

'Try it anyway,' Simons insisted.

'No need. I compared the description with missing persons reports,' she began.

'What's that got to do with anything...'

'This woman must've been living somewhere, as someone, under one of her aliases. She must have dealings with people. Someone must know her. If she's been involved in a shooting and gone underground, then whichever alias she was living under must have vanished.'

'It's all a bit of a long shot,' he said irritably.

'That's what I thought too. But an art dealer, Liliana Marshall, was reported missing the day before the shooting. A curator at Christie's thinks she might have been abducted. I asked her to describe her and send a photo if she had one. She emailed an old press cutting with a photo of Liliana Marshall.'

'Let me see,' Simons said.

Gakhar showed him a picture of a black-haired woman with glasses, an academic type. Her face was attractive but her expression was stern.

'She's hardly the seductress type,' he said off-hand.

'Exactly,' Gakhar said. 'This is who she is when she's not the seductress.'

'She doesn't look like the other women to me,' he shrugged, 'But show it to the marksman if you like.'

'I already did,' Gakhar smiled. 'It's her.'

JULIA

Coniston, Lake District, 2001

Dimitriev woke to find the bed beside him empty. Had she ever been in it, he wondered. Had it just been a dream brought on by the painkillers and the wound. His mouth was dry and his head ached almost as much as his shoulder. He raised his head off the pillow, taking care not to move his shoulder, knowing the wound would heal more quickly if he was still. Even the simple act of raising his head hurt his shoulder. He saw a bottle of sports drink beside his bed and another of water, and sipped from both through the nozzle. Looking around the room, he saw bright floral curtains hanging from a wooden pole, illuminated by the sunshine outside. The room was small, with cheap pine furniture and walls painted a creamy white. The carpet was a cheerful shade of red. The image of the fairytale cottage in the wilderness returned to him from the night before. He guessed he was inside that cottage now. He drank again, knowing that the blood loss from his wound would have dehydrated him dangerously. He continued slowly and deliberately until both bottles were finished.

A click at the front door and she was there in the doorway. Her hair was blonde now, with an attractive luster, shorter than before and tied back in a neat ponytail. The ill-fitting trouser suit and silk blouse of the art dealer had given way to a beige woolen sweater, faded blue jeans and hiking boots of a wholesome country girl.

'How are you feeling?' she asked.

'Rough, but not too bad, considering.'

'I have some clothes for you, and more medical supplies. I'll need to change your dressing soon, whenever you're ready.'

'You make a good nurse, Tatiana Zykova,' he said with a grateful smile. 'Actually, a good doctor.'

She looked at him with such sadness in her eyes that he wondered if she was offended. 'You don't look like Tatiana any more,' he said, almost to himself. You don't look like Liliana Marshall any more, either. Who are you now? What should I call you?'

'Julia McKenzie.'

'Well thank you for saving me, Julia McKenzie. You would have been better off with me dead. You still would be.'

'I don't think so,' she said. 'If the Alpha team find us again, I might still need your help.'

He laughed and new pain shot through his shoulder. 'I don't think I'd be much help,' he said.

'Not as you are, that's why you need to recover,' she said seriously.

She went to the kitchen and returned later to spoon hot food into his mouth. He had no appetite but knew the importance of putting energy into his body. 'Where are we?' he asked.

'A place I discovered several years ago in the northwest of England in an area called the Lake District. I saw this cottage for sale. It was so remote that I decided it would make a perfect safe house.'

'We taught you well,' he smiled.

'Should I be grateful?' she said, more harshly than she'd intended.

'No,' he said, raising his hand from the bed despite the pain.

'Listen, Julia, you don't have to help me. You can leave me for the authorities. They don't have much to charge me with, and with diplomatic immunity, I'll simply be expelled and sent home.'

'If they class you as a terrorist you'll find the British are not as forgiving as the rest of the world believes.'

Dimitriev's head rested back on the pillow. She was right, he knew. 'Even so, I don't want to put you in any more danger. I ask only one thing. Call General Levkov and inform him about Prokop. Tell him to investigate him. Will you do that for me?'

'No I won't, Vasili. You can call Levkov when you're well enough to move. I won't have anything more to do with The Organisation. I'm sorry.'

'Very well,' he nodded. She fed him another spoonful and he chewed slowly.

'Your cover as an art expert is blown. Will you start again, build a new one?' he asked.

'No. The Havilland job was my last. I have enough money now. I won't work again.'

'What will you do?'

'I'll go someplace far away, where no one asks who you are, or what you've done. Where no one wants to know which side you're on. A place with no sides. I don't know where that place is yet, but I'm going to find it.'

'It sounds like a good place,' he smiled sadly.

'It is,' she assured him, preparing another spoonful for him. 'A beautiful place.'

Coniston Water, Lake District

Julia walked beside Vasili on the shifting pebbles beside Coniston Water.

It was morning and the lake was calm and serene. A boat was moving slowly on the opposite shore, half a mile away, with a handful of tourists aboard. It was September and the summer crowds had gone, but there were always visitors in this area, drawn to the beauty and romance of the lakes. They continued until they reached a jetty and strolled to the end, where they stood and watched the ducks gliding by.

'Are you tired, Vasili?' she asked. 'Do you want to rest?'

'I would like to sit here for a while,' he answered.

They sat on the edge of the jetty, their feet dangling near the water. 'I almost forgot,' she said with a smile. 'There's someone I'd like you to meet.'

Vasili glanced back along the jetty. There was no one in sight. Julia reached into her bag and handed him a passport. 'Colonel Vasili Dimitriev, meet Dr. William Khan, a British citizen and a Doctor of Philosophy, no less.'

Dimitriev examined the passport. It was suitably worn, as a passport would be if it had been used for some time. Inside, he saw his photo looking noticeably younger than he did now. It was an expert forgery, he would have expected nothing less from her. He slipped it into the breast pocket of his jacket. 'It feels strange, to be a citizen of the former enemy,' he said seriously.

'You get used to it,' she said.

'I imagine you do.'

A sparrowhawk hit the glassy surface of the lake at speed,

creating a smooth ripple of circles and rising a moment later with a small fish in its talons. Dimitriev watched the water returning to its mirror-like calm.

'The water's so still that they set speed records here,' she told him. 'A man called Campbell set one here before the war. Later his son did the same, but his boat hit something, a wave or a piece of driftwood, I don't remember. It overturned and sank. He died. They still find parts of the wreckage from time to time.'

'It's not how I imagined the English countryside,' he said.

'We're near the Scottish border,' she said.

'Scotland! Yes, this is more how I imagined Scotland.'

'I'll take you there one day, if you like,' she said.

'I would like that,' he smiled, and she saw a flicker of enthusiasm in him. It was good. She needed to build on it, to kindle it until it was a real flame once more.

'You can see the lochs, it's what they call the lakes. They're quite something.'

'And taste the whisky,' he grinned.

'You like whisky, Vasili?'

'The single malts – Glenfiddich, Glenlivet, Glen... something-or-other, I forget the names. There are hundreds of different makes, as diverse as our vodkas.'

'Then we'll visit the Highlands,' she smiled. 'But today, I think we've gone far enough. We need to return to the cottage and rest. There's just one more place I'd like to take you on the way back.'

They walked to the tiny village of Torver and Julia led Vasili into the old black and white inn that stood on the corner of the main road. Inside was typical of the pubs in the area with a low ceiling, oak beams and a welcoming log fire that took the edge off the chill coming in off the water. Dimitriev took a table in a quiet corner while Julia went to the bar. She returned soon after with two tumblers of amber spirit and set them down.

'Whisky?' he asked, delighted.

'Glenfiddich,' she smiled.

He held his tumbler up before the log fire and watched the flames dance in the golden liquid. 'It's been a while since I tasted it.'

She raised her glass to him. 'Your health.'

'Nazdrovie,' he said looking her straight in the eye.

'Don't drink it all at once,' she warned.

He laughed at this and swirled the tumbler in circles beneath his nose, inhaling the spirit's bouquet. 'Funny how things change. There was a time when I was teaching you about life here.'

'I'm sorry, I didn't mean to patronise you,' she said.

'I know how to appreciate good whisky. Things have changed in Russia too. We can get all sorts of things now, even single malt.' He sipped the whisky and rolled it around his mouth before swallowing. He nodded appreciatively. She was happy to see him enjoying his whisky. She took a sip of her own. 'There's something else we should drink to,' she said, setting her glass down carefully. He did the same, sensing it was something important.

Her fingers brushed the table top lightly, tracing over the grains in the old wood. 'In Berlin, when Svetlana entered Cleary's house, Cleary was about to shoot me. He was about to kill me. I wasn't fast enough to get away. Svetlana came in at that moment. He shot her instead of me.'

She watched Dimitriev's eyes to see his reaction. His gaze

was steady, it was impossible to tell what he was thinking. She needed to continue and say it all now. 'He hit her twice in the chest with his last two bullets. I took her pistol and fired at him, but he took cover in the kitchen. Svetlana was alive but bleeding out fast. I wanted to get her out of there. She ordered me to run, but I didn't. I swear it, Vasili.' Tears pricked her eyes. She went on. 'Then I saw her die. She was dead, Vasili, I swear it. I saw the spirit leave her. I hope you believe me. It was only then that I left.'

He stared at her, his eyes fixed and cold. She went on, wanting to say it all while she had the strength. 'I hated her, Vasili. I'm sure you know. After our first mission in France she had my target killed, a young man with a wife and child, Michel Benoit. I still remember his name. Others I have forgotten, but his I remember. She was tying up loose ends. She did it to protect me, to protect The Organisation, but it broke my heart Vasili. The strangest thing of all was that I didn't even love him. I just felt something for him. Do you understand, Vasili? She took that away from me. After that I never felt anything again.' She held his gaze. 'I blamed her for that, for everything that had happened to me, and then she gave her life for me without a second thought, Vasili. Without a moment's hesitation. I saw how much she loved me. It was in her eyes when she died.'

Dimitriev held the top of his whisky glass in his fingertips and moved the glass in circles, skating on the surface of the table. 'I often wondered how she passed her final moments.'

'She died quickly. There was no pain.'

'That's not what concerned me,' he said, his voice barely above a whisper. 'Svetlana was never bothered by pain. She wasn't alone when she died. That makes me glad.'

They sat in silence, the gentle murmur of the other guests the only sound in the darkened pub.

'There was one more thing she said before she died,' Julia said finally. 'It's the reason I brought you here. She told me to raise a glass of Starka with you. I promised I would. I've been waiting a long time to do it.' She smiled apologetically, 'There's no Starka here and the vodka they serve, well, it's not the same. It's too ... I don't know ...' Words left her and tears came instead.

'It wasn't your fault,' he said.

'Even so, I'm sorry,' she said, drying her tears with the back of her hand. She glanced around the room to see if any of the other guests were watching, not wishing to draw attention to herself or Vasili, but Vasili had chosen their spot well and they could not be seen easily.

Dimitriev raised his glass. 'Let's do as she wished,' he said. She picked up her whisky, raised it level with Vasili's and looked him in the eye, blinking back the tears that threatened to return.

'Svetlana,' she said firmly.

'Svetlana,' he repeated.

She threw back the glass quickly, all thoughts of savouring the whisky forgotten, and welcomed the cleansing sting of the spirit on the back of her throat, strong enough to take away her sorrow, and Vasili's, if only for a moment.

Harlesden, North London

Lieutenant Colonel Miroslav Arshan entered the dining room. Two of his remaining team, Konstantinov and Markevich, had spread newspaper over the table and were busy cleaning weapons. It was a good sign, a mark of their professionalism. Under normal circumstances each member of the Alpha team would be responsible for maintaining his own weapons, but Arshan had been speaking to General Prokop in Moscow and Kitaev had been cooking their evening meal, so Konstantinov and Markevich had cleaned their weapons too. Arshan could see they were enjoying the calming ritual of stripping down, cleaning, oiling and reassembling the beautifully engineered killing machines. They were taking their time to perform the tasks they could do in a matter of seconds if the need arose. Both needed something to occupy their hands in the long hours of waiting. Arshan knew that feeling well enough himself, and the deaths of Alexandrov and Saburov were weighing heavy on all their minds. Alexandrov had been the team's medic. They were all trained in first aid and field dressing, but Alexandrov was a surgeon and they were butchers in comparison. If they were injured now, their chances of survival were far slimmer. Saburov had been their cook and store master. People who didn't know the military had no idea how important supplies were to a team: the difference between comfort and misery, between good morale and bad. Over time it could easily be the difference between success and failure, between life and death. Kitaev had taken over Saburov's role of cook while Konstantinov, who spoke flawless English, had taken charge of supplies. He'd bought a carton of Marlboro cigarettes and the ashtray on the table was filled with butts. Though it was only mid afternoon, the curtains had been drawn and the lights were on. The room was filled with cigarette smoke and the smells from the kitchen. More newspaper had been placed near the wall and the weapons that had been cleaned had been placed on it. Arshan examined their arsenal, confirming what he already knew they possessed: one L96A1 sniper rifle belonging to Kitaev, two Uzi submachine guns belonging to Konstantinov and Markevich, and his own AK74 assault rifle. They had also recovered Saburov's Skorpion after he'd died, but they had failed to retrieve his pistol, or the AK74 and the pistol Alexandrov had been carrying. The loss of the weapons was not a problem. New weapons could be acquired. The loss of the men was a far greater problem. They had both been first-rate Spetznaz whom he'd both liked and admired. The team's combat effectiveness had been diminished, although he knew they still had the capability to accomplish their mission. Dimitriev and Zykova were highly trained agents, but one was wounded and past his prime, and the other a woman, a swallow, trained in seduction. Against four Spetznaz, the odds were still heavily stacked against them.

Konstantinov and Markevich had laid out the remaining pistols on the table: two FN Browning High Powers favoured by themselves, Arshan's Serbian-made Zvezda, and Kitaev's Beretta, plus two back up Spanish-made Stars that they were cleaning. The weapons corresponded with Arshan's mental list. Everything was as it should be. He felt a surge of pride in his squad, and admiration for the men who served with him. They were the best of the best, trained under the toughest conditions to accomplish their mission under the most testing circumstances. They were Spetznaz. While other countries had special forces that he respected, none had been trained as they had, to adapt to the most challenging of conditions with such cool professionalism. The reason for his confidence was simple: no Western country ever put its soldiers at such risk during training.

After their first contact with Dimitriev and Zykova in Harlesden, his team had regrouped at the designated safe house in northwest London and he'd established a secure line to Moscow. The conversation with General Prokop had not been easy. Prokop had listened in silence while he described the escape of Dimitriev and Zykova, his words tumbling out to fill the silence on the other end of the line. He had forced himself on, categorising the failures so far, including the deaths of Alexandrov and Saburov, careful not to avoid any detail that could later be held against him. When Prokop finally answered, his voice had been calm, so calm that Arshan had found it all the more unnerving.

Arshan called Kitaev in from the kitchen to join the others. 'I just spoke with General Prokop,' he told them. 'We will continue in our mission until it is accomplished. We are to set up a new safe house near Guildford, a town to the southwest of London. The search for Tatiana Zykova is being led by the Surrey police force whose headquarters are there. For the moment we will simply monitor their correspondence and wait until we get a lead on her location. Our mission is to reach our targets before the police do and execute our mission, as ordered. Pack up your kit tonight. We leave this place in the morning for a town called Woking.'

Coniston, Lake District

Julia woke to the rhythmic creaking of the floorboards coming from the bedroom beside hers. It was a good sign, the sound of Dimitriev exercising. She went into the kitchen, her bare feet silent on the cold tiled floor. She switched on the kettle and smoothed the chequered red tablecloth before laying two place settings. She poured orange juice and set about making toast and eggs. Outside, the weather was gloomy, but the cottage was warm and snug, like a cottage deep in the forest in one of the fairytales from her youth. She made tea and served it with no milk, just fresh lemon and cane sugar.

Dimitriev emerged from the bedroom. His T shirt was damp with sweat and his face pale. There was a towel over his shoulder.

'Come and eat,' she said with a smile.

'I need to shower,' he said.

'Eat first, while it's hot.'

He looked at her, and she could see the thoughts flowing through his mind.

'Please,' she said, hoping to cut the calculations short, to get him to engage with her once more. He had been silent for the last two days, since they had drunk a toast to Svetlana, only answering when spoken too, single words, yes and no. She needed him to re-establish contact with her. They needed to decide what to do. He wiped the sweat from his face with the towel and sat at the table as requested. She served him a plate of eggs and handed him his tea, which he accepted gratefully. She could smell him, his sweat, the warm, sweet, acrid smell that she remembered from long ago. It mingled with the smells of breakfast, and made her feel at home in this lonely corner of the world.

'I heard you exercising. I hope you weren't putting too much pressure on your shoulder.'

'I still can't put any weight on it,' he said forlornly.

'Don't be in such a hurry, Vasili.'

'I can't wait until it heals. It'll take too long.'

'Let me check your dressing,' she said, rising from her seat. 'I need to make sure you haven't reopened the wound.'

'Finish your food first,' he ordered, but she ignored him and knelt on one knee beside him. Slowly she reached up to the sleeve of his T-shirt and pulled it aside. There was a streak of fresh blood showing through the bandage. 'The wound has reopened,' she said. 'It's too soon to train on it.'

'It's nothing,' he said, but his pallor told her it was not nothing.

She rose swiftly and stood, leaning against the sink, her arms folded across her chest. 'Finish your eggs, then I will redress it. It might need new stitches too, and that is going to hurt.'

He ate quickly, his body hunched over the table. 'There's no need to redress it. I don't have time for that. I need to leave today.'

'You can't leave. You're wounded.'

'I need to contact Levkov, return to Moscow. I can't wait around any longer.'

He pushed the remains of his food away and rose from the table, taking up his towel and heading for the shower. She didn't stand in his way. When he emerged from his room thirty minutes later, his bag was packed. Julia stood before the door.

'You're not leaving, Vasili.'

'Don't stand in my way,' he said.

'You won't catch me unprepared this time,' she warned.

Dimitriev took a step forward, his eyes boring into her. Her eyes met his and he saw the determination in them. She was prepared to make him stay, with force if necessary. He estimated his chance of success, with one arm and a serious wound, against Julia, who had learned his system so well. The odds were little better than even. However he had a way of improving them dramatically. He drew his pistol from his bag and aimed it at her forehead.

She stepped forward until the barrel was inches from her face. 'You remember that day in Siberia when we went to the church in the forest and you showed me the Rublev?' she asked calmly.

'Stand aside,' he warned. His jaw hardened, steeling himself for what he was about to do.

'How do you think you found me so easily – an art historian specialising in Russian art and religious icons – I'm surprised it took you so long, Vasili.'

She let his mind go where it needed to realise the truth. 'Shoot, Vasili' she said softly. 'It is the only way I'll let you go.'

He held the pistol to her for a half minute before lowering it. His arm hung limp by his side. She turned the kitchen chair around to face him. 'Sit,' she ordered. 'I need to look at that wound.'

He obeyed without a word, raising his arms so she could remove his sweater and undershirt, and sighing deeply to distance the pain as she stripped the bloodied bandages away.

Tarn Hows, Lake District

Julia drove north through the pretty grey-stone village of Coniston, following the signs for Hawkshead, then turned onto a minor road and parked beneath the branches of an autumn oak. She led Vasili down a short track through a patch of birch trees that reminded him of their homeland. They came to a lake surrounded by spruce and pine and the path followed the lakeshore. They went with it.

'How pretty it is here,' Vasili said. 'Like a picture.'

'It's called Tarn Hows,' Julia explained. 'It's man-made, two small lakes joined together into one, and the surroundings are all landscaped. I chose it because it's a good distance for you to walk. It takes an hour to get around.'

'Perfect,' he said with a smile. It was the first she'd seen from him in a long time.

'I'm glad you like it,' she said.

'It's beautiful, but not like our country. In our country the beauty is natural.'

She took his arm and they walked on the lakeside path. 'Yes, our lakes are beautiful, but there are no footpaths for people to walk on and enjoy them.'

'Is that a bad thing?' he asked. 'Only the most dedicated get to see the beauty of our lakes.'

'Is that what you believe?' she asked.

'I believe God made them without paths,' he smiled. 'He gave us free will to forge our own path, if our desire is strong enough.'

'Do you still pray, Vasili?' she asked.

'Yes, of course. I've been praying a lot recently, seeking

guidance.'

'What does God tell you?'

'He's been silent,' he said, shaking his head. 'And you Julia, do you pray?'

'I learned from a young age never to wish for anything.'

'Praying is not wishing,' he said quietly.

'Then what is it, Vasili?' she asked gently.

'Praying is asking for strength so we can achieve our wishes – the strength to forge our path.'

'It makes sense when you say it. But God would never listen to me.'

'Why do you say that?'

'Too many sins,' she said with a bitter laugh.

'God listens to us all, even sinners. Especially sinners. I know, because he listens to me.'

'Then why has he been silent?'

'He has not been silent. I was wrong to say that. I've simply not been able to hear him. My ears have been deaf to his words because my heart has been closed to his love.'

'You believe it will open again?'

'I know it will. I am a man of faith.'

'I envy you, your relationship with God,' she said.

'You can have the same,' he said seriously.

'I don't think so.'

A cold breeze came down through the narrow valley that ran between the Cumbrian peaks and whipped up the leaves around them. A fast moving ripple ran across the surface of the lake, small white lines of foam ran, as if skating on thin ice before falling and vanishing into the cold water.

'You have walked here before?' he asked.

'Several times.'

'Alone?'

'Sometimes. Not always. Why do you ask?'

'I want to know if there has been anyone in your life, Julia?'

'You mean anyone significant?'

'Yes.'

'It has been difficult, with my work and my past. No one can ever know who I really am. And how can there be love, without such knowledge?'

'A lonely way to live,' he said.

'I know no other way,' she said.

'How about you?' He looked at her in surprise. 'Has there been another woman in your life, after Svetlana?'

'No,' he laughed at the suggestion. 'There has only ever been one woman for me.'

She nodded, understanding, though it hurt to hear it.

'Svetlana was my student for several years before we were married,' he continued. 'We spent a lot of time together and we grew close. You know how close training can be, how it can forge a bond between two people that's hard to break.'

'I know all too well,' she smiled sadly. She was losing him with every step. It hurt, after what she had gone through, after being so close to him again.

'It was Levkov's idea for us to marry,' Vasili said quietly. He kept his gaze ahead, speaking matter of fact: 'A married couple is less suspicious on a mission. That was what Levkov said. It was common, in those days, to marry for the sake of the motherland.'

'I had no idea,' she said breathlessly.

'No one did.'

'Svetlana loved you. It wasn't fake.'

'I know.'

'You were such a beautiful couple: the perfect couple.'

'Perfect in the eyes of The Organisation,' Vasili said.

'But not in the eyes of God?'

They walked on in silence, her mind turning over the new information. She clung to his arm, afraid that if she let it go she might never hold him so close again. He stopped and withdrew his arm from hers. She didn't resist. He took her hands in his.

'When we arrived in the cottage, that first night, you slept beside me.'

'I needed to be sure you were safe,' she said, her eyes on his chest, not daring to look at his face.

'I thought it was true but later I wondered if it was a dream.'

'I wanted to be nearby, in case you needed me.'

'I did.'

His rough thumbs brushed across the backs of her hands, tracing the rise and fall of the tendons that ran to the knuckles. 'I do.' He let out a breath. 'When I said there has only ever been one woman for me, I wasn't talking about Svetlana. Ever since you and I flew to Krasnoyarsk and you berated me for not taking you to England, there has only been you.' He smiled at the memory and she laughed too, despite the tears in her eyes, distorting her vision of him against the pristine lake.

'That was a cheap trick,' she said. Then her face grew serious. 'And there has only ever been one man for me, Vasili. Ever since you asked me to dance to that ridiculous waltz.'

He drew her into his embrace slowly, and held her, his cheek against hers, his hand caressing the back of her neck, as the golden leaves blew around them. Finally their lips met and they kissed, and for the first time they were together not as soldiers, but as a man and a woman, unfettered by duty or obligation.

'Will you sleep beside me again, Julia McKenzie?' he muttered in her ear.

'Yes,' she whispered. 'I will sleep beside you again, Vasili Ivanovich.'

Surrey Police Headquarters, Guildford

DCI Simons hunted for his mobile phone. He could hear it ringing in one of the pockets of his coat hanging by the door. Why didn't people call his landline? He hated his mobile phone. By the time he'd found it, it had stopped ringing. He saw a missed call from DI Childs of the City Police and called him back.

'Been looking into this Liliana Marshall,' Childs told him. 'Got one of our guys doing a bit of forensic accounting.'

Simons chuckled. 'Is that what you call it?'

'Why, what do you call it?' Childs asked, nonplussed.

'Having a nosey through someone's old bank statements – that's what we used to call it,' Simons answered.

'Yes, well it's not far off that,' Childs said cheerfully. 'Anyway… turns out we got some juice once we scratched beneath the surface.'

'Juice?'

'Yeah. One of Liliana Marshall's off-shore accounts in Jersey paid out to several others, including a private account in the name of one Julia McKenzie. The account's been dormant for several years, but it's showing several large cash withdrawals recently. The first was in West London on the day of the shootout. The second was in Manchester a few days later.'

'You think Julia Mckenzie is one of her aliases?'

'It's a distinct possibility.'

'London and then Manchester – it's not much to go on.'

'No. But then there was a third withdrawal, yesterday, in Kendal.'

'In the Lake District?'

'Yep.'

'That's a bit more like it.'

'I've got one of our specialists looking deeper into Julia McKenzie, to see if there's anything else we can find on her.'

'Tell him to pull his finger out. This is an emergency now. This woman's been shooting up half of north London.'

'I'll call you as soon as I get anything,' Childs assured him.

'Simons shut his phone. Have you ever been to the Lake District, Mena?'

'I'm a Yorkshire lass,' she frowned. 'It's on the wrong side of the Pennines for me.'

'It's lovely up there. You'll like it. We used to go regularly when David was a boy.'

'If you say so,' she said.

'I do. Pack for a couple of nights.'

'Now?'

'We'll leave first thing in the morning. It's a long drive.'

*

In a house in a quiet suburb of Woking, Arshan replayed Simons' phone conversation with DI Childs to the other members of the Alpha team.

'They believe Tatiana Zykova is in a place called Kendal in the Lake District.'

'Should we go there now?' Kitaev demanded.

'No, we wait…' Arshan answered.

'For what?' Kitaev asked.

'There's no point going to Kendal without a better idea of where they're hiding,' Arshan said. 'When the inspector leaves, we'll follow. He'll lead us to both of them.'

'How are we going to follow a police car without being noticed?' Kitaev asked.

'Easily,' Markevich grinned. 'I planted a tracking device on his car while he was in London earlier today.'

'And where's the Lake District?' Kitaev demanded.

'North,' Arshan said. 'We're going north.'

Coniston, Lake District

Julia and Vasili undressed slowly. They had waited more than fifteen years for this moment, and there was no rush now. There was no urgency in their movements, no fumbled kisses or clumsy embraces, no frenzied ripping of clothing. Instead they undressed with an economy of movement that was a graceful dance, each admiring the other's performance, before stepping close to one another. She held his gaze, reveling in the delicious anticipation, holding onto it for as long as she could, knowing it would never be the same after the first time.

Her eyes left his and travelled down to the livid scar on his shoulder. The bandages had been removed and the wound, despite its ugliness, was healing well. She ran her fingertips softly over the scab and bent forward, slowly, and her lips brushed over it, delicate as a gossamer, kissing it, healing it. Her tongue flicked at it playfully, wetting it with her saliva and then licking it up. His hands brushed her hair aside so he could watch the antics of her lips and her tongue. Saliva was a healing agent, he knew, but she pressed hard enough to cause fierce pricks of pain to shoot through his shoulder and down his spine, into his loins. The sensation was electric. Her fingertip sought his penis and found it already erect. She brushed it gently, then cupped his scrotum and massaged, never taking her lips from the scar. She heard him sigh. She had never seen Dimitriev lose control before, he'd always been in perfect control. Now she could feel the faintest tremor in his thighs. She felt herself grow suddenly wet and wanted him inside her urgently, but there would be time for that later, plenty of time. Instead, her fingers began to stroke his penis again, this time more firmly. This would be Vasili's moment, she would make it perfect for him. He groaned again, and she pressed her teeth gently on the wound. He gasped in pain and she felt his penis twitch in her hand. Then she felt herself lifted off her feet, Vasili's hand in her hair, pulling it back hard to expose her throat. She closed her eyes and let him do as he wished. She felt the sensation of his lips hard on her throat, heard his harsh breathing and felt his rough stubble on her chest as his lips descended, seeking her breasts. His teeth held her nipple in them hard, until she cried out in delicious pain.

With a simple movement of his hips he took her down, ignoring the bed, and laid her on the thin rug that covered the floorboards. The impact sent the breath from her body. As she struggled to inhale, she felt his penis enter her and thrust deep inside her. She cried out, surprising herself at the sound. It was unlike any she had uttered before – a primal cry from somewhere deep within, a release of feelings locked inside for so long that she'd forgotten their existence.

Dimitriev grunted hard, the sinews of his neck and shoulders standing out like cable, the strength she had known before holding her tight now, holding her still while he thrust into her. For a fleeting moment she was aware she had never felt safer than she did at that moment. As his thrusts grew harder and more urgent any awareness of her own thoughts vanished, engulfed by the flames that curled up from her loins, marking the beginning of a long and violent climax building inside her.

*

Fifteen miles away, a police Mondeo turned off the M1 motorway and joined the A590 that would take it into the wild beauty of the Lake District.

Ten miles behind the Mondeo, a silver Primera followed. The driver, Kitaev, took care not to exceed the speed limit. There was no need. The tracking device would take them all the way to the Lake District, and beyond, to Zykova and Dimitriev, if the inspector knew what he was doing.

Kendal, Lake District

Simons and Gakhar sat in a café in the centre of the old market town of Kendal that was the gateway to the Lake District. They examined the photo of Julia McKenzie that they'd got from the bank where she had made a cash withdrawal two days earlier. The manager had taken some time to retrieve the photo taken automatically by the cash machine – such requests from the police were rare in Kendal – but eventually, with the aid of a younger colleague, he'd managed to produce the photo.

Apart from being blonde, Julia McKenzie didn't resemble the CCTV photo of Nadia Antonescu in the slightest. Gakhar took the *Matryoshka* file from her briefcase and took out a photo of another blonde woman taken some years earlier in Chicago. 'Look Chief, this looks more like her. She could be Julia Mckenzie's younger sister,' she said hopefully.

'They look different to me,' Simons said bluntly.

'It's not only the looks, Chief. That woman from MI5, George Smith, she told us this woman adopts a whole new persona.'

Simons frowned but Gakhar went on. 'If I had to be a woman living here it would be her, Julia McKenzie.'

'You'd be Julia McKenzie?'

'Laugh if you want,' she said, replacing the photos in the file.

'I'm not laughing Mena. It's just not a lot to go on.'

'No offence Chief, but George Smith also said she relies on people seeing her like that. Men, mainly…'

'Seeing her like what?' Simons demanded.

'The woman they want to see. When a man sees what he wants to see, he looks no further.'

Simons pushed his half-eaten sandwich away and stirred his tea.

Mena munched on her sausage roll, speaking between mouthfuls. 'It's easy if a woman's prepared to do it.'

'Do what?'

'Give up who she really is. It's not something I could do. Sometimes I wish I could.' She saw the doubt in Simons' eyes and shrugged. 'Sorry, women are complicated, Chief.'

'Even you, Mena?'

'Even me.' She nodded seriously. 'People see a Pakistani woman and they think I must be a Muslim who prays five times a day and is waiting for an arranged marriage. Then they hear my accent and realise I'm from Yorkshire, so they assume I eat Yorkshire pudding with my Balti...' Simons grinned at this, '...none of which is true, by the way,' she added forcefully. 'I left home to get away from all that. But even down South, it's still who people think I am. When they find out I'm a copper, they think I got the job to make up the ethnic quota. They don't believe I might actually want to be one.'

'I have to admit, you weren't what I was expecting,' Simons said gently.

'What were you expecting?'

'I guess it was the devout Muslim designed to make up the quota.' He shrugged apologetically. 'I guess I was wrong.'

She popped the last of her sausage roll into her mouth and he watched her chew. 'Does Yorkshire pudding go with Balti?' he asked lightly.

'Actually, it's dead nice,' she smiled.

'I'll have to try it next time I'm in Yorkshire.'

She grew serious. 'What I'm trying to say is it's easy to adapt

on the surface, but to change who you are on the inside …
that's difficult. Most people can't do it. The woman we're after,
she lives her whole life being someone else. When one cover is
blown she just adopts another.'

'Like a snake,' Simons said quietly.

'Even a snake only changes its skin,' Mena said. 'She
changes everything.'

'I haven't thought of it like that before,' Simons said.

'It must drive her insane,' Gakhar said quietly.

'That's a very real possibility,' Simons nodded grimly.

His phone rang. He listened intently for a minute before
hanging up. 'That was DI Childs of the City Police. There's a
property registered to a Julia Mckenzie in Coniston, no exact
address, but that doesn't matter. I know Coniston well. We
used to go boating on the lake. It's little more than a village.
Everyone knows everyone, especially out of season. If she's
there, we'll find her.'

*

Anita Bradley held the photo of Julia McKenzie at arms length
and squinted at it through her bifocals. 'Yes,' she smiled. 'She's
been in the store a couple times recently. Don't know her
name. Seems ever so nice, though.'

'Do you know where she's staying?' Gakhar asked urgently,
feeling Simons tense behind her.

'No idea. I haven't seen her around Coniston, so she's
probably in one of the holiday cottages outside.'

'Which one?' Simons demanded.

'I have no idea,' she said, taken aback by the intensity of the
police officer's questioning.

'Where would be a good place to start?' Gakhar asked more gently.

'Try the Broughton road and the little lanes off it,' she said. 'That's where a lot of visitors stay.'

Gakhar smiled and took back the photo. Simons was already out of the door and striding to the Mondeo. She caught up with him. 'Shouldn't we call for backup Chief?'

'As soon as we're sure of her location,' Simons told her. 'We don't want to call out the cavalry for no reason.'

A590, Lake District

Vasili revved the white Astra hire-car hard. Julia knew it had been some time since he'd driven and she could see he was enjoying the sensation on the twisting country lanes. She thought about telling him to slow down – they didn't want to draw attention to themselves, not now when they were so close to getting away – but she couldn't bring herself to spoil his enjoyment. A police Mondeo rounded the bend ahead and Vasili hit the brake. The Mondeo was also travelling fast and the cars stopped nose to nose, one yard apart.

Vasili gestured to the police car to come forward and threw the Astra into reverse. There was an entrance to a field twenty yards back where two cars could pass. It was always a good idea to let the police have right of way. He reversed and the Mondeo followed him, coming forwards. Julia scanned the faces inside: a white middle-aged male officer driving and a young South Asian woman beside him. She saw the woman say something to the man and both sets of eyes locked onto hers.

'Stop the car,' she told Vasili.

'They can't pass yet,' he said, still looking over his shoulder. 'Just a little further.'

'Now!'

He hit the brake. She was out of the car before him, striding to the Mondeo, pistol drawn. Vasili followed a moment later with the machine gun he'd kept under his seat. Julia opened the driver's door. 'Get out. Both of you. Now.'

The driver emerged slowly, his face pale. 'Take it easy, we're not armed. I'm Detective Chief Inspector Jeremy Simons and this is Detective Constable Mena Gakhar.'

'I don't care who you are,' she told him. 'Tell her to get out now.'

Simons turned to Gakhar. 'Get out Mena,' he said softly.

Vasili opened her door and dragged her out to where Simons was standing.

'I should tell you that armed police are on their way,' Simons told them. 'Give yourselves up now. It'll be easier all around.'

Julia laughed. 'We should play poker some time, Detective Chief Inspector Simons. You'd lose quickly.'

'I assure you it's true,' Simons said seriously.

She smiled at Vasili. 'Armed police? Do they even have such a thing in England?'

'England only has bobbies on the beat,' he said with a shrug. 'No guns.'

'Don't be a fool...' Simons began. She hushed him with a pistol in his face. 'There are no armed police.'

'What are you going to do to us?' Mena asked, fighting back the tears.

'That's what we need to decide,' Julia told her.

She spoke swiftly with Vasili in Russian and he reversed the Astra past the field entrance, then drove the police car into the field, parking it beside the tall hedgerow where it could not be seen from the road.

'Get in,' Julia ordered.

'Oh God,' Mena began to cry. 'They're going to kill us.'

Simons found his voice. 'Listen Liliana... Nadia... Julia... whoever you are, don't make this worse than it is. You're not charged with murder. Let us take you in and I promise you we can work something out.'

'Detective Gakhar's right,' Julia said coldly. 'I should kill you.'

She trained the gun on him once more and he felt his leg begin to tremble. He thought of Patricia, his wife, and how he wished he was sitting beside her now on the sofa watching a crummy American cop show. How little the silly stunts of the detectives would bother him now. He thought of his son David in Australia, and how he would never see him again, never put his arms around his broad shoulders, shoulders once so small that he could envelope them in two hands. He thought how he would never hold David's son Jack as he'd once held David, never meet David's wife Andrea, never kiss her affectionately on the cheek or hold her hand in friendship. He wondered if he would feel the bullet entering his brain before it ceased to function. He screwed his eyes tight shut, awaiting the answer. He would find out soon, one way or the other. He waited. Nothing. No answer. He felt a surge of anger, not with his killer but with himself, followed by remorse. Such remorse. His obsession with finding this seductress had caused his own death. That was somehow understandable but Mena would die too and that was unforgivable. If only he'd been able to let it go, to sign off on George Petersen's death as a suicide but something about the woman had drawn him. He wondered what it was exactly. She was standing before him now, he had only moments to find out. He opened his eyes.

She'd lowered the gun. She was as beautiful as he'd imagined, though with none of the guile he'd been expecting. She could have been any rich country woman holidaying in the area, riding horses and sailing on the lakes, only a hint of something behind the eyes told him of the woman she really was. Not coldness, as Mena Gakhar had suggested earlier, but rather a fierce determination, a spark of something, excitement perhaps. He looked at the silent Russian man with her and then he knew it: they were lovers.

She smiled at him with surprising warmth. 'What do you take me for Detective Chief Inspector? A cold-blooded killer? Get in the car.'

Dimitriev disabled the police radio and slashed the tyres as Julia bound the officers securely to their seats with rope and tape from Vasili's kit bag. She leaned into the door and whispered in Simons' ear. 'If you come looking for us again, I *will* kill you.'

'We'll perish out here,' he said.

'Oh don't be so dramatic,' she laughed. 'Someone will find you sooner or later. This is England not Siberia.'

*

Twenty minutes later, four men appeared in the field. For a moment Simons couldn't believe his luck. He and Mena shouted to them but the men simply stared at them and talked among themselves. Suddenly Mena stopped shouting. Simons stopped a moment later.

'It's them.'

'Who?' he asked.

'The men from the gun battle in Harlesden.'

Simons knew it was true instantly. The lean hard bodies and cold eyes of the four men were those of a special forces team. He saw the men talking and knew again that his life and Mena's hung in the balance. 'Look away,' he told Mena urgently. 'Don't look at their faces.' It was all he could do, apart from pray that the men would leave them be. He saw Mena shaking, her head turned down and away and pressing into the passenger door. He saw the back of her neck, exposed. He felt such terrible shame for what he was putting her through.

When he glanced up again, the men had gone.

Khodinka Airfield, Moscow

General Levkov lifted the receiver to his ear without a word. He recognised the voice on the other end instantly, despite the hollowness and delay on the long distance line.

'Vasili Ivanovich. You found her?'

'I did. You must investigate Prokop.'

Levkov was silent, stunned by the revelation, and its implications for The Organisation. General Prokop was Head of the Sixth Directorate in charge of Signals and Surveillance – the same level as himself. Taking him down would be akin to one head of the Hydra attempting to sever another. He fought to remain calm, using all the powers of control he'd learned through his decades in the most brutal and dangerous information-gathering service in the world.

'You have evidence?'

'I have a bullet-wound in my shoulder that says he sent an Alpha team to terminate us both.'

'How do you know it was Prokop?'

'He was in Berlin when Tatiana Zykova was betrayed. He was manning the signals room. He alerted Cleary as soon as the listening device went live. And now he's the only one who knew about my operation, except you, General. Prokop is the connection.'

'Return to Moscow and bring Zykova with you. I will need her evidence and yours.'

'I can't do that.'

'Bring her in,' Levkov ordered.

'I'm resigning,' Dimitriev told him. 'That is permitted these days, is it not? And if my years of service mean anything to you, you won't try to find me. I wish you well. You were a good teacher, Gennady Fyodorovich. The best. Good luck in your coming battle.'

The line went dead. Levkov replaced the receiver and sat back in his chair. His mind was already calculating how to begin the deadly chess game that would result in Prokop's ruin. Or his own. For when two heads of the hydra fought only one lived. The other died.

*

One floor below Levkov's office, a powerful American-built computer had already locked onto the source of the call and Prokop was summoned immediately. He entered the signals room where two of his officers were hunched over their desks.

'Have either of you listened to the conversation?' he asked.

They both answered no. He looked at their faces. If they were lying, they were very good. 'Leave,' he ordered.

They obeyed.

He activated the playback of Levkov's call and his jaw hardened as he listened. The Alpha team had failed in their mission to silence Zykova and Dimitriev. Now the final act of his long battle against the Soviet Union was about to play out. It was a battle that had, in truth, ended long ago. His enemy had died, cut open and slaughtered from within. His mother country, Ukraine, had achieved freedom from its oppressors. Now the battle was simply one for his own survival.

The call to Levkov been made from Manchester airport. He picked up the phone and dialed the Alpha team leader Lieutenant Colonel Arshan to give him this information, with orders to complete his mission immediately. He had to remove the evidence against him before Levkov made his move.

CIA Headquarters, Virginia

Charles 'Chip' Hermon had only just begun his shift. His extra large coffee cup was full to the brim. He'd added all four plastic cups of thin cream and four sachets of sugar to the watery brown drink. It was terrible coffee, but you got a lot for your money and the low-level signals analysts at Langley were notoriously poorly paid.

Another day of routine stretched out before him, monitoring transmissions, coding and filing the sound files, batching anything unusual for analysts higher up the food-chain. A few years ago he'd dreamed of one day becoming a CIA-man, a player in the greatest game of all. Now he knew the stark reality: spying was nothing more than gathering information, cataloguing information, filing information. Being a spy had more in common with being a librarian than one of the smooth action heroes he'd watched on the big screen.

He was about to take his first sip of coffee, needing the caffeine kick to keep his attention on his work, when he noticed a flashing icon on his screen. He wondered if there was a bug in the system. It was the kind of icon he'd only seen before during training drills. He clicked the icon and read the message, then put his coffee down slowly. He wouldn't be needing it any more. A Flagged Word had been identified and immediate action was required. Level 5 Command must be alerted at once – highest priority.

Chip had Level 3 clearance, higher than most others at his pay grade due to the sensitive nature of his work. His direct boss had Level 4 clearance. Above him there was only one more grade, Level 5, the head of operations James Cleary. He'd never met or even seen Cleary, and only knew of his name but Chip knew the procedure well enough. He would have to deliver the message and its content personally to Cleary. He printed off the message, exited the program and left the room casually to avoid arousing interest among his colleagues. He didn't want to be stopped now that something mildly interesting was about to happen. He was about to deliver a top-secret eyes-only message to a Level 5 spook. He took the elevator up two floors and walked along the corridor to Cleary's office.

'I need to see Mr. Cleary,' he told the young man outside.

The gatekeeper looked up unhurriedly. 'Mr. Cleary is unavailable. Can I help you at all?'

'I need to see him personally,' Chip replied.

The gatekeeper smiled at Chip. It was the self-satisfied smile of an insignificant man who controlled access to the most powerful man in the division. 'If you could tell me your name and what it's regarding I might be able to arrange something when Mr. Cleary gets back from Toronto next week.'

'Sure,' Chip returned the smile. He was going to enjoy this. A lot… 'Could you tell him Chip Hermon from Signals had a message for him marked 'Immediate Action, Level 5 Eyes-Only' which he needed to hand-deliver to him personally but that you – his *Secretary* I guess you'd call it – asked him to sit on it until he got back from Toronto, so he should pop down whenever he's ready and I'll give him the message.'

The gatekeeper's smile was replaced by an angry frown. 'Why the hell didn't you say? Go in.'

Chip knocked and entered swiftly. Cleary was hunched over a file of paper three inches thick. He appeared relaxed, with his tie loosened and his jacket off. He looked up slowly and examined him coolly. Chip noticed the livid red pock-marked skin, like that of a reptile burnt in the desert sun. He wondered if he would end up the same way if he stayed in the job too long.

'Chip Hermon, sir,' he said briskly. 'Just picked up a Level 5 Eyes-Only on the international chatter. A telephone conversation originating in the UK and received in the GRU headquarters in Moscow. A flagged word was used on two occasions.'

'Has anyone else seen the message besides yourself?' Cleary asked deliberately. His voice was soft and rasping. Chip guessed it was due to the disfigurement he noticed on Cleary's throat. He had the sense that his answer was important.

'No.'

'No one but you?'

'No one but me.'

'What was the flagged word?' Cleary asked absently, though Chip had the feeling he was under close scrutiny.

'I've no idea, sir. It wasn't marked on the message. The word was programmed as a flag some time prior, I don't know when, and the message was flagged automatically by the system.'

He handed the paper to Cleary, and Cleary read it without comment. His face showed no emotion, not even a flicker of interest, and for a moment Chip wondered if he'd be reprimanded for wasting the Chief's time. Cleary folded the paper neatly, twice, and put it into his jacket pocket.

'You did the right thing, bringing this to me, Agent Hermon. Now, where is the original message?'

'Still on the system,' Chip answered.

'I need you to delete it and to remove all trace of it. Is that possible?'

'Yes. I can do that, sir.'

'I want to see you do it. I'll come to your terminal.'

'There's no need, sir,' Chip told him. 'I can do it here, now, if you'll allow me to use your terminal.'

'Even better. Go ahead.'

Cleary moved his chair aside and Chip's fingers moved in a blur over the keyboard. Two files appeared on the screen, the first a sound file, the second a written transcript of the conversation in Russian and English, both created by the system software automatically with no human involvement. The accuracy was such nowadays that human evaluation was rarely needed.

'Shall I delete both files?' Chip asked.

'Play the audio first,' Cleary ordered. Cleary's Russian was fluent and he wanted to hear the name spoken again before he erased it forever. The first voice came over the speaker, deep and calm. It was familiar but he couldn't place it. Then he heard a voice he knew very well, that of General Gennady Levkov, an old adversary from the day when he'd known the names and faces of his enemies.

Cleary put on headphones and listened to the exchange that followed. The voices had been cleaned up and slowed automatically, to make the conversation more intelligible, and he had no difficulty in following it. He heard the name of his long-time mole within The Organisation, Prokop. It was ironic that Prokop's treachery should be unearthed now, so many years after the Cold War had ended. He felt no emotion for Prokop, the man was a traitor and he despised traitors. He wondered how painfully Prokop would die now that there was a semblance of change in Russia. Would he die in torment or face a swift, merciful death by firing squad. He found he didn't care one way or the other. Prokop had long since outlived his usefulness to the CIA. But Prokop had not been the flagged word. Prokop was a GRU general and as such well-known to the intelligence community. His name would set off no alarm bells in the CIA. It was later in the conversation when the name Zykova had been mentioned that the flag had been raised.

Cleary removed his headphones. 'Where did this call originate?'

Chip punched more keys and the location came up, along with a map and a satellite view of the area, 'Manchester airport, Terminal 3.'

'Thank you. Now erase all files relating to this message if you please Mr. Hermon.'

Chip complied. Something in the Director's tone made the job less exciting than he'd imagined, and he felt uneasy being so close to Cleary's silence. He wondered what long buried emotions the message had evoked and decided he had no wish to find out.

'Done,' he said.

'Now I'm going to ask you a question,' Cleary said deliberately, 'And I want you to think carefully before answering. Is there any trace of the message itself, or any log that it was received at all, on this, or any other computer or system?'

Chip knew the answer immediately, but waited a moment to show he'd given it due consideration. 'None whatsoever, sir.'

'Good, thank you for bringing it to my attention,' Cleary said, 'anything further on this subject and you contact me again, day or night, here's my direct number,' he said handing

Chip a card. Chip pocketed the card and left the room quickly, not bothering to gloat at the gatekeeper who was deliberately avoiding his eye. He hurried down the corridor. He wanted to be away from Cleary's office now, back at the familiar surroundings of his desk, his computer, his files and his coffee cup. The visit to Level 5 had unnerved him more than he'd expected it would. Maybe working as a librarian wasn't such a bad way to spend the day after all.

Manchester Airport, England

Julia and Vasili boarded the flight to Athens separately. They had bought their tickets the day before, booking separately and paying in cash. They had sat apart in the airport lounge and now they sat on opposite sides of the aisle at the rear of the plane, ostensibly strangers to anyone who didn't know different. The position afforded them a good view of the other passengers. There were no obvious threats.

They had tossed a bag containing all their weapons into the Manchester Ship Canal and abandoned the Astra in the city centre before taking a bus to the airport. It would have been foolhardy to try and bring weapons through airport security. They would acquire new weapons when they arrived. Vasili had contacts in Greece who could get them any weapons they wanted, for a price, and arrange for the two of them to disappear without trace. Both carried only a single piece of hand luggage and a large roll of cash. The less they carried over from their old lives the better.

The air stewards shut the doors. Julia breathed a sigh of relief. She had to force herself to avoid looking at Vasili and smiling. They were away free. They were safe. The 'Fasten Seatbelts' sign lit up and the captain's voice came over the speaker system. They were being held at the departure gate for a short time while a routine safety check was being carried out. They would be on the move shortly. Julia shot a glance at Vasili and saw that he shared her concern.

Outside, Terminal 3 was being evacuated as a bomb disposal team checked for the suspicious package that had been reported. They found nothing, not even a forgotten bag. The call was finally dismissed as a hoax. Inside the cocoon of the aircraft, only the pilot knew what had been happening. Sixty minutes had crept by before he announced he'd been given the All Clear and they would be on the move just as soon as a few late-arrivals had boarded.

The front door was opened by the air steward and Lieutenant Colonel Arshan entered, followed by the remaining members of his Alpha team, Konstantinov, Markevich, and Kitaev. They were shown to seats at the front of the plane by the steward but Arshan ignored him and strolled down the aisle towards the rear. His gaze was fixed straight ahead but his peripheral vision took in each passenger as he went. Julia knew that with his training, there was no doubt he would recognise her and Vasili.

A stewardess emerged from the rear and asked him to return to his seat but Julia felt his eyes on her for a second longer than the other passengers. Arshan smiled apologetically to the stewardess and returned to the front. Watching his retreating back, Julia felt a cold fear descend, fear of an agent who was trained as she had been, by the best of the best. Two of his team had already died trying to silence her, but she knew he would continue his mission until he completed it successfully or died in the attempt.

The aircraft lurched forward and the whine of the Rolls Royce engines rose until the power shook the plane. The pilot released the brake and the flat grass and square buildings of the airfield flew past. Next a green and brown patchwork of fields appeared in the window, quickly being replaced by the white glare of the low cloud that hung over Manchester.

Julia looked across at Vasili. He appeared calm. He was thinking the same as she was. The Alpha team had no weapons. They would not have risked bringing them through the tight airport security. They might improvise weapons aboard the plane, but even if they did, it was unlikely they would use them on a crowded aircraft, with the possibility of a hostage situation developing. They might try at Athens airport but that too was unlikely. Too much security, too many armed guards, too many cameras. No, they would wait. They would stalk her and Vasili like wolves waiting for the right moment to strike, the moment that afforded them the best chance of escape after the kill and make a clean exit. The Organisation wanted no trail back to its lair.

That meant in all likelihood, no attack would take place for at least five or six hours, not until they were clear of Athens airport. Which meant that despite the proximity of four of the world's deadliest soldiers hell-bent on killing her, Julia knew she needed to relax. If she didn't the tension would leave her exhausted by the time the wolves descended. She forced herself to lean back in her seat and slow her breathing, pushing the tension from her body with her mind, until she felt herself settled like still water. She glanced across to Vasili, wondering if he agreed with her assessment of the situation. She saw that he did. He was asleep.

Washington Dulles Airport, Virginia

The security guard at Washington Dulles Airport recognised the CIA badge immediately. He saw plenty of them, working as he did, so close to CIA headquarters at Langley. Nevertheless he held it up beside the reference sheet he'd been issued and went through the checklist to ensure it was genuine. The reason for his extra caution was the paperwork that had been handed over along with the badge – a permit to carry an agency-issue firearm on board the aircraft. He checked the permit too and finally compared the agent's passport picture with the man before him. The face was the same, there was no doubt, even the passive expression was the same, but he sensed that not far beneath the surface, the agent was burning to get on the plane. He wondered why.

'Please go through, Director Cleary,' he said smartly.

'Thank you,' the director answered with a half smile.

'And enjoy London,' the guard added. Director Cleary did not reply.

Athens Airport, Greece

Hector Nicolaides drove his yellow Mercedes to the front of the taxi rank. For the price he'd paid for it, he could have bought a brand new Peugeot, Skoda or Mitsubishi, but he had paid for a Mercedes C-class with over 100,000 kilometres on the clock, a car that, he believed, would do another 100,000 more before he parted with it. Ever since he'd been a young boy, he'd shared his father's love of cars. Not sports cars which he rejected for their lack of comfort and useful space, but beautifully engineered vehicles like the Mercedes that transported you serenely, safely, effortlessly, to your destination.

He could have settled for a leaner engine and enjoyed better fuel efficiency, but the 2.8-liter engine retained a reassuring purr of effortless power on the rare occasion that he needed it. There were good business reasons for the Mercedes, too. Every taxi driver knew that taking travelers from A to B was the least profitable of all aspects of the job. It paid far better to become a personal tour guide for those wishing to see the wonders of Athens in comfort and style. Americans would pay the most for such a service, followed by the British, Germans and Japanese. Other nations of Europe tended to bargain harder, while Eastern Europeans bargained so much that there was little point in wasting a day with them. The Americans and Northern Europeans appreciated the well-rehearsed explanations he provided on the way to each of the city's sights. The combination of the most stunning sights of the classical world, the personal service of the driver, and the soft local wine combined to make his clients pay well over the odds. He also believed the timeless quality of the Mercedes added an extra dimension to the whole experience and to the size of the tips he received.

The couple that approached him now was the right age. The man was in his forties, bronzed and handsome, with a physique that told of many hours in the gym, the woman ten years younger, beautiful, lithe and elegant, walking with the grace of a model or a dancer. Neither carried any luggage apart from a small bag, and he struggled to decide which country they came from. He was still wondering when they opened the door and entered with an urgency that surprised him.

'Drive!' the man ordered in Greek.

Hector was about to turn and smile at the passenger and ask, 'Where to?' since it was important to show each new passenger who was the boss in his taxi, and establish a little personal rapport at the beginning, but he caught the man's eyes in his rear view mirror, boring into his, and his question stopped in his mouth.

'Now,' the passenger added. The voice was quiet, but Hector felt the need to oblige and pulled away swiftly from the airport terminal.

'What is your name?' the passenger demanded.

'My name is Hector, what is yours?' Hector asked, his tone light and friendly, eager to diffuse the sense of unease he now felt in the presence of his new passengers.'

'It's good to meet you, Hector,' the passenger said, ignoring Hector's question. 'Do you offer city tours?'

'If it's a city tour you want, you got into the right taxi, my friend,' Hector said proudly. 'We can begin right now, if you like. I will take you to the Acropolis first, where you can see the Parthenon. Then the Archeological Museum. After that we can go to your hotel so you can freshen up. I'll return in an hour and take you to the old quarter of Plaka, where you can wander in the cobbled streets and have dinner in a traditional taverna.'

Hector swung the Mercedes onto the E94 heading northwest to Athens. A hundred yards behind, another taxi, this time an Opel, turned the same way.

'How much do you charge for a tour?' the passenger asked.

Hector's eyes flicked from the man to his silent companion. She was blonde. It was not her natural colour, and her hair was cut a little too short for his liking, but the overall effect was still quite special. She regarded him coolly, awaiting an answer to her companion's question.

'Three hundred Euros,' he said lightly, hoping he might get away with such an extortionate price. They looked wealthy enough.

'I will give you a thousand if you make a different tour,' the man said.

Hector recovered his surprise quickly. He raised both hands off the wheel in apology. 'It's too late to include Delphi or Corinth, they're too far away. But we can go tomorrow. It's not a problem. I can take you all the way to Meteora if you like, where you can see beautiful monasteries built on the tops of mountains.'

'I don't want to go to Delphi,' the passenger said. 'I want to go to Piraeus.'

Hector was confused. 'Piraeus is the port of Athens,' he explained, 'I thought you knew, you speak Greek so well, I just assumed ...'

'I know Piraeus,' the passenger said sharply, 'But I want the tour first.' He leaned forward until his mouth was near

Hector's ear, 'Do you see the taxi behind us?'

Hector glanced in his rearview mirror and saw the Opel trailing them. He nodded.

'When we arrive in Piraeus, I don't want that car behind us. Do you understand?'

Hector shrugged.

'Get rid of it, and there's a thousand Euros in it for you.' The passenger held up a wad of notes for Hector to see. 'Fail, and you get nothing.'

From the passenger's expression, Hector saw he might also risk something far worse than not getting paid. He continued driving smoothly. It had been many years since Hector had raced around the streets of Athens in the small hours of the morning against other foolish young drivers, drivers with too much pride and not enough sense. He'd seen too many accidents on the roads of his beloved country. Nowadays he congratulated himself on the smoothness of his driving, the careful gear changes that didn't crunch the mechanism, the delicate touch on the clutch and brake that would keep those parts functioning for years, the considerate treatment of the tyres, to keep the tread as good as new. Then he dropped two gears and floored the accelerator. The tyres screeched an instant protest before finding their grip and sending the Mercedes surging forwards. A thousand Euros was a thousand Euros – he could buy new tyres and brakes with plenty to spare.

The Mercedes snaked through the traffic on the three-lane highway. It was busy, as always. Many of the cars were hire-cars, moving slowly while their drivers got accustomed to the controls. Hector checked his mirror. He couldn't see the Opel now. Losing it had been easier than expected. His passengers stared through the rear window. He wondered who would be chasing these two, and why. Perhaps they were drug dealers? Their expensive attire suggested it, but they didn't seem the types. He kept his foot down on the accelerator, though not to the floor, not wishing to attract the traffic police unnecessarily.

The highway entered the suburban sprawl of Athens. With its high rise blocks and the dull shops and factories, there was nothing to suggest they were in the capital of the classical world. The yellow Opel reappeared in his mirror. He cursed silently to himself. He imagined the driver had been offered an equally big incentive to stay with him, or perhaps a more serious threat. He threw the Mercedes right across two lanes and off the highway, down an exit road to the intricate streets of the suburbs. It would be easier to lose the Opel there. The Opel followed, three cars behind on the curving slip road. The traffic lights at the intersection ahead were green. Hector sped across. The Opel followed, pulling out to overtake one of the cars between them to a loud salvo of horns. Hector stepped on the gas, heading to a grid of small, interlocking streets he knew four blocks ahead where he'd be able to lose the Opel. The next set of traffic lights were turning red but Hector sped through. The Opel followed, overtaking the stationary car before it and causing a new blare of horns. Hector saw it clip a blue delivery van and swerve into the opposite carriageway, narrowly missing a white Fiat. Crossing the road so late had been suicidal, and Hector wondered what incentive the Opel driver had been given to take such risks. The promise of money was a powerful incentive, but to cross an intersection so late wasn't worth any price. The other driver must have been in fear of his life. He looked again in the rearview mirror and into the eyes of the dark-haired man who controlled him now, and wondered what danger his own life would be in if he failed.

He hit the accelerator hard and raced onwards, amid the sound of new horns, towards the tightly woven streets of Koukaki in the centre. Before them the proud columns of the Parthenon rose from the ancient citadel that was the Acropolis, built on top of the rocky limestone bluff and towering over the modern city below. The familiar picture of the cradle of Western civilization came and went between the shapeless modern blocks of the new city.

Hector shot another glance in his mirror. The Opel had fallen further behind after swerving at the intersection. He threw the Mercedes into a hard right and tore down a narrow side street. If he'd continued to where the streets were even more dense, many were blocked off and he risked getting stuck. He turned left and right in quick succession before accelerating northwards. The dramatic rock and pale stonework of the Acropolis came into view once more.

In these narrow streets life went on almost unchanged from what it had been centuries ago. Market traders still set out their stalls, though instead of selling fruit and vegetables, cheeses and oil, they sold smoothies and souvenirs. People still drank small cups of coffee in small pavement cafes, though it was usually espresso now rather than traditional Greek coffee, slow-cooked on the stove in a long-handled copper pot.

Flooring the accelerator again, Hector felt the old heart of the Mercedes burst into life, the willingness to please in the old frame, and thanked his stars that he'd chosen a powerful car for his work. He was almost at the end of the street when he saw the Opel skid around the corner, smoke rising and mixing into the dust and smog of the Athens afternoon. Hector was forced to slow urgently to avoid an old woman carrying a watermelon in a string bag, then took a series of tight turns, left, right, right, left, through the narrow streets. Coming to the junction with a main road, he paused just long enough to check the traffic and glance in his mirror. The Opel had gone. He pulled out and raced away up the two-lane road, heading northwest, towards the main road that would take them to Piraeus. Red traffic lights stopped them three hundred metres on, and Hector drummed the steering wheel nervously with his fingers, waiting for the lights to change. His passengers scanned the street behind them for the Opel, but it was not to be seen. Hector breathed a sigh of relief. He'd done it.

The lights changed to green and he pulled away slowly with only a cursory glance in his mirror. He saw it again. The Opel was a hundred metres behind and moving fast. Hector saw his passengers exchange tense glances. He accelerated again, undertaking a slow moving car in the middle lane. His years of driving in this city, his city, had given him an innate knowledge of the traffic systems of the city, and he could predict the changes of traffic lights to the second. The lights had been red for three seconds by time the Opel raced across the junction. He watched it narrowly avoid two cars on the far carriageway and weave across the junction, tyres pawing at the ground like an angry racehorse seeking purchase on the smooth road surface. Then it was swept aside by a white SUV travelling at speed. The impact pushed the Opel sideways across the junction and out of sight. All that remained in Hector's mirror were stationary cars scattered haphazardly across the junction, and people gawping or running in the direction of carnage unseen.

St Petersburg, Russia

General Kupchenko no longer travelled to the Finland Station or stood beneath the statue of Lenin. He no longer stayed at the Hotel Europa and drank a silent toast to his fallen comrades at the bar. When he returned to the city of his birth – known once again as St Petersburg rather than Leningrad – he stayed in his comfortable dacha by the sea, and had his driver Somov take him to the Piskarevsky Cemetery to pay his respects.

The dacha was situated on a rise overlooking the sparkling Gulf of Finland. It was spacious and compared to most dachas, which were little more than log cabins – well appointed with electricity, heating and hot and cold running water. Kupchenko rarely used the heating, preferring the modest warmth of the open fire. There was no need to heat such a large place when he was alone except for Somov, who stayed during the day and slept in the nearby barracks at night.

Most of the time he reread old books from his library or played chess against a machine so old that he could, on occasion, still beat it. However on this day he'd felt like taking a walk and had taken a path through the larch forest to the seashore. He'd followed the rocky coastal path for half a mile before arching back inland. It had been a fine spring morning, the air crisp, the sun bright, and the Baltic Sea sparkling blue and silver for him.

On his return Somov lit a fire and served sweet lemon tea without being prompted. He'd also followed him on his walk from a discreet distance to assist him if he got into difficulty. Ten years earlier Kupchenko would have objected to being nursemaided this way. Now he found he didn't mind. Let Somov follow him, and drive him, and chop wood for his fire. He would enjoy these small privileges in the time he had left.

Somov had brought in the two briefcases of files from the car and placed them beside the table by the window. They were the files he intended reading during his stay at the dacha. The view from the large window over the gulf would make the tedium of working on them a little more bearable. He sipped his tea and thought of his wife Ludmilla, and how she would have loved the dacha. She would have invited endless family and friends to stay, served cold *okroshka* on the terrace in the summer, and baked warming *pirozhki* in the winter. How she would have played music and sung her favourite patriotic songs, as they had done in their youth. He wondered what she would have made of the CD player in the dacha – his memories of her were memories of wireless radios and gramophones.

Somov's voice interrupted his reverie. 'Sir, there is an urgent call for you.'

He'd not heard Somov enter. He chided himself. His foolishness was getting too much, even for an old man. He didn't ask who it was, but simply rose from his armchair and moved to his desk. He lifted the receiver and Somov transferred the call from the other room. He waited until he heard Somov hang up.

'First Deputy Chief Kupchenko?' the caller said.

Kupchenko recognised the voice immediately. It was Levkov, whom he'd recruited personally in the late sixties. Levkov had been one of his finest choices and he'd followed Levkov's rise in The Organisation with more than a little pride over the years. 'Gennady Fyodorovich, is there any need for such formality between us?' he said slowly.

'General, please listen carefully,' Levkov said. 'I received a call from England, from Colonel Vasili Dimitriev, an hour ago. I've been trying to get hold of you ...'

'I'm on vacation,' Kupchenko grunted. 'What's so urgent?'

'Dimitriev's been in contact with a former agent, Tatiana Zykova.' Levkov waited, knowing that the old general probably remembered agent Zykova better by a another name, if not several other names.

'Tatiana Zykova has been missing since the mission in Berlin in 1989,' Kupchenko said. His mind was as sharp as ever for things that mattered.

'Yes. Dimitriev says she has implicated a traitor high within The Organisation.'

'Who?'

'General Prokop.'

Kupchenko knew Prokop. He'd never liked the man, believing him superior and conceited, but he'd never suspected him of being a traitor, *the* traitor they'd been seeking for so many years, a ghost they'd not even been sure existed. Prokop had risen through the ranks as a signals officer, and a good one. Kupchenko's blood ran cold at the thought of all the classified material that had passed through Prokop's hands over the years.

'You have proof?'

'Not yet. But I have the word of Dimitriev and that is enough to warrant an investigation.'

'Why is it enough?' Kupchenko demanded. He needed more than the word of a colonel delivered via telephone from England to investigate a general like Prokop. Levkov breathed out silently, steadying his voice before speaking.

GORAN POWELL

'Do you believe you can ever really know another man's heart, General? See into his soul so clearly that you would put your life in his hands without a moment's hesitation?'

Kupchenko had known four such men in the siege of Leningrad. He had put his life in their hands, and they in his, countless times in the 900 days that the Nazis had pounded his city to dust.

'Your point?' he demanded.

'Dimitriev is such a man.'

Kupchenko replaced the receiver without another word.

Port of Piraeus, Athens

Julia ate the grilled Souvlaki and warm flat bread slowly, forcing herself to chew and swallow with deliberate movements of her jaw. Vasili did the same. They drank water instead of wine and afterwards sipped strong sweet Greek coffee. When the sun dipped over the horizon, casting the ramshackle backstreets of Piraeus into a more somber mood, they made their way to the Mikrolimano marina. Vasili walked twenty paces ahead of her on the other side of the road. It was basic *Maskirovka*, to change what was being sought, in this case a couple, into two individuals, and basic field craft, to spread the target in case shooting began.

The marina was busy with vessels returning from a day at sea. Tourist boats disgorged red-faced passengers with souvenirs from the nearby islands and local fishermen unloaded their modest catch. The waters off Piraeus were among the busiest in the world and fish were not in plentiful supply.

Vasili entered a local bar at the end of the marina to search for the man he knew and trusted, a boat owner whom he'd worked with before. Julia didn't follow. Instead she joined a party of German tourists disembarking from a ferry, sitting among them on the quayside, within sight of the bar. She chatted in fluent German to an old lady travelling by herself, her senses still alert for any sign of the Alpha team. If they had survived the crash, they would still be searching for them.

Vasili emerged from the bar and sat beside her. 'Theo will meet us at his boat in five minutes and take us to Hania. We'll be there in a little over six hours.'

'Hania is in Crete?' she asked.

'Yes. I know a forger in Crete, a good one, based in Iraklion. He'll create new identities for us so we can cover our tracks properly. We just need some time.'

A short middle-aged man emerged from the bar. His skin was dark and leathery from long days in the sun, his hair black and curly, thinning on top. His limbs had the wiry strength of a boatman, but his short-sleeved shirt was stretched tight across a growing belly. He headed away from them towards the far side of the marina without glancing in their direction. That was good, the mark of a professional.

'That's Theo,' Vasili told her.

Julia didn't answer. Her attention was already elsewhere. A tall, rangy figure was approaching from the other direction, his face silhouetted by the harbour light behind him. Despite his athletic physique he limped, revealing he'd been in a recent accident. His hand was raised to his ear. He was speaking into a mobile. Vasili saw him too. They ran at the lone agent, knowing their best chance was to take him down before his comrades joined him.

Lieutenant Colonel Arshan saw the approaching figures and replaced his phone in his jacket. He withdrew the axe and utility knife he'd bought in a hardware store that afternoon and smiled. His guesswork had been correct. The targets would attempt to leave via Piraeus in a small boat. The passenger lists on the larger ferries made them too easy to trace. He had also guessed the marina correctly. Yet it was not guesswork, knowing your enemy, it was a skill he had learned at the same school where the renowned Colonel Dimitriev had trained. There was only one difference now. He was in his prime. Dimitriev was past his. He had been injured in the left knee and left elbow in the crash, and there was a livid bruise on his temple where his head had struck the window, but Konstantin, Markevich and Kitaev would be there in less than minute, and he was confident he could hold them off until they arrived.

Julia and Vasili withdrew the steak knives they'd pocketed in the taverna and split left and right. There was no talk of tactics, both knew how to give themselves the maximum advantage by attacking Arshan from two sides.

Arshan strode backwards now, without taking his eyes from them, prolonging the time to their engagement and giving his companions more time to join him. He moved to his right towards Julia, the weaker of the two, hoping to engage her first and use her body to block Dimitriev's attack. Then she was on him. The serrated knife lashed out and down to cut his left hand holding the utility knife. She was fast, but he was faster. He rolled his hand away and made to slash her biceps. She withdrew just in time. He used his forward momentum to bring down the axe in his right hand. As he did, his vision disappeared. She had thrown something in his face. The smell was familiar. Pepper. A cheap trick but surprisingly effective.

His strike was redirected low and he felt it being swept before him. She'd deceived him. Her first attack had deliberately been a fraction slow. She'd set him up, had him do what she wanted, and now she would kill him. He threw himself into a forward roll, following the direction of his axe swing, knowing his only chance of life was to move away from her. He felt the sting of her jagged blade across his ear as he rolled. He was lucky to be alive. He rolled twice more to create distance and allow his vision to clear, then rose with his feet on the edge of the quay, his heels overhanging the edge. The dark form of Dimitriev came towards him now at speed. He wasn't ready to face Dimitriev, not yet, and sprang back in a twisting dive into the sea.

'Vasili!' Julia shouted, knowing he was about to follow Arshan into the water and finish him. It was the right tactic with Arshan weakened but now there was a new more urgent threat: three figures approaching fast. Vasili turned and saw Julia lying prone on the ground. He was surprised because she'd not been injured. Her tactic came to him a moment later. She was thinking faster than he was. He needed to keep up. He moved away, drawing the assassins to him. They ignored Julia's prostrate form, believing Arshan had killed her, and approached the live threat, Dimitriev. They fanned out to advance on three sides, Konstantinov with a claw hammer and a folding knife, Markevich with an axe and a chisel, Kitaev with an antique army knife bought in a tourist shop.

'Is that woman alright?' The question came from an elderly Swedish woman who had just emerged from the cabin of her motor-launch. Her husband appeared a moment later and surveyed the scene before him open-mouthed.

'Go and fetch security,' Dimitriev told them calmly. They hesitated, then the woman left the boat and ran away down the marina while her husband returned to the cabin and locked the door.

Dimitriev stood relaxed, his arms by his sides, the trace of a smile on his lips as the three moved in for the kill.

'Are you praying, colonel?' Konstantinov asked.

Dimitriev's gaze rose slowly and he fixed Konstantinov's eye. 'I am.' He spoke with exaggerated slowness, then dropped his voice, forcing them to listen intently. 'Praying for the soul of your comrade, whose body is in the harbour.'

Konstantinov was about to answer when he sensed

movement behind. Dimitriev's words had occupied his attention and now it was too late, Julia was upon him. He spun away just as her blow struck the back of his neck. His movement took away a little of the force, but it was enough to knock him out. As his mind blanked, his last thought was that she'd chosen well. A knockout was instant while cutting or stabbing was not. He might have fought on, even with a serious wound, for thirty seconds before bleeding out.

Kitaev swung around to attack Julia, leaving Markevich with Dimitriev. He held the antique knife in the traditional saber grip and kept it forward, knowing the extra length was his advantage over Julia's smaller blade. They circled slowly, every sense hyper-alert. Kitaev tested with a feint – a backhanded cut to her blade hand. She snatched it away and stepped in, lightning fast, blocking his knife hand with her left and thrusting for his belly. Kitaev smashed down onto her forearm with the back of his palm but Julia had been expecting it. She used its energy to redirect her knife in a tight circle to his throat. Kitaev sensed it and brought his knife across to block her knife arm and cut. She switched her stab to a downward cut and slashed his wrist. Kitaev felt his blood ooze into his fingers. He ignored it. There were more urgent things to attend to. Julia had redirected the flow of her knife into a stab to his eye. He blocked with his left hand and brought the blade in his bloodied right down to cut her. She dropped to one knee and his knife sliced air. Julia cupped his ankle with her left hand and stabbed hard into the inside of his thigh, opening the femoral artery that carried blood from the heart to the legs. She continued to drive forward, unbalancing him and sending him crashing to his back. With his femoral punctured Kitaev knew death was close. He put it from his mind and stabbed at

Julia. She caught his wrist and pinned him with her knee.

'Lie still and hold your wound. You might live.' Then she was gone. It was pointless pursuing her, Kitaev knew. He would be unconscious before he caught her and dead moments later. He pressed one hand hard on the wound and worked quickly with the other to fashion a field dressing using a handkerchief in his pocket and his belt.

To his surprise, Markevich saw that Tatiana Zykova had bested Kitaev and was approaching fast. In the same moment Dimitriev was upon him. Markevich marvelled at his enemy's approach, so subtle that he hadn't registered it, even in his highly trained peripheral vision. The kick caught his wrist, already broken in the car accident. The agony caused him to release his axe. He ignored the shocking pain, channelling the hurt into a cold desire to kill Dimitriev. He lunged forward and thrust the chisel in his left hand at the older man's throat. Dimitriev twisted aside and smashed his fist into Markevich's liver with shocking force. Markevich bent to absorb the blow and drove the butt of the chisel handle into Dimitriev's left shoulder. Markevich had seen the bullet in London hit Dimitriev in the shoulder and he knew it would be agony for him.

Dimitriev felt his left side go numb. He smiled – it was God's will. He didn't question it. He loved God. God would never harm him. God had been merciful, leaving him a good hand, his right hand, and that hand still held a knife. He slashed it upwards across Markevich's triceps, severing the tendons and rendering his left arm useless. Markevich's right elbow swung around, striking him hard on the jaw and Dimitriev fell, rolling nimbly, waiting for his head to clear. Markevich bent to collect his axe from the ground, giving

Dimitriev the split second he needed to roll to his feet. But Arshan had reappeared from the water and struck Dimitriev's carotid with the hard inside of his forearm. Dimitriev went down, doubly dazed now, turning to drag Arshan down with him, knowing Arshan was unarmed and hoping to use him as a temporary shield to escape Markevich's axe. Arshan overcame his surprise that Dimitriev was not unconscious – he had no idea why not. He dropped to seize the knife from Dimitriev's hand while he was stunned.

Markevich caught the approach of Julia in the corner of his eye and turned. She sent a feint to his left which he ignored as he swung his axe for her neck. But her feint was not a feint, only her eyes had appeared uncommitted. She drove her blade hard across his left hand, slicing his fingers and causing the chisel to fall from his hand. At the same time she stepped inside the axe swing and threw him over her shoulder onto the concrete quay, dropping her left knee to impact his head a moment later. He was out cold.

Julia saw Arshan and Dimitriev fighting for the blade. She took Markevich's axe and brought the blunt end down on Arshan's skull.

Dimitriev rose and they surveyed the bodies on the marina. 'We should kill them,' Dimitriev said.

'Yes.' She replied. But neither moved. It wasn't so easy to kill your own kind.

'There they are!' It was the old Swedish tourist approaching with two security guards in tow and a moment later, Julia and Dimitriev were running to the far end of the marina and Theo's waiting boat.

*

Arshan forced himself back to consciousness by will alone. He saw Konstantinov sitting beside Kitaev, pressing his hand on Kitaev's wounded thigh and talking to him to prevent him going into shock. Arshan heard Kitaev laughing grimly at something Konstantinov had said, and not for the first time he marvelled at the courage and professionalism of his comrades. He shook Markevich awake, massaging his bruised temples and swearing softly beneath his breath. Once again he had underestimated his targets and they were lucky to be alive. He ordered Markevich to search the marina for a fast boat and waited beside Kitaev and Konstantinov for security to arrive. It took the two uniformed guards two minutes to appear, the smell of ouzo and cigarettes strong on their breath. Arshan waited until they'd radioed for an ambulance before knocking them out and taking their guns, one pistol and one sub-machine gun. He knelt beside Kitaev, who was pale but still conscious. 'Wait for the medics. We'll spring you from the hospital once we've taken care of the mission.'

Kitaev nodded grimly. It was the only option. He would die quickly from loss of blood if he tried to accompany Arshan in the chase.

*

Julia and Dimitriev emerged from the cabin where they had been checking one another's bodies, searching for puncture wounds that may have gone undetected in the battle. They were both unscathed. Julia extinguished the torch and sat on the deck away from Theo in an area of deep shadow. Theo wanted nothing to do with her, to know as little as possible about her, she knew. That was good – Theo was a pro.

There were no lights on the boat, nothing to alert another vessel to their whereabouts. Only a half-moon and the stars lit the ocean, casting a silver web across the gentle waves. Ahead, red and green dots told of three larger ships, ferries or cruise liners making their way across the water. Behind, the lights of Piraeus grew dimmer in the distance. Soon the lights would disappear altogether and they would be alone on the open water. Free, until they reached Hania.

She noticed a light behind them that was not getting dimmer. It was getting brighter. It was a boat, approaching fast. Dimitriev saw it too, as did Theo, who pushed the engine to maximum. It was no use. Theo's old wooden speedboat was no match for the state-of-the-art motor launch that had tracked them with its on-board radar. Within three minutes the launch was bearing down on them, the tall white prow high above them, powerful arc lights illuminating their own craft. Dimitriev went into the cabin and reappeared with a spear gun and a flare. The launch drew alongside and Arshan's figure appeared on the prow. He fired a submachine gun blast across the deck and the old wood exploded in splinters. Dimitriev returned fire with the spear gun, missing Arshan by half a metre. Arshan smiled. It had been an excellent shot for such an inaccurate weapon. Theo turned the boat away and the launch sped past them, turning tightly for another attack.

'We should give ourselves up and spare Theo,' Julia told Dimitriev.

'They'll kill him anyway,' Dimitriev said, taking aim with the flare. 'Get below.'

'I'm staying with you.'

There was no time to argue. The launch approached fast. They took cover and Dimitriev shot the flare just as Arshan opened fire. The gun was hopelessly inaccurate. He missed by several metres. More bullets thudded into the deck as the launch roared past. The speedboat slowed.

'One of the propellers has been hit,' Theo told him.

The launch came back around fast and caught up to the ailing speedboat. Arshan stood on the deck. Dimitriev took Julia's hand and they stood together, taking no cover now, waiting for the end, a clean end, a proud end, not cowering in a corner or begging for their lives. The launch pulled alongside and the muzzle of Arshan's gun was upon them.

They waited, but no bullets came. Arshan held them in his sights for thirty seconds while the launch curved away. Julia felt his gaze on her long after he had disappeared into the darkness.

'What happened?' she murmured. 'Is it over?'

'Levkov won his battle with Prokop,' Dimitriev told her. 'The assassination order has been rescinded.'

'How do you know?' she asked.

'Nothing else would make the Alpha team give up,' he said softly, turning to her, finding her lips in the darkness, feeling the warmth of her tears on his cheek, holding her so tight that nothing could ever pry her from his grip again.

Lake District, England

An incessant knocking woke DCI Simons from his dream. He'd been walking among strangers on a broad windswept beach, then running as the tide had begun to come in fast without warning. The water was up to his knees. The heavy wet sand tugged at his feet, slowing him. The others were far ahead of him now, running normally. The dream was familiar, he'd had it before. He was glad to be awakened from it.

An unfamiliar face at the window, a voice he didn't recognise. He was in a police car. Mena Gakhar was sitting to his left, talking to the stranger. Simons' mind began to clear. The man was a farmer. They were parked in his field. The farmer produced a penknife and begin cutting Mena's bonds.

'Are you alright Mena?' Simons asked, his voice little more than a croak.

'I'm fine, apart from sitting in my own piss for ten hours,' she said. 'How about you?'

Simons smiled weakly. His own seat was damp too. It was the least of his worries. He tried to be patient as the farmer cut away Mena's bonds carefully and methodically. He had to force himself not to struggle against them pointlessly now that he was about to be freed. He was desperate to reach for his phone, to call his wife, to tell her he was safe. To tell her how much he loved her.

'I'm fine,' he told her, his eyes glistening as he smiled. 'Same as you. I'm just fine.'

Khodinka Airfield, Moscow

Prokop fought to control the tremor in his left hand as he held the lighter to another cigarette. He'd played the deadly game for so long, during a time of such danger, it was ironic that his denouncement and arrest should come now, when they were at peace with the old enemy.

In the end, Levkov had not needed the testimony of Dimitriev or Zykova to prove his guilt. Once Cleary's arrests had been compared with his own involvement there had been too many links to be written off as coincidence. First Deputy Chief Kupchenko had questioned him personally. Under the old man's icy gaze his defences had crumbled quickly and he'd confessed everything. Now he was simply tired, so tired that all he wanted was a swift end. The irony was that ten years ago, his wish would have been granted. He would have endured several days of drugs and torture to ensure he'd spoken every word of his treachery before being killed in the usual way – fed alive into the incinerator. But now, with the new government, it had been ten years since anyone had been incinerated. It had been four years since anyone had been executed by firing squad. He had begun to fear his court martial might become a show trial to enhance the image of the new bureaucracy. So he was almost proud of his former colleagues when they decided to maintain a firm grip and ordered his execution just two days hence with no room for appeal.

Throughout the night he had replayed his reasons for betraying the Soviet Union – he never deigned to call it the motherland, it was no mother to him. His family was from Ukraine and it had suffered under the yoke of the Russian communists like no other land. As a boy his mother had told him stories of a famine so bad that her neighbours had eaten the bones of their dead children to survive the winter. His grandparents had died in that famine, and his father, his elder brother and his little sister, who had been a baby. But his mother had lived. She had been strong. She had remarried after some years and given birth to one more son. Him. Growing up, she had instilled in him a hatred for the Soviets as passionate as her own. But she had also encouraged him in his studies at the Soviet school, and later at the university in Moscow, where he had excelled. She had died one year before his graduation. She had never seen him receive his degree, or enter the Red Army as an officer of the signals corps, or learn that through his hard work and talent he had achieved a post in military intelligence.

The American CIA man James Cleary had approached him on his first foreign assignment in Sophia, and Prokop had jumped at the chance to gain retribution against the empire that had ruined his homeland. Soon, the simple act of his betrayal was reason to continue, he had no option to back out. Cleary gave him none. Countless times over the years he'd thought he would be discovered. In Berlin it had been close. Now that Levkov had denounced him he felt almost relieved. The waiting was over. He would know peace at last. He pulled on the cigarette. The guards had allowed him to keep a supply that would see him through to his final hours, and now, he was down to his last packet.

The sound of a heavy set of keys jangled in the iron door. 'Time to go, *General*,' the guard said sarcastically.

He rose unhurriedly and stubbed out his cigarette beneath his shoe. The guard's mention of his rank gave him the strength he needed to walk out of his cell upright, unaided, his head held high, his jaw set firm. The first of three guards led the way down the dank corridor and two more guards followed behind. At the end of the corridor the lead guard unlocked a low metal door. The door opened into a small courtyard surrounded by high walls of smoke-blackened brick. The farthest wall was pock marked with countless bullet holes.

Eight soldiers stood in the yard, each with a rifle. They looked so young, little more than boys, fresh-faced and handsome, still rosy cheeked with the flush of youth. There was only one officer, a colonel whom he recognised, but whose name he didn't recall.

'Over there,' the guard told him, pointing his gun at the far wall. Prokop complied and the guard offered him a cigarette without prompting. The brand was Pall Mall, the same as Prokop smoked. He took one and the guard lit it for him and stepped away. He wondered at the generosity of the guard, that he should spare a cigarette even for a traitor. He wondered if it had been offered in goodwill, or simply as a means to keep his prisoner calm and prevent a scene.

Those in the firing squad who were not already smoking lit up too and the little courtyard was filled with mingling cigarette smoke. The prisoner and his executioners continued their silent ritual, joined by the pull of tobacco, until Prokop threw down the butt and clasped his hands tight behind his back to hide his growing tremor from the young men.

'Do you require a blindfold?' the colonel asked.

'No, I will look the men in the eye,' Prokop said proudly with only the smallest quaver in his voice.

The colonel shrugged. 'Prepare,' he told the firing squad. The young men threw down their cigarettes and trained their rifles on the general's chest. The space where his service medals had hung was now blank, but other than that, he wore the full dress uniform of an army general. It was not a target that any of the young men would forget in a hurry.

Prokop felt his left knee begin to tremble, quickly followed by his right. He felt his bladder loosening. He fought with all his power to maintain his rigid stance so that he might die with dignity.

'Fire!' the colonel shouted, and in the split second before the bullets tore into his breast, Prokop was filled with gratitude to the young officer for giving his order so promptly.

Kendal, Lake District

Simons knocked gently on the door to the small private room in the Westmoreland General Hospital. There was no answer. He opened it slowly, and saw Mena Gakhar in her police uniform, staring at herself in the mirror. She turned to look at him, her eyes slow to recognise him.

'Morning, Mena,' he said softly. 'How are you feeling today?'

'I'm not sure. I'm trying to work it out myself.'

'Are you up to leaving? If you're not, it's fine. We can stay a bit longer.'

'No, I want to go,' she said. 'I hate hospitals, always have. I don't want to stay a minute longer.'

The ward sister had checked them earlier that morning and given them both the all-clear. They had suffered nothing more than dehydration and a frightening ordeal that had left them shocked and dazed. Simons had spoken with the Chief Superintendent who had ordered both him and Mena to take some leave, and Simons had no intention of disobeying. He told Mena and she nodded. She could do with a break.

'Have you spoken to your family yet?' he asked gently.

'Yes, I spoke to mum and dad, and my little brother, Rafi.' She smiled at the thought of them. It brought sudden tears to her eyes. She brushed them away hurriedly. 'I didn't tell them what happened. They wouldn't rest until I left the force.'

Simons closed the door and took her hands. 'They worry about you, it's understandable.'

Fresh tears came and she turned away.

'You've had a hell of a shock Mena. So have I.' His hands went around her and he pulled her gently to him. She stiffened,

348

then held him too. His hand touched the back of her head.

'I'm sorry I put you through such an ordeal,' he said.

'It wasn't your fault,' she said.

'I wanted to tell you in the car, when we sat there all that time, but I couldn't.'

'There was no need,' she said, shaking her head to reassure him further. 'I knew it wasn't your fault. It's our job.'

'Even so, it was stupid. Dangerous. George Smith from MI5 warned me and I still went charging in like a bloody fool.'

They held each other a moment longer and then Simons released her gently.

'Funny,' Mena said with a small laugh. 'When we finally caught up with her, she wasn't who I was expecting at all.'

'I know what you mean,' Simons said. 'She surprised me too. Although I don't really know what I was expecting.'

'Some sort of an act, I suppose,' Mena offered.

'Yes, that's it,' Simons nodded. 'Some sort of act.'

'But she wasn't acting,' Mena said. 'She was… real. We saw the smallest doll.'

Simons frowned, not understanding. 'The Russian doll, don't you remember?' It's what George Smith called her. I think all the other layers were off. We saw the smallest doll.'

Simons smiled. 'Maybe we did. But I'd be quite happy if I never saw it again.'

'Me too,' Mena nodded.

He stepped away and opened the curtain. It was overcast outside with a grey cloud that threatened rain, but he wanted to be out there, moving, not in here, waiting. 'Your family's in Bradford, isn't it?' he asked.

'Yes. Why?'

'I thought we could go back that way. You could stop in and

pay them a visit.'

Mena smiled. 'That would be nice, if you don't mind. It's been a long time since I've seen them.'

'I don't mind at all,' Simons said happily. 'In fact, I'm thinking of doing something similar myself.'

'Really, where's your family?' she asked, taking up her bag and heading for the door.

'A little farther,' He grinned. 'We have a son in Australia and I think it's high time that we paid him a visit.'

EVALINA

Hania, Crete, 2001

The waters in the ancient port of Hania were calm, the quayside silent and still. Julia looked out through the cracked glass of the cabin window. It would be another hour before the local fishermen arrived to leave on the dawn tide, but already it was light enough to make out the Venetian skyline. 'It's so pretty here,' she said quietly.

'It's very pretty,' Vasili smiled. 'All of Crete is pretty.'

They were waiting for Theo to return. He had gone to buy a car for them. With their own car no one would see them enter or leave Hania. No taxi driver, no bus driver, no car-rental clerk. It was the first of many steps to removing all trace of themselves, to disappearing completely.

'Where will we go from here?' she asked.

'I know a place in the hills,' Vasili told her. 'Very remote. A good place to wait while we get new papers.'

When Theo returned it was with an ancient Renault Clio that was certainly not worth six thousand euros, however they accepted the car gratefully and the boatman offered no money in return.

Thirty minutes later they had left the wakening streets of Hania far behind and were climbing into the White Mountains of the interior. When the road finally levelled they were a thousand metres above sea level on the Omalos plateau. Beyond the little village that gave the place its name, two houses stood alone on a rocky track off the main road. Vasili roused the owner of one house and was given keys to the other, a well-appointed guest lodge. They were the only visitors, and Vasili paid the owner handsomely to ensure it stayed that way.

They slept until lunchtime, exhausted from their journey that had not stopped since leaving Coniston some 24 hours earlier. When Julia woke she found the room cold despite the quilt and the midday sun. She pressed her body against Vasili's for warmth. His arm encircled her and they lay together in silence, waking slowly. She placed her hand over his, and entwined her fingers with his.

'You bring me to Crete, and it's colder than Siberia,' she grumbled lazily.

'It's beautiful up here, you'll see. Tomorrow I'll show you a sight you won't forget.'

She could hear the excitement in his voice though she couldn't see his face.

'What about today?' she asked.

'I'll drive into Iraklion this afternoon. I know a forger there.'

'Is he good?' she asked absently.

'The best,' Vasili assured her. He touched the back of her neck, brushing her skin with his fingertips. 'Before he makes up the papers, there are a few things we need to decide.'

'Like what?' she asked, enjoying the gentleness of his touch.

'Like whether we should be married, for example,' he said, matter-of-fact.

She turned with a frown and squinted to see his face in the dim light. 'Is that some sort of proposal, Vasili?'

'Yes it is,' he nodded.

'Is that because it's easier for a couple to forge an identity if they're married?'

'No,' he said quickly.

'Are you sure? It's not just a clever idea you got from The Organisation?'

'No,' he grinned, 'It's an idea I got from God.'

'God, you say?' she snorted. 'Really Vasili …'

'Yes, from God,' he told her forcefully.

'God is speaking to you again, is he?'

'Yes he is.'

'Well I'm happy for you. But are you asking me to marry you, Vasili, because if you are, it's hard to tell from the way you're talking in circles.'

He laughed. 'Yes I am. So let me begin again.' He cleared his throat. 'Julia McKenzie, will you…' he stopped. 'No wait, that's not right. That is not your name. In fact, wait just a moment longer, please. There's something I wanted to give you first.' He saw her scowl lessen and sighed. 'It's not a ring. I'm sorry. I should have got one. I will get one. It's something I've been meaning to give you for some time but I never seemed to find the right moment.'

He opened his wallet and removed a slip of card concealed inside the lining. He handed it to her and she saw it was a small, faded black and white photo. A dark woman with kind eyes was sitting erect on a chair, the faintest hint of a smile on her lips, and an infant was standing at her knee – a girl. She knew the girl, though she hadn't seen her for many years. Images from dreams came tumbling back, and long-forgotten voices calling her name. She turned the picture over. Written in a neat hand, in faded black ink, she read: *Eva, aged 3*.

'I found it in your file,' Vasili told her gently. 'It was the only thing I could take. Anything else would have been noticed.'

She studied the photograph for some time before speaking,

summoning the courage to ask: 'What else did you find?'

'Your grandparents were from Spain,' he told her. 'They fought for the Communists during the civil war and escaped to the Soviet Union when the fascists won. For several years they worked to overthrow Franco but he was too strong. They found life in the Soviet Union was not the ideal they had believed in and fought for. They were vocal in their criticism of Stalin. Too vocal. Eventually they were denounced as foreign spies and sent to Siberia. They died in a work camp, but they had a daughter, and she survived. She grew up in Magadan and married a Kyrgyz man she met there. This man died a year later of tuberculosis, but not before giving her a daughter – you. After Stalin's death you and your mother were allowed to move to Leningrad. You lived there for three years with her, until she was taken ill and died. I don't know the cause. The death certificate just says ill-health. That's all I know. I thought you should know too. I'm sorry if it hurts you.'

'Don't be sorry. Never be sorry, Vasili,' she said, stroking the back of his neck at the hairline, feeling the soft stubble that she liked to run her fingers through. She smiled through her tears.

'So, will you marry me Evalina Petrovna?' he asked.

'My mother used to call me Eva,' she said, her words barely audible.

He smiled. 'Will you marry me, *Eva*?'

Samarian Gorge, White Mountains, Crete

Vasili had visited the forger in Iraklion the day before and set the forger's work in motion. Today, he was planning to show Eva something memorable while they waited for the forger to work his magic.

They rose early and dressed quickly, leaving the lodge just as the sun cleared the White Mountains. The high plain was bathed in a welcoming light despite the chill in the air. Leaving early meant they would avoid the bulk of the tourists arriving from the coast later to visit the spectacular Samarian Gorge, one of the longest and deepest in Europe, it was a chasm a thousand feet deep that sliced through the mountain range all the way to the sea on the south coast of the island. They strolled across small, misshapen meadows of wild flowers, bright yellow snow crocuses and white tulips tinged with purple and green. The surrounding ridges were lined with cypress. A prickly oak marked the beginning of the gorge.

They followed the narrow mule track that wove its way lazily into the chasm. As the sun rose higher the pale limestone that gave the White Mountains their name shone like polished silver and even the shaded areas of the gorge had a subtle light all of their own. The gorge had been cut by a river that still ran along the bottom of it, fed by fresh mountain springs. The river appears and disappears at intervals, and stepping stones had been positioned at the places on the walk where the trail crossed the water.

'You were right,' she said, unable to keep the wonder from her voice, 'This place is incredible.'

'I knew you'd like it,' he said.

'You like it too.'

'I do,' he replied. 'If we're lucky, we might just see an agrimi.'

'What's that?' she asked, enjoying Vasili's relaxed smile, the twinkle of mischief in his eyes.

'A little wild mountain goat with a black stripe on its back,' he answered.

'I'll keep an eye out for him,' she said.

They continued for an hour at a leisurely pace, enjoying the beauty of the gorge in silence, until the trail led them to an outcrop overlooking the ruins of the old village of Samaria, after which the gorge was named. They stopped and stood side by side, gazing at the small collection of square tumbledown remains of the little houses that had once been a working village.

'You like Crete, I can see,' she said happily.

'Do you plan to stay here once the new identity papers are done?' she asked.

'No, we need to leave Crete,' he answered seriously. 'But if you like Greece, we could stay here.'

'I know why you like it,' she laughed. 'All those churches and monasteries I saw coming up here, the grizzly old priests with long white beards ...'

'I like it, I admit it,' he laughed. 'But there's another reason too. Do you remember in Coniston, you told me about a place you dreamed of going where no one asked which side you were on. A place that has no sides.'

'I remember,' she said.

'I know such a place,' he smiled. 'An island.'

She laughed.

'Don't laugh,' he went on, 'this place is so remote, it doesn't even appear on the map. No one would ever find us there.'

'Is it deserted?' she asked, unsure if she was ready for such a life.

'No,' he grinned. 'Not quite. It's near a larger island. There's a small harbour with fishing boats, a few shops, a local school, and a church. And a ferry that goes across to a bigger island. We'd be safe there, together, away from the world.'

'It sounds perfect,' she smiled.

They entered the gorge, passing only the occasional hiker along the way, and stopping to drink the plentiful icy water that emerged from natural founts and danced down the cliffs to the river below. They stopped at the top of the Iron Gates, where the walls of the gorge came within fifteen feet of one another and fell in a chasm a mile deep to the rocky riverbed below. Here they sat side by side, a short way from the footpath, to eat the rustic bread, olives, and local mountain cheese that the lodge owner had packed for them, and to drink a small flask of wine.

The hiker who came down the path was travelling alone. He was American, it was obvious from his clothing, expensive and neatly pressed. Vasili glanced at him, then looked away to avoid catching the man's eye – the fewer people who saw his face, the better. Eva watched his approach a little longer. There was something familiar about him but his features were shadowed by his cap and his eyes hidden behind dark glasses. Even his mouth and chin were hard to see beneath a short grey beard. She couldn't place him. Something else alerted her to the hiker who approached so casually – perhaps it was the very casualness of his approach. He was avoiding looking at them too deliberately. She reached into her backpack for the hunting knife she'd taken from the lodge but it was too late. The hiker's pistol was out and aimed at her.

'Throw the bag aside, Tatiana Zykova.'

It was the voice of a man she'd met long ago only different now, softer, weaker, changed forever by the hairpin she'd embedded in his throat. 'And stay where you are, Colonel,' he added, turning the gun on Vasili.

She saw that Cleary had swapped his revolver for a modern Taurus with a suppressor. It was a good idea to silence the shot. In the limestone gorge it would be heard for miles. The magazine contained 15 rounds and could be emptied in seconds. This time Cleary would make no mistake.

'I've been waiting to meet with you again for a long time,' he said, removing his sunglasses with his left hand so he could see her face more clearly in the shaded gorge.

'I don't know who you think I am mister, but you've got the wrong person,' she said.

Cleary smiled. The hair was different, blonde this time, and cut to a middle length, even her skin was a different shade. She was good, he had to admit. Over the years he'd found out all he could about her, and dreamed of this moment, the moment of his revenge. Her eyes were wide with surprise and terror. He looked at her right cheek. There had been a burn there once, he was sure. His gun had exploded inches from her face. But some rich plastic surgeon had no doubt worked his magic, and this too had been concealed, changed, altered forever, so no trace of that moment remained.

'Really, mister, I don't know who you are, but I think you're mixing me up with someone else,' she said again. Her acting was frighteningly good. Cleary smiled in amazement, admiring her craft, despite the hatred he felt for her.

'Mixing you up with someone else, like who?' he sneered.

'My name is Michaela Banks, and this is my husband, Tony. We're from London. Perhaps you're looking for that couple over there,' she said, pointing behind him. For a moment he imagined it was a cheap trick, but then he heard footsteps on the gravel track and turned to see a man and woman walking towards him, a friendly expression on the woman's face, until she saw the gun in his hand and froze. She was middle aged, with light brown hair, tanned and pretty, and for a moment, Cleary wondered if he really could be mistaken. The woman began to scream. She was not Tatiana, Cleary saw it now. But she was a witness and she would have to be silenced, as would her companion. He fired and the woman fell, her mouth still open in amazement. His second shot struck her companion, killing him instantly, the muted report of the gunshot absorbed quickly in the gorge. Cleary swung the gun around to cover a possible attack. Both Eva and Vasili had launched themselves at him when he'd fired his first shot, but Eva had been closer and she was moving with shocking speed. He saw her spinning form in the air and felt the dreadful force of her kick explode in his abdomen. The power smashed him back against the thin wooden railing at the cliff edge. He hit it hard and heard the old wood crack and crumble. The rest happened slowly, so slowly he had time to examine each moment as it passed: his hands flailing, the wood giving way beneath his hips, his boot scrambling on the loose gravel, seeking purchase, finding none. The realization that he would fall, that he had no means of preventing it. The determination to take her life before he died. The struggle to bring his gun to bear on her. Her eyes on his, a look of curiosity, as if to say that if he could shoot her now, she would accept it, not try to evade it. The idea filled him with a final excitement that blocked out the terror of the coming fall. He grinned as he fought to bring the gun forward, to hold it steady, to pull the trigger. He fired once. Again. Again. Again. The last three shots had all gone high, their muffled reports mixing with the roar from his throat, and of the river rapids below, fast approaching, but, he wondered, had the first shot found its target?

EVA

Unnamed Island, Cyclades, 2012

Father Christodoulou made his way up the stony path that meandered through the olive grove. As a young priest he'd been excited at the prospect of tending the beautiful little chapel built on the hilltop, with its views over the picture-book harbour. Its elevated position had made it seem closer to God, and at the time, it had been what he'd sought – to be closer to God. It would be his own St Catherine's Monastery on Mount Sinai, the place he dreamed of visiting one day. But now, on weary legs that had walked the same path for almost four decades, he knew God didn't reside any more in high places than he did in low, any more in isolation than he did among people. God could be found in all these places, if one knew how to seek him. However others felt now as he had felt then. They sought isolation, beauty, and peace, and if such things made them feel closer to God, then he would help them in their quest.

So he walked uphill among the sparse olives trees that offered so little respite from the sun, admiring their gnarled beauty as he did. Each one was so irregular, so unlike its neighbour, so unlike the carefully cultivated trees of the mainland. These were island trees, small, dry, contorted by the wind, whose bitter little fruit was so important to the lives of the Greek people, and in particular, the islanders. Beyond the olive grove, almond and carob trees grew wild on the hillside, filling the air with a sun-baked sweetness that offset the salt of the sea. A small herd of goats blocked his path to the monastery, refusing to part even for a priest, and he was forced to go around them. A donkey flicked its tail lazily at the flies. Crickets jumped before him in the yellow grass.

The bell on top of the chapel came into view, then the dazzling white dome of the roof. The man who maintained the chapel repainted it each summer, and its whiteness appeared extraordinarily pure against the blue Aegean sky. The same man also swept the floor inside, and cleaned the altar, and dusted the icons that hung on the walls. He tended the small garden outside and maintained the olive grove that belonged to the church. Since he'd begun to care for the trees, they had produced a decent harvest of olives, some of which the man sold in the town. The rest he made into olive oil that he labelled 'Blessed Oil' and sold to tourists who visited from the main island. The man had bought the two old buildings that had lain empty nearby and converted one into a home and another into a café that sold cold drinks and souvenirs. Father Christodoulou could see him now, tinkering with an ancient Honda motorcycle, so engrossed in his work that he didn't notice Father Christodoulou, but the man's wife did. She was standing in the doorway of the café, and waved to him. Hers was a smile he never tired of seeing. She wasn't young any more, but hers was an ageless beauty, and the happiness in her eyes made her more beautiful still. Father Christodoulou was about to go inside the chapel when she called to him. 'Wait a moment please father.'

She disappeared inside the café and emerged a moment later. 'I have something for you.'

Her Greek was remarkably good considering she hadn't spoken a word when she'd arrived. Father Christodoulou had married the couple shortly after their arrival. It had been a brief, intimate service comprising just the three of them in his tiny chapel. He had never asked where they had come from, sensing that it was God's will he didn't know, however he'd heard Greek spoken with the same accent by the many Russian priests he had met during his younger days at the holy mountain on Mount Athos, where priests from the orthodox faith all over the world gathered in the most holy of places.

She offered him a wine bottle with no label. 'Please, take it.'

'Wine is not for me, my dear,' he smiled, 'But thank you.'

'It's olive oil, Father,' she explained. 'From the first press. *Virgin oil.* The best.'

He saw the humour in her eyes and couldn't suppress a smile.

'You are very kind, but really, I can't take it. The two of you have worked so hard cultivating the grove, I can't deprive you of it.'

'Please Father, I insist,' she said, pressing the bottle firmly into his hands – so firmly that for a moment he was startled by her strength. 'If not for you, then for God.'

Father Christodoulou had the feeling, and not for the first time, that it was easier to give the woman what she wanted than to oppose her. He wondered about her, as he often had over the years. She fascinated him, though he could not be sure why. Did she mean it? Was the oil really for God? Was she devout? Her husband was, of that there was no doubt. But she kept her feelings hidden, and Father Christodoulou found he had no way of telling what they were.

'For God then,' he said, accepting the oil, knowing it would taste good, and all the sweeter for knowing it was a gift from her.

At this he was treated to a beaming smile and he saw that her faith, or lack of it, mattered little. What was faith when he saw such happiness in her eyes, in her soul? He smiled and made a mental note to give thanks in his private prayers that evening. The woman may not have found God, but God had found her.

ACKNOWLEDGEMENTS

The number of people helping me to get my writing into shape seems to grow with each new book. I would like to mention some of them here, and to thank all of them for the time, expertise and care they have shared so willingly.

They are: my wife Charmaigne, my sister-in-law Genevieve, my sensei and brother-in-law Gavin Mulholland, my sister Sasha and my parents Michael and Vanda. There are also those from my karate dojo who have given me valuable input: Andrew Reynolds, Clare Brown, Jake Hoban, Cassandra Derham, Mike Thornton and Frances Little. And no list of thanks would be complete without a nod to my talented business partner and good mate Adrian Nitsch for his inspired cover design.

CHOJUN

A novel by Goran Powell

A typhoon brings the renowned karate master Chojun Miyagi into the life of young Kenichi Ota, who must prove himself before he can enter the master's inner circle. As once-peaceful Okinawa prepares for war, master and student venture to China in search of the deepest meaning of karate.

After the attack on Pearl Harbor, the tides of war turn against Japan and an American invasion fleet approaches Okinawa. Kenichi is conscripted as a runner for the Japanese general staff and finds himself in the epicenter of the Battle of Okinawa. In the aftermath, he must fight again to rebuild the shattered hopes of his people and to preserve his master's art of karate.

REVIEWS

Riveting... very highly recommended!
Lawrence A. Kane

Remarkable, it's that good!
Kris Wilder

Goran Powell has a marvelous way of capturing the tone of Asian storytelling
Loren W Christensen

Covers the relationship between student and Sensei beautifully
Nick Hughes

An exciting next-step in the evolution of how karate's history is told
Mike Clarke

Detailed, meticulously researched and absolutely compelling
Geoff Thompson

Beautifully written, skilfully blending the real life of Chojun Miyagi with the fictional character of his student, Kenichi Ota.
Karen Van Wyk

All the excitement and emotional highs and lows you can handle.
Andrew O'Brien

Enthralling... hard for me to put it down before finishing it
Violet Li

A SUDDEN DAWN

Historical fiction by Goran Powell

The life of Bodhidharma is one of myth and legend, 'A Sudden Dawn' is one version of his story. Born to the warrior caste, he gives up a promising future as a soldier to become a monk and seek enlightenment. After many years of searching in vain, he becomes enlightened in a single moment.

Bodhidharma accepts a mission to China to spread the Buddha's teachings. On the way he meets an unlikely disciple, a Chinese fugitive named Ko. Together they venture to Emperor's palace in Nanjing and beyond to a temple in the mountains, Shaolin. But there are powerful forces at work to destroy the Indian master and Ko's violent past catches up with him at the temple gate, where a deadly reckoning must take place.

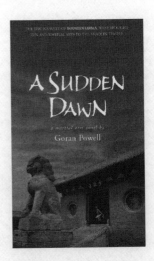

REVIEWS

Bridges the gap between training and spirituality…
Faultless and fabulously entertaining.
Combat Magazine

The book martial artists have been waiting 2000 years for
Chris Crudelli

Destined to become an epic tale of the warrior's journey
Patrick McCarthy

Inspirational, beautifully written, I loved it
Geoff Thompson

Weaves fact and fiction to produce a powerhouse of a page turner
Iain Abernethy

You can feel the hot breath of battle on your neck and the cool
of the temple's damp hallways on your legs
Kris Wilder

As good as James Clavell's 'Shogun'
Lawrence Kane

Superbly crafted characters, surges with action
Loren W. Christensen

Walk alongside one of mankind's greatest legends
Gavin Mulholland

WAKING DRAGONS

A martial artist faces his ultimate test

Non-fiction by Goran Powell

The 30 Man Kumite is one of karate's toughest tests, reserved for senior black belts with years of experience. One person fights a line-up of thirty fighters, one after another, full contact, moving up the grades to face the strongest, most dangerous fighters last.

Waking Dragons is a true account of Goran Powell's 30 Man Kumite and the lifetime of martial arts that led up to it. He covers the fitness training and mental preparations required for such a brutal test, talking openly of the conquest of fear and the spiritual growth that is at the heart of the traditional martial arts.

REVIEWS

One of those rare books you want to keep reading because it's so good, but fear reaching the end because then it will be over
Richard Revell, Waterstones

Quite simply, this book is impossible to put down
Traditional Karate Magazine

An exciting and tense read with lots of action
Martial Arts Magazine

The author's journey is one in which we can find great wisdom, information that all martial artists should know.
Lawrence Kane

It inspired me, and I know it will inspire you."
Geoff Thompson

It will shine light into the darkest reaches of your psyche
Graham Wendes

Whilst he relays the fight sequences in almost terrifyingly brutal detail, what really hits you is that the real battles are won and lost in the mind
Doug Wood

As a non-martial artist, I found it an eye-opener into that world and the training involved is described in incredibly accurate detail
Ingrid Charles

ABOUT THE AUTHOR

Goran Powell is a freelance writer and martial arts author who holds a 5th Dan in Goju Ryu Karate. He works in London and teaches and trains at Daigaku Karate Kai, one of the UK's strongest clubs.

In 2006 he published his first book *Waking Dragons,* an autobiographical account of his training for the 30 Man Kumite, one of the ultimate tests for a martial artist. An instant bestseller on Amazon's Martial Arts listing, *Waking Dragons* has become required reading in karate dojos worldwide.

Goran's first novel *A Sudden Dawn* was published in 2010, telling the story of the legendary Bodhidharma who brought Zen and martial arts to the Shaolin Temple, and winning awards for Historical Fiction from USA Book News, eLit, and LivingNow. His second novel *Chojun* tells the story of a young Okinawan boy who trains with the world-famous karate master Chojun Miyagi as war looms in the Pacific. In 2013 *Chojun* collected five awards including Winner at Eric Hoffer, and Silver at the Benjamin Franklin Awards.

For the latest on books by Goran Powell, find him on FaceBook or visit:

goranpowell.com

Printed in Great Britain
by Amazon.co.uk, Ltd.,
Marston Gate.